P9-CAO-903

"*The Poison Artist* is an elegant, gripping, hair-raising gothic chiller, a wicked mix of Poe, *The Silence of the Lambs,* and *Vertigo.* Settle in for a long night of reading — once this one grabs you, it doesn't let go." — **William Landay, *New York Times* best-selling author of *Defending Jacob***

"Jonathan Moore has written a wickedly smart, emotionally complex novel that will haunt you long after you turn the last page. Whether you find it seductively terrifying or terrifyingly seductive, in my mind, *The Poison Artist* is better than Hitchcock." — **Lou Berney, author of *Whiplash River* and *The Long and Faraway Gone***

"With *The Poison Artist,* Jonathan Moore has given us a brilliant debut thriller, confident, mesmerizing, edgy, and very cool. So much happens on every page, it's almost dizzying. Hitchcock should come back from the grave and film this story." — **Howard Norman, author of *The Bird Artist* and *Next Life Might Be Kinder***

"Moore has a great gift for the macabre and creepy." — ***The Times***

"This is a cinematic and phantasmagoric treat . . . Obsession and violent death collide in an elegantly written thriller." — ***Independent***

"*The Poison Artist* takes an old film noir setup — man meets femme fatale and starts to fear that she might be even more dangerous than she looks — and brings it into the modern world . . . a superior cat-and-mouse story, with an effective twist in the tail." — ***Mail on Sunday***

"A noirish, atmospheric tale . . . Uniquely sinister . . . Like Agatha Christie, Jonathan Moore is a writer who gets you hooked on a plot where poison is the cold, clinical method of execution. *The Poison Artist* is a debut that's both an exemplary psychological crime novel and a masterful exercise in intoxicating dread. It's a strange, sensual story to be savoured like the finest single malt whisky." — ***Crime Fiction Lover***

"This thriller's twists become as dark and intoxicating as the bars where the mystery begins."
— *Sunday Mirror*

"Jonathan Moore expertly weaves together the murder hunt and Caleb's descent into the demimonde existence of Emmeline, with the San Francisco setting evoking the dreamlike state of Hitchcock's *Vertigo,* for a compelling psycho-thriller that releases its poison just the way I like it: slowly and with a wicked grin."
— *Crack*

"Moore's evocative prose infuses this unusual tale with smoldering noir elegance."
— *Curled Up with a Good Book*

"There are some books that are just perfect for curling under the covers on dark nights. *The Poison Artist,* part gothic, part CSI, is one of those books, set in a perpetually fog-shrouded San Francisco that is dark and dangerous."
— *Reviewing the Evidence*

"Moore writes beautiful, careful prose and presents readers with an atmospheric story . . . Where he excels is in the sensuousness of his writing: food, sex, alcohol — he fully engages all of the senses . . . Absinthe, oysters, the painter John Singer Sargent, a classic car, and a string of disturbing deaths . . . make this dark tale memorable."
— *Kirkus Reviews*

"With crisp dialogue and skilled plotting, this atmospheric novel — fittingly set in a dark and foggy December in San Francisco — is an engrossing thriller by an author to watch. Give this one to readers who like forensic thrillers but would also be drawn in by the creepy mood."
— *Booklist,* **starred review**

"Exquisite . . . The sympathetic, though brutally flawed hero and the shocking, Hitchcock-esque finale make this psychological thriller a must-read."
— *Publishers Weekly,* **starred review**

BOOKS BY JONATHAN MOORE

Redheads

Close Reach

The Poison Artist

The Dark Room

The
POISON
ARTIST

JONATHAN
MOORE

Mariner Books
Houghton Mifflin Harcourt
BOSTON   NEW YORK

First Mariner Books edition 2016

For information about permission to reproduce selections
from this book, write to trade.permissions@hmhco.com or to
Permissions, Houghton Mifflin Harcourt Publishing Company,
3 Park Avenue, 19th Floor, New York, New York 10016.

www.hmhco.com

Library of Congress Cataloging-in-Publication Data
Moore, Jonathan, date.
The poison artist / Jonathan Moore.
pages cm
ISBN 978-0-544-52056-1 (hardback) — ISBN 978-0-544-54643-1 (ebook)
ISBN 978-0-544-81182-9 (pbk.)
I. Title.
PS3613.O56275P75 2016
813'.6 — dc23
2015004343

Book design by Brian Moore

Printed in the United States of America
DOC 10 9 8 7 6 5 4 3 2 1

For Maria Y. Wang, M.S.B.

ONE

AFTER HE CHECKED in and got up to his room, Caleb stood in front of the full-length mirror screwed to the bathroom door and looked at his forehead. In the back of the cab he'd stopped the bleeding by pressing his shirt cuff against the cut, but there were still tiny slivers of glass lodged under his skin from the tumbler she'd thrown. He picked them out with his fingernail and dropped them on the carpet.

Then the blood started again: a thin runner that dropped between his eyes and split on the rise of his nose to descend in twin tracks toward the corners of his mouth. He looked at that a moment, the blood on his face and the bruise just getting started on his forehead, and then he went to the sink and wet one of the washcloths. He wrung it out and wiped the blood off, then went and sat on the floor with his back against the closet door. The little blades of broken glass glittered in the weave of the red carpet.

It was good glass. Murano crystal, maybe. They'd bought a set of the tumblers at the Macy's fronting Union Square a year ago at Christmas, right after she'd moved in. There'd been ice-skaters going in circles on the rink beneath the lit-up tree, and they'd stood there awhile, side by side, to watch them. She'd been so warm then, as if there were embers sewn into her dress.

Radiant.

That was the word in his mind when he pictured her. Even now. It was a dangerous path to stroll down, but what wasn't?

1

He picked one of the shards out of the carpet and held it on the pad of his fingertip.

On their third date, they'd walked on the beach across the road from the western edge of Golden Gate Park. She'd taken off her sandals, had slapped them together a few times to get the sand off them before putting them into her purse. The Dutch windmill and some of the big cypress trees were breaking up the fog as it streamed in off the ocean. Bridget was holding his hand and looking at the blue-gray gloom of the Pacific. She'd cried out suddenly, falling into him as her right knee buckled.

"Ouch. *Fuck.*"

"What?" he said. "What?"

She was hopping on one foot now, her arm around his waist.

"Glass, I think. Or a shell."

He helped her to a concrete staircase that led up the seawall to the sidewalk. She sat on the third step and he knelt in the sand and took her small bare foot into his hands. It was tan and slender, and he could see the Y-shaped white mark where the thong of her sandal had hidden her skin from the sun. For a second, he saw up her leg, the skin smooth and perfect all the way to her pink panties. She saw his eyes' focus and blushed, then used her hand to fold her skirt between her thighs.

"Sorry," he said.

She smiled.

"My foot, stupid."

"Right. Your foot."

The piece of glass had gone into the soft white skin in the arch of her foot. It wasn't bleeding until he pulled the shard out, and then the blood came. It trickled to her heel and then dripped onto the bottom step. Bridget made a low gasping sound. When he looked up at her, she was biting her lip and her eyes were closed.

"You got tissues or something in your purse?"

"Yeah. Take it. I can't look."

He took her purse and found the plastic-wrapped package of tissues. He pulled out a handful and folded them into a thick pad and then pressed it against the cut, holding it tight. She made the gasping sound again.

He didn't know her well. Not then. He'd come to know her sounds, would know the difference between a gasp of pleasure and one of pain, or the quick way she would draw a breath when she was afraid, like a swimmer getting one last burst of oxygen before a wave washes over. But that afternoon, on his knees at the edge of the beach with her foot in his hands, he didn't know any of these things yet. She was the girl he'd met at a gallery opening two weeks ago. The beautiful shy girl in a thin-strapped black dress, who, it turned out, had painted half the work in the show. He didn't know much about her except that he wanted to know everything.

"Am I hurting you?"

"I just really don't like blood."

"Pretend it's paint."

She laughed, her eyes still closed.

"I'll carry you to the car, so the cut stays clean."

His car was a quarter mile away, to the north, where the beach ended and the cliffs began.

She opened her eyes and looked down the beach.

"Can you manage it?"

"Easy," he said.

And it was. She hooked her elbow at the back of his neck and he lifted her up and carried her in his arms, and thirty minutes later, when he parked outside his house on the slope of Mount Sutro, he carried her inside. He cleaned her foot with hydrogen peroxide and covered the cut with gauze and tape, but that came off in his bed soon enough, and neither of them noticed. The wound traced the patterns of her pleasure in blood on his sheets as he knelt before her and learned the first of many lessons about the woman he would come to love and to live with. Later, when they realized her cut had reopened, he took her down the hill to the hospital, where they cleaned the laceration a second time before closing it with stitches.

They hadn't spent a night apart afterward, until now.

He sat on the carpet with the washcloth against his forehead and thought the simple artistry of the pattern was something she wouldn't have missed. It might even please her a little, might make her smile in that quiet way she did when the paint covered the last empty places on the canvas and the shapes came into focus as though a fog had blown clear. Broken glass at the beginning; broken glass at the end. He pulled the washcloth away and looked at it.

"Blood in, blood out," he said.

Like a rite. The code of some secret society. Their sect of two, now disbanded. He wadded the washcloth and threw it into the bathroom.

He'd left the house with nothing but his wallet. No phone, no keys. He'd walked down the hill to the UCSF Medical Center, called a cab from a pay phone. He stood waiting for it, thinking maybe Bridget would drive down. Double park in the ambulance loading zone and come running to him. To apologize, to ask him to come back.

But if she'd come, it was after the cab rolled up, so he was gone.

The bar at the Palace Hotel was called the Pied Piper. A Maxfield Parrish painting hung across the back bar and gave the place its name — ninety-six square feet of light and shadow and menace, the children leaving the safety of the walled city of Hamelin to follow a monster with a face as old and as cruel as a rock.

It wasn't the first time Caleb had taken shelter in a painting, giving himself over to the canvas until both the room and the world holding it went black and silent. Some paintings were made for it, maybe. When he found them, and sat close enough to see the individual brush strokes, the room would eventually tilt toward their frames, as if the mass of the earth had recentered itself. Drawing him closer, drawing him to the world hidden beyond the veneer of paint.

He blinked and looked at his watch. It was a Saturday afternoon, not quite two o'clock.

There were three people in the bar, total, counting the bartender. Caleb pulled out a stool and sat, elbows on the glowing mahogany. The only real light in the place was aimed at the painting, and the bartender gave him time to study it again before he finally came over.

"You like it?"

"Always have."

The bartender had been studying *The Pied Piper of Hamelin* too, but now he turned back to Caleb.

"Hotel commissioned it," he said. "Paid six grand, in 1908. Parrish knew it'd hang in a barroom. He wanted men to sit where you are, to look up and maybe recognize a kid — to think of their own kids, waiting at home. And then not buy that second drink."

"Does it work?"

"I don't know. I don't think so. You know what you want?"

"Jameson, neat. And a pint of Guinness."

"Look at a menu?"

Caleb shook his head, then looked down at the bar. Someone had left the local section of the morning's *Chronicle*. It had been folded twice so that only one headline was visible:

CHARLES CRANE MISSING 10 WEEKS
POLICE: "WE NEED LEADS"

Underneath the headline was a picture of a heavyset man wearing a dress shirt and a tie. Caleb studied the photograph, then flipped the newspaper and pushed it away. He knew what it was like, having your picture run under a headline like that. Being missing wasn't always so hard. Sometimes the hard part didn't start until they found you. If you couldn't give the right answers, people looked at you sideways for the rest of your life.

He looked back at Maxfield Parrish's painting. In the foreground, the Piper led a group of children under a dark, spreading tree. Rough ground. To keep up, the youngest children were scrambling on all fours over broken rocks. The Piper, his back stooped and his hair hanging in stringy ropes, strode in the middle of them.

The bartender put a tumbler on the wooden plank in front of Caleb and poured two fingers of Jameson.

"Thanks."

"You got it."

Caleb drank the whiskey in one long swallow and set the glass down when the bartender came back with the pint of Guinness.

"I'll have one more of those."

"Now we know," the bartender said.

"What's that?"

"The painting doesn't work."

Caleb shook his head.

"No kids at home, or anywhere. So it wouldn't work on me."

The bartender took the bottle of Jameson from its shelf on the back wall. He poured the drink and pushed it back to Caleb.

"Car accident?"

"Huh?"

"Your forehead. Car accident?"

"No. Girlfriend. Ex-girlfriend, I guess."

"I'm sorry."

"It's okay." He paused and picked up the pint glass. "I mean, it's not okay. It's not. But it's okay you asked. The rest, no."

"That one's on the house, then." The man was pointing at the fresh whiskey.

"Thanks."

The bartender bent down and came up a moment later with a clean towel wrapped around a handful of ice.

"Thanks."

"Looked like you needed it, is all."

"Is it bleeding?"

"No."

Caleb took the towel and held it against his forehead until the heat of the wound drew the melting ice water through the cloth. It felt cool on his skin. He held it awhile and then set it down.

A woman in a black satin dress walked into the bar and looked the place over. Her hair was as dark as her dress, falling just past her shoulders so that it half obscured the choker of pearls she wore. She looked at each man in the room, her lips pressed lightly together as if in concentration.

Then she turned and left.

Her dress had no back to it at all, and her skin looked as soft as a white oleander petal. Caleb watched her leave, and then there was a silence between him and the bartender like a cloud passing by. When it broke, the bartender held out his hand.

"I'm Will, by the way," the bartender said. They shook.

"Caleb."

"What's the ex-girl's name?"

"Bridget."

"She's got good aim."

Caleb took a long drink of his beer.

6

"I'm not sure if she meant to hit me or not."

"Steer clear till you figure that out."

"Yeah," Caleb said.

He let his eyes go back to the wall behind the bar.

The woman in the black dress had been at least thirty feet from him, but he could still smell her perfume. It was a dark scent, like a flower that only blooms at night.

After the third Jameson, he paid his tab and walked back to his room. He looked out the windows as he made his way across the lobby. It was dark now. The woman in the backless satin dress stood near the valet stand, where there would be no warmth for her. She couldn't have heard him, couldn't have seen him. But she turned, slowly, and met his stare. He nodded to her and then went up the stairs to his room.

He woke in the dark of his room near midnight, sober again.

Even before he placed himself, he was aching.

He swung his feet to the floor and sat drinking a bottle of mineral water, and then he picked up the phone and dialed his home number. By the fourth ring he knew she wasn't there and he hung up. He was hungry but didn't want to eat, and he didn't want to be awake but knew he couldn't sleep. More than anything, he wanted not to be alone, but he remembered how it had gone with Bridget in the morning and the way it had all come to an end before he'd walked out of his house. He knew he would be alone a long while.

He went to the bathroom and took a shower. Then he dressed in the only clothes he had, and went out of his room and down the stairs again to the lobby. He stood at the threshold of the Pied Piper, but it was crowded now, and loud. Standing room only at the bar.

He left and walked out of the hotel, standing on the corner of Market and New Montgomery in the blowing cold. Fingers of fog moved down Market Street and mixed with steam from the street vents as it blew toward the bay. If it weren't midnight, he could walk up to Union Square and stand by the ice rink and the lit-up tree to watch the skaters and scratch open that warm memory until it was flowing and sticky.

He wondered where Bridget was right now.

That was a trap, but he went there anyway, picturing her in the cold fog and the dark, crying. Or in her studio on Bush Street with a bottle in one hand and a brush in the other, slashing the canvas with paint. Or maybe she wasn't cold, or alone, or thinking of him at all —

Across the street there was a bar. It looked open, but it was very dark. The only true light came from the sign outside, each letter traced in red neon:

H

O

U

S

E

of

SHIELDS

Cocktails

He stood with his hands in his pockets and looked at the sign. A few of the letters had bad transformers and flickered. After a while, he crossed the street without looking for traffic, and went to the door.

There were ten or fifteen people in the place, but the only sound as he walked in was the distant, metal-on-metal screech of a streetcar grinding its way down Market Street, and then the door closed behind him and there was silence. There was no music. A few faces looked around from the bar to see who had come inside with the draft of cold air, and after they registered him and marked him as nothing of consequence, they turned back to their drinks and to each other and to the low murmur of their conversations.

Other than the bar and a few vacant booths, there was nothing to the place. He went to the end of the bar away from the group and took the middle of three stools. An empty reservoir glass with a slotted spoon sat on the bar to Caleb's left. There was a faint lipstick mark on it. One of the two bartenders came over and took the glass away and wiped down the bar. He looked at Caleb but didn't say anything.

"Jameson," Caleb said. "Neat. And a Guinness on the side."

The man went away to get the drinks, and Caleb looked around. The high ceiling was painted black so that it disappeared into the shadows. The wall behind the bar was paneled in dark, oiled wood, and the front wall of the room was split up by thick, wooden columns and recessed alcoves holding bronze art deco goddesses. Each nude statuette held aloft an olive branch, and from those twigs sprouted soft incandescent bulbs that gave the only light in the place. This was a high temple of alcohol; there was nothing on offer here but drink. The bartender came back with the Jameson and Caleb took that and drank it, then waited for the beer.

He smelled her before he saw her, that shadow-flower scent, and as he turned to his left the room blurred a bit from the whiskey, but steadied when his eyes settled on her. She was sitting on the stool next to him. Her hands were folded atop a black clutch bag. She pivoted at the waist, and eyed him head to belt and back again without moving a muscle in her neck. Then she smiled.

"He took my drink. I wasn't quite finished with it."

"I'm sorry," Caleb said. "I thought this seat was empty."

"Your seat was empty. I was sitting here." She reached out and used a lacquered fingernail to trace a small circle on the bar top in front of her. "And there used to be a drink sitting here."

She spoke with an accent he couldn't identify. It wasn't a voice that came from another place, but maybe a voice that came from another time. Or maybe that was the dress she wore, and the choker of pearls, and that dark perfume. As if she'd stepped out of a silent film, or crawled down from one of the alcoves where previously she'd been holding up a bronze olive branch, casting light and shadow. She could have been anywhere from eighteen to thirty-five, but whatever her age, she didn't belong to this year or even this century. She reminded him of a painting, but he couldn't wholly remember which one — maybe it was one he'd just dreamt. Seeing her was like finding something that had been lost for centuries, then restored to its rightful place: he was in the hush of a museum near closing time. He felt the distant heat of the overhead spots and the spent awe hanging in the gallery's air, like old dust.

He leaned toward her.

"What were you drinking?" he heard himself ask. It didn't take much more than a whisper — the room was that quiet. "I'll buy you another one."

"Berthe de Joux," she said. "French pour."

He waved the bartender over and repeated the name of her drink; the man nodded and came back a moment later with a tray. He put a clean reservoir glass between Caleb and the woman, poured an ounce of the green absinthe into it, and set the silver slotted spoon across the top of the glass. He put a sugar cube on the spoon and then set a small carafe of ice water on the bar. He nodded at Caleb and then went back to the group at the other end of the bar.

"You pour it," she said. "I like to watch the *louche*."

"I don't know what that means."

"Drip the water over the sugar cube, until I say when."

"All right."

The carafe must have been in a freezer before the bartender filled it with ice water. His fingertips melted through a scrim of frost when he picked it up. He held the carafe above the sugar cube and began to tilt it, but she stopped him. Her fingers were light and cool on his wrist.

"Higher," she said. "It has to be a little higher."

She moved his hand until the lip of the carafe was nearly a foot above the sugar.

"That's right," she said. The way she let go of his wrist was like being kissed by her fingers. "Go on. The slowest drip you can."

He watched the sugar cube melt through the slotted spoon into the absinthe. The liquid in the glass changed from green to milky white, the cold water precipitating something from the spirit. He could smell a mix of bitter herbs now. Wormwood and rue. Anise.

"Stop."

He put the carafe down. She took the drink and dipped in the slotted spoon to get the rest of the sugar, and then she sipped it with her eyes closed. Her eyelids were dusted with something that might have been crushed malachite. When she opened her eyes, she smiled again and put the drink down.

"Your forehead," she said.

She reached to him and touched the wound with the tip of her

10

forefinger and then showed him the drop of blood. It looked black in the darkness of the room.

"Are you hurt?"

"I'm okay."

She rubbed her forefinger against the pad of her thumb until the blood was gone, and then she took another sip of her absinthe. He had never seen anything like that. Anything like her. She finished her drink in one last sip and set it down. Then she stood from her stool. Her clutch was still on the bar. She put her hand on the back of his neck and leaned toward him until her lips were next to his ear.

"I have to go," she whispered. Her perfume wrapped him like a cloak. Her left breast brushed his arm, nothing between her nipple and his skin but the slippery silk of her dress. "But maybe I'll see you sometime. Thanks for the drink."

She stood and took her clutch. He watched, immobilized almost, as if she'd struck him with a curare-tipped dart.

"Wait," he said.

She smiled, that same half-smile that crossed Bridget's face when a painting was almost done, when whatever final form she'd held in her imagination was about to pass over into the canvas.

"What's your name?" he said.

"Next time. Maybe."

She turned and left, her hair swaying against her naked back as she walked away from him.

TWO

THE KNOCKING WOKE him up. He came from somewhere deep and black and finally opened his eyes, rolling in the bed to look first at the door and then at the window. The light outside was very bright, and the knocking started again. He looked at his watch and saw it was noon.

"Housekeeping."

The door opened an inch and caught on the chain. The maid shut it, then knocked again.

"Housekeeping. Sir?"

"Gimme a sec," he said.

He looked down. He was still dressed. He stood and went to the door.

"I'll be out in ten minutes," he said.

"That's fine, sir."

He pushed the door to be sure it was locked and then he went into the bathroom. He bent to the sink and washed his face, then took one of the glasses and stood drinking tap water. One dream still lingered, clinging to him like a film of night sweat: the long series of knocks on the door, and how he'd climbed from the bed and crossed the room, entranced with sleep but believing he was awake. He'd put his eye to the peephole.

She was in the hallway, curved and distorted by the fisheye lens.

Not Bridget, but the woman in the black silk dress. He'd stepped back and watched the door handle move until the lock stopped it from going any further. It came up, then twisted down, harder this time.

He hadn't moved. He'd been holding his breath and leaning against the wall for support because he was still too drunk to stand unsupported. Finally he heard her walk away, and then the chime of the elevator and the creak of its doors parting. It was only then that he went back to bed.

Caleb would have forgotten this dream but for the maid's knock. Even now it was getting away from him, something slippery and alive that did not want to be lifted from the water. He let it go. There had been others, worse dreams, but those had already escaped and were just ripples now. He checked his back pocket for his wallet, and headed out. Before he got to the hallway, though, he stopped with the door half open. He woke up all the way then, if only for a moment, and felt the shock-current ripple down his spine and tingle through his arms to his fingertips.

There was a little dot of blood on the door's white paint, a few inches above and to the right of the peephole. Right where his forehead would go.

Caleb got out of the taxi on Haight Street, across from Buena Vista Park. He was still a couple miles from his house, but the air inside the cab was close and hot, and he thought if he didn't get out soon, he'd be sick. It was better once he started walking. Going west on Haight Street brought him out of the sunshine and into the fog.

Over the course of the next three blocks, someone had taped and stapled identical flyers to every telephone pole and lamppost. They fluttered from all the tree trunks, from the public trash cans at the intersections. They were tucked under the windshield wipers of parked cars, where a passing rain had soaked them to the glass. On each page, a grainy black-and-white photo of a man was topped with the words:

HAVE YOU SEEN CHARLES CRANE?

He paused in front of one, looking at the man again. Twenty-five years ago, his own picture might have plastered this same street. A phone number was repeated sixteen times in vertical columns at the bottom of each flyer, and someone — Crane's wife, perhaps — had scissor-snipped between each number to make tabs that passersby could tear off.

But every flyer was intact. No one had taken a number. No one had seen Charles Crane.

The cold wind helped him keep his pace. By the time he cut through the corner of Golden Gate Park and turned south toward the heights of Mount Sutro, there was rain in the wind and he was genuinely cold. He came to his house the back way, leaving the road behind the medical center and walking along the footpath beneath the eucalyptus trees. The fog here was medicinal, scented with camphor, and he breathed it deeply as he walked. He hopped down a retaining wall and landed on the wet pavement of his own street, and then walked the last bit up to his house. Bridget's Volvo wasn't parked anywhere in sight.

He followed the paving stones through a low front garden and came to his door. He pressed the doorbell, listening to the chimes inside and knowing she wasn't home. He could walk back to the hospital and call a locksmith from his office. He knew that.

Because of the incline, no houses were built on the other side of his street. Looking over his shoulder, he saw nothing but the cement retaining wall and a few parked cars. Above the wall was the ascending, forested slope of Mount Sutro. No one would see what he was about to do.

He balled his fist and swung it at the plate glass.

The water coming from the kitchen tap was freezing cold this time of year, and he held the fingers of his right hand under the flow and watched the crimson mix of blood and water swirl in the stainless-steel sink basin. He kept his fingers under the stream for five minutes. Then he opened the bottle of peroxide with his teeth and poured it over his hand, watching the effervescence of oxygen bubbling up from the open wounds.

Afterward, he walked through the house, looking at the empty closets, at the blank spaces on the walls. The bookshelves in the living room were denuded and there were no more art books on the coffee table. In the master bathroom, he opened the mostly empty medicine cabinet and found a bottle of Tylenol.

Except for the broken glass in the entryway and the blood on the floor that marked his path from the door to the kitchen, the place was perfectly clean. The only painting Bridget had left behind was a well-executed copy of John Singer Sargent's *A Parisian Beggar Girl*. She'd painted it herself, as a gift to him, and it still hung on the bedroom wall. The girl stood in dirty white like a cast-off bride, her back against a plaster wall. She held out her left hand, palm up and fingers curled. A hint of blood marked her sleeve, or maybe it was just a strip of red cloth she'd wrapped there. Caleb had never been sure, and he'd never asked Bridget.

Other than the begging girl, she'd taken every trace of herself out the front door. She'd swept up the broken pieces of the tumbler she'd thrown, had righted the lamp he'd knocked over when the glass hit him.

She hadn't left a note.

When he found his cell phone on the counter, he checked it. There was a message from the lab, asking him to call his graduate fellow. Half a dozen emails from a grant auditor at the National Institutes of Health. It could all wait. There was nothing from her. Not even a missed call.

He spent half an hour using scrap wood from the garage to board the broken window, and when he finished cleaning up, he went inside and lit the gas fireplace in the living room. He took off his shoes and lay on the couch, pulling a tartan throw blanket over himself. He stared at the redwood beams in the ceiling.

They used to make love here, on this couch, with the fire going and the lights of the Sunset District down below, the patio doors open so the sea wind could sweep the room. He dug his phone from his pocket and turned it off. That was gone now. Bridget was gone. He could tour the house again and look at all the empty spaces if he needed to prove it. He thought of the woman from House of Shields, the slippery cold silk of her dress when her breast brushed his arm.

The phone in the kitchen had only finished half of the first ring before he was awake and rising from the couch, throwing the blanket aside and coming around the living room wet bar to enter the kitchen. He got it by the second ring.

"Hello?"

"Caleb."

He leaned against the wall and then went to the floor. The sound of her voice, just the one word, his name coming from her mouth, was that strong.

"Where are you?" he said.

"In my studio. But don't come here."

He didn't know what to say. It had gotten dark while he'd slept, and the only light came from the fire in the living room. From his low angle on the floor, he saw a drop of blood he'd missed earlier. A little splash on the baseboard, close to the china cabinet. It was black in the firelight.

He found his voice.

"Will I see you again?"

"I don't know. Maybe. But not soon."

They were silent a long time, but he could hear each breath she took.

"Why'd you call?"

"I don't know," she said. "Maybe I shouldn't have."

"It's okay."

"I'm glad to hear you think so."

"Wait — don't hang up."

He waited, not sure if she'd cut the connection or not. He looked at the blood on the baseboard and thought of what he'd seen on the hotel-room door, above the peephole. The question slipped out before he knew he was going to ask it.

"Do I sleepwalk?"

"Jesus, Caleb."

"When we —"

But she hung up before he could finish. He wasn't even sure what he meant to ask. The microwave clock said it was nine p.m.

He hadn't eaten in more than twenty-four hours. Maybe he was ready for something. He looked at the bare tabletop and listened to the silent house. The only sound was the low whoosh of gas in the fireplace. A clock ticking in his upstairs study. There was food in the refrigerator, things he could just heat up. He took a step further into the kitchen, then stopped.

Nothing was going to make this feel any better, but staying here would be the smart thing. And he had to go to work in the morning.

Instead he walked down the hall to his bathroom, turned on the shower, and stripped down. In fifteen minutes he'd showered and re-bandaged his fingers, changed into fresh clothes, and put on a jacket. He went into his garage and backed his car into the street.

THREE

THE PIED PIPER wasn't crowded, and he easily got a spot at the bar. Will came and was about to say something, but the words stopped and his eyes flicked down to Caleb's right hand. There were little circles of blood at the top of each bandage. He must have been squeezing the steering wheel too hard. But he couldn't remember the act of driving here, couldn't say what route he'd taken or how long he'd spent. The only thing he remembered was parking on New Montgomery.

"It's nothing like that," Caleb said. "So don't go there."

"Okay."

"I didn't have my keys, and she was gone. I didn't want to call a locksmith."

"I hope you own and don't rent. So she left, then? Bridget?"

"Yeah," Caleb said.

"Maybe this time, you wanna look at the menu?"

"I think I better. I'll skip the Jameson, but a Guinness would be good."

"You got it."

Will handed him a menu and went to draw the beer.

The steak held his interest for at least the first half, but after that he slowed down and worked on the Guinness, splitting his attention between the painting and the doorway. Sitting up every now and then and closing his eyes, trying to recreate in his mind the scent she carried. He didn't know if nightshade was a flowering plant, or if its flowers bloomed at night, but the word was right. It was dark, something occulted. You might lose yourself in the shadows just looking for it. Looking for her.

"Refill?"

He looked up and saw his empty glass in Will's hand.

"Yeah."

"No problem. Steak okay?"

He nodded, then turned back to the door.

When Will came back and put the Guinness down, Caleb turned to him.

"Last night, that girl who came in here, the one in the silent-film-star dress — you seen her before?"

Will drummed his fingers on the bar top.

"Last night. Girl. Silent-film-star dress. You gotta be more specific," he said. "Five hundred people came through last night. Lot of them were girls. In dresses."

"She walked in, walked out. When there were just three people in here. Right before you told me your name."

The bartender just looked at him and shook his head.

Caleb understood. He had cuts on his fingers and his forehead, and a pair of thin-sounding explanations. If Will didn't want to tell him anything about one of his other customers, that was probably just good sense. He let it go.

"Then let me ask you this," Caleb said. "Absinthe. That's legal now?"

Will relaxed and moved down the bar. He came back with a deep green bottle in each hand.

"Law changed five, six years ago."

"This is the real stuff? What Van Gogh and Toulouse-Lautrec drank?"

"The real deal, from France. Made with wormwood."

"You got Berthe de Joux?"

Will looked at him for a second before nodding.

"Not many people ask for that one."

Caleb pushed his plate away and put his elbows on the bar.

"Probably not."

"You'll want the French pour, I guess. That's with a sugar cube —"

"And ice water," Caleb said, finishing for him. "There must be oils dissolved in the alcohol, and the sugar and cold water precipitate them out of solution — that's what makes it cloudy, right?"

"You a chemist?"

"Sort of."

"When it gets cloudy like that, when you mix in the ice water, the French call that the *louche*."

"What's that mean?"

Will shrugged. He took the two bottles and put them away, then came back with the Berthe de Joux and the rest of the paraphernalia of an absinthe cocktail. He poured an ounce of absinthe into the glass and laid the slotted spoon atop it. He set the sugar cube on the spoon and handed Caleb the carafe.

As Caleb poured, Will stood and watched.

"*La fée verte*," he said as the drink started to change color.

"What's that?" Caleb asked. "The *verte* part, what you just said."

"The green fairy," Will said. He took the carafe. "That's what they called it, those guys. Van Gogh, his crowd."

"All that hallucination stuff, it's not just a myth?"

"You're the chemist," Will said. "Enjoy."

Caleb held the glass under his nose and breathed in. He closed his eyes and he could picture her perfectly. The way she'd touched the back of his neck while she breathed her thanks into his ear, her hand cool and light. The nightshade scent of her. He imagined her ivory fingers gripping the edge of a theater's screen, her muscles trembling as she pulled herself out of a silent film and into this world. He put the glass to his lips and drank the absinthe in one slow swallow, then set the glass down and put his elbows on the bar and his head in his hands.

At midnight he walked out of the Palace Hotel and stood looking at the red neon sign: HOUSE OF SHIELDS. When the letters flickered, there was a low buzz. An empty paper cup blew down the middle of the street, rolling in tumbling, uneven arcs. There was a black SUV parked next to a fire hydrant ahead of him. The only other car within two blocks was his own. It didn't surprise him at all when it began to rain.

"This is pointless," he said.

He started for the door to the bar, but it opened before he reached it. Two men came out. The older one was adjusting a gray fedora but stopped when he saw Caleb. He put out his arm to check the man behind him, who moved to block the door.

The older one looked down at Caleb.

"You going in?"

He had gray stubble and a salt-and-pepper mustache. He looked tired, but not like he'd been drinking. He reached into his overcoat and brought out a leather badge holder. Caleb saw the golden, seven-pointed star. There was just enough light to see the words on it before the man snapped it shut and put it away.

"I was. Inspector."

"You a regular here?"

"Getting to be, maybe."

"You here last night?"

Caleb nodded. The detective turned to his partner.

"Let me have it, Garcia."

The other man handed over a white rectangle of paper. It must have been a photograph, but Caleb couldn't see it. The detective was holding it to his chest, to keep its surface dry.

"What time were you here?"

"Midnight, till maybe past two. I'm not sure."

"Let's do this in the truck," Garcia said. "C'mon, it's raining."

"Fine," the older detective said. "We'll do it right. You mind sitting in the car with us?"

"What is this?"

"Just some questions."

"About last night?"

"Let's talk in the car, like Garcia said."

"What's wrong with talking right here?"

"It's raining," Garcia said.

"It's just a few questions. We're not driving anywhere."

"All right."

They walked to the black Suburban, Caleb in between the two detectives. Garcia reached into his coat again and came out with a key fob. He hit a button and the truck's fog lights flashed as the doors unlocked. The older detective opened the rear door for Caleb.

"Push over. I'll sit next to you."

"Okay."

He slid across the bench seat and the other man got in and shut the door. Garcia got into the driver's seat, slammed that door, and then reached up to switch on the dome light.

"Better now?" the older one asked his partner.

"Yeah."

The man next to Caleb turned and held out his hand, a business card between two of his fingers.

"Inspector Kennon. Guy up front is Inspector Garcia — he grew up in L.A., doesn't understand about weather."

Caleb reached for the card and Kennon took in the Band-Aids that wrapped each of his fingers. Garcia was watching in the rearview mirror, his brown eyes steady on Caleb's when they met in the glass.

"So you walk into House of Shields around midnight, leave at maybe two a.m. That right?"

"Yeah."

"What'd you drink?"

"Jameson and Guinness. Three rounds, maybe."

"Come alone or with a group?"

"Alone. And I left alone."

"From the city, or you here on business?"

"I'm from the city. What is this?"

Kennon ignored him.

"What happened to your forehead?"

"Look, it's none — I got in a fight with my girlfriend on Saturday morning. She blew up and threw a glass at me. I left the house to cool off and came down to the Palace Hotel to spend the night. Right there." He pointed out the window, but Kennon's eyes never moved from his face. "I came over to the bar around midnight and had some drinks."

"What was the fight about?"

"Personal stuff. I don't see what that has to do with this."

"What's this have to do with?" Kennon asked. His wire-rimmed glasses had slipped low on his nose, and he was looking over them at Caleb.

"Why don't you tell me?"

He pulled the handle on his door and opened it a crack, so they couldn't lock him in.

"Close the door," Garcia said.

"You want me to close it, you put me under arrest. You just want to ask me questions, go ahead. But the door stays open."

Kennon just pushed up his glasses.

"Leave it," Kennon said. "It doesn't matter. He doesn't want to talk, he can go."

"Fine," Garcia said. "Let him get wet."

"And the hand?" Kennon said, facing Caleb again. "She do that, too?"

"Didn't have my keys, so I punched out a window. It's not against the law. I own the place."

"You mind showing some ID?"

"Sure."

Caleb leaned to reach his back pocket. Kennon's hand disappeared inside his overcoat but came out empty when he saw Caleb's wallet. Caleb got his driver's license and tossed it on the seat. Kennon took it and looked at it briefly, and then passed it up to Garcia. Garcia set it on a clipboard and started copying off the information.

"That address current?" Kennon asked.

"Yeah."

"Nice street. What do you do for a living, Mr. Maddox?"

Garcia stopped writing and looked up without turning around.

"I run the toxicology research lab at UCSF Medical Center."

In the rearview mirror, Garcia's eyes snapped over to look at Kennon's, and then he bent back to his clipboard. The pencil made a dry scratching noise.

"You a doctor?"

"Not a medical one. Ph.D."

"We met before?" Kennon asked.

Kennon was older, probably a year or two away from retirement. He'd have been a young patrol officer when Caleb was twelve. It was an easy enough calculation, and Kennon had apparently already done it, or he wouldn't have asked. Caleb felt the absinthe in his blood, warm and alive. He wanted to take it and wrap himself in it, wanted to disappear down inside himself where there would be no questions and no answers, where the only thing was the clean burn and the memory of the woman's lips next to his ear.

"Mr. Maddox?"

"I don't think we've met," Caleb answered. "If we did, I don't remember."

"You're probably right. I talk to so many people, after a while they all blend together."

"Yeah."

Garcia reached back and handed Caleb the license. He slid it into its holder, put Kennon's business card behind it, and then stuffed the wallet into his pocket.

When he looked up, Kennon was holding out the rectangle of paper Garcia had given him earlier. Caleb took it and looked at the four-by-six black-and-white photograph. It was a blow-up of a driver's license photo. A middle-aged guy in a white shirt and tie, a light gray background.

"Know him?"

Caleb held the picture closer to the light.

"Know him? No."

"But you've seen him."

"Maybe last night, at the other end of the bar. There was a group of men. Six, seven. A couple of them turned around, checked me out when I came in. He might've been one of them."

"Checked you out how?" Kennon asked.

"Just — you hear a door open behind you, you turn around. See who's coming. That's all."

"It bother you?"

Caleb shook his head.

"I'd have done the same."

"If you saw any of the others he was with, could you pick them out?"

"Maybe if I saw pictures."

"Could you describe them?"

"No."

"You talk to him?"

Caleb shook his head.

There was a stretch of silence and they listened to the rain hitting the metal roof. Then Kennon tapped the window with his gold wedding band. Garcia turned around.

"Start the engine if you want. Get some heat going."

Garcia put the keys in the ignition and cranked the engine. He let it idle a while and then he turned on the heater. Caleb felt the warm air around his ankles. He could still taste the absinthe every time he breathed out. *Next time,* she had said. Like a promise.

"You see him leave?"

"Huh?"

"You been drinking tonight?"

"I had dinner at the Palace Hotel. So, yeah."

"You eat dinner, you have a drink," Kennon said. "One goes with the other."

"I didn't say that."

"The guy in the photo. You see him leave?"

Caleb shook his head.

"I don't think so. I left after last call. There were still some people in there. I don't know if he was one of them or not."

"You talk to anybody while you were in there?"

"The bartender. To order drinks."

"That it?"

"Yeah."

The lie came out easily, without hesitation. He didn't understand what had happened between him and the woman in House of Shields, but he'd already decided he wasn't going to talk about it with anyone. Especially police inspectors who wouldn't state their business. He'd tell them everything about his fight with Bridget before he'd tell them what it had felt like to sit next to the woman, to have her whisper in his ear.

"There's no television in there. No music. You didn't talk to anybody. You bring a book or something?"

He shook his head.

"I was just sitting there."

"Just drinking. Thinking about your girlfriend."

"And minding my own business. I didn't pay much attention to anyone else — and I was pretty drunk."

"Where'd you go after that? After-hours place?"

"Just across the street. Back to my room."

"Valet working that time of night?"

"I don't know. I wasn't driving. I just walked across the street."

"Anyone open the door for you?"

"No."

"Which door did you use?"

Caleb turned and looked out the SUV's window at the hotel across the street. He saw the valet stand, where he'd seen the woman. When she turned around and met his stare, it was as if she'd been waiting for him.

"That one," Caleb said, pointing at the door he'd used.

"You went straight up to your room?"

Caleb nodded. "And I didn't leave until noon — maid woke me up."

Kennon looked at Garcia in the mirror for a moment, then pushed up his glasses and had another long look at Caleb's forehead.

"Well, Mr. Maddox," he said, finally. "Thanks for your help."

Kennon opened the door and got out, then waited while Caleb came across the bench seat and stepped back into the rain.

"Think of anything else, my number's on the card. Office on the front, cell on the back."

Kennon shut the door and started around the hood of the Suburban to get in next to Garcia.

"Wait a sec," Caleb said.

Kennon paused and put his hand on the hood. Garcia switched on the headlights. The beams lit up the raindrops falling onto the already wet and glistening street.

"This guy in the photo, what'd he do?" Caleb asked.

"Him? He didn't do anything. He's dead."

Kennon reset his fedora and went to the passenger door. He climbed in and then the Suburban rolled off. Caleb stood with his hands in his pockets and watched the truck. It went a block, then paused behind his parked car for a moment, headlights on his license plate. It pulled back into the lane and took the next left without signaling.

FOUR

CALEB SAT IN his car with the heater running. He stayed until he stopped shaking, until the rainwater evaporated from his hair and his coat.

"Just go home," he said.

Just go home, and go to work in the morning, and wait for Bridget to call. Sit by the fire for a while and then go to sleep in your bed. If you can't sleep, if the smell of her hair on the pillows won't let you, then pour a good nightcap. Or two. Knock yourself out. But just go home.

He got out of the car and locked it, then walked the block and a half to House of Shields. He stepped inside and waited by the door as it closed behind him, letting his eyes adjust to the darkness. There was a different bartender tonight. Just the one. Aside from him, Caleb was the only person in the place. He came across the room, his wet feet clipping on the tile floor, and took the place he'd had the night before. He ran two of his fingers lightly across the leather top of the stool next to him.

The bartender came over.

"You still open?" Caleb asked.

"Till two. But nothing clears a place like cops. Even a nice place. Hit the lights, roaches scatter. They talk to you outside?"

"Yeah."

"Thought I saw you. They had you awhile."

"They're thorough. I'll give them that."

27

"It wasn't my shift last night," the bartender said. "So I couldn't help them much. But I'd seen that guy a lot. It's weird, him disappearing. Turning up dead."

"They give you any details?"

"Just said they found him. His body. That it looked suspicious. They were trying to trace who he was with, where he was last night."

"Who was he?"

"A banker. A lawyer, maybe," the bartender said. He shook his head. "I never asked him. His name was Richard. You didn't know him?"

"Last night was my first time in here."

"It's not always this way, you know? Our customers getting killed. I'm a little freaked out, tell you the truth."

He looked up from the wineglass he was drying, and Caleb noted what was getting to be a familiar movement of the eyes: a slow drift from his forehead to his fingers, then back up. A little click somewhere. The sound of one thought connecting with another.

"So am I," Caleb said.

He shrugged and saw the bartender relax. The man put away the wineglass, the tension coming out of his shoulders. He turned back to Caleb.

"You know what the weirdest thing is?"

"I guess not."

"His car. He always drives here, parks out front. Has a couple drinks, then drives home. I've seen it, his car. On my cigarette breaks. It's a BMW, one of those SUVs?"

"Okay."

"When I came to work today, I saw it five blocks down the street."

"On New Montgomery?"

The man nodded.

"And I didn't think anything, because I didn't know he was missing. Then the cops come, and everything's going nuts, and I take one of the detectives —"

"Kennon?"

"Yeah, Kennon — so, I take Kennon down the street and show him the car. They run the plate and tow it away."

"Okay."

"So you know what's weird?"

"No."

"They come back two hours later, and they're questioning people, and I overhear a lot of it. And from what they're saying, they found out from his friends that Richard — guy who got killed — he filled the tank at that station on Harrison, right before he came here."

"Half a mile from here," Caleb said.

He looked to his left, at the stool she'd used last night. He wanted to put his hand on it again, but stopped himself.

"That's it. But this is the weird part. The detectives, they take the BMW to the yard after I show it to them. And when they come back, when they start questioning the regulars, they let on he'd driven twenty miles after filling the tank."

"Yeah?"

"And they didn't find the body anywhere near here."

"Where'd they find it?"

"I don't know — but not here," the bartender said. "So whoever killed him must've been waiting outside, right? They go somewhere together, in his car. Guy kills Richard, dumps him, then drives back and ditches the car. That's what I think."

"Makes sense," Caleb said. "But why drive back?"

"I don't know. Maybe he'd parked his own ride around here, needed to get it," the bartender said. "What're you having?"

Caleb looked at the empty stool again.

"Berthe de Joux."

The bartender tilted his head and looked at him.

"French pour?"

"Yeah."

The man came back a moment later with the tray, setting out the glass and the spoon. He put the drink together except for the water, which he left for Caleb to pour himself. When Caleb was done, he stirred it with the spoon and looked up at the bartender. There was already hesitation on the man's face.

As if he knew Caleb was about to tread on something special. Something forbidden.

"You know a girl, comes in here and orders this? Dark hair, green eyes? I need to find her."

The bartender looked down, put his hands in his pockets. Then he looked back at Caleb.

"You a cop too?"

"No." He held up his hands, palms out. "Honest. I just want to see her again, is all."

The bartender took a tumbler off the back wall and poured a finger's worth of Fernet-Branca into it. He drank it down and wiped the back of his mouth with his sleeve and then refilled the glass with ginger ale from the soda gun.

"There's —" He stopped and looked at the door, then turned back to Caleb. "I'll say this. There's a certain *type* of girl. I'm not talking about anyone in particular. Just a type, comes into high-end places like this, orders things like absinthe. Comes in alone, and usually leaves that way. You get me?"

"Not really."

"This type of girl only goes to a certain kind of place. House of Shields is one of them. Across the street, the Pied Piper, is another, but that's a little big for this type. A little crowded. So it's not quite right."

Caleb looked down at his drink. He ran his fingertip along the rim. She'd probably used this glass before. Her lips had been on it. There was no mark, but as he traced the rim, the cool, smooth crystal, he was sure of it. But he had no idea what the bartender was talking about.

"What are some others? Other places this type of girl goes?"

He brought the glass to his lips and took a sip. It was perfect. Delicious and cold, the full force of the herbs tugged out of the spirits by the cold water.

"You might try Bourbon and Branch. The Bar Drake, half an hour before it closes. Slide. Places like that. You know what I'm talking about?"

"You're saying these girls are part of a scene?"

"If it's a scene, it's so new or so deep underground, you're not going to find anything about it. If it's got a name, I don't know it. Girls like that, they just show up sometimes."

"Have another drink and put it on my tab."

The man poured a dram of the coffee-colored spirit into a clean glass. He left the bottle on the bar.

"She wouldn't go to the same place two nights in a row. She — they — might not even go out two nights in a row. You might not see them for a month. So if you're looking for one of them — I don't know."

"You don't know what?"

"Maybe she has to come to you."

The man was useless. Caleb wasn't looking for a kind of girl. He was looking for the one who'd been on the barstool next to him. The bartender hadn't seen her but wouldn't just say it.

"All right."

Caleb stood and leaned over the bar and took the ballpoint pen from the chest pocket of the bartender's shirt. He took his drink off its paper napkin and turned it over so he could write on the dry side:

Next time, I want to know your name.

He wrote his cell number and signed his name. There had to be a better way to do this. Something that would make her look for him, that would call her out of the shadows. But this would have to do for now. He folded the napkin into a triangle and took a fifty-dollar bill from his wallet. He handed the note and pen to the bartender.

"When you see her," he said. "Give it to her."

He finished his drink in one swallow, put the bill behind his glass, and walked out.

Even then, he didn't go home.

He drove through the quiet city, passing the homeless huddled next to their shopping carts near the subway grates on Market Street, and then up Nob Hill, where he idled the car for half an hour just beneath the entry steps to Grace Cathedral, its filigreed stone mullions and tracery and stained-glass windows dark and dripping with mist.

An antique coupe drifted past, trailing a cloud of steaming exhaust. Its white-walled tires and ghostly smoke-gray side paneling were just a blur through Caleb's rain-wet windshield. He watched it go. No sounds at all except the rain on the roof and the old coupe's tires swooshing along the wet pavement.

Then it was gone and there was just the rain again.

Caleb wound down to Union Square and circled its empty ice rink, the glittering tree attended by drifting knots of homeless men. And then, ten minutes later, without quite meaning to, he was parked opposite Bridget's studio on Bush Street. He could see into the alley that ran between her building and the one next to it, the brick walls of each building zigzagged with fire escapes, and the alley itself cluttered with dumpsters. Bridget had four windows on the third floor, two facing Bush Street and two facing the alley and the fire escape.

They were lit up.

She would be in there with the space heaters running, her easel standing in the middle of the small room. The canvases would be stacked along one wall and it would be more cluttered than usual now: she'd taken so much from their home. She might have bought a sleeping bag somewhere — there was an Army-Navy store around the block — but even with the heaters running, it would be cold up there. It wouldn't matter. Bridget carried a fire in her. You could lie down with her in a snowbank and it would be all right.

He thought about calling her. Even picked up his phone and punched in the password to use the keypad. But then he stopped. If he called her, she might look out the window, and if she did, what would she think? There might be a law against what he was doing. He didn't know. He just wanted to see her. For a while, he let go of House of Shields and the woman whose name he hadn't yet learned.

He just wanted Bridget.

Wanted to be invited upstairs, to be welcomed into her warmth.

It was after four a.m. when he left, and nearly five when he got home. He parked his car askew in the garage, watched the door roll down, and then went into the house. He'd forgotten the fire, which had been on all night. At least the living room was warm.

He poured a last drink and had it on the couch.

FIVE

HE HEARD FOOTSTEPS on the tiles in the main laboratory, a fast pace that came to a stop outside his office. His door was almost closed. A man spoke, not to him. Maybe to one of the secretaries or lab techs working in the main space.

"He in yet?"

Caleb had enough time to switch off his computer screen and swivel in his chair to face the door. His secretary poked her head in.

"Dr. Newcomb's here. But he hasn't got much time — he's got to get back to the medical examiner's office."

A tall man in a hurry, Henry Newcomb opened the door and stepped around Andrea.

"Caleb — just the guy I needed to see."

He swung the door shut, just missing Andrea's head, and stretched out his open hand. Caleb stood and reached across to shake with him.

"Henry."

"How's it — Jesus, what happened to you?"

Caleb fell back into his chair and motioned at the couch opposite the desk. Henry lowered himself into it, his knees higher than his hips.

"Bridget left," Caleb said.

"That was her parting shot?" Henry asked, touching his own forehead.

"Yeah."

"When'd you tell her?"

"Saturday. It was bad."

"I hate to say it—"

"But you told me so."

Henry smiled, but it was a sad smile. There was a long tug of history in the look on his face, a line that led back nearly thirty years.

"What's Bridget—thirty? Thirty-one? When Vicki was that age, there was no way I'd have done something like that. No *way*."

"You were right. Bridget was right. But it's not like it can't be undone," Caleb said. "I can fix it."

"That's not the point. The point is to talk to her *before* you pull shit like that, not after. Jesus, Maddox. But she can tell you that."

"If she ever talks to me again."

Henry leaned back on the couch and nodded. He gestured at Caleb's right hand.

"Don't tell me you hit her back."

"No. Hell, no. I'd never."

"You'd never," Henry said.

"I'm serious."

"You remember the whole thing?"

"Jesus, Henry. I wasn't drunk."

"That's not what I'm talking about."

For a moment, Caleb felt like they were playing chess. Except Henry was the only one who could see all the pieces. Caleb didn't know what he stood to lose, but he was sure he couldn't win anything in a game like this.

"She threw the glass, I left. When I came back, I was locked out. Punched through a window to get in. You know a glass cut when you see one. Come on."

He held up his hand and spread his fingers. He'd taken off the bandages to see if the scabs would hold. Henry looked at them and nodded.

"That was stupid."

Caleb let that pass in silence. His work phone rang; he looked at the number.

"Just the lab techs."

"You doing okay? I guess you know how you look."

"I had too much to drink last night. I know what you're thinking, but this wasn't like that at all. So don't start—I'll be all right."

"It's just, you know, I'd hate to see —" Henry stopped and looked up. "You've been doing so well, since you met Bridget."

"I thought you weren't going to start."

"I'm done. That's all I'm gonna say."

"Okay, then."

Henry looked at Caleb's hand until he put it on his lap, under the desk. Then Henry shifted his long legs and leaned back on the couch.

"I came looking for you this morning," Henry said. "We got a problem down at the ME. Got some results back, had us scratching our heads for a couple hours. Then I thought, 'Mad Dog Maddox can solve this.'"

Caleb smiled at that, the old name.

"Mad Dog's not at the top of his game. But I could use a distraction."

"And my side gigs are always fun, right?"

"Always."

"You got time now? I can take you down, lay it out."

"Give me a minute. I'll meet you out front."

Henry reached for the door but stopped when Caleb raised his hand.

"Yeah?"

"This job, I'll be getting samples?"

Henry nodded.

"I'll bring the cooler. But let's get the ice at your place."

When Henry was gone and the door was closed, Caleb swiveled back to his computer. He'd been writing a letter to Bridget, writing and rewriting and not getting anywhere. And he'd also been browsing the Internet, reading about underground bars and speakeasies in San Francisco. Places a certain type of girl might go. Places he'd be seeing soon. He'd gotten a lot further with that than with the letter. He emailed the list of bars to himself, deleted the letter, and shut off the computer. If anyone came into his office, he didn't want his life sitting on the screen. It was starting to get too complicated to explain.

As he was standing, Andrea opened his door ten inches and looked through the crack.

"Joanne's been hunting for you."

"I got her message."

"There's a new box of samples in the lab fridge. Patient charts sitting on top of it."

"When'd that come in?"

Andrea shrugged. "I don't know. Joanne found it. That's what she wanted to tell you."

"UCSF patient charts?"

"No. From the VA."

Now Caleb nodded. He'd contracted with half the hospitals in the Bay Area to deliver sample sets, if they could get them. Because of the population it served, the VA hospital found more volunteers than every other hospital put together. Veterans were prone to volunteer. And they had plenty of what Caleb was studying.

"Their delivery guy's been here so many times, he probably just walked right in and stuck it in the fridge," Caleb said. "Maybe Sandy was on the phone and he didn't want to bother her. No big deal."

"What if we'd missed it? Don't we need to sign for something?"

Caleb shook his head. "But we didn't miss it," he said. "Look, I gotta go help Henry. Email me if anything comes up."

Andrea ducked out. Caleb started around his desk, but then he stopped. He rolled his chair back and knelt on the floor. He'd been nonchalant a second ago, but now it bothered him, this idea of Andrea's. No one from the outside should be coming into the lab without at least signing in and getting a visitor's badge. A person who could get in and leave a box of samples in the refrigerator could just as easily slip in and take something away.

And there were things in this lab that shouldn't get out.

He opened a mahogany cabinet under the desk, exposing the refrigerated safe behind the wooden door. From the outside, it looked okay. The steel was still gunmetal black, and unscratched. The digital keypad glowed a soft green. He punched in the combination, heard the electronic bolts withdraw into the door, and then opened the safe. A wash of cold air spilled out. Inside the fluorescent-lit box, everything looked fine. The four sample vials were intact, and the plastic bags that held them still bore red seals with his signature across them.

Caleb closed the safe and listened to it lock, and then went out to meet Henry.

. . .

"Let's grab a coffee, kill some time till five o'clock," Henry said. "Nobody stays late anymore. Not this close to Christmas."

"Sure," Caleb said.

Henry was going to show him things he shouldn't see. Better to do that in an empty office.

They parked on Valencia Street and went into a coffee shop between a used-appliance store and a dive bar. The girl who served them had piercings in her face, hoops and sharp spikes of silver skirting her mouth as if she'd tried to sew it shut. Caleb wondered if it hurt. To lean your head back and let someone run curved needles through your lips. Did she do it to punish herself? Maybe there was pleasure in it too. He stood waiting for his coffee with his hands on the scarred countertop, and his thoughts skipped to Bridget. She'd been crying with her face between her knees, and then she'd exploded when he knelt beside her and put his hand on the back of her neck. He thought of the girl in House of Shields, her cool fingers so light on the nape of his neck that even the memory of it tightened his chest so intensely with a mixture of longing and expectation that it was difficult to breathe. A feeling both wonderful and frightening.

As if she could step out of any shadow at any moment; as if he might go insane if she didn't.

"You coming?"

"Sorry," Caleb said. He wasn't sure how long he'd been staring at his coffee.

He took it from the counter and followed Henry to the back of the shop, where they sat opposite each other in a pair of overstuffed chairs. Henry leaned forward, his elbows on the small table between them. He looked around the room and studied the other customers. There was a kid wearing headphones, watching something on a laptop. A man with a briefcase next to his chair.

"You want, we can save it till we get back in the car," Caleb said.

Henry leaned a little closer and kept his voice down.

"We can talk in here. The basics, anyway." He glanced at the man with the briefcase again, and then looked back to Caleb. "I'm worried our toxicology lab is missing something. Consistently."

Caleb shook his head.

"Marcie Hensleigh's running it, right? She's a good scientist. I co-authored a paper with her once."

"She's fantastic," Henry said. "But so what? A lab's only as good as the worst tech handling the samples. Or the worst industry rep who calibrates the equipment—"

Henry lost that thought and leaned across the table.

"I wish I had you in there," he said. "You'd get it right."

"You know why that wouldn't work," Caleb said. "If I got called to the stand."

"But I still wish."

Henry looked around again. No one was paying attention to them. But he lowered his voice to just a whisper anyway.

"These budget cutbacks. Christ. Our equipment's all shit. Half's outdated. A quarter should work but doesn't. If our office weren't in the SFPD basement, I'd think someone was breaking in and sabotaging it."

"You're joking."

"I'm not."

"Probably just a lab tech, never got the right training. Or got it and forgot it. That stuff's delicate."

"Obviously. But it leaves me in the same bind, and now I've got a problem."

"How big?"

Henry held his hands in the air, three or four feet apart.

"Big," he whispered. He looked down. "Maybe."

"How many?"

"Seven, that we know about. Some might've just drowned. They all came from the bay. Maybe it's not that bad."

"Lab didn't find anything? At all?"

"We found alcohol. Most were too drunk to drive, but not so drunk they'd walk the wrong way off a pier."

Caleb looked down at his coffee and tried to put his head into the problem. It was easy to see how good this could be for him. A way to bury himself with work until Bridget either came home or faded away. Until the buzzing neon sign outside House of Shields finally went dark in his head. He tried to think like a scientist, because that was the way back. Careful thought and hard work had always been the way back for him whenever the neat lines in his life started to blur, whenever things that shouldn't be important grew into the hooks that anchored everything. Even if Henry's hunch had nothing to it, it would be an all-consuming exercise.

Instead, he opened his mouth and said, "Any idea where they'd been drinking? The names of the places?"

Henry nodded, mistaking the question for an attempt to narrow the range of possibilities.

"We ran that down, but there's no pattern. Seven bodies—but fifteen, twenty bars. No overlap. The only thing in common is they were all high-end. Upscale. Maybe there's something for the detectives to follow up on. But from a toxicology standpoint, I don't see it."

Caleb had a couple sips of his coffee.

"What makes you think there's a toxin at all?"

Henry leaned all the way across the wobbly table and whispered.

"Because none of these guys has a good reason to be dead. I think it's murder. I just can't prove it."

The days were so short now. By the time they parked in the police lot under the I-80 overpass, it was just past five and the sky had been dark nearly half an hour. Caleb followed Henry along the chainlink fence rimming the county jail, then through a back entrance into the Hall of Justice. The building was a seven-story concrete rectangle, as drab and severe as a Soviet apartment block. Caleb had never figured out if it was grim by design or if that was just a result of economics and function.

They took the stairs to the basement level, and Henry swiped his key card to bring them through a series of locked doors in the medical examiner's suite until they were standing in front of a four-body portable cold chamber unit. Music was playing from somewhere. There always seemed to be a radio left on down here at night. Maybe it made it easier to work in the morgue by yourself.

"You mostly hear about overcrowding in the jail," Henry said, nodding at the portable cold chamber. "Got it here, too."

Caleb was carrying a small Styrofoam cooler and he set this on an empty stainless-steel autopsy table next to its drain hole. He opened the cooler and looked at the glass sample vials he'd brought.

"Come over here—there's coats and gloves."

Caleb went to the wash station and took a white lab coat off one of the wooden pegs. He buttoned it up and then pulled on a pair of latex gloves. Henry handed him a pair of protective glasses and a surgical mask.

"You did the autopsy already?" Caleb asked. He glanced down into the sink and saw an aluminum tray with a scatter of scalpels and saws that hadn't been washed yet. A pair of long-handled pruning shears leaned to one side in the basin. The black blades were flecked with bits of tissue.

"Yesterday, late evening. They found him in the afternoon. Tourist on the Golden Gate Bridge spotted him, called it in. A police boat came out and got him. Soon as he came in, I bumped him to the head of the line."

Henry took a jar of Vicks from his pocket and held it out, raising an eyebrow. Caleb waved it off, then changed his mind when he saw Henry dip his finger in and wipe some of the cream on the inside of his surgical mask.

"You moved him up because the others bothered you."

Henry nodded, then pulled on a pair of gloves and slipped the mask up from his neck to cover his mouth.

"He wasn't a jumper?"

"Those're easy to spot. Broken ribs, punctured lungs. Torn aorta, lot of times. Besides, they've got cameras up there now. Been at least four days since anyone jumped."

They went back to the portable cold chamber. It was divided into four sections, each accessed by a square steel door. The chamber had to preserve a chain of evidence, so each door was separately locked. Henry keyed open one of the doors, then pulled the cadaver tray out on its slide tracks. The body was covered with a green sheet. Henry wheeled a metal autopsy table alongside.

"You want the feet or the head?" he asked.

"Head."

They eased the cadaver tray off its tracks and set it on the autopsy table. Henry shut the cold storage chamber, and then they wheeled the table into the main workspace. Except for the lingering smell, these places always reminded Caleb of industrial kitchens. Deep stainless-steel sinks lined one wall. Farmer's market produce scales hung above the sinks, where the drips would be easiest to clean up. The cutting tools lined an entire wall.

"Who took the tissue samples?" Caleb asked.

"Marcie."

"Any embalming fluids used?"

"No. I didn't freeze him, either. And we put the organs back inside the chest cavity before we sewed it up. I knew you'd need to take a look at this."

Henry took the sheet and pulled it back so the cadaver was exposed from the knees up. Caleb stared, too tired to be shocked by the sight of the corpse.

"I thought this was supposed to look like a drowning."

"The face? You get that when a body comes from water. They sink, then go along the bottom. Face down. There's a strong current under the Golden Gate when the tide changes. So he'd have been hitting things at a good clip."

This man's face looked like he'd been thrown from a moving car. Caleb knew part of it was just the normal, post-autopsy distortion. During the examination, Henry would have cut around the man's scalp, would have folded his face down past his chin before using a cranial saw to get at his brain. Afterward, a mortuary assistant would have fit the skull back together and stapled around the incisions. Faces never looked quite right after that. But this man's face was worse than usual. It was abraded and sliced, as if he'd washed back and forth on a barnacle-covered rock. The tip of his nose was gone and his chin bone was visible through a deep cut.

The man was completely unrecognizable.

He might have been the man from House of Shields. It was certainly possible. But Caleb wasn't sure. He wasn't sure he wanted to know, either.

"Looks like there's bruising around the cuts," Caleb said. "Bleeding under the skin. I thought dead bodies didn't bleed or bruise."

"Can't say. Floaters are hard. They'll get postmortem wounds and go on bleeding. Especially when they're floating head down."

"You can't say from the autopsy that he just drowned?"

Henry shook his head. "That's the problem with drowning. There's no bright-line test. He had middle-ear hemorrhages. You see that in drowning victims — no one knows for sure why. But it's not conclusive. You could see mid-ear bleeding from a head trauma. An electrocution, even. Same for the pink froth we found in his trachea."

"What about fluid in the lungs? I thought that's what you guys look for in a drowning."

"Sure. But after ten, twelve hours in the water, there's no way to say if it's drowning or pulmonary edema from heart failure. Head injury can do it too."

Caleb nodded and pointed at the man's left thigh and buttock. Each had been torn open.

"Shark do that?"

"Little one, probably. Looks even worse if you roll him over. There're sevengill sharks in the bay. Threshers. They'll scavenge a corpse."

"What about these bruises?" Caleb asked. He touched the man's shoulder just above his right clavicle. There was a deep, fresh-looking bruise there.

"Shoulder-girdle bruises," Henry said.

When Caleb just looked at him, Henry explained.

"Sometimes, when a guy's drowning, he'll start panicking. Struggle gets so violent, he tears his own muscles. Maybe that's what happened."

"Or?"

"Or maybe someone tied him down by his chest and shoulders while he was having some kind of seizure. Big straps, so there's no rope marks."

Henry turned to look at the cadaver. Behind his protective glasses, the lenses of his silver-framed eyeglasses caught the harsh overhead light and glared.

"You mean a drug-induced seizure."

"Yeah," Henry said. His eyes seemed to follow the course of rough sutures holding together the Y-incision on the man's chest. "That's what I'm talking about. They all had those bruises, you know. All seven. What'll you need here?"

Caleb closed his eyes and forced himself to think about it. He was so exhausted, he almost tipped over. But he held on to the raised edge of the cadaver tray and worked through it.

"Blood from both ventricles, if there's any. If his heart was still beating when he breathed in saltwater, magnesium concentration in the left ventricle could be a little higher. I'll want slices of everything," Caleb said. "Brain, lung, liver, kidneys."

He put his gloved thumb and forefinger on the man's left eye and pried it open. Then he looked at the right eye. Both were still clear and turgid.

"Doesn't look like Marcie took any fluid out of his eyes, but I'll want it."

"What else?" Henry asked.

"If there's no urine, get some bile. Cerebrospinal fluid. Subcutaneous fat and skeletal muscle. If you saw anything that might be a needle injection site, take the fat and muscle around it."

Henry looked at the cadaver. Little bits of sand and algae still clung to the folds of his skin.

"Might need a talk with Marcie. She's not as thorough as she used to be," Henry said. He was walking to an instrument tray. "Anything else?"

"Just a printout of her report. You do yours yet?"

"Holding back till you and I sort this out," Henry said. He took a fine-bladed scalpel and pointed to a desk on the other side of the room. "Her report's in that green folder."

"What about time of death? Got an estimate?"

This wasn't an imperative for Caleb's work, but drugs in a dead body degraded like everything else. Knowing how long the man had been dead would help him figure out what kinds of chemicals had been in his system before he died and they started to break apart.

Henry looked at his feet while he thought.

"He was definitely alive at two a.m. on Sunday morning. Bunch of witnesses can put him in a bar called House of Shields, right till closing. Closing's at two. After that, it's hard to say. They pulled him out of the water a little after three o'clock yesterday afternoon — you okay?"

"Yeah. I'm just not feeling so hot. Go on."

"Well — see the maceration on his hands? Those prune wrinkles? Takes time to develop, especially in cold water. These aren't too far along. He probably wasn't in the bay more than eight hours. I'd guess he either died in the water, or right before he went in. So time of death is just around sunrise, Sunday morning."

"Got it," Caleb said.

His thoughts tumbled down a dark alley. Bridget stood at one end and the woman from House of Shields waited at the other. Kennon and Garcia were in the shadows. He closed his eyes and thought of the woman's touch, the way she'd frozen him on his barstool with nothing more than a whisper of breath across his earlobe and a brush of her hand. What would it be like if she put her arms around him? If she let the length of her body slip against his?

"Take Marcie's report and go sit down in my office. You need it. I'll get you when I'm done."

"Thanks. I'm not — It's the body, I guess."

"They do that."

Henry dropped him off at the UCSF Medical Center at eight o'clock. He stood with the Styrofoam cooler in his hands and watched his friend drive away. Then, when the car was gone, he set the cooler on the sidewalk and dug out his cell phone. He turned it on and waited for it to connect to the network. There were no voicemails or new texts. Just an endless scroll of emails from work.

He was putting the phone in his pocket when he changed his mind. He dialed Bridget's cell number, tucked the cooler under one arm, and walked to a concrete bench next to the hospital bus stop. She answered it quickly.

"What do you want?" she said.

She could have said anything in that tone and he'd have known this conversation was going nowhere. He lowered the phone from his ear, his thumb over the button to cut the connection. Then he brought it back up.

He made a sound, but it wasn't even a word.

He couldn't think what he'd wanted. Her first words had burned that thought to its foundation.

"What did you want?" she asked. "Jesus, Caleb. You made this call, not me."

"Your voice. I wanted to hear your voice. But this isn't it."

"Yes it is. This is my voice. This is my voice saying *Fuck you*. This is my voice saying *Don't call—*"

He hung up, then switched off the phone. He cocked his arm to pitch it into the street, but stopped himself.

He'd need a phone. This phone.

There was a chance, however slim, that someone else would call. He'd left this number on a napkin at House of Shields. He calmed himself with that thought, however desperate it was. Then he turned the phone back on, pocketed it, and carried the cooler into the lab.

He knew she was nearby, the woman from House of Shields.

He'd spent his life finding things no one could see. Poisons, pathogens. Some people didn't even believe they existed until he showed them how to look. He knew more about her than he had about anything else he'd searched for. He knew what she looked like, knew the perfume she wore. That wasn't all. He knew the temperature of her skin, the pressure of her breath in a whisper, the shade of her eyes in a dimly lit room. The shape of her naked back, like a violin carved in ivory. So she could be found. He would study the problem until he saw the secret way in. The hidden passage, the swinging wall.

He took Henry's samples and transferred them to a cold storage unit, doing it entirely by touch and feel. He'd closed his eyes. It was easier that way, in the false darkness, to remember the scent of her perfume. If he wrapped his mind around her—if he protected his memory of her the way he'd shield a candle flame with a cupped hand when he walked room to room to check his house in a storm—then the memory wouldn't fade. He could huddle up close to it for warmth and let it sustain him until he found her.

If that wasn't faith, then there wasn't any such thing.

SIX

HE KEPT A small flashlight on his keychain for the sole purpose of having a way to light the footpath when he walked home from the lab after nightfall. He'd seen a bobcat once in its beam, the wild cat's eyes green-gold in the light for an instant before it ran growling into the shadows. Tonight he saw nothing but eucalyptus leaves and mud on the path. When he got home, he used the light to check that his boarded-up window was still intact.

It was midnight when he sat cross-legged on the floor in front of the coffee table with a pad of heavy drawing paper and a set of charcoal pencils. He'd spent three and a half hours in the lab, building a calibration curve and then running the first set of samples through the gas chromatograph and the mass spectrometer. He wasn't finished, but he'd seen enough to know Henry's hunch wasn't misguided. But that wasn't on his mind now. He could finish it in the morning, and then go see Henry.

He took one of the pencils and looked at its tip in the firelight, then practiced with it on the first blank sheet in the sketchpad. A rough sketch to start with. Lines and a little shading. He gave himself ten minutes for it, closing his eyes now and then to shield the memory and let it grow bright again. When he was done, he turned the paper to the fire and looked at it a long while, making adjustments until he was satisfied it was right.

It wasn't until Bridget moved in that his childhood habit of drawing developed any kind of focus. She would stand behind him sometimes at the kitchen table, reaching around to guide his right hand with hers, her cheek on his shoulder. Her voice had been soft but sure. She'd wrap his finger in a scrap of chamois and use it to blur the shading and the lines. When the lesson was over and they moved on to something else, their fingers were blackened with carbon as if they'd been hauled in to a police station. Printed and booked for a crime.

When he got better, she would model for him.

There was a clawfoot tub in the master bathroom. She would sink into it and lie still with her eyes closed and her arm trailing from the side, one finger just touching the wooden step. He would sit on the floor against the wall and sketch her, and they would talk quietly like that until the water got cold.

So he was confident he could draw the woman, could capture in charcoal the way she'd looked that night. He ripped the rough sketch from the pad and set it aside. Now he repeated the same drawing, but the execution was more precise. There was no more experimentation.

She'd taken ahold of his wrist to move his hand until the carafe was at the right height. That was the instant he captured: the second just before she let go of his wrist, two of her fingers already off and her index finger brushing along the rise of his tendon as if feeling for his pulse. The crystal reservoir glass stood on the bar between them, covered by the silver slotted spoon and topped with a cube of sugar. He drew this from a perspective just behind his left shoulder, so the side of his head was a shadow in the lower right corner of the drawing. From this angle, the loveliness of her face and the interaction of their hands could play across the main space of the sheet. Shading darkened half her face and torso, but this only set the rest of her off. Gave her depth and shape. The rest of House of Shields came through in hints. A gilded lamp leaned from the shadows. A bottle on the back bar glowed from the chiaroscuro darkness. He knew now that there was a dead man on the far side of this scene, where the background went to full black. But that man wasn't a part of this. The light and the focus were drawn to her. Drawn to their hands together, to the story of longing set in motion by that touch.

. . .

It took two hours to finish it, drawing without pause. His hands were black with carbon, and bloodied where the scabs had pulled free. He went to the kitchen and washed them, then came back to the coffee table carrying a good fountain pen. On the left corner of the drawing, he wrote the same note he'd put on the napkin at House of Shields.

He could take the drawing upstairs to his study, scan it, and print a hundred copies. But something in him knew she would only respond to an original. You couldn't simply mimic the motions of a prayer if you expected it to work. You had to say it anew each time. On your knees.

He stretched his arms and moved his shoulders around to loosen them, and then he sharpened the charcoal pencil and started again.

Once, while she was in the tub and Caleb sat drawing her by candle-light, Bridget had opened her eyes. She'd brought her head up from the edge of the bath, her hair dripping onto her shoulders and her breasts, and she looked at him.

"Why didn't I find you sooner?" she asked.

"I'm hard to find."

"I know," she said.

"You know what?"

The candle flames whickered when he sat up from the wall.

"What you said. That you're hard to find. But they found you — so I could."

She closed her eyes again, put her head back onto the rounded lip of the bath. She relaxed, let her body slip into something very close to sleep, so that he could draw her.

Of course, he'd never told her about being lost. He didn't know what she knew, or what she guessed. For a moment, he just stared at her, the charcoal pencil motionless in his hand.

"Draw," she said, without opening her eyes. "It's okay."

He started again, and that was as close as they ever came to the blank space in Caleb's history, the blind fog that Henry called the lacuna. She must have known most of it, and maybe it was better that way. If she knew but hadn't wanted to talk about it, then maybe she never would. More than anything, he didn't want to talk about it.

The pencil's tip trembled against the paper as he began filling in the shadows beneath the raised tub.

When he woke on the couch in the cold December light, he walked into the kitchen, where he'd laid out the drawings on the granite countertop. He thought by daylight they'd look amateurish. Laughable. That their failed conception and execution would finally purge House of Shields from his mind. But the drawings were better than any he'd ever done. She was so lovely that if he closed his eyes and balanced himself against the counter, he could feel his entire body pulling toward her, like a compass needle swayed off its true course by an anomaly in the shape and tug of the earth.

He made it to work almost an hour before lunch.

During the night, he'd been too lost in the drawings to drink anything, and that was a mercy this morning because he'd slept so little. Andrea caught him as he was shutting the door to his office.

"They're waiting upstairs, in the conference room."

"Who's waiting?"

"Joanne. And that man from NIH."

He stared at her, trying to place it.

"The grant review?" she offered.

"Oh, shit. Sorry."

By the time he came in, his graduate fellow and the NIH grant auditor had given up on small talk and were just staring at the rolled-down screen. The visitor's badge clipped to the auditor's lapel said his name was Dr. Greckin. Caleb couldn't remember if he'd ever spoken to this man or not. He followed the man's eyes and looked at the screen. The lead slide was the title of his last paper:

QUANTIFICATION OF PAIN:
A SYSTEMATIC APPROACH TO UNDERSTANDING
SUFFERING

Maybe not his best title ever. But the work was good. Caleb dimmed the lights and let Joanne start the slide presentation. He watched without a word. Every time Dr. Greckin stopped her to ask a question, Joanne would stare at Caleb, waiting for him to speak. When he didn't, she would shrug and answer the question herself. She was doing fine, but Caleb wasn't making either of them look good.

At the end, Greckin stood and began gathering handouts from around the table.

"Dr. Maddox, this was interesting, but—"

"But what?" Caleb said.

It was the first he'd spoken since the meeting started, and he regretted it right away. He'd meant it as a simple question, but the words were bits of broken glass in his throat. The man thumbed through the stack of printouts and then looked at Caleb.

"They're not what we asked for. We understand the theory. We need the backup data. That's all—just hard data."

"It's almost ready."

"All we need is a little support to justify the money. It's a lot of money."

"It's coming. We're getting new samples almost every week."

"Good."

The man shook Joanne's hand on his way out. Caleb came around the conference table and held out his hand.

"Glad to finally meet you," Caleb said.

Greckin shook his hand, but looked at Caleb with his head half-cocked.

"We met twice," he said. "In September."

Caleb watched him until he was gone. Then he turned to Joanne.

"It's not a problem," he said.

She looked at her laptop screen, started closing out of the slide presentation.

"That's good. Because it looked like a problem to me."

"I've got more than he knows. Some of the new sets are really good."

"You might've given him a hint," Joanne said. She slammed her laptop closed and put it into her shoulder bag. "I could've picked a lot of programs. I signed on with you because I wanted to do some hard science—in a lab with full funding."

"We've got full funding. And we'll keep it."

"And what was that last bit? You don't remember Bethesda? We were there for three days."

"Sorry," he said. He stepped past her, into the hallway. "It's been a hard week."

She called after him, but he didn't stop. When he got to his office, he shut the door and locked it. He sat behind his desk, closed his eyes, and put his thumbs on his temples. When Bridget threw the glass, she'd done more than just knock him down. He needed to get up, though. To get back to where he'd been last Friday, before the fight. The data wasn't coming in as fast as the NIH wanted, but what was coming was good. He could put it all together by the deadline and keep at least that much intact.

Joanne knocked and called his name. When he didn't respond, she tried the door handle. It jerked up and down but didn't turn. She slapped the door in frustration and walked away.

He waited until she was gone, then sat up and switched on his screen. It took him an hour to force his mind into Henry's problem, but once he was in it, he stayed with it to the end.

The hostess led Caleb past the bar and the tables in the front of the restaurant to the grotto-like back room, where Henry was waiting at a half-circle booth. Caleb slid in and let the hostess put the napkin across his lap.

"Sorry," Caleb said. "Had to go home first. Shower, change clothes."

He'd shaved and put on a better suit, had then taken the time to comb his hair well. The bruise on his forehead was turning yellowish, but it looked all right in the low light. The light in Farallon's back room was dim enough to hide nearly anything.

"I ordered wine," Henry said, looking at his forehead. "You gonna be okay with that?"

Caleb held up his right palm, as if giving an oath.

"I won't go crazy. Maybe just six or seven bottles before dessert."

Henry smiled.

"Good. You'll like this one. But if we're having six more bottles, we'll need cheaper ones." He looked at Caleb and added, "Seriously, though. Take it easy."

The sommelier came and uncorked a bottle of Cabernet Sauvignon, poured a swirl of it into Henry's glass, and waited for Henry to nod. Then she filled Caleb's glass, topped Henry's, and left the bottle on its coaster. Henry watched her go, then turned to Caleb.

"Bridget's still—"

"Yeah."

"Wanna talk about it?"

"No."

"Okay." Henry sipped his wine. "What'd you find?"

"Your guy drowned. Magnesium in his left ventricular blood was elevated. He breathed in seawater while his heart was still beating, then died before it finished circulating."

"So Marcie's report is right? There was nothing else?"

"Marcie's calibration curve is flawed," Caleb said. "She used a sodium fluoride blood preservative, which is standard, but she didn't calculate the right compensation to account for it in the tests. And her preservative's contaminated—someone must be pouring one bottle into another to save shelf space, then accidentally mixing in other stuff—but Marcie, some of what she picked up, she probably wrote off as preservative. Noise in the data. Other stuff, she just missed. I can't explain why. It wasn't hard to find."

"Shit." Henry pushed his wine away. "What'd she miss?"

"You'd need a pen and paper, and you'd need to be ready to write fast, because it's a long list. But the two standouts were thujone and vecuronium."

"Vecuronium's a muscle relaxant."

"A fast one," Caleb said, nodding. "Shoot a guy with ten milligrams, he'll be on the ground in sixty seconds. Put him in the water, no chance he'd make it. This guy's blood was full of the unmetabolized drug. If he hadn't died, his liver would've eliminated it in eighty minutes. So he was incapacitated when he hit the water."

Henry took his wineglass by its stem and slowly twirled the Cabernet inside it. A waiter approached, but Henry waved him off.

"So it's murder."

Caleb nodded. "That much vecuronium, no way he could've gotten into the bay without some help. So, yeah. Murder."

"We're gonna have to go back, run the other six."

"You want, send Marcie to my lab. Let her run the other six on my equipment."

Henry looked up.

"Give her a clean way out? She finds it in your lab, then I know the problem is my equipment and not my toxicologist?"

"Something like that," Caleb said. "Who knows? You're a smart guy. Maybe you could parlay that into a budget increase."

Henry laughed, but the change dropped off his face as quickly as it had come.

"They catch a guy, it goes to trial, some defense lawyer's gonna ask why the first six reports said 'drowning' and then we go back and find a bunch of stuff we missed."

That was Henry's problem to figure out. Caleb just did the science. But now something else was bothering Henry.

"And what about the shoulder-girdle bruises?" Henry asked. "If he had a muscle relaxant, he wasn't thrashing. So how'd he get the bruises?"

Caleb drank some of his wine and thought how to explain it.

He wasn't quite sure when he'd last eaten, or what that had been. He'd been living on loneliness and obsession since Saturday night. He was getting a break from it now, with Henry, but as soon as he left the restaurant and was alone again, it would come back. But that was all right. It was like pulling out thorns. Maybe it was better to just work them out and take the pain.

Bleed until it was better.

"Caleb?"

"Sorry," he said. He put his wineglass down, saw it was empty. "I think the shoulder-girdle bruises are where the thujone comes in."

"I've never heard of thujone."

"Neither had I. Had to look it up. It's an organic. A ketone, pretty close to sugar. But it's a poison. High dose, it'll cause thrashing."

"I don't get it. Why mix that with a muscle relaxant?"

Caleb almost smiled. This had taken him the longest to puzzle through. He still liked his work enough to appreciate it when the pieces fit together neatly.

"It didn't make sense until I started looking at the metabolites — the breakdown of the drugs in the system. And the timing. That's critical. This guy got vecuronium twice. You can read the metabolites in his liver like tree rings. First dose was about four hours before he died. When his liver cleared it, he got thujone — a lot of it. Then he got another shot of vecuronium, right before he went in the water."

Henry nodded.

"I see what you're saying. Someone shot him with muscle relaxant to get him under control. Took him somewhere safe, strapped him down and did something to him for three hours. Then shot him with muscle relaxant again and dumped him in the bay to die."

"That's pretty much it. Except, there's one other thing," Caleb said. "I've been researching the physiological effects of pain. How it changes the body, at a chemical level. And I'm getting good at it — still trying to get NIH funding to finish what I started. Learn how to measure it."

"You told me," Henry said. "A while back. But I thought you were just looking for the poisons, what Marcie missed."

"I did a breakdown of things his endocrine system pumped out the last three hours he was alive. Ran the histamines, too. Shit's off the charts. Before he died, he went through as much pain as a man can take. Three hours, maybe more. Total, unbearable agony."

"So it's not just a run-of-the-mill murderer, is it?"

"Not at all," Caleb said. "This is new science. So new you probably couldn't get it into court. But I thought you should know."

"Should we order?" Henry asked.

When he left the restaurant, Caleb went to the garage where he'd parked his car. The folder with his drawings was in the trunk. He took it out and tucked it under his arm. He'd done five drawings altogether. Just thinking of it now made his right hand cramp up. He'd cut the edges of each with a box knife and a straight edge, and had put them inside oversized stationery envelopes. Because he didn't know her name yet, there'd been only one way to address them. He'd scanned one of the drawings, then cropped the image on his computer, singling out her face. He'd printed five copies of that onto heavy bond paper. After trimming the images to neat squares, he'd pasted her face over the flaps of the envelopes like wax seals.

He walked west on Post Street, away from Union Square.

Men stood in the shadows of gated doorways and asked for change. These were Henry's people. His customer base, just filling in the days until it was their turn to visit Henry's basement on Bryant

Street. One man came out of his doorway and followed Caleb with a crumpled prescription for Oxycontin.

"You fill it, and we'll split it," the man said to Caleb's back.

Caleb turned south on Jones and dropped down the hill to the intersection with O'Farrell. This was Bourbon and Branch, but the sign on the corner was just a plain, backlit white rectangle extending from the building's side:

ANTI-SALOON
<><><>
LEAGUE
San Francisco Branch
Est. 1920

His reservation wasn't until eleven. He decided to walk around the block. Though he'd never been here, he knew the rules were strict. You couldn't ring the buzzer before your time. And that was fine with him. To have structure to the search. Rows and columns. He knew how to conduct a search like that.

Fifteen minutes later, he came back to the corner of Jones and O'Farrell. He pressed the buzzer and looked at the speaker mounted on the wall. The brass grate was covered with a patina of green oxide. Whoever was on the other end made him wait. But he didn't press the buzzer again. Finally there was a break of static from the speaker.

"Password?"

"Bitters and rye," he said.

The door clicked open. He felt his way down the dark hallway and stepped into the main room of the speakeasy. When he came into it, and saw the pressed-tin ceiling, and the way the glass-spiked chandelier lit the room like a snarl of burning teeth, the shadows cloaking the rest of the room in thick velvet, he knew this was the right bar. She could glide across this dark space and materialize onto a stool next to him the way fog settled into the valleys between the hills, nestled there in the cool shadows, and became something solid. Something real enough to touch. To taste. He knew she'd been here, as surely as he'd felt the touch of her lips on the absinthe glass at House of Shields when he'd traced its rim. He sat at the bar and waited for the bartender to work his way over.

"Yessir?"

"Let me have a Martin Mills. Make it a double."

That would set him back two hundred dollars, if they even had a bottle of it. But he thought it would get the bartender's attention.

It did.

The man ran his hand along the front of his black tie and down the gabardine-covered buttons of his vest. He leaned against his side of the bar.

"Neat?"

Caleb nodded.

"You want a back with that?"

"Glass of ice water."

The man used a stepping stool to reach the niche in the wall with the Martin Mills. He poured it into an old-fashioned glass and brought it over with the ice water. Caleb took the glass of bourbon and slid one of the envelopes back across the bar in exchange. His finger was above the portrait he'd pasted to the flap.

"She comes here sometimes," Caleb said. "Keep it behind the bar, where you'll remember it. When you see her, give it to her."

The man hesitated, and Caleb slid the envelope an inch closer.

"What is this?" the bartender asked. He hadn't touched the envelope.

"I need to see her again. I don't know her name."

The man looked at the envelope a long time, his hands on the bar. Then he took it and put it out of sight. He nodded at Caleb and brought the bottle of Martin Mills back. He added a quarter of an inch to Caleb's glass.

"You'll need it."

"Tell me about it."

He stayed ten minutes at Bourbon and Branch, finishing his drink. The bourbon was smooth and clean, a low fire. When he stood from his stool to leave, he slid three hundred-dollar bills under his empty glass. He could afford that, for now. And there'd be new funding coming in a few months.

Then he was wandering back toward Union Square, pulling his

coat close against the wet wind and sidestepping the beggars who'd staked their places with flattened boxes and scraps of blankets.

By three a.m., he'd covered ten miles and had delivered all five envelopes. He'd found two teller machines during the night, drawing cash to replenish what he was leaving on bar tops. He'd drunk Martin Mills and old Scottish single malts, and at the last place, up in North Beach, he'd had Berthe de Joux. In that basement-level speakeasy, instead of a carafe of ice water they'd given him a crystal reservoir held aloft by a silver statuette of a nude Venus. To start the drip, he only had to twist a tap on the reservoir's side.

The bartender hadn't taken the final envelope until Caleb pushed it another inch across the bar to show the corner of the bill beneath it.

Now he was walking down Powell Street, listening to the cable rattle in its guide path under the tracks in the middle of the street. At the intersections of eastbound streets, when the fog broke, he could see the curving lights of the Bay Bridge on its transit to Yerba Buena Island. He was twenty blocks from his car, but needed the walk before he'd be ready to drive anywhere.

SEVEN

CALEB WAS ON the couch with a wet washcloth rolled up and draped over his eyes when the doorbell rang. He sat up and looked at his watch. Three in the afternoon. Bridget taught a painting workshop at the Academy of Art University on Wednesday afternoons, so it wouldn't be her. Of course, he was supposed to be at work too, so if her life had become anything like his, maybe she was on the doorstep.

The bell rang again.

"Coming."

He tossed the washcloth on the coffee table and glanced in the dining room and kitchen on his way to the foyer. The house was still pretty clean. Since coming home on Sunday afternoon, he'd spent almost all of his time in bars or at work, and hadn't eaten anything at home. So he hadn't had time to tear the place apart. But he didn't look so great himself, which he knew without looking in a mirror. He'd fallen asleep on the couch at five a.m., still wearing his suit. Two hours later, he was up just long enough to leave a voicemail for Andrea to tell her he wouldn't be coming in till the late afternoon. If at all. Then he was asleep in the same spot, the phone still in his hand.

He reached the door and opened it without looking through the peephole. The man on the doorstep was using the side of his palm to brush beads of rain off the front of his overcoat. He looked at Caleb and nodded.

"Went to your office first," he said. "But they told me to come look-ing for you here. Remember me from Sunday night?"

"Detective Kennon," Caleb said.

"*Inspector* Kennon," the man corrected. "SFPD's old-school."

"Sorry."

Kennon glanced to the right of the door, pointing with the fedora in his hand.

"That the window you punched out?"

Caleb nodded.

"Girlfriend back, or you here alone?" He was looking at Caleb's rumpled suit and untucked shirt, at the half-formed scabs on Caleb's fingers. He could probably guess the answer to that one.

"It's just me. What's going on?"

"I wanted to ask a few follow-ups, see if I can figure out who was in the bar that night."

"Just questions?"

"That's all."

"All right, then."

Caleb didn't open the door any more than he already had, and he didn't move back to let Kennon in. Kennon looked at the porch and then leaned to look past Caleb into the house.

"It'd be easier if we did it inside," Kennon said.

Caleb didn't want to let him in. When he'd answered the door, the detective's eyes had moved quickly across his face, and then he'd nodded slightly, as if he'd just checked off the last box on some unseen list. Kennon knew something about him, or thought he did. Maybe the easiest way to send him away would be to give him what he wanted. Or maybe, for a thing like this, there was no easy way. Caleb stepped back and opened the door.

"Want a cup of coffee or something?"

Bridget had owned the coffee machine, so there was just an empty space on the counter between one of the knife racks and the toaster. Caleb turned on the flame under a teakettle and dug in the back of the cupboard until he found the French press he'd used before she'd moved in.

"Where's Garcia?" he asked.

"Running down something else. But I finished my stuff, figured I'd start at the beginning. See if I can't shake anything loose that didn't come down the first time."

Kennon was sitting on one of the stools with his elbows on the kitchen counter. Caleb stood opposite him. When the kettle whistled, he poured the water into the press and then a moment later, after pushing the grinds to the bottom, poured coffee into mugs. He passed one to Kennon, sliding it over the black granite.

"Thanks. Smells good."

"I don't know what else I can tell you," Caleb said. "I told you everything I remembered when we talked in the car."

Kennon either didn't hear him or simply didn't care to acknowledge what he'd said. He looked around the kitchen, studying the countertops and the walls, then pivoted on his stool and looked at the dining room and, beyond that, the living room.

Then he turned back to Caleb.

"How's that hand? Getting better?"

Caleb looked at the backs of his fingers.

"Okay. Not paying much attention to it."

"Out late again last night?"

"Yeah."

"That a regular thing for you, or just something you started after the girlfriend left?"

"New thing, I guess. Since Bridget left, I've —"

But he couldn't finish the sentence. At least, not without telling Kennon more than he was willing to tell. He looked out the kitchen window, into the fog blowing over the rail of the deck.

"You what? Since Bridget left, what?"

"I don't know. I haven't been handling it well."

"Your secretary said you'd been coming in late this week."

"You talked to Andrea?"

"Sure."

Kennon left it at that. He picked up his mug and held it just in front of his chin, breathing in the coffee steam with his eyes closed. Then he took a sip, set the mug down on the counter, and turned it to look at the emblem on the front.

"Stanford, huh?"

"Yeah."

"Undergrad, or for the Ph.D.?"

"Ph.D. I went to Cal for undergrad."

Kennon rotated the mug until the university's seal faced Caleb.

"Those are good schools," Kennon said. "Selective."

Caleb nodded.

"Any trouble getting in?"

"No."

The inspector looked at Caleb and laid his hand on the leather document folder next to him. He opened its cover an inch and looked inside it, then focused again on Caleb.

"Now you're researching pain at UCSF."

Caleb had been bringing his mug to his lips, but he put it down on the counter. Some of the coffee sloshed over the side.

"Must've been a long sit-down you had with Andrea."

"Nah. Don't get on her case. She just told me you'd been feeling bad this week. Said to come find you here. But I Googled you. One of your papers came up, and I read the abstract."

Caleb nodded. That was fine. It wasn't Andrea's fault he wasn't in the office when a homicide detective came looking for him.

"If you want, I've got a couple extra copies of the journal."

Kennon turned down that offer with the back of his hand, then wrapped his palm and fingers around the mug again. It was cold in the kitchen, with all the west-facing windows taking the full force of the wind.

"I wouldn't understand it. But it looks like interesting stuff. And how's a guy get into studying pain, anyway? I mean — there some kind of background there?"

Caleb couldn't help flicking his eyes away from Kennon's face to watch the detective's fingers tapping at the corner of his leather document folder. He wanted to reach across and take it, wanted to flip it open and see what was inside. The man was going to his lab, talking to his secretary. He was checking up on Caleb, and there'd be more on the Internet than just the academic articles and the patents. Caleb started to bring his hands together, but then stopped and kept them where they were. It wouldn't help anything to seem nervous.

"Nothing like that," Caleb said, looking out the window now. "No background, or whatever you want to call it. It's just an interesting problem of chemistry, of physiology. Kind of thing I'm good at."

"How's that work?" Kennon asked. "Running blood through a mass spectrometer, figuring out how much pain someone's been in."

"Chemicals. Guy gets hurt, his endocrine system responds. Adrenaline, endorphins. Damaged cells dump out different histamines. There's paracrine signaling going on—that's cell-to-cell communication—with compounds like prostaglandin and thromboxane. Bunch of other stuff. Pain leaves markers, and I'm following them. To quantify it."

"So you can say, like, 'On a scale of one to ten, this guy's suffering is a nine point five.'"

Caleb nodded.

"It'd help doctors. Patient comes in, says his pain's unbearable, asks for a narcotic. Oxycontin, morphine. Guy might just need an aspirin. And maybe the grandmother in the room next door's in nonstop agony but she doesn't want to say."

"Don't know about doctors," Kennon said. "But cops and DAs will love it."

"How's that?"

"Capital murder, penalty phase. Get an expert on the stand, have him tell the jury how much the victim suffered. That'd be like a magic bullet—for getting death sentences."

"I hadn't thought of that."

Kennon shrugged.

"Kind of stuff I think about," he said. He brought his coffee to his face and breathed in, but didn't drink any. "And pain's not the only thing you're studying right now."

"I've got several things going. Totally different projects."

Kennon set down his cup.

"I saw another paper. The thing with DARPA and the frog guy."

"Herpetologist. Dr. Reed-Giles."

"Lot of red tape, dealing with toxins like that? What's it —"

"Batrachotoxin."

"Batrachotoxin, right. Kind of hard to pronounce. But I mean, you don't just keep it in the house, do you?"

Caleb turned and looked over his left shoulder, wondering if he'd left any of the bloodstains on the kitchen floor. He couldn't see any. He looked back at Kennon, who was still studying him, waiting for an answer.

"The median lethal dose is ninety micrograms — a couple grains of salt," Caleb said. "And all you'd have to do is touch it."

He reached across and took Kennon's right hand, turning it over on the counter so it lay palm up. Kennon tensed his wrist but didn't try to pull his hand away. He looked at Caleb, let Caleb uncurl his index finger against the granite.

"This a paper cut, right here?"

"Yeah."

He let go of Kennon's hand.

"That's all it'd take. It'd look just like a heart attack. So the answer to your question is yes, there's red tape. A lot of it. And no — I wouldn't keep it around the house. It's in the lab. Signed and sealed, and in a safe."

Kennon nodded and took his hand off the counter, brushing his thumb across his fingertips before wiping his palms down the front of his jacket. Caleb poured the rest of the coffee into Kennon's mug.

Caleb stared out the windows at the gray-white blur.

This was such a good city for a girl who wanted to stay unseen. By daylight, it was hidden half the time. Secretive. At night, when the rain came in and the streetlights were an amber haze, and you were trudging alone down an empty trolley line because it was three a.m. and you were drunk — when you stopped to catch your breath at the top of a hill and caught sight of the bay and its black water reflecting the city like a sheet of shattered glass — in those moments, the city was a dreamscape. A dream she moved through as freely as the fog.

Kennon was watching him.

"There anything you wanted to ask me about?" Caleb said.

"You said you might be able to recognize the other people in the bar that night if I showed you pictures."

"You've got pictures?"

Kennon nodded and tapped the leather document folder on the counter next to his coffee mug.

"We talked to all the bartenders, made a list of the regulars. Then we found pictures of them. Found some others, too. People who might've known the victim."

"You're not saying these are the people who were actually there that night," Caleb said. "These are just the people who might've been there."

"That's right."

Even with that caveat, Caleb felt a prickle of interest. He reached across the counter and put his hand on the leather folder.

"May I?"

"Please."

Caleb slid the folder across and opened it. Inside was a manila envelope.

"In here?"

Kennon nodded, and Caleb bent the copper tabs back and opened the envelope. He pulled out a half-inch stack of photographs printed on high-gloss inkjet paper. He went through the forty pictures quickly, thumbing them onto the counter in a loose stack. The pictures were a mix of driver's license photos and candid shots culled from the Internet. Most of the regulars were men, and the few women weren't even close. When he got to the end of the stack, he went through it a second time, a little more carefully now.

Midway through, he set aside one of the photographs.

"This guy, I think, was down at the end of the bar."

"Okay. Anyone else?"

"I don't think so. I was pretty drunk by the time I got in there."

"You went through that in a hurry the first time. Looking for someone in particular?"

Caleb felt the skin around his eyes tighten. When he looked up, Kennon was watching him closely.

"There was a bald guy — came in, had a drink, and left. I thought I might recognize him, is all."

"That it?"

"Anyone else tell you about him? The bald guy?"

Kennon just looked at him, another of his long pauses. The bartender surely would have remembered the girl who'd ordered absinthe. Kennon would have talked to him, either in the bar or down at the station, in one of the interrogation rooms. So if Kennon didn't know about the girl already, the bartender must have held out on him. There were plenty of reasons a man might not want to tell the police about a girl like that. Or else Kennon knew about her but wanted to see how far Caleb was willing to go to lie for her. But when Kennon spoke again, he changed the subject entirely.

"Maddox — that wasn't always your last name, was it?"

Caleb shook his head.

"My mom remarried when I was fourteen. She changed her name."

"And yours went along for the ride."

"Something like that."

Kennon nodded, then drained the rest of his coffee. He pushed the empty mug back across the counter, to Caleb. Then he just sat, his fingers tapping on the stone as he looked at Caleb.

"Mr. Maddox," he finally said. He scooped the photographs off the counter and slipped them back into the envelope. He put on his fedora. "Thanks for the coffee, and the time."

After Kennon was gone, Caleb stood on the back deck for half an hour, leaning against the redwood rail and letting the cold mist blow into him until his suit was soaked. On the night after it ended with Bridget, all he'd wanted was to go somewhere quiet. Some place he could sit and drink whiskey, and think about her. As if by sitting on a barstool and concentrating on his memories of Bridget, the two of them together, he could bring everything back. She had loved him so much, so fiercely, until her hand found the tumbler. If there'd been anything wrong, some little crack that widened on its approach to last Saturday, he'd missed it. And now he'd lied at least twice to a homicide detective who'd known Caleb's true name. He was helping Henry with something he shouldn't touch at all because he was a witness. He thought of Bridget less than he thought about a girl he'd met for five minutes in the dark.

Five minutes that spun through his mind in a ceaseless whirl.

Her hand on his wrist. Her whispered breath brushing his earlobe. Her naked back, waiting for his touch. The silk dress she'd worn had been so gossamer-thin that if she'd reached to unclasp the strap at the back of her neck, if she'd let it slip past her hips and down to the floor, it would have pooled at her feet and spread there like spilled water.

She was like a dark star passing overhead. She eclipsed everything that guided him, but he couldn't see her. He looked out at the grid of avenues below the hill. Streetlamps were flickering and coming on, though it wasn't quite four in the afternoon. He went inside and stripped off his suit, then took a shower and dressed. When he came back to the living room he sat on the couch and picked up his phone.

He dialed Henry's cell number.

"Just wanted to see what's up. This a bad time?"

"It's a perfect time," Henry said. "I was about to call you."

"Something happen?"

There was a rustle from Henry's end of the line. Caleb could picture him looking around the office, cupping his left hand over the phone's mouthpiece.

"They brought in another one," he whispered. "Just now."

Caleb was silent, staring at the fire. Henry went on in his low voice.

"There'll be a crowd in here for the autopsy. Inspectors from SFPD, some guys from the Marin County sheriff's office. But if you can, come by around eight."

"I can make it. This new guy, he's like the others?"

"Looks like. Same shoulder-girdle bruises. No ID yet, and he's been in the water a while."

"What's a while?"

"More than eight weeks. When you come, bring your cooler. And don't eat a big dinner."

"Sure," Caleb said. He paused, remembering why he'd called. "Guys coming in for the autopsy, those the same detectives working the other case?"

"Yeah. Once the rest of the lab results come back, if they're what we think they are, SFPD will probably go nuts. Put together a task force, set up a tip line. But right now, there's just two inspectors."

"They any good?"

"The lead guy, Kennon, is the best in the city. Maybe in the state. Been on the force so long, he's seen everything twice. I don't know his new partner, but if he's working with Kennon, he's probably good."

"They know we're talking?" Caleb asked. He put his feet on the coffee table and laid his head on the backrest.

"Christ, no. And it'll stay that way. That's trouble I don't need."

"Okay. Good. I'll see you sometime after eight."

. . .

Caleb parked a few blocks from the Hall of Justice and walked past drunks slumped in doorways. He sidestepped a scattering of street-walkers headed to a bus stop after the evening's run of bail hearings. He wedged the cooler under one arm, took out his phone, and called Henry.

"I'm half a block away. Everybody else gone?"

"Just me and the dead," Henry said. "I'll meet you by the back door."

Henry hung up and Caleb put his phone back into his pocket. He followed the chainlink fence and then stood close to the back wall of the Hall of Justice, where he'd be in the shadows and where the rain, falling at an angle, wouldn't reach him. He wondered if Kennon and Garcia worked in here. Probably they had desks in the downtown headquarters. But they'd be in and out of this building all the time: it had the bodies.

The steel door opened, sending a shaft of light across the broken asphalt.

"Caleb?"

"Over here."

They shook hands and Henry held the door for him. They didn't talk until they got down into the medical examiner's suite. They went into the main autopsy room and suited up at the wash station.

"Go heavy on the Vicks," Henry said. "Or you'll be sorry."

"I'm already sorry."

Caleb put a glob of the cream inside his mask and spread it around. Then he wiped the excess under his nostrils. The menthol vapors made his eyes tear up. After he put on his gloves, Henry led them to the portable cold storage unit. Henry took out his keys and opened the locked chamber adjacent to the last victim.

"Got a tentative ID, but we won't release it till the family's been notified," Henry said. He looked sideways at Caleb. "Know how you ID a guy who's been in the water eight weeks?"

"No. And I'm not sure I want to."

"Guy soaks that long, his skin loosens up. You cut around his wrist with a scalpel and then you can peel his hand off in one piece. Like taking off a glove. Fingernails and everything. Turn it right side out, and put your own hand in it. That'll stretch out the maceration wrinkles. Then you've got on this glove. You get an ink pad, and get a print. Like going to the DMV."

"You actually did that?"

"That's standard."

"Remind me not to eat at your house anymore. Unless Vicki cooks."

"I was wearing gloves."

"Yeah — two pairs."

Henry opened the cold chamber door and rolled the cadaver tray out on its slide tracks. The corpse was covered with a sheet. It looked like a big man. He had maybe seventy pounds on Caleb.

"Already got samples for you — made two sets while I was getting Marcie's. But I thought you'd want to see this."

He pulled the sheet off.

EIGHT

"GOOD GOD," CALEB said. "Is that —"

He turned away, pressing the surgical mask tightly against his face.

"What?"

"Is that," he waved his hand at the cadaver, but still couldn't finish. He took a couple shallow, testing breaths, then tried again. "Is that . . . normal?"

Henry nodded.

"Adipocere. They used to call it corpse wax. You stick a body in deep, cold water for a month, it'll happen. Bacteria get in, hydrolyze the fat. Turn it into soap. Cutting through this guy's stomach was like working on a bar of Ivory. Remember Cub Scouts? When we made the soap carvings?"

Caleb nodded, still pressing the mask against his face with the fingers of his left hand.

"Just like that," Henry said. "Smelled worse, though."

The cadaver looked like something from Madame Tussauds Chamber of Horrors. The man was bloated, and there were crevasses in his flesh splitting down as deep as his rib cage, where small sharks and crabs had focused their scavenging. But saponification had turned the corpse hard and yellowish so that he looked like a work of wax sculpture. It was grotesque, but it was so far beyond anything Caleb had seen before that it didn't seem quite real. Caleb looked at the body's right arm. All the skin was missing from his hand. Gray-pink muscle clung to white bone.

Caleb blinked away the menthol tears and swallowed.

"You wanted to show me something?" he asked.

"Yeah. Check these out."

Henry put his index and middle fingers on the man's neck, as though he were checking the jugular for a pulse. There were two red holes in the skin there, about an inch apart. Each hole was the diameter of a small pencil eraser.

"Holy shit," Caleb said. "Those look like —"

"Cutaneous current marks."

"What?"

"Electric current marks. From a stun gun."

Caleb bent down and looked at them more closely. He was holding his breath, pressing his lips together behind the surgical mask so that nothing got in. The holes weren't deep at all. They'd looked like punctures, but from close up he could see they were thin abrasions. Surface burns.

"Yeah," Caleb said, after he'd stood and stepped a comfortable distance away from the cadaver. "Makes sense. Anything else you wanted me to see?"

"Step over here, to the other side."

Caleb came around the end of the cadaver tray. Cold air was pouring out of the open stainless steel-chamber and pooling on the floor at their feet. He stood on the slick tiles next to Henry.

"Look at this," Henry said. He was touching the other side of the man's neck.

"Needle mark?"

"I think so," Henry said. "I think the adipocere let us see it. When the fat hardened into wax, it preserved the needle hole. Made it wider, even."

Henry took the sheet and covered the corpse again, then pushed the tray back into the cold chamber. He closed the door and locked it.

"Let's wash up and sit down in my office a minute. Bring that cooler. I'll give you the samples."

Henry's office was nice enough, but it was still in the basement of a public building. And in a morgue. Caleb sat on the worn leather couch and looked at the degrees on the wall behind Henry's desk. They'd gone to Cal together, but afterward Henry had gone east for medical school and Caleb had gone west across the bay for his Ph.D. Henry shut the door, rounded the desk, and sat in his chair. He had a pair of Tiffany desk lamps, almost ridiculously out of place in the concrete-walled basement office. He switched them on, then cut the overhead fluorescent tubes by flicking the switch on the wall behind his computer monitor.

A two-inch-long cockroach was sneaking along an electrical conduit bolted to the wall just below the ceiling. Caleb watched it.

"Get you a drink?"

"Jesus, yes," Caleb said, looking away from the insect.

He'd washed his face twice in a bathroom sink, but the smell of menthol was still running through his nose. The Vicks hadn't masked everything, though, and even now, on the couch, he could smell the drainpipe stench of the morgue.

Henry leaned down and opened a lower desk drawer. On the back wall, the roach slipped and fell. It landed on the frame of Henry's Yale diploma, clawed its way back to the conduit, and carried on. Henry came up with a pair of cloudy glass tumblers and a bottle of Jim Beam.

"Still keeping it classy," Caleb said.

Henry had been unscrewing the cap from the bottle, but he paused and looked up.

"This morning, I did an autopsy on a ten-year-old girl. All I had was her head. I go through the motions, write a report. Cause of death? How the fuck should I know? All I have is a head. Marcie took samples, but I don't know if she's really doing her job or not. So when I come in here and pour a drink, is it classy? I don't know. Do I care?"

"Make mine a double," Caleb said.

Henry smiled in that thin, tolerant way of his.

"Always the same Caleb. At least there's one thing I can count on."

Henry poured the drinks and passed one of them to Caleb. He reached across the desk and they clinked the rims of their glasses together. Caleb took a sip of the bourbon and breathed the warmth out through his nose. The colored lampshades threw a pattern of light that highlighted the water stains on the wall. Some previous occupant of the office had hidden the worst of these with a framed René Magritte lithograph. *The Treachery of Images.* Caleb stared at that, the pipe and the French script beneath it, and then closed his eyes. He leaned back on the couch, the tumbler cupped in his hand.

"First guy we looked at, his neck was all torn up," Caleb said.

"Crabs did that."

"So if he'd had the stun gun marks, you wouldn't have seen them?"

"That's right. The other six, too — all torn up. Crabs. Marks might've been there, but we wouldn't have seen."

"Okay. Same for the needle marks?"

"Yeah."

"Where'd they find the guy today?"

"Same as the last one. Going under the Golden Gate on the falling tide."

"He was bobbing around in the bay for eight weeks, and no one saw him till now?"

"He wouldn't have been floating most of that time. When a body goes in the water, it sinks — doesn't float until decomposition builds up enough gasses inside to make it buoyant. That could take either hours or days. But this guy's got some marks on his back. Impressions. They look almost like big hex nuts — inch and a half, two inches across. In a line across his shoulder blades."

Caleb opened his eyes and brought his head up.

"You think he got wedged under something?"

Henry nodded and sipped his bourbon.

"He's drifting along with the current, on the bottom, and gets jammed under something," Henry said. "Stays there, eight, maybe ten weeks. Then, in the last couple days, he gets jostled loose. He's buoyant now. So he pops up, starts floating on the outgoing tide."

"How come the crabs didn't pick him apart like the others?"

"I don't know."

"The tissue you got for me, that includes skin samples?"

"Yeah."

Caleb closed his eyes again and put his head back on the cushion.

"What are you thinking?" Henry asked.

But Caleb just shook his head. He didn't really know yet. He just had a hunch.

· · ·

He parked in his garage at midnight after dropping the samples in his lab. He'd started the initial run of tests, then spent an hour answering emails. Now he came into the house and stood looking at the shadows. Listening. There was a soft creak, like someone taking sliding steps in socked feet on the wood floor in one of the other rooms. It came again, from somewhere else. Then there was just silence.

"Bridget?"

He waited, but there was no reply. Of course she wasn't here. It was just the house settling on its pylons. It did that all the time, but at night it was quiet enough to hear it. Caleb walked the rest of the way into the living room and turned on a lamp and the gas fire. His heart had flicked awake for a moment when he'd thought Bridget was in the house, but now he felt himself going back to sleep. He wanted to eat, but couldn't imagine going through the effort of finding something, of putting food into his mouth and chewing it. He dropped onto the couch and the moment he kicked off his shoes and put his feet on the armrest, his phone rang.

He pulled it from his pocket and looked at the screen. A San Francisco number with no name to it. A pay phone, maybe. He swiped the screen and put the phone to his ear.

"This is Caleb."

For a second there was only silence. He was suddenly sure of what he was about to hear. His entire body went tense. The world underneath him was made of paper stretched drum-tight over a void. The slightest wrong move and everything solid could tear out from beneath him. He closed his eyes and held so still that he might have been asleep.

"Caleb," she said.

Her voice was just as it had been before, in House of Shields: a whisper as cool as a night breeze, the accent impossible to place. On the second syllable of his name, her tongue would have brushed just behind her upper teeth, and then she'd have closed out the sound with her lips together, like a blown kiss.

He didn't speak because he couldn't. She'd frozen him with just a whisper.

When he didn't answer, she went on.

"That was the most beautiful thing, what you did. No one's ever done anything like that for me."

He rolled off the couch and moved on his knees to the skirt of stones around the fireplace. He leaned close to the flames to be in their light and warmth.

"I needed to find you," he said.

"Because you want to know my name?"

"Yes."

"Should I tell you now?"

"Please," Caleb whispered.

"Emmeline."

"Emmeline," he repeated. The sound felt like three low waves gently washing past him. "Where are you?"

"It's not where I am that matters. It's where I'll be at three a.m. Will you meet me?"

"Yes. God, yes."

"Good. Come to Spondulix. I know you won't be late. But don't be a minute early, either."

"I'll come."

"Not before three."

He started to answer, but she was already gone.

By the time he'd showered and dressed in a clean suit, it was only twelve thirty. It had been nine hours since he'd talked to Kennon, but that could just as well have been a decade ago, on another continent. The same went for seeing Henry in his morgue, or coming home a few moments ago to a flutter of hope that Bridget had come back.

Emmeline, he thought.

And just by thinking it, he could smell her. He let that take him for a moment. It was like walking into a midnight garden. He thought of honeysuckle hanging from a trellis, the leaves and white blooms beaded with cold rain. He steadied himself and looked back at his computer.

Spondulix was a few blocks from Grace Cathedral, in an alley reaching off Powell Street. But he couldn't find anything else about it. Other than a single pinpoint on the map, it was a blank space on the Internet. That didn't matter. She had chosen the place, and she would be there. So it was the right place, whatever it was.

He had more than two hours to travel just five and a half miles. But as exhausted as he'd been since Saturday, now he had too much energy to stay in the house. He took his keys and his coat and went out to the garage. He drove down the hill and through the Inner Sunset, the avenues empty of traffic. Some of the houses had Christmas trees in their windows, strings of white lights trimmed along their porch rails and under their eaves. The rain started again as he crossed Golden Gate Park, and then he was driving down Geary to the slow rhythm of his windshield wipers. The heater had just started to blow genuinely warm air when he parked in front of Mel's Drive-In at one in the morning. He shut off the engine and sat looking at the blue and red neon lights lining the front of the diner. For the first time since Saturday night, not only was he hungry, but he knew he could actually eat.

Caleb had finished his omelet and was waiting for the waitress to refill his cup of coffee when his phone rang. He pulled it from his pocket and looked at the screen, expecting to see another pay phone number.

But it was Bridget.

Two in the morning, and it was Bridget. He swiped the screen and brought the phone to his ear, shielding his mouth with his left hand.

"This is Caleb."

"Where are you?"

"I'm out. Eating a late dinner. Where are you?"

"At the house — your house. I'm outside. I came to drop something off for you. Something I made. But the garage door was open, and your car was gone, and I saw the front window was broken. So I was worried."

Caleb leaned to the side and hunched closer to the phone while the waitress reached across from the other side of the table and refilled his coffee. He met her eye and nodded. Then he whispered into his hand.

"I guess I just forgot to close the garage. I've been — busy. Henry's got something going on, and I've been down at his office. And in the lab."

"Are you okay? Caleb?"

"Yeah."

"All right," she said. He could picture her standing in the drive-way, leaning against the side of her Volvo. Looking at the broken, boarded-up window and wondering how much of the story he wasn't telling her.

He could tell her to go inside, to wait for him. That he was just down at Mel's and he'd be back in ten minutes. And he came close to it, but in the end he said nothing at all. After a while, Bridget broke the silence. She was always the one to do that, to take a breath and put her head down, then come across whatever gap lay between them.

"So anyway. I have a thing for you," she said. "I was going to put it on your doorstep, where you'd find it in the morning when you went for the paper. But you haven't been getting your papers. They're all stacked up. So I'll put it in the garage, with the papers. And I'll close the door for you."

"Okay. Thanks."

"It's nothing. I mean, no — that's not true. It's *something*. I worked on it awhile. Since before, you know, what happened Saturday. Because I know how you are. I knew you'd like it, like to sit and look at it. And when I finished it, I still wanted you to have it. Maybe tomorrow, after you look at it, we can try talking."

"Okay."

"You asked me a question that time, right before I hung up on you —"

"Don't," he said, too quickly. He didn't want to know. Not now.

"But —"

"It's *okay*, Bridget. Forget it. All right?"

"Okay," she said. "But, Caleb?"

"Yeah?"

In the pause, he felt the floor shift as if a fault had slipped.

"I'm really sorry I threw the glass," she said. "I shouldn't have done that. I had a right to be mad. I still have a right to be mad. But I shouldn't have done that."

"It's fine," he said.

"No, it isn't. None of it is. Not what you did, not what I did. But please, let's talk in the morning, okay? Or the afternoon?"

"Okay."

"Good," she said.

There was another silence between them, and again, she was the one to break it. He hated that he could make her do that, make her come across to him. When she spoke, her voice wasn't much more than a tearful, warm whisper.

"Bye, Caleb. I love you."

She hung up right away, as if she didn't want to know how he'd respond.

NINE

WITH HALF AN hour left to kill, he parked on Taylor Street, at the bottom of four tiers of steps spilling away from Grace Cathedral's main entrance. He got out and locked the car, then walked halfway up the wet steps and stood looking at the darkened rose window. He started on a slow walk around the cathedral, watching the shadows of its buttresses and the faint gleam of the polished bronze friezes on the Ghiberti doors leading to the baptistery. This was Bridget's family's church: she'd come here since she was a little girl. When her parents emigrated from France, they chose it because it reminded them of Notre Dame—never mind that it wasn't Roman Catholic. It was the building that mattered. Now the columbarium in the bell tower held their ashes. Caleb turned the corner and went into the deeper shadows beneath the naked branches of sycamore trees as he climbed the hill past the Cathedral School.

For Bridget, this building was like an island in time. It brought the past and the future together. She could stand in its nave before the altar and remember herself in her first communion dress, knowing—both then and now—that in the future she would stand here again to receive a different rite. As if all three strands of time were woven into a braid by their common connection to this spot of ground. She'd brought Caleb, and taken him through the main sanctuary on an empty Saturday night, explaining this to him.

Yet he'd done what he did, without telling her about it for months. And now, in twenty minutes, he was still going to do what he'd come here to do. He put his head down and turned the next corner, walking slowly east on Sacramento Street. When he finished his circuit, he checked his car and looked once more at the rose window. Then he turned his back to it and walked down California Street. Toward Spondulix. Toward Emmeline.

A few nights ago, he'd walked past this alley without even noticing it. He'd been too drunk to see much except his feet on the pavement. But even now, mostly sober and having studied a map, he almost walked past it. It was that narrow. He stood at the mouth of the alley with his back to Powell Street and looked ahead.

A hundred feet down, a parked car took up the width of the lane between the buildings. There was less than a centimeter's space between its passenger side and the brick wall of the adjacent building. On the driver's side there was just enough room, maybe, for someone to open the door and squeeze out. It was hard to tell its color in the shadows, but he thought it was the same ghost-gray antique coupe he'd seen drift past Grace Cathedral in the rain and fog on Sunday night. It was parked facing outward. He was looking at its chrome-plated headlamps and the silver statuette on its hood. It was too dark to be sure, but he thought the trunk was open.

Spondulix, if it existed at all, must be somewhere down the alley, past the coupe. He looked at his watch. It wasn't quite three, and she had been insistent: he could be late, but not early.

He put his hands in his pockets and walked down Powell Street. He took a left on Pine and then circled the block, lingering in the spots of light across from the Ritz-Carlton's marble-columned façade to check his phone and then turn it off.

When he completed the circle and came back to the alley's entrance, it was five minutes past three. He stood at the dark mouth of the alley. The gray coupe was gone. The way up the alley was clear.

"Hello, Caleb."

He turned, and there she was. Ten feet up Powell Street in the shadowed doorway to a shuttered delicatessen. He had walked past her without seeing her, because he'd been focused on the alley.

"Emmeline."

She was wearing an off-the-shoulder black dress. It was sleeveless, but she wore black silk gloves that went past her elbows. Her hair was as dark as volcanic glass, and fell loosely about her shoulders and curled inward beneath her chin and across her breastbone to frame her face. The light of the streetlamps glowed in the fine drops of rain caught in her hair.

"Shall I show you the way?"

"Please."

She came to his side, switching her black clutch bag from her right hand to her left so she could take ahold of his arm. There was nothing shy in that touch. The side of her body pressed up against his, and because of that, and the way she walked as she led him into the alley, he could map out the violin curve from her shoulder to her hip.

"Here we are," she said.

They were standing beneath a small canvas awning above a painted wooden door. Brass lettering mounted in the door might have spelled out *SPONDULIX*. It was too dark to tell for sure. There were gas lamps on either side of the door, but they were unlit. The only light came from the streetlamps on Powell, and they were a long way off.

"Is it open?" Caleb said.

"For us."

She put her gloved palm on the door and pushed it gently. It swung open and Caleb was looking down a staircase. Whatever Spondulix was, it was underground. From the bottom of the stairs came the flickering light of candles.

"Go ahead," she whispered. "I'll close the door."

She let go of Caleb's arm and he felt her fingertips at the small of his back. He went four steps down the stairs and heard her move behind him. She closed the door so that it was entirely dark on the stairway except for the candlelight down below. He heard her throw a deadbolt lock, a jingle of keys. Then the lovely nightshade scent of her perfume was with him, and she'd come down the few steps that separated them. Her hands came around his shoulders and rested lightly on his clavicles.

"Go on," she said. "It's all right."

The stairs were too narrow for them to walk side by side, but she stayed close to him till they reached the bottom. Then the hallway widened some and she was next to him again, taking his arm and leading him through an arched doorway and into the bar.

The single room of the bar was like a jewelry box: exquisitely crafted, plush with red and black velvet. Sparkling. It was also completely empty. The ebony wood floor was freshly mopped and still had wet streaks from its scrubbing. There was a baby grand piano on a small raised stage in one corner. A pair of votive candles flickered at one end of the bar. Half a dozen more of them rested on the table of the largest corner booth, their combined light glittering in the crystal pendalogues of the unlit chandeliers. She led him toward the candlelit table. A half-full bottle of Berthe de Joux was there, together with a carafe of ice water and a pair of reservoir glasses already topped with slotted spoons. A little silver platter held a small stack of sugar cubes.

"Will you make the drinks?" she asked.

"Yes."

"You remember how?"

"I do. You could say I studied it. While I was looking for you."

She smiled and let go of his arm. Then she slid into the booth, looked up at him, and tapped the velvet seat beside her.

"You must be freezing," he said. "Can I give you my coat?"

"Could you?"

She leaned toward the table and let him put the coat around her shoulders. She didn't put her arms through the sleeves but reached up from inside it and pulled the lapels together so that she wore it like a cloak.

"Thank you."

"It's nothing," he said. He looked around the empty bar. "Is this place yours?"

"No."

"You're the manager?"

"No, I don't work here," she said. "But it's okay, Caleb. I promise you."

"All right."

She tapped the seat next to her again, and this time he sat. She moved over, closing the gap he'd left between them. Then she rested her cheek against his shoulder.

"Pour the drinks."

He reached for the bottle and uncorked it. He poured just over an ounce into each glass, pushed the cork back into the bottle, and set it down. He put sugar cubes atop the spoons and then took the carafe and poured the ice water the way she'd taught him at House of Shields. High and slow.

"I'm glad you found me," she said, without lifting her head from his shoulder. "I'd like for us to be friends. I don't have any others. Do you believe that?"

He paused in pouring the second drink and looked down at her.

"No," he said. "I don't."

"Well, it's true," she said. "Finish pouring that one. We'll have a toast."

When the second sugar cube had melted through the spoon and into the absinthe, he stirred both drinks and set the spoons aside on a saucer. Emmeline sat up and moved back on the velvet bench so she could hold her drink and face him. He moved to touch the rim of his glass against hers, but she pulled hers back.

"This is the toast," she said. "It's a promise. Two promises. If I'm your friend, I'll never lie to you. And I'll never hurt you. Do you believe that?"

"Yes."

"And what about you? You'll promise me those two things?"

"Yes."

"You *promise* me?"

"Yes."

"All right, then."

She reached toward him with her glass and they clinked the heavy crystal rims together. Then she put her glass to her lips, closed her eyes, and sipped the absinthe. He did the same. It was a mix of such opposing sensations that it felt like a balancing act. Bitter wormwood and rue leaning into the sweetness of the sugar and anise, the chill of the ice water pulling against the alcohol's heat. She put the glass on the table and sat with her eyes closed for a moment. Then she looked at him.

"Just because I promised not to lie to you doesn't mean I'll answer anything you ask. But if I answer, it'll be the truth. You understand?"

"I think so."

"Good." She picked up her drink and finished it. "Finish yours, and then let's have another. Don't you want another?"

"Yes."

He picked up his glass, swirling the absinthe and breathing in its vapors.

"Did you spend a long time on it? Making the drawing?"

He nodded, and sipped his drink. Her eyes were following the fingers of his right hand. The scabs were almost complete now. When he put his glass on the table, she took his hand and used her gloved fingers to coax his fingers flat on the black tablecloth. She brushed her fingertips in circles along the edges of the wounds. She'd done something similar to his forehead in House of Shields, getting his blood on her bare finger within a minute or two of meeting him.

"You didn't have these before."

"No."

"You have to be careful, Caleb."

"I will be."

She slid one of her hands under his, then placed the other atop his, so that she was pressing both sides of his fingers with the cool silk of her gloves.

"Why don't you ask me a question? I know you want to. You have a lot of them."

He had so many questions, he didn't know which to start with. He couldn't even begin to understand the effect she had on him. It was like one of Henry's cases—a tangle of interacting compounds and forces so complex that he would need a week in his lab to sort it all out. He finished his absinthe and refilled both of their glasses. He put the slotted spoons into place, topped them with sugar cubes, and began to drip the ice water into Emmeline's glass.

"It isn't a test, Caleb. You can just ask me a question."

"All right."

"Pour it slowly," she said. She moved one of her hands to his right knee. "That's right."

"You said you didn't have any friends. Why is that?"

She took her hand off his knee, then tucked both her arms away inside his coat where he couldn't see them. She drew the coat tightly around herself again.

"It wasn't always that way. I used to have one. A friend, I mean. A man. We traveled together, place to place. He raised me, but he wasn't my father. When I got old enough, we —"

She stopped, and looked at him. When she blinked, he saw the powdered malachite eye shadow she wore.

"But I don't have to tell you everything, do I?"

"No," he said. "Not unless you want to."

Caleb finished pouring the water into her absinthe and moved the carafe so he could pour into his glass. He could already feel the first drink moving into him, meeting his blood and coming alive there. The second glass would be even better, would wrap his skin the way her perfume and the touch of her cheek on his shoulder enveloped him. Carried him.

When she didn't say anything else, he asked another question.

"What happened to him?"

"He went away one night. That was normal enough. When he'd leave, I had to wait for him. That was the rule, from when I was little: I had to stay wherever we were sleeping. The motel, an apartment. In the old days, before we had much money, sometimes I had to sleep in the car, parked out in the woods. The last time he left, he didn't come back. I waited a week. And then I did what we always did."

"Which was?"

"I moved on."

When he finished making the absinthes, she reached her arm out of the coat and took her glass by its stem. She brought its rim up against his, one soft click of crystal to crystal, and then she drank the whole thing, in one swallow.

"How long ago was this?" Caleb asked.

"A month ago. Maybe two," she said. She looked at Caleb. "I think he's dead."

Caleb looked through his drink at one of the candle flames. The absinthe darkened the fire and tinged it green. He picked up the glass and drank it all at once, just as she had.

"You think this is bad," she said. "This worries you."

He looked at her face, her wide green eyes captured in the candle-light and shadows of this empty, shut-down bar. He'd promised not to lie to her. So he nodded.

"Yes. It's— I don't know what to think. About any of this, I guess."

"You can leave if you want. I won't hold it against you."

"No. I don't want to leave."

"Good," she said. She leaned her cheek on his shoulder again. Her left hand was curled on her lap and her right hand rested on his leg, just behind his knee. "There's one thing I have to do before we leave here. I want to give you something, so we're even. You gave me the picture. But I can't draw like you. So make us a third Berthe de Joux. I probably need a third, to do this right."

He took the bottle and pulled its stopper out, liking the wet, hollow *plonk* of the cork coming free.

"Pour this one like we're at home," she said. Her cheek was still on his shoulder. "Like we're not in a bar, but we're at home, a home we can always stay in, and we're about to go to bed. This is the last drink."

He poured it that way, slowly filling the reservoir of her glass and letting the meniscus of absinthe rise past the bulb of the reservoir until each glass held a full two ounces. He put the sugar cubes on the spoons, his hands steady and his vision lucid with the pulse of the spirit he'd already drunk. Emmeline sat up from him and took her drink when he was finished. He had many more questions, but now wasn't the time. She was so beautiful that when this night ended and he went back to his house alone, he would want to lie on the couch with his eyes closed, remembering the way she was right now. He didn't want to interrupt this with questions. She brought the glass to her lips and drank, then met his eyes and smiled at him with half her mouth.

"Stand up, Caleb," she said. "So I can get out."

He slid out of the booth and stood at the end of the table above the light and smoky heat of the candles. Emmeline put her glass on the table and then brought her right hand to her mouth. She bit down on the fingertip of her glove, holding the silk in her teeth as she slipped her hand out of it. She put the glove on the table and then did the same with her left hand. She looked up at him and saw he was watching.

"I can't play with my gloves on," she said. She stood, leaving her gloves on the table. She took her drink, then looked at Caleb. "Bring a candle. I'll need a little light."

He took one of the votive candles inside its thin shell of warm glass. Emmeline held his arm, leading him across the ebony floor toward the small stage. She let go of his arm and stepped up to the raised platform, pulling the piano bench back and sitting down before the keyboard in a single movement of silk and shadow. She set her drink on the narrow sheet music shelf above the keyboard.

"Come stand over here with the light," she said. "Over to the side so there's no shadow on the keyboard."

She hit the first couple of notes as he stepped past the bench. She was so light on the keys that he could hear the wooden hammers coming down on the wires and the felt-padded dampers as they moved in to still the vibrations. He could hear the creak of the right pedal as she touched it with her foot. The first few notes were like a scattering of rain on a window overlooking the sea. Warm and intimate.

He recognized it right away when she began to sing.

Her voice was just a whisper, and that made it work. He'd never heard a woman sing this. Tom Waits, who wrote it and sang it, had a voice like smoking flint. The song was so beautiful because you'd never think his voice could say anything so tender. Emmeline's voice was as smooth and polished as the stem of the glass in front of her. But when she sang in a whisper and the breath caught in her throat because she was trying so hard to be quiet, and some parts of the words were simply lost to silence, it had almost the same effect.

It was an end-of-the-day song. An end-of-it-all song.

Emmeline paused before the penultimate verse, her foot on the sustain pedal so that the last notes she'd struck carried into the break while she picked up her glass and drank it off until nothing was left but a slurry of sugar. She set the glass down and finished the song, running out of breath as she whispered the last words, her fingers slipping a little, missing the cadence of the final notes. She moved her foot off the pedal and Caleb heard the dampers fall all the way across the board. With that felt-hushed thump, the room went silent. The flame in his hand whipped and sent up a thin runner of smoke as he breathed.

She looked up at him.

"That's it, I guess."

Caleb didn't know what to say. She'd done it again, immobilized him.

"You should go," she said. "I'll clean up."

"All right."

He stepped closer to the piano and set the candle on its lid, then moved toward the edge of the little stage.

"Wait."

She stood and came to him. She took the empty glass from his hand and set it next to hers. They didn't kiss. It was better than that. She shrugged off his coat and put it around his shoulders, and then wrapped herself around him, her cheek pressed just beneath his collarbone. He put his face down into the dark nest of her hair. It was still wet from the rain, and cool, though his own hair had long since dried.

"Thank you," she said. She held him tightly. "We'll keep our promises, right?"

"We will."

"Go on home. I'll see you."

"You'll call me?"

"Soon."

She let go of him and sat again on the piano bench, her back to him. He looked at her a moment, her bare white shoulders and the raven-spill of her hair in the candlelight. Then he turned and showed himself out.

TEN

HE DIDN'T GO home. That would have been impossible.

He wandered up to California Street, then back toward Grace Cathedral. He felt like he had a second heart, something that beat a
countercadence to his normal pulse, so that he was both out of control and twice as alive. Part of that was the absinthe. He knew that.
But most of it was Emmeline. He would have stayed in that underground bar with her, drinking absinthe and listening to her sing at
the piano, until the sun burned itself to ashes. He jaywalked across
California Street and then stumbled west, toward the church and his
car. For a minute, he stopped and leaned his shoulder against the
wrought-iron pole of a streetlamp, holding his arms across his chest.
Steadying himself, keeping the remnants of her embrace close to his
skin. Then he went on.

He drove into the Tenderloin and stopped outside an all-night bo-
dega that existed for no reason but to flout every liquor law known
to San Francisco. He went in and asked for absinthe. Berthe de Joux.
When the man just gave him a blank look, he bought a bottle of Jim
Beam. Then he went back to his car and drove to the Inner Sunset,
winding up to Parnassus and parking at his spot in the medical center. He took off his coat and wrapped it around the bottle of Beam,
pausing next to his car to close his eyes and absorb the smell of Emmeline's perfume. She'd been so close to him, for so long, that he was
permeated with it. As if he'd swum across a river to reach her.

. . .

He was wide awake when he sat at his desk at five in the morning, sipping bourbon straight from the bottle and chasing it with black coffee he'd brewed in the break room. He used his computer, setting out a plan for testing the samples Henry had given him, the slices of tissue from the saponified man.

He had a hunch about the skin samples.

The first man he'd seen had been coated in silt and algae; the second man had been jammed against the ocean bottom for weeks in one spot. The sand, and anything in the sand, would have worked into his skin. It would have filled the microscopic crevasses and packed the pores. There was an opportunity there, maybe. He took another sip of the bourbon and began to build a calibration curve.

The next time he called Henry, maybe he'd have something better than a cause of death. He might have a plan, a way to get them close to the killer.

At eight in the morning, Andrea knocked on his door and stuck her head in. He had just enough time to put the bottle of bourbon on the floor, out of sight. But he knew how he'd look.

"You doing okay, Caleb?"

"Yeah."

"Can I get you anything?"

"No. I'm fine."

"Can I leave at lunch? Maggie's school let out for Christmas break, and I don't have a sitter lined up. Nick's got her till one, but after that, he's gotta work."

Caleb waved his hand at the concern on her face.

"It's fine. Take as long as you need."

"Thanks, Caleb."

"It's nothing. It's slow around here anyway."

Andrea looked down at her fingers on the outer door handle. She was confused, he thought. Maybe embarrassed for him. He hadn't been in the lab enough this week to have an opinion on how busy things were. He was less than a third of the way through his unread email.

"Joanne's been looking for you," Andrea said. "All day yesterday. I think she's worried about the grant. She had a conference call with some guys in Bethesda."

That got Caleb's attention. He pulled his chair closer to the edge of the desk, bumping the bottle of bourbon at his feet. It tottered on its glass bottom but didn't tip over.

"She needs to talk about something, she's got my email."

"You'll be in all day?"

"No. I've been here all night. I'm heading home in an hour or two. I just need to finish running something."

Andrea nodded and backed out of his office. She shut the door.

The sun had only been up an hour when he got back to his house. He waited for the garage door to roll up, then drove inside. There was a paper-wrapped package leaning against the inside door, a stack of bagged newspapers in front of it. He looked at them a moment before shutting off the car. Part of him wanted to just throw the transmission into reverse and drive back down the hill, then out of the city. North, south, or east — it didn't matter as long as it was away from all the points of pressure twisting in on him. Bridget and Emmeline; Henry and Kennon; Joanne and the National Institutes of Health. Instead, he hit the button on the sun visor and watched in the rearview mirror as the garage door closed. When it was down, he switched off the car's headlights and sat in the dark with his eyes closed. After about a minute, he realized the engine was still running. He shut it off, then got out of the car, holding his breath against the exhaust. He took Bridget's package and brought it inside.

He put Bridget's gift on the dining table but didn't open it. It was a painting, and it would be beautiful. But he wasn't ready to look at it. Even with Bridget all but standing in the dining room, he couldn't let go of Emmeline. Her perfume's scent was on his coat; the memory of her hands lay upon his skin.

"Jesus Christ, Caleb," he said. "Come on."

He put the coat over the back of a chair, then walked to the phone on the wall. He unplugged it, then took out his cell phone and turned off its ringer. There were decisions to be made, and they would have to be made soon, but so long as neither woman could reach him, he could stay balanced in between. He took the bottle of Jim Beam and had one last long pull from it, then chased it with cold tap water from the sink, leaning down to drink straight from the faucet. He hadn't been in his own bed since getting out of it on Saturday morning, but he thought it wasn't time yet. The couch would do for today, again. At least it was close to the fire, and he needed that.

He kicked off his shoes and turned on the fire, then lay on the couch under his tartan blanket.

It started as soon as he closed his eyes.

The couch began to spin and his mind spun with it, the previous day's images caught like rafts of debris in a whirlpool. He saw Kennon in his kitchen. Then the soap-rotten corpse. Henry holding up his own hand to demonstrate how he'd peeled the man's skin off like a glove, in search of prints. He heard Bridget's voice on the phone and saw the waitress's eyes as she poured his coffee. There was Andrea looking at the doorknob because she was embarrassed for him. Embarrassed by the state of him.

And he saw the shadows swaying in Spondulix as he stood above and beside Emmeline with a candle, lighting the keyboard for her as she played. Then Kennon was asking who he'd been looking for when he'd flipped through the stack of pictures too quickly, after his rush to find Emmeline drove him through the snapshots at a finger-fumbling sprint. He felt his face burn again with the shame of being caught in a lie, and then there was the smell of the morgue and the sound of the cockroach running along Henry's office wall, chitinous claws on damp concrete.

The memory-pool widened.

He saw Bridget — saw the first time she'd stood before him wearing nothing but her panties, her other clothes spread across his floor where she'd shed them. She held her forearm across her tan breasts and came up to him with hesitant steps so she would not break open her wound, closing the distance between them because she was too shy that first time to stand afar and be seen. He remembered the way his hands had fit around her bleeding foot barely an hour before that moment.

Emmeline was pressing his sliced-open fingers between her silk-lined palms. Her cool whisper, *You have to be careful, Caleb.* There was a painting on the wall behind her. He couldn't see it for the shadows, but it made him cold.

Emmeline's breath brushed his ear: *We'll keep our promises, right?*

He finally wrapped his thoughts around Emmeline, wound them tightly enough to keep his mind from drowning in the day. It was like holding on to a tree to stay in one place against the force of a flood. He clung to her, latching on to the memory of her arms around him as they said good night, no space between them at all. His face in her hair, the beaded rain cold on his skin. He held on to her until the flood subsided, until the spinning images of the day finally dried up, and then he followed her down the stairs again and back into the darkness of the hideaway bar under Nob Hill. The bar no one knew about. The bar that was open for them, and only for them, when the rest of the city was a rain-wrapped dream.

Buried in those shadows, he slept at last.

He didn't remember getting up, or going to the dining room to get his jacket from the back of the chair. But he must have. When he woke, well past nightfall, the jacket was rolled into a pillow between the crook of his elbow and the side of his face. He stayed like that a while, his cheek on the soft wool of the jacket, watching the fire and not wanting to look at the time.

When he did get up, he went into the kitchen. According to the microwave clock, it was a minute past midnight. He turned on the flame under the kettle, then washed the French press, which was still sitting in the sink from after his conversation with Kennon. While the water heated, he found his cell phone and checked it.

One missed call from Bridget, eight hours ago. No messages, no texts. And no calls from pay phones.

He set the phone on the counter, upside down, so he wouldn't see the screen if it lit up. He went upstairs to his study and got his laptop computer, a hardbound copy of the *Physicians' Desk Reference,* and a spiral-bound atlas covering the Bay Area. The kettle was whistling when he came back to the kitchen. He booted the laptop and logged in to his remote office connection, tying himself into the lab's network. After a few sips of coffee, he started where he'd left off: analyzing data from the initial tests he'd run on the tissue samples cut from the saponified man. Interpreting the chromatograph signatures and the spectrometer printouts, working backwards from the metabolites to build a story about the man's last few hours alive.

They couldn't have been pleasant, those last three or four hours. By the time the clock showed six a.m., he was sure of that much.

By sunrise, he was showered, shaved, dressed, and sitting in the same booth at Mel's he had the morning before. He ordered an omelet and a short stack of pancakes. Coffee and orange juice. While he waited, he took out his phone and dialed.

"I wake you?"

"Christmas vacation — kids are out of school. They got me up at a quarter to five. Vicki sleeps with earplugs," Henry said. "So, lucky her. What's up?"

"Any chance you can miss work today?"

"It's possible."

Caleb could hear a television in the background. Cartoons, maybe. Henry's kids were talking above the show's volume.

"It'll be worth it. I promise. How's *Toe Tags*?"

"She's fine."

"Engine's fixed?"

"Three, four weeks ago. Swapped out the heat exchanger."

"The morgue can spare you. Let's meet at the wharf — eight thirty work?"

"All right," Henry said. "I'll make it. Want to tell me what we're doing?"

"We're gonna figure out where the bodies are getting dumped," Caleb said.

He saw movement and looked up. The waitress was standing across from him with the coffeepot. Caleb put his hand over his mouth and whispered.

"I gotta go. Call me if you can't make it."

Caleb parked in a public garage near Fisherman's Wharf and walked over to the pier. There were flyers taped to all the parking meters. He stopped to look at one, crouching low enough to read it.

HAVE YOU SEEN JUSTIN HOLLAND?

The text ran above the picture of a handsome thirty-year-old man in a business suit. Caleb stood and turned around, scanning the empty block. Identical flyers plastered every vertical surface for two blocks. But the fringe of phone numbers at the base of each flyer was untouched.

He bought sourdough rolls and takeout containers of chowder at a restaurant in the Pier 39 concourse, carrying the food away in a brown paper bag. He found Henry on a bench near the locked gate that accessed the marina's floating docks.

"You're early," Caleb said.

"Because you always are. What's that?"

Caleb hefted the brown paper bag.

"Lunch."

"I meant the backpack," Henry said, nodding his chin at the black strap on Caleb's left shoulder.

"Some gear for getting samples. Maps. Stuff for you to read."

"We'll be out long enough to need lunch?" Henry asked. He stood and began leading them toward the gate.

"Gotta cover fifty nautical miles. We might be out all day."

"Good thing I topped off the tanks last week."

"I'll pay you back for the fuel," Caleb said. "This was my idea."

"If it's about the murders, it's on me. It pans out, I'll get reimbursed."

Henry unlocked the gate and held it open for Caleb. They walked down the sloped gangway to the floating docks, then followed a path between sailboats and cabin cruisers until they reached *Toe Tags*. Henry had bought her from a retired medical examiner in Los Angeles. Not just because of the name—though Caleb was certain the name played an outsize role in Henry's decision—but also because she was a beautifully kept trawler: thirty-six feet of oiled teak and polished bronze from stem to stern, with steering stations both in the protected pilothouse and aloft on the flying bridge.

Caleb hadn't been aboard since the summer, when he'd come with Bridget. Henry and Vicki had taken them for a weekend at Angel Island while their kids were with Vicki's parents. The four of them sat up late around the boat's dinette table, drinking wine and lingering over a dinner Caleb cooked, talking by the light of the oil lamps mounted on brass gimbals around the cabin.

Bridget's way of saying thanks for that trip now hung on the teak bulkhead in the saloon, and when Caleb unlocked the pilothouse door with Henry's keys and stepped into the cabin, he stood looking at it. She'd painted it at dawn, after rowing ashore alone while the rest of them slept, then standing on the dock and looking back at the boat in Ayala Cove, back across the stretch of water toward Tiburon. The warm glow of lights from inside the boat's cabin shimmered atop the ripples in the calm anchorage.

To Caleb, this painting captured everything important there was to know about boats, and about Bridget. There was the dark water, and the darker hills in the distance beyond it, and the dawn sky was the gray-purple bruise of a day that would bring wind and rain. And yet there in the center of this, the boat sat so gracefully upon the water. Comfortable and at ease in the dark cove, beneath the uncertain sky.

She would keep you warm, carry you through any passage.

"She talking to you yet?" Henry asked, leaning in the doorway.

Caleb turned away from the painting.

"She called. Yesterday, I think. And she dropped off a painting for me."

"So things are looking up?"

Caleb shrugged.

"Hard to say," he said. He handed the key ring back.

"Don't tell me your girlfriend's complicated. No one would believe that."

"Yeah."

"Maybe I was too hard on you, when we talked before."

"Probably not."

Henry stepped past Caleb and sat at the wide helm seat in the starboard corner of the cabin. He fit the key into the ignition and started the engine. Its cylinders caught right away and then chugged along with a lazy rumble.

"Gotta idle her a while, warm her up before we go. Sit down. Tell me what we're doing."

ELEVEN

THEY SAT OPPOSITE each other at the mahogany dinette table on the port side of the cabin. It was cold inside, and the windows were fogging with their breath, but that would clear soon enough. Henry had switched on a pair of small space heaters, and their wire coils were already starting to glow nicely. Caleb could feel the vibration of the engine coming up through his elbows, which rested on the table-top. Outside, a flurry of rain whipped across the deck.

"The soap man, you identified him?" Caleb said.

He wanted to be able to think of him as a person instead of a hor-ror sculpture. A name would help.

"Family confirmed. Name was Charles—"

"Charles Crane?" Caleb said.

"How the hell did you know that?"

"He was in the newspaper. There were flyers up and down Haight Street."

Henry tilted his head, then accepted it with a nod.

"I thought the family and the police were keeping it quiet," Henry said. "Anyway, he was a software engineer. Last time anyone saw him alive was at the bar in the Drake Hotel. Nice, upscale kind of place."

"And the first guy I looked at, what about him?"

Caleb already knew this man's first name from talking to the bartender at House of Shields, but he couldn't tell Henry that. He wanted to help Henry, and he didn't mind helping Kennon, but he'd drawn a circle around Emmeline in his mind. A circle that contained everything about her, about their relationship. He didn't understand why it was there. Maybe Emmeline had slipped into his thoughts with her promises, set its boundaries with her song in the dark, and sealed it with the press of her body against his. He'd lie to his best friend before he'd risk her.

"Richard Salazar," Henry said. "Partner at a law firm on Market Street."

"Makes it easier, having names."

"You get over it."

Caleb let that go without saying anything. Even Henry had cracks. He'd seen that for himself. The work was getting to Henry, putting him on edge. Things like having to do an autopsy on a ten-year-old girl's head. Henry's daughter was about that age. And for that, Caleb wanted to give his oldest friend something. Wanted to give him facts he could use to put at least one problematic case to rest. He tried to think how to explain it.

He sat tracing his fingers in the woodgrain patterns of the table. Outside, a gull landed on the rail and tucked one of her feet up into her feathers, out of the rain. Caleb watched the gull through the fogged glass, and then looked back at the table.

"Same person who murdered Richard Salazar murdered Charles Crane," Caleb said. He looked up and saw Henry was watching him closely. "It was harder to trace in Crane, but the chemical signatures were identical — vecuronium, followed by a wallop of thujone. Three or four hours of torture. Intense pain. Then another shot of vecuronium to get him in the water."

Henry nodded.

"This means the others are probably linked too."

"Yeah."

They sat listening to the rain hitting the decks and running down the sloped windows of the pilothouse.

"So we'll need to run the tests on the others. Either send Marcie to your lab, or have you come in and look over Marcie's shoulder. But what're we doing on the boat?" Henry said. "How are we supposed to find the dump sites?"

"Crane's skin samples."

"What about them?"

"You said he had hex bolt marks across his back, right?"

Henry nodded.

"Marks like that, he'd have to get wedged under something pretty quickly after he went in the water?" Caleb asked.

"That's right. Before he went into rigor. He stiffened up around the bolts. Like a wax mold, cooling down. And he had livor mortis — his blood settled and left bruise marks on the side of his body facing down. Most bodies in the water don't do that. They stay moving, the blood doesn't settle. So if he had livor mortis, he was wedged under something early on. Within the first hour."

Caleb pulled a sheaf of paper from his backpack and set it on the dinette table between them. Printouts from his lab.

"Which means," Caleb said, "if we can figure where he got stuck, we'll know he went into the water somewhere nearby. The bay's got currents, but they're not random. We can map them, come up with a probable entry point. Wherever the victims are going in the water is probably close to where they're getting tortured. Somewhere safe for the killer. Maybe his house. Maybe just a place he uses."

Henry glanced down at the paperwork. It was mostly charts and graphs. Tables of chemical symbols.

"What'd you find?"

"High concentrations of sodium hydroxide and pure aluminum. You know what those are, together?"

Henry shook his head.

"The two most common ingredients in drain cleaner," Caleb said.

"Okay."

"It gets even better. His skin — the silt packed in the pores of his skin — had traces of synthetic estrogen and progestogen. Also the metabolites of acetaminophen, fluoxetine, and citalopram. Now, tell me — where would you find drain cleaner, birth control pills, Tylenol, and the two most popular antidepressants in America, plus a hundred other drugs and common household cleaners?"

"I — I don't know."

"It's easy," Caleb said. "Sewage treatment plants. The outflow vents."

Caleb reached into his backpack and pulled out his atlas of the bay. He set it on the table but didn't open it.

"They treat the sewage, but only biologically," Caleb said. "Not chemically. The effluent's mostly sterile. But if you take a birth control pill and a Tylenol every morning, and your boyfriend's on Prozac, and sometimes you pour Drano down your kitchen sink—all that stuff goes into the bay pretty much the same way it went down the toilet or the drain. And that's probably why Crane didn't get torn up by crabs. He was stuck in a biological dead zone."

Henry took the printouts and leafed through the pages. He pushed them back across the dinette table to Caleb.

"So we're cruising to sewage treatment plants?"

Caleb nodded.

"I got them mapped out. There's five within ten miles of the Golden Gate Bridge, on the current paths. If we get silt samples, I can match one of them to the profile I got from Crane. Each one's got a different signature, I bet."

"Because the people at the other end of the pipe flush different stuff."

"Exactly," Caleb said. "Say a hundred thousand women taking birth control live in houses connected to the South San Francisco plant. So that effluent will show high marks for estrogen. Maybe the Treasure Island plant has less than a hundredth of that, but everybody there's on Zoloft. Who knows, until we take the samples? But I bet one of the five samples will match what I found in Crane's skin."

Henry took the atlas and opened it to the page Caleb had marked with a sticky note. He studied it awhile, then slid the book back across the table.

"Sewage samples," Henry said. "On my day off. That's great. What'd you bring for lunch?"

"Clam chowder. Sourdough rolls."

Henry gave that tolerant smile of his.

"Put it in the fridge."

It was too cold and wet to go up on the flying bridge, so Henry worked from the inside steering station. He pushed the transmission into forward and they wound out of the marina, going no more than three knots. They passed an empty dock draped in sleeping sea lions, then motored along the side of Pier 39 until they cleared the breakwaters and entered the open bay.

"Where to?" Henry asked.

"We'll start with the Southeast San Francisco plant, then work around the bay counterclockwise."

"Down near Islais Creek?"

"That's right."

Islais Creek was south of China Basin and the AT&T ballpark, five nautical miles down the shoreline from Pier 39. When they were past the no-wake zone, Henry opened the throttle until *Toe Tags* pushed through the flat water at six knots. He steered southeast, parallel to Embarcadero Drive.

"How're you getting the bottom samples?" Henry asked.

Caleb got his backpack from the bench at the dinette table and opened it. He'd tied an empty soup can to a two-hundred-foot length of parachute cord, and had used duct tape to fix a handful of lead weights to the can's lip. He held it up.

"When it hits the bottom, the weight should tip it so it digs in and fills with silt when I start pulling it up. If I bring it up nice and slow, the silt shouldn't wash out."

Henry looked away from the window and studied the can and string Caleb was holding.

"You make that all by yourself, or did NASA pitch in?"

"This is all me."

"Amazing."

"I know. Want me to make some coffee?"

"Now you're talking."

Yerba Buena Island was less than a mile to port, but Caleb could see it only on the radar screen. The rain was coming heavily now, and *Toe Tags* was bobbing in low waves rolling up from the south. A pair of cormorants swimming on the rain-pocked swells saw the boat and dove beneath the surface at the same time.

"When we get to the site, you know exactly where the effluent pipe is?"

"Supposed to be about three hundred yards straight out from the mouth of the creek. Not too deep. Maybe eighty feet."

"I'll try to hold in one spot. When you're sampling, stand in the bow. Prop wash at the stern will screw you up."

Caleb nodded. They still had twenty minutes until they reached the creek's mouth. Henry looked out the starboard windows and then out the stern windows, back along the industrial shoreline leading up to the bridge.

"Long way to drift," Henry said.

"Tidal current runs this way. Straight north. Then it curves between North Beach and Alcatraz to head out to the Golden Gate."

"Still a long way."

"Some of the others are closer. But I thought it'd be better to get them all."

"So if I have to testify about it, I can say we checked them, ruled them out."

Caleb nodded. That had been exactly his thought. He knew how careful Henry was on the stand. He liked to show the jury the methodology he used, liked to impress them with the weight of skill and knowledge underlying his findings.

The mouth of Islais Creek cut through an industrial wasteland, each bank lined in gray concrete and rusted iron. A huge sign on the shore faced out to the bay and announced, in red block letters: NO ANCHORING — UNDERWATER PIPE. Henry put the engine in neutral and they drifted up into the wind until they came to a stop. Then he gave pulses of power to the prop to hold their position.

"What's our depth?" Caleb asked.

Henry glanced down at the depth sounder's display.

"Twenty-five meters." He put his finger on the color display and traced the line of hazy green dots. "Looks like a soft bottom."

"Think what's down there."

"Check this out," Henry said. He traced a red blur on the depth sounder display. "That's the pipe. Looks big enough to drive a bus through."

"We're right on top of it?"

Henry nodded and looked up from the display. "You got some latex gloves?"

"Yeah."

"Try not to spill any of that shit on my nice clean deck."

The cold rain was blowing at an angle, so that it hit his face in spite of the hood. He went up to the bow and leaned over the water. Henry kept the boat aimed into the wind, steady over one spot. Caleb coiled the parachute cord in his hand, then tossed the can so that it hit the water ten feet in front of the bow. He let the thin rope pay out as the weighted can sank, feeding out line until loops of it floated on the water because the can was already at the bottom. Then he started to draw it in, pulling slowly and gently, hoping the lip of the can would tip into the silt and dredge along it before it started coming up.

In a minute, he could see the can in the dark water under the bow pulpit, and then it was dangling in the air. He lifted the can up over the rail, poured off the water, and looked inside. There was an inch of black muck at the bottom. It smelled like dead fish. He took the glass vial from his pocket, slipped the rubber stopper out, and poured a teaspoon of the liquefied silt inside. Then he stopped the vial, put it back into his pocket, and dropped the can back into the water, shaking it on the end of the rope until it was clean.

"Success?" Henry asked when Caleb stepped back into the warmth of the cabin and shut the door.

"Yeah." He took the sample from his pocket, showed it to Henry.

"I'll call Jacques Cousteau, let him know what we've accomplished here."

"Don't forget the Patent and Trademark Office."

"You should label that vial."

"I brought stickers."

He sat at the dinette table and peeled off his gloves. Then he took the stickers and a marker from his backpack. Henry had put *Toe Tags* back into gear and was bringing her about.

"Where to now?"

"Northeast side of Treasure Island."

"All right."

"If we figure out where the bodies are getting dumped, what do you think Kennon and Garcia will do with it?" Caleb asked.

"I don't know. Outta my league. But I think they'll take anything they can get. Talking to them, it sounds like they're stuck."

"How's that?"

"These cases are hard—killers who murder people they don't know," Henry said. "There's no link between any of the victims, no connection between the victims and the killer. No motive. No witnesses."

"None that are talking, anyway."

"Yeah," Henry said. "If the killer's meeting these people in bars, someone must've seen something. But Kennon hasn't found anyone yet."

"The vecuronium is a solid lead. They running with that?"

Henry nodded.

"They are, but it's slow. Checking every hospital, every pharmacy. See if there's any missing. If anyone's been getting it without a good reason."

"They think it's a doctor?"

"Don't you?"

Caleb hadn't thought that much about it. But he nodded.

"Doctors would be good suspects. Or nurses. A pharmacist, even. Not because of the knowledge it'd take —"

"The knowledge is nothing. Anyone could figure that part out," Henry said. "It's the access."

"Yeah."

"Vecuronium's not common anymore," Henry said. "They've got better stuff for surgery."

"It's still around."

"But you can't just pick it up on the street. It's not like there's a black market for it. So it's someone who's got access to a hospital, or a pharmacy. It's gotta be."

Caleb's phone started to ring inside his pocket.

"You wanna get that?" Henry asked.

Caleb pulled it out and looked at the screen.

"It's Bridget. I better. I'll go outside."

He stood on the aft deck, close to the back of the cabin, where he was out of the rain and wind. The wake was a trail of green and white froth leading across the dark water, the low swells rolling underneath it.

Bridget was crying.

He had the phone to his ear, holding it close so that he could hear her sobs, trying to discern if there were any words in there. She'd been crying since he answered the phone and he hadn't heard her actually say anything yet. It had been almost two minutes.

"Bridget?"

"I — I don't want — Caleb —"

"Bridge?"

"I *miss* you."

"Honey," he whispered.

"I can't do this."

"You don't have to do this," he said. He wasn't even sure what they were talking about. He was looking at the bay, the cold water the color of wet slate. He wondered how deep it was, how many bodies they were passing over. People nobody bothered to look for anymore.

"I do. I have to — I just can't. I miss you."

"Bridget, I don't know —"

"Tell me you love me. Don't make me wait for it. Tell me."

"I do love you. You know that."

"Do you really?"

She fell into a long series of sobs. He'd once read something that came back to him now. There was a pheromone in women's tears, a chemical signal held over from some cave of prehistory, meant to be a subtle tug on the men it touched. It would be on her face and on her phone, would get onto her fingers when she wiped her cheeks, so that everything and everyone in contact with her would be brushed with the invisible hue of her loneliness. It would disperse like that, one hand to another, through the city. A single drop of ink spreading in clear water until the glass goes dark.

"Bridget," he said, whispering. "I'm so sorry."

"I can't do this, Caleb. I really can't."

"Can't do what?"

"This. What we're doing now — what *I'm* doing. I thought I could, when I left. But now I don't know."

He didn't know what to say, so he said nothing. He cupped his hand over the phone so the wind wouldn't scream into the silence.

"Caleb," she whispered. "I thought about it. What you did. Maybe you did it the wrong way. Maybe you should have told me sooner. But I could get past it, because I think I know why you did it, what you were trying to save us from. I think —   Are you even still there?"

Finally, the silence stretched to a length even she couldn't cross. She hung up.

Caleb returned the phone to his pocket, but didn't go back inside. He moved around to the side deck and faced into the rain, letting it wash him with its cold touch. But he knew nothing would clean away the thing he'd just done. She'd been holding her hand out, and even then, when she'd given him that chance, he'd been thinking of Emmeline.

"You okay?"

"I guess," he said. He took off his raincoat and hung it on a peg next to the door. "It's — I don't know."

"Complicated?"

"It's more than that. It's a fucking disaster. I don't know what's happening anymore."

He sat down again. They were about to pass under the eastern span of the Bay Bridge. The white tower, rising five hundred feet above the water, disappeared into low clouds.

"You want, I can ask Vicki to —"

"No," Caleb said. "I mean, that's nice of you. And I know she'd try. But I don't think it'd help."

"You're right."

Henry drained the last of his coffee and then pointed ahead. Parts of the old Treasure Island naval station were poking through the white-gray blur.

"You said it's on the northeast corner?"

"Yeah. Here," Caleb said. "I'll get the chart."

The last stop, after samples from Oakland and Tiburon, was the Sausalito-Marin sanitary plant, a mile south of the Sausalito Ferry landing. By the time they found the end of the discharge pipe, it was half past three in the afternoon, and there would be only another hour of true light.

"I'll try to keep us in one spot," Henry said. "Current's pretty strong, and the wind's running across it."

Caleb looked through the window at the shore. It sloped up steeply from the water and was forested in cypress trees and bay laurel. To the south, a finger of heavy fog was working in beneath the bridge.

There would be a fortress wall of it over the Pacific, moving slowly toward the city.

"We're only a mile and a half from the bridge," he said.

Henry nodded.

"This is a good site," Henry said. He was matching the engine's speed to counter the force of the tidal current, tapping back the throttle lever with two fingers to nudge it to a balance point.

"We'll see if the samples match up," Caleb said. But he already had a feeling about this one. It was so close to the bridge, and Henry was right about the current. The flow of water cut a smooth trail through the surface ripples, a meandering lane marked at its edges by bits of sea foam and floating debris brought to the bay by all the recent rains.

Caleb put on his raincoat and fresh latex gloves. He took the last vial from his backpack and went out on deck, kneeling to untie his sampling can from the rail. Because the current was so strong, he had to toss and retrieve the can three times before he got it to dig into the bottom and bring up a sample. He poured the watery sludge into the vial and tamped the stopper into it.

When he was back inside, with his rain jacket off, he sat at the front of the cabin close to one of the space heaters. It was colder in Sausalito than it had been in other parts of the bay, either because it was closer to the open Pacific or because the daylight was almost gone. Caleb held his hands over the heater, shivering a little.

"Since we're here, mind if we do a little experiment?" Henry asked. "I want to let this current take us. See where we end up."

"Fine with me."

Henry steered *Toe Tags* into the current line and then dropped the transmission into neutral. As the engine loped at a low idle, the boat lost its forward momentum, bobbing gently in the low waves. She began to drift sideways, the bow pointed toward Sausalito and the port rail facing San Francisco. Caleb glanced at the GPS screen. They were drifting south in a two-knot current.

"You want some more coffee?" Caleb asked.

"Sure."

He went in the galley to make it, taking his time because his fingers were still cold. The cuts on his right hand were stiffening up as they healed.

"Current's picking up," Henry said, still at his place behind the helm. "Another half a knot."

Caleb bent to the freezer and got the bag of coffee beans. He filled the grinder and turned it on, shaking the beans back and forth through the blade. After he had the machine set up, he went into the head, shut the door, and filled the sink basin with hot water. He washed his hands and his face, then took his phone from his pocket and looked at it. He'd turned off the ringer after Bridget's call, but she hadn't called back or sent any texts. There were no messages or other missed calls. Emmeline had promised to call again soon, and as he thought about that, his chest tightened. He wanted Emmeline to call; he also wanted to go find Bridget and make her happy again. He wanted to let everything go, to find a dim room with a painting, where he could sit and stare at the canvas until everything else was just an inconsequential blur in the background.

"Caleb," he said to the tiny mirror above the brass basin.

There was a right way out. He knew that. But he saw no course that would let him have everything he wanted.

"You're a fucking asshole."

He looked at himself in the mirror and nodded. At least he could be honest when he talked to his reflection. That was something.

Caleb poured coffee into clean mugs and then brought them up to the helm station. He handed Henry one of the mugs and then looked out the window. They were about a hundred yards from the shore, drifting along the headland between Horseshoe Bay and the north tower of the Golden Gate Bridge.

He brought his mug up to his lips and started to take a sip.

In another minute they would drift into the wall of fog coming under the bridge, but for now, the line of sight was clear between the bow and the rocky shore.

Because of that, he had no trouble spotting the body.

TWELVE

"HOLY *SHIT*," CALEB said. "Henry, you see that?"

He put his coffee mug down on a shelf and pointed through the front window. The naked body was floating face-down within twenty feet of a cliff face. The water was dark-looking, flecked with foam and floating sticks. There must have been an eddy in the tidal current there.

Henry followed the line of Caleb's finger. He nodded and turned to the bulkhead, taking a pair of marine binoculars from a teak bin. He put them to his eyes and adjusted the focus with his index and middle fingers. He offered the binoculars to Caleb, but put them away when Caleb shook his head.

"Can't get *Toe Tags* in there, that close to the rocks," Henry said. "No room to maneuver. How you feel about taking the dinghy? The dinghy, and a rope."

"Tow him back?"

"I'll stay out here, hold a position in deep water. You bring him back and we'll put him on the swim platform at the stern."

"I can do that."

"All right," Henry said. "I'll move us up so we drift back to this spot while I get the dinghy ready."

"What should I do?"

"Go out on the bow and keep a lookout. Make sure it doesn't go anywhere. Here — take these."

Caleb took the binoculars from Henry and went to put on his raincoat again. He stepped out of the cabin and then walked along the side deck up to the bow. Beneath his feet, he felt the deck vibrate as Henry throttled the engine to maneuver the boat into a position for launching the dinghy. He put the binoculars to his eyes and watched the body, but the lenses quickly beaded with rain. He wiped them on his shirt, then held the binoculars back up, this time using his palms and fingers to shield the lenses.

It was hard to tell much, even with magnification. And it was starting to get dark. The motion of the boat slowed — Henry had dropped it back into neutral. He heard the cabin door open and shut, and he turned and saw Henry on the side deck. He was holding an orange life jacket, a plastic oar, and a long length of white rope.

"Need a hand with the dinghy?"

"I got it. Stay on the body."

The dinghy hung from a pair of davits on the stern. Caleb could hear Henry working on it, pulling the canvas rain cover off, then tinkering with the outboard motor. Finally he heard the pulleys creaking as Henry lowered the little boat into the water.

"You ready?"

"Coming."

Caleb came back to the aft deck and looked over the stern rail. The dinghy was bobbing lightly in the water, bouncing against the swim platform mounted to the transom.

"Better put on this life jacket," Henry said.

Caleb took it and slipped it over his head, then ran the webbing strap behind his back and clipped the plastic buckle shut.

"I put a paddle in there, just in case you have trouble with the motor."

"Should I expect to?"

Henry looked at the outboard.

"Been a while since I used it. But it should do okay once it starts. When you get to him, rope him around the chest. Don't even try to get him in the dinghy. You'll tip over. Just get the rope around him and drag him back."

"Okay."

"Here, take this."

Henry's hand came out of the pocket of his khakis holding a small waterproof flashlight.

"Thanks."

Henry swung open the transom door and Caleb stepped through it to the swim platform. Then he alighted onto the wooden seat of the wobbly dinghy, moving quickly to lower his center of gravity before the small boat flipped.

From less than half a mile away, one of the foghorns at the base of the Golden Gate Bridge blew a long, low blast.

"Let's try and do this quick," Henry said. "Before it gets dark or that fog comes any closer."

Caleb nodded and turned around, facing the dinghy's stern. The outboard was a little two-stroke Mercury. Caleb primed the carburetor by thumbing the red rubber bulb on the front of the motor, then adjusted the choke and yanked on the pull-cord until the engine caught. He let it run a moment in neutral, then looked up at Henry.

"Okay," he said. "I'm good."

Henry tossed Caleb the painter line, and Caleb put the outboard into gear. He puttered slowly away from the swim platform, then throttled up and steered toward the shore. He was too low in the water to see the body, but there was a sea cave at the base of the cliffs, near where it had been floating. He could see the cave, so he aimed for its mouth.

He was fifty feet from the cliff face when he saw the pale shape of the body floating on the back of one of the waves. He put the motor in neutral and took out the paddle, closing the last of the distance with awkward strokes, trying to keep the dinghy level in the waves. He concentrated on the paddle, on keeping the boat from capsizing. When he looked up, the body was gone.

He laid the paddle across his lap and sat on the wooden seat, shivering in the cold and scanning the water. The waves were running into the sea cave, hitting the mouth and rushing inside with a rolling boom. He could feel the cold air blowing out of the cave each time a wave ran inside. The air smelled of salt and seaweed, but there was something else. It might have been his imagination, but he thought he could smell the body.

He twisted around on the bench, looking for it, one hand on the gunwale to steady himself. *Toe Tags* was two or three hundred feet away, silhouetted in front of the twinkling hills of San Francisco. Whole swaths of the city were invisible where the rain was falling heavily. Henry was up in the flying bridge, standing at the steering station. As Caleb looked, Henry switched on a high-powered spotlight. Caleb squinted and turned away from the white beam. The foghorn let out a low note, and Caleb felt another wash of cold breath from the cave.

Then he saw it. A moment later, Henry found it too, and lit it up with the spotlight. It was between Caleb and *Toe Tags*.

It must have been drifting in one direction on the back side of the swells while he'd been paddling with his head down. He turned around, stopping his stroke long enough to get out the flashlight. Holding it in his teeth, he knelt on the bottom of the boat and kept going until he felt the bow bump against the dead man's side. He ducked down and found the end of the rope Henry had given him. He tied it around the T-shaped handle of the paddle, then crawled on his knees and looked over the tip of the bow.

The body was right there, a foot below his eyes.

Something had taken a gigantic bite out of the man's thigh, stripping the muscle all the way to the white femur. The light hit the water in jerky flashes. The wound was dark red, and hadn't been blanched by the sea. He had an idea what that meant, and he worked as fast as he could.

"You okay?"

"Light's in my eyes," Caleb said. "Here, catch."

He tossed the painter line to Henry and killed the motor. When Henry pulled the dinghy alongside the stern, Caleb stepped to the swim platform and climbed quickly to the aft deck. Beneath him, *Toe Tags* felt as solid as Alcatraz.

"Let's get this dinghy on the davits and then we'll put the guy on the swim platform."

"We should hurry. I think something's out there."

Henry nodded, and they worked quickly. When the dinghy was up, Henry spread a bed sheet across the swim platform. Caleb pulled in the towline and the body came out of the darkness. Henry had turned on the boat's underwater lights so that the water was glowing from below. Cold, absinthe green. Henry leaned over the rail and caught the man's feet in a loop. Lifting together, one on each end, they got the body onto the swim platform atop the sheet.

"I think that bite just happened. Couple minutes ago, over by the rocks."

Henry aimed his light at the man, who was still face-down. The wound looked even wider out of the water. The bone was chipped and scored where teeth had scraped along it.

"Big one, I bet. Not a minnow, anyway," Henry said. He put his hand on Caleb's shoulder. "You see it?"

"Didn't see anything. But the body disappeared on me. Then popped back up, in a different spot," Caleb said.

"Close call, maybe."

Caleb looked at the water behind the transom. It was still lit up from below, still the same cold green. But the blood was gone now, dissipated by the action of the waves and the steady tidal current.

"You called this in yet? To Kennon and Garcia?"

Henry shook his head.

"Wanted to see what we've got first. But it looks like I'll need to. See that?"

Henry moved the light in a tight circle on the man's pale back. There were three sets of stun gun marks going up his spine. The current burns and the spacing looked the same as they had on the other victim. Caleb felt his muscles loosen up and his skin prickle with cold. He was soaked with rain.

"You got anything stronger than coffee?"

"Bottle of twenty-five-year-old Laphroaig. The one you gave me."

"Let's pour a drink. There's something I have to tell you. Before you call Kennon."

Henry looked at him a moment, then nodded.

He stepped down to the swim platform, crouching beneath the hanging dinghy. He covered the body with the other half of the bed sheet, then secured it with ropes so it wouldn't slip off the back when they got under way again. They were drifting toward the Golden Gate Bridge, and were getting nearer to the blind bank of fog. When the bridge's horn sounded, it was close and loud. Caleb could feel it in his stomach.

THIRTEEN

HENRY TURNED OFF the overhead lights in the cabin. The only light came from the glow of the space heaters, from the instruments and the LCD screens around the steering station. He put *Toe Tags* in gear and trimmed the throttle until they were making headway toward San Francisco at two knots. He sat at the helm and watched the radar screen closely until they were clear of the fog.

"You know where to find the scotch?"

"Yeah."

"I'll take however much you're having," Henry said.

Caleb found the scotch and the tumblers and poured a finger's worth into each glass. He brought one to Henry and then sat opposite him.

"Kennon's come to talk to me," Caleb said. "Twice."

Henry looked at him sharply.

"What?"

"I was in House of Shields the night Richard Salazar was murdered. I was one of the last people to see him alive."

"Wait, you're — you're telling me, you're a witness?"

"I was just in the bar. I didn't talk to him. I didn't see anything happen."

Henry put his drink down on the chart table, hard. Whiskey sloshed over the rim and soaked into a paper chart of the bay.

"You're a witness that a homicide detective talked to *twice,* and you got involved in this with me? Jesus Christ, Caleb, what're we going to do if they put you on the stand? You were on the scene the last time anyone saw Richard Salazar alive. You touched his body in the morgue. You ran tests on his tissues and came up with a cause of death. You touched *another* body and connected it to the case. Then you came out here and spotted a third body, and you were alone with it for fifteen minutes. The defense would go nuts with a guy like you."

"Henry—"

"And what if they dig any deeper, Caleb? You ever think about that?"

"I don't think Kennon even has to," he said. "Dig deeper, I mean."

Caleb swallowed some of the whiskey.

"What are you saying?" Henry asked.

"That he might've been there," Caleb said. "He's nearly sixty. He'd have been a patrol cop back then. One of the first on the scene, maybe."

"Been there which time?" Henry asked. "For your dad, or after?"

Caleb just shook his head. He didn't know about that.

"I know, it's—"

"You know? You don't know anything! When the fuck were you going to tell me?"

"I just—I didn't think it mattered. When I pitch in for you, we keep it quiet. So I didn't think it was gonna be a problem."

"Until now," Henry said. "Now it's a big fucking problem. We're on a boat with a dead body. We can't very well dump it back in the water and hope someone else finds it. I'm the fucking chief medical examiner. I have to call it in. And Kennon's gonna be standing on the dock when we get there."

Caleb looked at the city in the distance. For a moment, Henry faded out. Bridget was in there somewhere, in that play of light and darkness on the steep hills. And Emmeline, too. He couldn't even remember what day of the week it was. How could things have gotten so out of control, so quickly? He'd woken up on Saturday morning feeling good about things. Happy about the holidays, to spend Christmas with Bridget.

"I'm sorry," Caleb said, quietly.

"Shit."

"What if I'm not on the boat anymore when you dock?"

"What?"

"What if I'm not on the boat anymore?" Caleb said. "You call it in and tell Kennon you were out by yourself. That you're coming in now and you'll meet him at the marina."

"And where will you be?"

"There's the fuel dock at Gashouse Cove. We'll pass it on the way to Pier 39. You don't even have to stop. Just get me within jumping distance of the dock. Then go on down the shore another mile and pull into your slip."

Henry drummed his fingers on the helm, then picked up his tumbler and drank off half the whiskey in one swallow.

"Jesus, Caleb," he said.

He was silent a while, just steering. Caleb knew better than to interrupt him. He just needed time to think it through. Finally, Henry nodded.

"I guess that might work," he said. "Beats the alternative, anyway."

"It'll work. Just get me within five feet of the fuel dock, and I'm gone."

Henry looked at him, then finished his drink and put the glass back on the chart table.

"Tell me this. And tell me the truth. Is Kennon looking at you as a suspect?"

"A suspect? A *suspect*? Henry — I'm a witness."

"Did Kennon tell you that?" Henry asked. His voice was thick and urgent. "Did he tell you, in those exact words, that you're not a suspect?"

"He just asked me questions. Asked where I was, asked for help identifying people."

Henry looked away from him.

"Shit," he muttered. Then he looked back at Caleb, caught his eyes and held them. "If he comes to talk to you again, you watch out. You understand me? You think very carefully about what you say to him. And don't you ever tell him a lie."

"I just went into House of Shields, after Bridget left. I was staying at the Palace, and all I wanted was a quiet drink. I was in the wrong place at the wrong time. Kennon's the best detective in California? That what you said? If he's that good, I don't have anything to worry about."

Henry tapped the throttle to slow the boat down even more. A tanker was passing in front of them, five hundred yards ahead, steaming toward the Golden Gate and the open Pacific. They watched it pass, a city of lights moving at ten knots. When it was gone, *Toe Tags* rocked in its wake. Henry pivoted on his seat and faced Caleb again.

"Caleb, you're a scientist, so you think in terms of true and false," he said. He was speaking calmly and quietly. There was no anger in his voice anymore. "You don't understand police work, so let me explain something to you. For a detective, being good and being right don't always match up. They don't even have to match up. Kennon's good. Very good. But that doesn't mean he'll be right every time. So if he comes at you again, you fucking better be careful."

"Now you're starting to scare me."

"Then maybe you're getting the point."

Caleb jumped off the side of *Toe Tags,* hit the wet surface of the fuel dock at the Gashouse Cove marina, and skidded to his knees. He stood and brushed himself off, adjusting his backpack. His kneecaps and palms stung. He watched *Toe Tags* slide away, churning a white path in the black water. The sheet over the body had blown loose at the bottom. A stiff foot stuck out. Caleb looked around, but the marina was empty. He hitched up the pack, walked up the gangway, and stepped ashore.

He cut across the Fort Mason Great Meadow and in front of Ghirardelli Square, then walked half a mile down Beach Street until he reached the parking garage where he'd left his car. Five minutes later, he drove out of the garage and continued down Beach Street to Embarcadero. Pier 39 was across the street. A white van from the medical examiner's office was parked on the brick-lined pavilion in front of the Aquarium of the Bay. Its yellow lights were flashing and its back doors were open. It was flanked on one side by a police cruiser and on the other side by a black SUV. A uniformed policeman stood watch over the three cars, but it was too cold and rainy for there to be much of a crowd. Caleb merged onto Embarcadero going southeast. He drove slowly, rubbernecking to the left, but didn't see anything else. Just the three vehicles and their lone guard, the yellow lights of the morgue van flashing across the front of the aquarium.

. . .

A few minutes later, as he was passing Pier 15, a pair of police cruisers raced by in the opposite direction. Their roof lights were flashing but their sirens were silent. He heard the sound of their engines, the wet rush of their tires carving through the puddles. Cars traveling in the other direction pulled to the curb to let them pass.

The lab was dark. But Joanne Tremont's office was lit up, the light spilling out under her door onto the gray linoleum. Caleb put his backpack in his office, and then went back down the hallway and tapped on Joanne's door.

"Yeah?"

He opened the door and leaned against the metal jamb.

"Caleb."

"You were looking for me?"

"Everybody's been looking for you. I was starting to get really frustrated, and then I heard."

"Heard what?"

"Back in August, when I started, you gave me a bunch of contact numbers," Joanne said. "Remember? So when I couldn't reach you, I tried the backup mobile number."

He gestured at one of the two chairs opposite her desk, and she nodded. He came in and sat.

"You talked to Bridget?"

"Yeah."

"I'm sorry. You shouldn't have to get dragged into stuff like that."

"She didn't tell me anything that was, you know, personal. She said she didn't know where you were. Hadn't seen you since Saturday. So I put it together."

"I'm sorry."

"Stop saying that. After I figured it out, I've been covering for you."

"With the NIH?"

She nodded and looked at her computer monitor for a moment. He couldn't see what she had on the screen.

"We still have until the end of January to get the additional data sets they're asking for. So it's not a big deal," Joanne said.

"That's a relief."

"I mean, it isn't a big deal, is it? You understand what they want?"

"I do. I'll have it."

She leaned back in her chair and yawned.

"Good, because that's the part I don't know much about. I can explain the theory and the process. But you've had all the data sets. Whenever they want to get into that, I'm out of my depth."

"I'll handle it," Caleb said. "I know they're asking a lot —"

"Twenty?"

"But it's not insurmountable. We're nearly halfway there. The VA hospital's coming up with new tissue samples every couple weeks. Think of their patient population — not just guys with the kind of pain we need, but guys with bad wounds who don't mind volunteering."

"Our kind of guys," she said.

Caleb nodded.

"I run them when they show up. The VA samples. The sooner, the better. And everything's lining up the way we've been saying all along."

"There'll be time?"

"We've got till the end of January."

"Last Friday in January."

"That's next year," Caleb said. "Plenty of time."

She smiled. They both knew it was a matter of weeks. He stood and turned to leave.

"Caleb?"

"Yeah?"

"I'm really sorry about Bridget. I know how much you liked her."

He nodded and left, shutting the door quietly. Before he went back to his office, he switched on the lights in the main lab and powered on the gas chromatography mass spectrometer. He checked the log-in sheet next to the machine. The only initials for the last week were Joanne's. He hadn't logged his own uses. Joanne was meticulous, followed all the procedures. But he went through the full maintenance checklist anyway, to be sure each stage of the analyzer had been properly cleaned and reset.

His equipment came from the far end of the quality and price spectrum, and made Marcie's little toxicology lab in the morgue basement look like a middle school science project. There were reasons the papers coming from Caleb's lab were a gold standard at conventions and in journals. His equipment was one of them. He'd taken the royalties from his early patents and reinvested in his facilities, so that his lab, even before he was invited to UCSF, was peerless. But the main reason was simpler: Caleb had checklists for everything. And he followed them, every time.

"Hey, Caleb?"

He looked up. Joanne stood at the far end of the lab.

"Yeah?"

"Did you check the readouts on the uninterruptable power supply?"

"Not yet."

"Just look them over before you run anything. When I came in, the door to the power supply closet was open, and when I shut it, I noticed the utility tunnel was open too."

He nodded.

"I don't know if someone's been in there," she said.

"I'll double check," Caleb said. "Before I run it."

"I can send an email to all the lab techs. Remind them to shut everything."

"That's a good idea," he said. "Go ahead and do that. We've got some new people."

"And some old people who've forgotten the rules," she said.

"Copy the whole staff, maybe."

He watched as she went back down the dark hallway. While the sample oven finished heating, he walked to his office and started planning the tests.

When he was leaving the lab at midnight, his phone vibrated in his pocket just as he was getting into his car. He shut the door, then took out the phone. It was a text message from Henry.

Call me.

He put the phone in the cup holder between the seats, started the engine, and drove out of the garage onto Parnassus. At the first red light, he changed his mind and put the phone on his lap. He dialed Henry's cell and put it on speaker.

"Got your text," he said when Henry picked up. "This a good time?"

"Yeah. They're all gone now."

119

"You're still at Bryant Street?" Caleb asked.

The light turned green and he shifted into first and let out the clutch. He wasn't sure where he was going, but it wasn't up the hill. It wasn't home.

"Cleaning up. Finished the autopsy."

"What's going on?"

"Big night here. And not just because of what we found in the water. You were right about Marcie. She's a good scientist. I shouldn't have doubted her."

Caleb took a right and started working through the quiet avenues toward Lincoln Way, which paralleled Golden Gate Park all the way to the ocean.

"What happened?"

"While we were poking around in the bay, Marcie spent the day in the lab. She'd taken apart her machines twice and couldn't find any hardware problems. So this time she brought in a software guy from Hewlett-Packard."

"And?"

"He found a virus."

"Jesus, where?"

Caleb nearly missed a stop sign. He saw it with just time enough to come to a skidding halt, the car fishtailing on the wet pavement. The phone fell into the foot well. When the car was stopped, he reached down and found it.

"Everything okay?" Henry asked.

"I'm fine."

"You driving?"

"Yeah. The virus, where was it?"

"Mass spectrometer's software package. The Hewlett Packard guy pulled the hard drive and he's taking it down to San José, see if he can figure out what the virus is."

Caleb put the car into gear again and drove the rest of the way to Lincoln. He took a left at the green light and drove west, toward the ocean.

"Her equipment — the computer tied to the spectrometer — is it networked?"

"No, that's the thing," Henry said. "It's a standalone machine. To infect it, someone came into the lab, uploaded it by hand. You ever heard of anything like that?"

"Viruses in spectrometer software? No."

"Me neither," Henry said.

"You think it's connected to these killings?"

"I don't know," Henry said. "Maybe we'll know more when we find out what it is. What it does."

At the intersection of Lincoln and Sunset Boulevard, Caleb hit a wall of fog. He slowed from twenty-five miles an hour to fifteen, and then to less than ten. The last thirteen blocks to the ocean would be a gray, blind crawl.

"How'd the autopsy go?" he asked.

"Same as the others."

"ID him yet?"

"Got a print match with DMV. Name was Justin Holland — an architect or something. Went missing two nights ago. I talked to his boyfriend to get the confirmation."

"Went missing from another bar?" Caleb asked.

"They haven't tracked it down, but probably," Henry said. "If he didn't use a credit card, like the others, we may never know. All the boyfriend knew was he was going to meet a client for dinner somewhere around Nob Hill. Never came back."

Caleb had to swerve around a car that had stopped in his lane with its hazard lights flashing. It appeared out of the thick fog so suddenly, it was as if someone had conjured it from a black cloak. Caleb twisted the wheel hard to the left and missed its bumper by inches. He drove another block, then put on his turn signal and got back into the right lane. He slowed to a couple miles an hour, then remembered Henry was still on the line.

"What about a cause of death?"

"The HP guy swapped out Marcie's hard drive with a new one. So she ran the toxicology. About an hour ago, she confirmed everything you've been telling me."

"Vecuronium?"

"Yeah," Henry said. "And thujone. She didn't go as far as you with the metabolites, the order of doses. But we've got the basic picture."

"I can give you a little more," Caleb said.

He glanced in his rearview mirror. There had been a car behind him when he'd pulled onto Lincoln, but after he'd gone into the fog, it had disappeared. The car he'd swerved to miss was lost as well.

"You already ran the effluent samples?" Henry asked.

"You'll probably guess what I found. Given where we found the body."

"It's the Sausalito plant, isn't it?"

"Sausalito. Without a doubt."

Henry sighed and Caleb knew he was thinking through things. Trying to figure out how he could get that information to Kennon without involving Caleb in any way.

"This is what you need to do," Caleb offered. "Have Marcie test the skin samples from Charles Crane. Now that her spectrometer's working, she'll find the sodium hydroxide, no problem. Probably the synthetic estrogen, too. Once she sees that, she'll know Crane was near a sewage treatment plant. So then tell Kennon to take a lab tech on a police boat to go pull effluent. Have Marcie test that. She'll get a match with Sausalito, and I'll be out of it."

"That'll work," Henry said. "And now that Marcie's up and running again, I can get her to test the samples we preserved from the other possible victims."

"I know you need to keep me in the shadows," Caleb said, "but you think you can keep me in the loop?"

"I'll try. This is gonna turn into a major shitstorm, though."

"And Kennon?" Caleb asked. "What'll he do next?"

"You just watch out for him. Remember what I —"

Henry cut off, and Caleb could hear a phone ringing in the background. He heard Henry pick it up and speak quietly into it, the words too muffled to hear. Then his voice was back on the line at full volume.

"Hey. I gotta go."

Henry hung up. Caleb put the phone back into the cup holder and finished his slow drive to the beach. He parked along the seawall opposite the Dutch windmill and got out of the car. He walked along the concrete wall until he found the stairs leading down to the beach, and then he sat on the step where Bridget was sitting when he'd pulled the glass shard from her foot. It was so foggy he couldn't even see the waves, but he could hear them heaving and breaking on the beach. He put the pad of his index finger on the gravelly concrete where Bridget's blood had fallen. That stain had long since been ground away by the sand and the rain, but he remembered where it had been.

When the cold found him through his raincoat, through the sweater he wore underneath it, he got up and went back to the car. He sat with the engine running and the heater blowing. He'd been awake for so long now that his face felt numb. He backed out of his spot and drove north along the ocean, then jagged at right angles through the numbered avenues above Golden Gate Park until he reached Geary Boulevard. He parked in front of a liquor store he'd visited a few times before — it was, in fact, where he'd bought the bottle of Laphroaig on Henry's boat — and saw through the lit-up windows that the place was still open.

He got out of the car, went in, and asked for Berthe de Joux.

FOURTEEN

HE DIDN'T OWN a slotted silver spoon or a proper reservoir glass. Instead, he used a handheld kitchen sieve balanced over the rim of a tall glass tumbler, and he poured the ice water from a glass pitcher. The sugar cube melted into the spirit, and the drink turned from green to foggy white. He left the makeshift absinthiana on the counter and took the drink to the kitchen table, holding a paring knife in his left hand. Bridget's package was there, still unopened. He slipped the blade between the edges of the wrapping paper, sliced through the tape, and took the paper off.

Under the brown paper, she'd wrapped the unframed canvas with a layer of gauzy foam sheeting. He took this away and then stood looking at the painting. He knew exactly what it was, and where it was, because he'd just been there. And, in any case, he'd never let the place drift more than arm's length from the center of his thoughts. She'd painted the beach across from the western end of Golden Gate Park. The beach on a foggy day, so the wet sand melted into the breaking waves, so the mist-laden air blowing off the ocean and the low-ceiling sky blended softly together. The painting's focus was clear at the center but blurred out to the edges, drawing his eye and fixing it on a single spot on the beach, at the bottom center of the painting, where a jagged shard of green-blue glass waited in the sand like a shark's tooth. Beyond that, cutting through the seawall to the left side of the painting, was the staircase.

There was a second canvas behind the first. He lifted it out and removed the foam wrapping.

This painting was a soft, cottony white. Gray lines of shadow ran across it at angles, so that the canvas did not look flat. A red S-shaped mark was smeared across the middle, as though Bridget had dipped her hand in red paint and quickly moved it across the canvas as an afterthought. It would be easy to mistake this painting for an abstraction. But he saw it for what it was: a still life. Though she hadn't titled it, he knew what the plaque would say if he'd found this in a gallery instead of on his kitchen table.

Bed Sheet, with Blood.

———

Bridget Laurent, Oil on Canvas

Either painting would stand alone, but together they told a secret story. She meant for him to hang them in his office, or somewhere in the house where guests might look at them. So that people would see her work and what she'd made for him without understanding the history linked to it. The wound and the intimacy that had followed. How she had been cut open and then opened herself to him.

Caleb sat on one of the chairs and drank the absinthe in one swallow.

When he woke on the couch, it was ten in the morning. He went to the bathroom and stood in the shower under a stream of hot water. He looked at the date on his watch and tried to piece together the day of the week. He'd talked to Inspector Kennon in his kitchen on Wednesday afternoon, and afterward had gone to the morgue to look at the carved-soap corpse of Charles Crane. Early Thursday morning, shortly after the last time anyone saw Justin Holland alive, he was with Emmeline in the bar under Nob Hill. He'd lost most of that day passed out on the couch, spinning through images. He'd spent Friday with Henry on *Toe Tags,* and Friday night in his lab.

Today was Saturday. A week now, since Bridget left.

All seven days were a blur. He'd been fully sober and awake for about ten minutes since last weekend. There were three things he remembered with lucid clarity, each tied to Emmeline. A few moments in House of Shields. An hour or so in Spondulix. Half a minute in his living room, frozen by her voice over the phone. She was like something that had drifted to earth from a dark place in the sky. Transfixing. Every time he tried to shut her from his mind and pull himself back to where he'd been last week, he thought of her voice as she sang to him by candlelight. That desperate, lonesome whisper.

I don't have any friends.

He tried to picture her as a little girl, sleeping in the back seat of a car parked on a dirt lane in the woods, left alone to wait for a man who wasn't her father. There was a moment in Spondulix when she'd almost pulled the shroud off that man, her life with him. But she'd stayed her hand, had backed away. He thought of the promises they'd made. Even now, looking through the haze of everything that had happened since, the vows didn't seem trivial at all. They had weight and consequence.

Park Chow on Ninth Avenue served brunch until two o'clock, and it had a fireplace. He parked on the street a block away and walked to it with his hands in his pockets, the wind in his face.

Then he sat at a table near the fire, drinking coffee and waiting for his meal. The side of his coat facing the hearth steamed as it warmed. He could smell the lanolin in the wool, but Emmeline's perfume rode over it. It was like stumbling into a clearing in the trees at night and being washed suddenly by moonlight. He touched his phone in his pocket, his sole source of connection to her, and as he did so, it began to ring.

He pulled it out quickly, looking at the incoming number. A pay phone, maybe. A prickle of electricity ran from his shoulders to his fingertips. He answered, hitting the screen with his thumb and moving his left hand to shield his mouth. She spoke before he did.

"Hello, Caleb."

He closed his eyes to take himself out of the restaurant. He didn't want to be anywhere but with her voice.

"Emmeline."

"Did you have a good time? On our date?"

"I did."

"It was a date, wasn't it?"

"Yes."

"I promised I'd call soon. Was this soon enough?"

Caleb bent toward the table, wanting to hold this conversation close. The ice under his skin told him that if anyone overheard, if there were any witnesses to his connection with her, he would lose her forever.

"It could've been sooner. But I'm glad you called. I wanted you to call."

"Were you thinking about me?"

"Ever since I first saw you."

"You'd like to see me again?"

"Please."

"Tonight, then. You can meet me at midnight."

It wasn't a question, and he didn't take it for one. She offered it like a gift.

"Thank you," he whispered. "I'll be there. Just tell me where."

"No," Emmeline said. "I'll call tonight with that. But at midnight, I'll be hungry. Can you cook, Caleb?"

"Yes."

"Will you make me dinner?"

"I'd love to," he said. He wondered if she planned to show him where she lived, or if they were going to slip into another closed bar. "Will I cook it there, or should I make it before I come?"

"I want to watch you. There'll be a nice kitchen. Everything you'll want. You can take your time — I won't rush you, or get underfoot. I'll just watch."

"What should I make?" Caleb asked. "What do you like?"

"Whatever you want — I'll be hungry. And I'll bring the wine."

"Okay," he said. "I'll think of something."

"Of course you will," she whispered.

He could almost feel her breath against his ear. He knew if she were sitting next to him, her cheek would be on his shoulder. And she would want to be near the fire, because she would be cold.

"I'll call you tonight," she said.

She hung up before he could answer.

When he opened his eyes, his plate was in front of him. The waitress had come and gone, but he hadn't noticed at all.

· · ·

The second level of the Parnassus parking garage at the medical center was mostly empty when he pulled into his space. He switched off the engine and sat with his eyes closed for a while before getting out of the car. He knew why he was going to such lengths to hide Emmeline. Whispering his phone conversations, leaving her out of anything he told Kennon. It was guilt. What he was doing to Bridget was shameful. She'd left him, but maybe that was just part of trying to stay. A way of telling him how she felt. Yet he was acting like they'd been apart for a year. He didn't want anyone to see that. He didn't want to see it himself, but that wasn't enough to change his course. Because when Emmeline called him tonight, he'd answer. When she told him where to go, he'd race there with a pounding heart.

Being at work now was the best thing.

It would hold his mind to something else. He could force himself into the NIH project, could begin the process of fixing the data sets the audit committee wanted to see. He opened his eyes and stepped out of the car. Deeper in the garage, he heard a car door slam, heard the double beep as remote door locks engaged. He walked out into the lane between the rows of parking stalls, heading for the stairwell.

"Mr. Maddox."

He stopped and turned, looking at the man who stepped out from between two cars.

"Inspector," he said. "Where's Garcia?"

Kennon waited until he'd closed the gap between them, and then he made a gesture with the back of his hand, a sweep to indicate some faraway place.

"Saturday," Kennon said. "With his family, I guess."

"Guys like you get days off?"

"He does," Kennon said. There might have been a smile there, but it was hard to tell. His salt-and-pepper mustache hid it. "Can we sit in your office a minute?"

"What's this about?"

"Marcie Hensleigh."

Caleb nodded and reached into his pocket to get out his access card.

"Sure, Inspector," he said. "Follow me."

. . .

There was coffee in the break room. Caleb wasn't sure who had made it, or how long ago, because the lab was empty. But it was still vaguely warm, and it smelled okay. He poured two mugs and heated them in the microwave, and then led Kennon to his office.

"Take the couch."

Caleb went around his desk and sat. Kennon put his overcoat across the arm of the couch and put his fedora on top of it. As he sat down, he took a small spiral-bound notebook from his back pocket. There was a nub of a pencil jammed into the notebook's wire coil, but Kennon didn't pull it out.

"You know her," Kennon said. "Right?"

"Marcie?"

Kennon nodded.

"We met at Stanford. She was a graduate student when I was doing a postdoc year, and we shared lab space. We coauthored a paper."

"You keep up with her at all?"

"Stay in touch, you mean?"

"Yeah, stay in touch."

"Not much. I see her at scientific conventions, and when we run into each other, we're friendly. So I know what she does now, for the city," Caleb said. He looked at Kennon. "What's going on?"

"What can you tell me about mass spectrometers?" Kennon asked.

Caleb frowned at his desk's leather blotter, as if resigning himself to being kept in the dark. He had a pretty good idea why Kennon had come, but he couldn't show that.

"What would you like to know?"

"For starters, how they work. What they do."

"You want all the details, or, like, the view from thirty thousand feet?"

"Let's start with the big picture," Kennon said. "Pretend I don't have a Ph.D. from Stanford. That I've just got a bachelor's in criminology and a semester of law school."

Caleb thought of Henry's voice when they were motoring back across the bay toward San Francisco. *You fucking better be careful,* he'd said. Kennon had the pencil in his hand, the tip poised above the lined notebook paper.

"Imagine you're standing out on the middle of the Golden Gate Bridge," Caleb said. "A good, strong wind's coming off the ocean, blowing into the bay. You've got a bowling ball and a volleyball, and you drop them both. Where's the bowling ball hit the water?"

Kennon looked up.

"Right underneath me, more or less," he said. "It'd fall straight down."

"That's right. Now where's the volleyball hit?"

"A little farther out. Farther away from the bridge. The wind would carry it some."

Caleb nodded.

"That's everything you need to know about mass spectrometry. I take a sample and put it into a heating chamber. Molecules get ionized by an electron source — they get an electric charge — and then carried along a racetrack by a magnetic field. There's an electromagnet that deflects them around a corner, just like the wind coming under the bridge. The lighter particles get deflected more than the heavier ones. They hit an ion trap at the end of the racetrack and a particle detector records where they hit."

"Then what?"

"Then you get an incredible amount of data. A spectrum of molecular weights. If you look at it on a chart, it looks like the EKG of a man on cocaine — crazy spikes and troughs. You run it through computer software, use libraries of data from known samples, and you can figure out the molecular components of just about anything. It's a little more complicated than that, but that's the basic picture."

Kennon spent a moment writing, the notebook balanced on his knee. Then he looked back up at Caleb.

"The software — where's it come from?"

"Depends on the lab and the machine. There's three ways to go. You can get off-the-shelf stuff that'll cost anywhere from five hundred to ten thousand dollars. You can get shareware for free. There's a government lab in Switzerland that puts out a good free program called SpecServe."

"And if you don't go either of those routes?" Kennon asked.

"Some of us use custom software."

"That's what you've got?"

Caleb smiled. His lab was the envy of the world. At least once a month he led scientists and foreign delegations on tours through his fifty-thousand-square-foot facility.

"I run an off-the-shelf commercial program called Spectral Wave. But I have three Cray clusters out there, so I also run parallel programs. I have a modified version of the Swiss program, and then I run a wholly custom one."

Kennon was writing fast, and looked up when he was done.

"What's a Cray cluster?"

"A modular supercomputer. You can buy as many pods as you want, and link them."

"Who modified the Swiss program you run?"

"I did."

"And you wrote the custom program, too?"

Caleb nodded.

"I thought you were a chemist or a toxicologist or something," Kennon said. He was watching Caleb closely, his gray eyes unblinking behind his wire-rimmed glasses.

"My undergrad was computer science. And most of the hard sciences overlap with CS now," Caleb said. "You can't get away from it."

"So you're running three programs, for what? Each crosschecks the others?"

"So I can verify my own results in one run. But I still don't see what any of this has to do with Marcie. Is she— I mean, I don't know what's going on. Is she in trouble?"

Kennon jammed his pencil back into his notebook. He pulled back the lapel of his jacket and Caleb could see the shoulder holster of the gun he wore. He put the notebook into his inner jacket pocket.

"Not in trouble, no," he said. "You mind showing me your lab? The equipment?"

"Sure," Caleb said. "I can show you around. The machines aren't powered up, so if you want a demonstration, it'll take a while to get everything hot."

"I just want to look."

"It'll be different from Marcie's lab," Caleb said. He stood and came around the desk, then paused at the door, waiting for Kennon to go out of the office first. "Her lab's a workhorse. And small. This is a research facility."

Kennon stood, and for just a second, while the inspector was in profile, Caleb saw a flash of red light come from the right-hand pocket of his suit pants. It was just a blink through the fabric and then it was gone. There was a thin rectangular bulge there. Caleb looked away quickly, out into the lab. He thought Kennon hadn't seen.

"You've been in her lab, then?"

Caleb started out the door, so that his back was to Kennon. *Don't you ever tell him a lie.* He hit switches on the wall that turned on the lights and the overhead ventilation fans. Caleb spoke without turning his head, just loud enough that Kennon would be able to hear him over the din of the fans.

"Sure," he said. "I'm friends with Henry."

"Henry *Newcomb?* The medical examiner?"

"Yeah—we grew up together," Caleb said. He turned and looked at Kennon. "What?"

"Nothing," Kennon said. "It's just, I talk to him a lot. And he's never mentioned you."

"That's funny."

"Is it?" Kennon asked. "You've known him your whole life?"

"Yeah."

"Except for the two months you and your mom were in Langley Porter, and the two weeks after that when you disappeared, you saw him all the time."

He'd known it would come up. Talking to Kennon in the back of the SUV outside House of Shields, he'd known. Now Kennon had brought it all the way out, had tossed it on the floor for both of them to look at.

"Isn't that right, Mr. Maddox?"

Caleb shrugged and led him into the lab, staying ahead so Kennon wouldn't see his face.

FIFTEEN

THOUGH IT WASN'T quite five o'clock, it was dark when he left the lab. He drove down to Lincoln, then wound through the park and into the Richmond district, taking random turns and watching his rearview mirror. Everything about Kennon put him on edge. When he was satisfied no one was following, he pulled over briefly and took out his phone. He called Henry, put it on speaker, and then kept driving.

"Yeah?"

"It's Caleb. You alone?"

"One second."

A background swirl of voices rose to a crescendo as Henry walked away from wherever he'd been sitting to find a more private place. A moment later, there was only silence.

"Sorry," Caleb said. "Didn't mean to interrupt something."

"It's fine," Henry answered. "Still at Bryant Street, but I'm outside the conference room. We're waiting on Kennon, anyway. What is it?"

"If Kennon's not there yet, it's because he was with me."

"He came to see you?" Henry asked. His voice dropped to a hush. "Again?"

"He asked about mass spectrometers. About the software. He wanted to get a look at my lab. Said it was about Marcie."

Henry sighed.

"We're in a pile of trouble for how we handled things yesterday. Marcie and I."

"The virus?"

"We shouldn't have given the hard drive to the guy from Hewlett Packard. It was a crime scene, and we screwed up Kennon's chain of evidence. He drove out to San Jose and got the drive, then turned it over to the FBI early this morning. They've got a cybercrime division, and they're all over it."

Caleb saw an empty parking spot and pulled over. He turned off the speakerphone and put the cell phone to his ear, lowering his voice so he wouldn't be shouting at Henry.

"They find anything yet?"

"You'll keep it a secret?"

"Henry—"

"Sorry. I know you will."

"You better know it," Caleb said. "What is it?"

Caleb looked in his rearview mirror while he waited for Henry to speak. There was a car at the far end of the avenue, stopped at the curb a hundred feet away. Its headlights were on but it hadn't moved for at least ten seconds. Then Caleb saw a growing bar of light as a garage door scrolled up on the other side of the street. The car took a sharp left and pulled into its garage. Caleb looked back out the windshield.

"You still there, Henry?"

"Yeah."

"What'd the FBI find?"

"The virus and the killings are connected. The virus interfered with Marcie's spectral analysis. It kind of sat between the analyzer and the graphic output algorithm. So it could call the shots between the two."

"You mean it changed the results?" Caleb said. "Skewed what Marcie saw on the graphs?"

"It targeted one thing. If the analyzer found something with a molecular weight of 637.73, the virus just tossed that out. So there'd just be a blank in the printed chart, like nothing was there at all."

"A dark spot in the spectrum," Caleb said.

"That's right. A hole."

Caleb breathed out and looked at his car's ceiling, running the math and adding the atomic weights until he'd built a molecule in his mind.

"It's vecuronium, isn't it? The dark spot, 637.73, that's vecuronium."

"You got it," Henry said.

"Holy shit."

"It's bad," Henry said. "I mean, Jesus Christ, he can get into my lab. In the basement of the police station."

Caleb put the phone back on speaker and started to drive again.

"He was in my goddamn *lab*," Henry repeated.

"Are there suspects?"

Henry coughed.

"Everyone with an access card is a suspect."

"How many people is that?"

"We don't know," Henry said. He was whispering, but his voice was edged with rage. "Every card's supposed to have a unique code number — so you know who's coming in and out. But someone in IT fucked up, and all the lab cards have the same code. And no one's got a list of who got a card."

"Don't you have security cameras?"

"Sure we do, but this must've happened months ago, before the first killing. The cameras record on DVR, and those get overwritten every thirty days unless someone pulls it."

"You're just finding all this out tonight?"

"Like I said," Henry whispered. "I'm in a pile of shit, and it's over my head. The FBI's been chewing me a new one the last two hours, and every time they take a break, they tag Garcia in."

"Kennon didn't ask me anything about viruses," Caleb said. "But I might've made things worse for you."

Henry breathed out.

"What," he said, slowly, "did you do?"

"You told me I shouldn't lie to him," Caleb said.

"Oh shit, Caleb."

"I mentioned what Marcie's lab looked like. Compared it to mine. But he already knew I don't see her socially. So obviously he wanted to know why I knew anything about her lab."

"So you told him we're friends?"

"That we went way back. And Henry — I think he recorded it."

"He was wired?"

"I think so. And that's not all. I'm sure he was there. Maybe for both — when they came for my dad, and when they found me. I don't know what that changes."

135

It was the first time he'd spoken of what had happened that directly in more than twenty-five years. But it didn't feel like a new turn. Every conversation he'd had with Henry in all that time, and every silence between them, had to carefully skirt those rocks.

Caleb took a right on Geary and made it through two intersections before a red light caught him. He flicked on his windshield wipers and watched them sweep away the beads of rain, watched the water run in streamlets down the edge of the glass, catching the colors of the traffic light.

"I thought that was sealed," Henry finally said. "Or that they kept your name out of it. At least, the part about the hospital."

"That doesn't mean people can't talk about it. There are the articles, and there are people who know. But if Kennon's who I think he is, it wouldn't matter. Because he was there."

"Do you remember anything else?" Henry asked.

"I remember everything about the hospital. Langley Porter."

"I meant from before that. And what happened right after."

"No," Caleb said, flatly. "Now what?"

"I don't know," Henry said. "If Kennon asks me what we've been up to, I'll have to tell him. I might get taken off the case. I might — but that part's not your problem. And if he asks me about the other thing — I don't know."

"If he asks, just tell him," Caleb said.

"Tell him what?"

"Whatever you think happened," Caleb said.

"Fine."

"I'm sorry."

"I know," Henry said. "Look, I gotta go. Garcia and the FBI guys are in there waiting on me. Kennon will be here any minute. Just . . . don't call me for a while, okay? I don't need that kind of trouble."

Henry hung up. Caleb drove another five blocks, the glow of the cell phone screen lighting his face from its place on his lap. Finally the screen dimmed on its own.

There was a good grocery store on Stanyan Street, across from the east end of Golden Gate Park. He wandered side streets for an hour until he got there, his thoughts descending through the full spectrum — Henry to Kennon to Bridget — before finally settling on Emmeline. He remembered the way she'd played the piano for him, holding back her voice as she sang so the words would remain a secret between them. If they were making love, if she needed to bite into his shoulder to soften the sounds of her pleasure, her voice would be that way.

That was enough to hold him, a stake deep enough to keep his thoughts from straying back to Kennon. To Bridget. He needed that. A place to turn, a point of focus. Anything that could carry him away. Jameson and Berthe de Joux were good, but Emmeline was so much better for it. He thought of her arms around him, her slim body pressed against his. So little between them.

When he got to the store, he parked and switched off the engine. He sat with his eyes closed, listening to the rain on the metal roof, thinking of the meal he'd cook for her. He took his time planning it, working through each step until he had the entire process. Then he got out of the car and buttoned his jacket against the light rain.

He was almost to the half-circle of light spilling from the store's glass front when three women exited the sliding door in a flowing knot, swift and graceful. They wore black cocktail dresses under their long coats, and each of them was carrying a bottle of wine. By the time he recognized them, he'd gone too far into the light to turn for the shadows without calling more attention to himself. He could already smell the tangle of their perfumes, could see the streetlights' reflection in their hair and in the polish of their jewelry. They saw him, and their conversation ended as if a door had shut on it. They stopped, and stood looking at him. The one in the middle spoke.

"Caleb? Do you remember me?"

She gathered the lapels of her trench coat in her free hand and pulled them together beneath her throat. Then she looked at her friends and flicked her eyes ahead to their car. The two of them looked at her and then at Caleb, and then one of them started toward the car. The other girl looked at Caleb a moment longer, and then followed.

When they were alone, Caleb nodded at her.

"How are you, Paula?"

She shrugged.

"We're going to see Bridget," she said. She raised the bottle of wine, then lowered it. "A little party, at her studio."

"That's good."

"That she has some company? Because she's too fucked up to go out? Yeah. That's good."

"Paula—"

"I know what happened, the fight you had, okay? She told me. It wouldn't have bothered a lot of girls. But Bridget's different. For her? That was a deep cut."

He put his hands in his pockets and stepped back from her.

"She couldn't have told you everything," he said. "Because she doesn't know everything. And she never let me explain."

Paula shook her head.

"It's not just that. It's everything."

"What are you talking about?"

"How she wakes up and you're not next to her? Because you went back to the lab? How even when you're with her, sometimes you're not— You know what I'm talking about, so don't look at me like that. Don't even think about looking at me like that."

"I'm not looking at you any way, Paula."

She took a step toward him and pointed the base of the wine bottle at his chest.

"And it's not just what she told us. It's what we told her."

"You told her what?"

"Come on, Caleb. This isn't 1950. You meet a stranger at a gallery opening, you don't just move in with him. You get a background check first. And if you don't do it, your friends will."

She stared at him, breathing out slowly. She'd lowered the wine bottle, but she was still holding it by its neck.

"If you read those stories," he said, "you know you didn't get the whole thing. They have gaps, and they admit it."

Even here, with Paula confronting him, he was thinking about the holes in the spectrum. A virus on the San Francisco medical examiner's mass spectrometer was inconceivable to him. There could only be a few dozen people in San Francisco who had the necessary skills to write a program like that, and he probably knew them all. Marcie Hensleigh and Joanne Tremont were both on the list.

Paula leaned to look past him, and he turned to follow her line of sight. Her two friends had backed off about twenty feet. They stood under a dim streetlamp, in front of their car. Rain angled through the lamp's hazy cone of light, and the girls stood with their coats bunched around them, watching Caleb. Their phone screens lit their faces. They were recording him, as if they thought he might strike out at Paula. He took a step away, to ruin their expectations.

He couldn't remember their names. But he was pretty sure the two of them had spent the night in front of his fireplace after one of Bridget's gallery openings. Drunk and draped around each other, wrapped in the blankets he kept near the couch. They hadn't thought there was anything wrong with him then, even if they had done a background check. Even if they had known they were houseguests of the late Caleb Ellis Sr.'s son.

He nodded at them, and then turned back to Paula.

"And besides," he said, "those stories don't have anything to do with me. They're about something that happened to me."

"I didn't say you did anything wrong," she said. Her voice was low and calm, and her face softened as she spoke. She'd been angry before, but that was gone now. "You were a kid. Your dad — he did what he did. But Bridget had a right to know, okay? So I told her."

"Okay."

He was glad for the distance between them.

"If it'd happened today, it would've been different," she said. "You know? They wouldn't have let you out of their sight. And then maybe at least the other thing wouldn't have happened."

"Sure."

"But Bridget still needed to know."

"Jesus, Paula."

He started toward the store, but she stepped to her left and cut him off.

"What do I tell Bridget?" she asked. "I'm going to see her in twenty minutes."

"Whatever you want. Clearly."

He went around her and into the store.

When he came back to his house, he put the groceries away and then took Bridget's paintings, carried them into the bedroom, and leaned them against the wall inside her empty closet. As if by shutting them away he could close off that part of his heart. Then he went into the kitchen, uncorked a Loire Valley Sauvignon Blanc, poured a glass for himself, and kept the open bottle on the counter. He'd need it in a few moments.

He knelt and opened a cabinet, taking out a pair of maple cutting boards and a stockpot. Emmeline wanted to watch him cook, and there would be plenty left for her to see at midnight when he arrived. But he wanted to make a stock and reduce it first, to save time later. He coarsely chopped carrots, celery, shallots, and an onion. At the store, he'd bought eighteen live oysters, and he sorted through these now, picking six for the stock and saving the rest for later. He shucked the oysters over the pot so that it caught both their meat and their liquor. Then he added the vegetables, threw in a sachet of bay leaves and peppercorns, and covered everything with a cup of the white wine and a splash of cold water.

While the stock came to a boil, he cleaned the cutting boards and the knives he'd used, and then stood with the wineglass, looking out the window at the incandescent fog below the hill, the ground-clinging clouds lit from beneath by sources Caleb couldn't see. There would be streetlamps down there, and Christmas lights blinking on the eaves of the row houses. Illuminated windows spilling the light of family dinners, front rooms brimming with guests. But all that was obscured. Caleb just saw a glowing blur of gray.

Tomorrow's Christmas Eve, he thought.

Bridget would go to Grace Cathedral just before midnight. If things had gone differently this week, he'd have been there too. It would have been his first service there. If they did a candlelight service, he'd have watched the firelight spread wick to wick from the front of the cathedral until Bridget lit her candle from her neighbor's flame before turning to him. Offering him, as ever, her heat and light. And then he would have held her right hand with his left, their white candles guttering hot wax onto the paper hand guards, the flames bending and smoking as the congregants sang. Going home, they'd have heard the midnight bells toll most of the way down Nob Hill, would have felt the bronze vibrations deep in their stomachs at each church they passed.

He didn't know how to approach Bridget, even in his thoughts.

He'd been standing in this spot when she'd thrown the tumbler last week. Now he moved close enough to the dark window glass that he could see the transparent reflection of his face. The wound on his forehead was mostly healed. The cut had scabbed over, and the split edges of the skin were crawling back toward each other, cells knitting a new matrix. The surrounding bruise had first faded to yellow, then dropped out of sight beneath his tan.

But a cut on the surface was never the whole story. Half an hour with Henry in his basement morgue could teach that simple lesson. He wondered if the past seven days could be explained by a few laws of physics, whether all of his actions since Bridget threw the tumbler—his nocturnal hunt to find Emmeline, the hours he'd spent with Henry's drowned men — were merely an equal and opposite response to what she'd done. Perhaps it carried much further past that.

Caleb turned when he heard the stock begin to boil. He walked to the stove and lowered the flame, then used a skimming spoon to strain the froth. He twisted the bezel of his watch to set a timer, and went to take a shower.

His phone rang at ten o'clock and he jumped for it, looking at the screen. But the number wasn't what he'd expected.

It was Bridget.

He set the phone on the kitchen counter and stepped away, watching it. Each unanswered ring pushed him into a deeper shade of darkness, a steep gradient that dropped away to black. He didn't want to think about what was in those shadows, all the way at the bottom. And he knew answering, just saying her name, would stop his slide and throw light all around. But he didn't pick up, because it would mean the end of a different sort of hope.

A darker desire.

After five rings, the call went to voicemail. He went to the refrigerator, poured another glass of wine, and cursed himself.

Emmeline called at eleven fifteen, and he answered right away.

She didn't talk immediately, so all he heard was the hum of their connection. Wherever she was, it sounded windy, and there was traffic. Cars on wet streets, squealing brakes as trucks eased themselves down one of the city's steeper hills. Caleb sank to a crouch on the floor in front of the refrigerator, the phone pressed tight against his right ear and his hand covering his other ear so that he was nowhere but with her.

She breathed in and he listened.

"Are you ready?" she asked.

"Yes."

"Two thousand seven Franklin Street. Can you find it?"

"I'll be there," he whispered.

"Don't bring your phone, okay?"

"Okay," he said. He'd have agreed to anything. He was standing in blinding darkness and her voice was a cold glow. Her voice was the only thing in the world, so of course he'd move toward it. It didn't matter what might lie between them.

"You remember our promises?"

"Yes."

"Say them," she said.

Her voice was a whisper, but there was a new note in it. It was something more than desire, past need. Desperation, maybe.

"I will never lie to you," Caleb said. "I will never hurt you."

"Because you're my friend?"

"I am."

"Then come to me. Find me."

SIXTEEN

THE ADDRESS SHE'D given on Franklin Street was in the northern part of the city. He had plenty of time to get there. Enough leeway that he could swing past one of the two other addresses he'd looked up before coming to the garage.

Joanne Tremont lived near Cathedral Hill. Marcie Hensleigh and her husband lived in Pacific Heights, just blocks from his rendezvous with Emmeline. He didn't want to see either of them, didn't want to talk. He just wanted to drive past their apartments in the anonymity of the night, wanted to idle awhile nearby and see if their windows were dark or lit. He wanted to watch and see. Joanne knew about spectrometer software, and she knew about pain. On top of that, she was nervous about the grant, which was the sole source of her income. So she was under pressure.

Marcie's possible motives weren't as clear. As a suspect, she seemed like a stretch. It would be a hard sell to Henry or Kennon. But Marcie had the skills to manipulate her software, and she had something Joanne lacked.

She had access to her own lab.

Of all the people in the world who could have written the virus, Marcie was the only person who could easily install it. So he went to her house.

He wasn't sure how long he spent on the street, parked in the heavy shadows beneath a row of eucalyptus trees. He kept the headlights off but left the engine running and in gear, his left foot on the clutch. There was an illuminated row of bay windows above Marcie's narrow garage, but he never saw her silhouette pass them.

He thought of getting out, crossing the street. Climbing her steps and poking his finger through the mail slot in her front door, kneeling to peek through that narrow slit. But there'd be no purpose in that. It was no way to learn about her. Finally, he looked at his watch and saw the time was short. Marcie could wait, but Emmeline couldn't.

He slowed to a crawl as he drove past the address, looking out the left window to see the house to which she'd led him. It was a huge Victorian, a sprawl of painted gables and pointed cupolas, three or four stories tall. It was in the middle of the block, but it had a side yard and a garden. All of the windows were dark and the curtains were drawn shut. He circled the block and found a parking spot one street over.

Walking back, with two grocery bags in each hand, he saw a light moving behind the curtains in the house. He climbed the two sets of steps to the porch and glanced at the bronze plaque set on the wall. There was just enough light from the streetlamps to read it:

SAN FRANCISCO ARCHITECTURAL HERITAGE
HAAS-LILIENTHAL HOUSE
1886

The house, and the name on the plaque, tugged at a memory, but he couldn't place it. Something about Henry, something that came at him back-loaded with a mix of emotions as counterbalanced and self-cantilevered as a glass of absinthe: a shimmer of arousal coupled to terror of the dark. Shame lay underneath both, indelible, like ink pushed under the skin. He knew that twenty-five years ago, in a place like this, his mother had set out on a frantic run, dragging a policeman by his shirt cuff and screaming Caleb's name. She'd dropped the metal cane she was supposed to use, so that she'd run with a jagged limp. Most of the bandages had come off by then, but the stitches were still there, meandering her cheeks and forehead until the gashes and skin grafts healed.

He hadn't seen that happen. The image of his mother wasn't a memory but was something he'd pieced together from what she'd told him. She was gone now, though. There was no way to ask her if this was the place, or if this was just another false echo in a city that was, for Caleb, full of them.

It could be the two glasses of wine, and the way the street slept under its blanket of fog so that everything was soft at the edges, the familiar and the unknown swirled together and set adrift. He reached for the door knocker, but before he could grip it, the front door opened. Emmeline held a brass hurricane lantern, its wick trimmed low.

"You found me," she said. "Will you come in?"

She held the door open for him and he stepped into the old mansion. She closed the door behind him and turned the heavy deadbolt. She was wearing a dress that was a shade of crimson so dark, it was almost black. It was sleeveless, and her bare arms were pale white in the shadows of the entry hall. She was barefoot, and when she walked up to him, she made no sound at all. She stopped when her toes were touching his. The lantern was between them, close enough to his stomach that he could feel its heat. She reached up and traced the back of her index finger under the line of his jaw.

"Thanks for coming," she said. Her perfume, as delicate as a single strand of spider silk, wrapped around him. "Follow me?"

"All right."

She led him through the dark house, the lantern throwing a circle of light around them as they moved through the high-ceilinged rooms. The kitchen was in the back right corner of the house. She'd set candles on the marble pastry table and on the countertops next to the stove. The stove itself was vast and complicated, a gas and electric wonder at least a hundred years old. It had six cast-iron burners and three different enamel-coated oven compartments. There was a wire filament bulb in the range hood, the only electric light that he'd seen burning in the house. It cast a warm amber cone down to the stovetop, drawing it into focus.

"You'll be able to cook here?" Emmeline asked. She was standing beside him, two of her fingers resting on his arm just above his elbow.

Caleb looked around.

She'd taken out pots and pans, had washed them in the sink so that they now lay drying on dishtowels on the stone counters. Beautiful old copper pots, an assortment of handmade carbon steel knives that glowed at the edges where they'd been recently sharpened on a whetstone. There was a heavy chopping block made of the interlocking end pieces of old hardwood, and there was a cast-iron grill pan that gleamed with seasoning. He could broil the oysters on that, and heat the rock salt in the matching iron skillet.

"I'll be just fine in here," he said.

Emmeline went to the marble pastry table and set down the hurricane lantern. She used the wheel on the side to bring up the wick. The flame licked and grew, bringing more light to the room. She turned to him, leaning against the table with her hands against its edges.

"Tell me the menu," she said. "So I can pick the wine."

"I hope you like seafood," he said.

"I like everything."

"We'll start with grilled oysters," Caleb said. "Snow Creek oysters, the little ones."

She nodded.

"Something sparkling," she said. "I have a Treviso prosecco. We'll have prosecco with that."

"And then pan-seared scallops, with wild mushrooms," Caleb said. "Truffle risotto, after."

"I brought a good pinot grigio. That will go with the scallops. Burgundy for the risotto."

"Dessert's nothing fancy," Caleb said. "Just chilled raspberries. A little bit of dark chocolate."

She smiled.

"We'll finish the prosecco with that."

"Should I get started?"

"Please," she said. "I'm hungry."

There was an old-fashioned icebox against the far wall. Caleb opened it, not sure what he'd find. The inside was split into upper and lower compartments, and a block of ice sat in the upper compartment. In the bottom, there were bottles of white wine, and the prosecco.

"You brought the ice?"

"Yes."

"All right to put a few things in here?"

"Of course," Emmeline said. "I'll be back. I need to find wine-glasses. And wash them. They'll be dusty, I expect."

She took the lantern from the table and walked out. It was so quiet in the house, and she was so gracefully silent in her bare feet, that he could hear the silken rustle as her legs brushed against the inside of her dress. He watched her go, then put some of the groceries into the icebox. When that was done, he went to the stove and figured out how to light the oven.

The house was a time capsule, a ghost of a San Francisco wiped out by the 1906 earthquake. It was a museum now, maintained well enough to look at, but most of the things in the kitchen hadn't been used in a long while. He twisted a knob on the stove and leaned down to the burner, smelling the gas coming out. That was good, but there were no pilot lights. He ripped a piece of paper from one of his grocery bags, set it aflame with a candle on the counter, and then used it to light two of the oven compartments. He shook out the paper and put it in the sink. When he turned, Emmeline was behind him, holding six long-stemmed glasses. A clean set for each wine pairing.

"You have that look," Emmeline said.

"What look?"

"When I told you about the man I used to be with, when I told you he disappeared," she said. She put the glasses down on the counter next to the sink. "I told you he was dead—probably dead. I said all that, and you were worried. Like you look now. It's because we're here, isn't it? In this house."

He nodded. But he owed her more than that. There was a lot more than the house on his mind, and he'd promised her the truth. He remembered the smell in Henry's morgue, the waxen-death smell of adipocere when Henry drew the sheet back on the corpse. The way Kennon stood in the lab, hands in the pockets of his trench coat, watching Caleb with his deep-set eyes.

And Bridget.

Even here, in the candlelit kitchen with Emmeline, there was Bridget.

"I —"

She came up close to him, put one palm on his sternum and the soft pad of her right index finger against his lips.

"Shhh, Caleb," she said.

She looked up at him, not blinking. Holding him with her eyes. Then, as if satisfied he wouldn't start to speak when she removed her finger from his mouth, she took him into an embrace. Her cheek pressed against the front of his left shoulder.

"It's better this way," she said. "We're safe here now. I promise you. Do you believe me?"

"Yes."

"This isn't where I live. It's not my house. You know that. But we're safe here. It's all right to be here."

"But how —"

"Don't ask how," she said, holding him tighter. "It's not always good to know how. Not yet."

Now she held him so close that he could feel the beat of her heart. He slid his palms up her bare arms and then let his hands fall down her shoulders to the small of her back, holding her against him.

"I'll take you to the place I live. I want to," she whispered. "I want to take you there now. But I'm not ready for that. Not quite yet."

"Okay."

"And you want to bring me to your house. You want to have me there, to know everything about me. But I think you're not ready for that either, are you?"

He nodded, then realized she couldn't see him.

"I guess not."

"So that's why it's good this way. It's safe. For both of us."

She pulled back from him, without taking her hands from his waist, and raised her face to his. The kiss that followed was as easy as turning a key in a familiar lock, opening the door, and coming home. Her lips were cool. And sweet, like the glass of Berthe de Joux she must have drunk before letting him inside the house. Her hands ran up his back, inside his jacket, smoothing his shirt against his skin. When it ended, she let go of him, and then she turned and stood with her back to him, her hands on the kitchen counter.

"Shall I pour you a glass of the prosecco while you make the oysters?"

He looked at the back of her neck, at the shape of her body beneath the crimson flow of the dress. He had never wanted anyone so badly in his life. The skin on his back was still reacting to her touch, the memory of it lingering as clearly as it would if she'd dipped her hands in red ink. As though she'd marked him, scribed her ownership down his back. If he'd had no shirt on, if they'd shared their kiss while standing naked against each other at the foot of his bed, he was sure she'd have ended that touch with her fingernails. Curling her fingers and raking the nails down the length of his back.

Ten parallel lines, shoulders to waist.

"Caleb?" she asked. She didn't turn. "Wine?"

"That's all right," he said. "I'll be busy for a bit."

"May I watch?"

"I want you to."

The gas fireplace in the dining room was burning with a blue-orange flame behind its brass grate, and Emmeline had carried more candles into the room, placing them in a scatter down the long walnut table. He brought in the plates, holding them with dishtowels because of their heat. The oysters lay on a bed of smoking-hot rock salt, three to a plate, each half-shell topped with a spoonful of the butter-rich fumet, then chervil and a teaspoon of golden caviar.

Emmeline had already poured the prosecco.

She was sitting on the right side of the table and had set a place for him at the end. He put her plate down, then his own. He pulled out his chair and sat. Emmeline took her fluted glass and held it up. He touched the rim of the glass against hers, and they each sipped. The prosecco was as crisp as a green apple, as clean as spring grass.

"Thank you," she said.

"It's —"

"No, Caleb. Don't make it small. Hear what I have to say. No one has ever done something like this for me."

Emmeline put her glass down carefully. She used her fork and lifted one of the oysters from its shell, slipped it into her mouth, and closed her eyes. He watched her, saw her pleasure as the flavors melted together. She swallowed. She put her fork on the edge of her plate and opened her eyes.

"Caleb."

"Really, it's —"

"You don't know what it was like. What my life's been," Emmeline said. He saw how close she was to crying, how the tears were about to run down the white curve of her cheeks.

Caleb put down his fork, reached for her hand. She took his fingers in hers and pressed them.

"He *owned* me. Like you own a dog. You think I'd have stayed in the car, out in the woods — he was gone for *days* — you think I'd have stayed there if he hadn't put a lock on the collar? A steel chain? I might have loved him, but did I get a choice? I was a *child*. When I had to make that choice — when I had to make myself love him — I was a little *girl*."

"Emmeline —"

"— oh god, Caleb, I'm sorry."

"No."

"Caleb, I'm so sorry."

He turned to her, finally catching her left hand. He took it in both of his. Her fingers were as cool as the fog blowing through the streets. With her free hand, she wiped her eyes.

"I shouldn't have said all that."

"It's okay."

"It's not."

"We promised each other," Caleb said. He ran the tips of his fingers down hers. "Never to hurt. Never to lie. And we're okay."

He squeezed her hand gently until she met his eyes.

"All right," she said.

"He took you, didn't he?"

She nodded.

"He did."

"But he's dead now."

"I hope so," she said. "God, I hope so."

She slid her hand out from between his and took her wineglass.

They touched the rims together and then she drank off her prosecco. A thin foam of bubbles lay at the bottom of her glass, lit by the candlelight.

"I'm sorry. The oysters — they're so good. And I've never had anything like them."

"Then let's eat them," Caleb said. "They're best when they're hot like this."

Afterward, he put the plates in the sink and began preparing the risotto. Emmeline opened the pinot and then she leaned in the doorway and watched him. She held the bottle by its neck, down at her hip. He could feel her eyes on him, watching his hands work. The way she leaned in when he picked up a twelve-inch knife and tested its edge against the pad of his thumb before slicing the wild mushrooms on the hardwood chopping block.

He turned to look at her once. Her eyes were dark, and wet tracks on her cheeks glittered in the candlelight. He started toward her but she stopped him by holding out one hand, palm out.

"Cook, Caleb."

"Right."

"You have me now," she said. She was leaning her head against the doorjamb.

"Do I?" he asked. He wasn't sure of anything.

She nodded.

"You have me. I'm yours. So cook. Because I'll still be here, after."

There was a thump from somewhere upstairs. He looked at the ceiling, then at her. It might have been the house settling. It was an old house, built of redwood. There'd be creaks and groans on a night like this. The wind and fog were streaming past the house, pressing it into its foundations. But what he'd heard sounded like someone moving.

"Stay here," Emmeline said.

"You want me to —"

"Stay. Cook."

She smiled at him, but it didn't change her eyes. Didn't lift the sadness from them. She backed out of the room. He heard her put the wine bottle on the dining table, then a moment later heard the wooden stairs as she climbed them to the second floor. He put the mushrooms and the minced garlic into a hot iron skillet. The thin layer of olive oil flared up, sizzling. He pictured her again as a little girl, left alone in a car in the woods. He'd imagined this before, had seen it in his mind since their night together in Spondulix. Something about it had caught him, and now she'd given him enough to understand why.

Now he had new details.

He saw the dog's training collar — a choke collar, its spikes pointed inward — circling her neck. A chain curved away, its end locked to an eyebolt fixed through the car's floor. The dark-haired little girl clawed at the closed windows, leaving bloody streaks. Autumn leaves were scattered on the car's hood, on its roof. More than a day's worth. Wet leaves were stuck to the windshield, to the side windows. The darker ones were the same color as the clawed lines on the inside surface of the glass.

From above, he heard a slide and a bang. It brought him out of the wet woods. He looked at the ceiling and heard a quiet cry. Something stifled. A sob cut off with a surprised palm across the mouth.

Then Emmeline was coming down the stairs. He turned when she came back to her spot in the doorway.

"Everything okay?"

"A window. I left a window open upstairs. While I was waiting for you."

He nodded.

"It smells good," she said.

"It should be okay."

Emmeline looked at the tip of her finger, then touched it to her lips.

"You're all right?"

"I caught my nail. It's nothing."

There'd been a drop of blood on her fingertip, but it was gone now. She'd sucked it away, one quick kiss to the wound.

"I can get you some ice," Caleb said.

She shook her head.

"Cook," she said. "I'll have a glass of wine. That's all I need. It's just a little cut."

She disappeared into the dining room and came back a moment later holding a glass of the pinot.

"This'll be ready in about half a minute."

"Should I get plates?"

"I have them. On the pastry table."

With a wooden spatula, he turned the scallops one last time, to check them. They'd seared to a nice golden brown, and when he leaned closer to smell them, he could tell they'd pulled in the flavors of the chanterelle and morel mushrooms. He lifted the skillet off the burner and arranged the plates, which he'd already garnished with chopped thyme and truffle oil. When he carried them into the dining room, Emmeline pulled out his chair. She'd poured his wine.

"That looks lovely," she said.

"Thanks."

He put down her plate and then sat. She stood behind him a moment, her hand on the side of his neck, under the collar of his shirt. He thought maybe she'd say something, but she didn't. She brushed her right hand along the curve of his ear, and then with a rustle of silk and a swirl of perfume, she pulled out her own chair and sat.

SEVENTEEN

IT COULD HAVE ended so many different ways.

But as he walked to his car, jangling his keys in his coat pocket and thinking about it, he was sure it could not have ended more beautifully. After the risotto, they'd sat on the floor in front of the fireplace in the main living room, using cushions from the sofa and leaning against the heavy coffee table. Emmeline had poured the last of the prosecco and they'd eaten the chilled raspberries with shavings of dark chocolate, Emmeline pressing up against him for warmth. She'd put her hand on his chest, where two of her fingers slipped beneath the placket of his shirt between the mother-of-pearl buttons to rest against his undershirt, next to his heart. They finished the dessert, then the wine, and when the last of it was gone, she'd leaned up to him again and kissed him.

Her lips had been cool and sweet.

Emmeline moved her body against his, and when he grew hard, she put one hand against his lower back and pressed him to her. She broke off the kiss and spoke with the corner of her mouth against his ear.

"It'd be easy, wouldn't it?"

"Yes."

"Here, in front of the fire."

"I know."

"You could take me," she said. "Any way you wanted."

He drew his hand down her back, bringing her closer. That midnight scent of her skin, the smell of moonlight and shadows, wrapped him and carried him.

"But not yet. We can't yet," she said. "You understand?"

"Yes."

He was dizzy now. There was the wine, but the real intoxicant was Emmeline. She was inside of him, running through his veins and crossing the barrier to his brain. The slippery silk of her dress, and her bare skin underneath it.

She brought her lips to his and put her hands on the back of his head. When that ended, that long and deep kiss, she held her forehead against his. Her fingers still ran through his hair. Her eyes were closed.

They stayed that way long enough, pressed together on the cushions, that their breathing fell into the same rhythm. In and out, together. She pulled back first, and he lay on his side with his head propped on his hand. They were close to the fire, and the cushions facing it were warm.

"You're not looking at me anymore," she said. Her eyes were still closed.

"I was looking at the fireplace."

"Do you see it?"

"Do I—?" But he stopped midstream, when his eyes focused. "Wait."

He stared at the heavy jamb supporting the left side of the mantle.

"It swings out, doesn't it?"

She nodded, her eyes still closed.

"A lot of old houses had things like that," she said. "And when enough people die, then the house has a secret."

He wasn't sure what had given it away. But he'd spent his life learning to find what other people couldn't see. That was, perhaps, his defining trait. He looked at the fireplace again. The dimensions were off somehow. The wall was thicker than it needed to be and the jamb looked light for its size. The house was too beautiful, too well designed, for these anomalies to have been mistakes of proportion or failures of aesthetics.

And where there was a reason, there was a way in.

"Is it okay?" he said. "I mean—"

She put her finger on his lips again.

"It's all right, Caleb," she whispered. "You can look."

But he was reluctant to leave her. His fingertips were at the base of her throat, and he could feel her shoulder and back pressed against his chest.

"Take a look," she said. She shifted, and then she was pushing him up. "You'll figure it out."

"And you?"

"Not me," she said. "I don't like going in places like that. I like it by the fire."

He stood, letting his fingers trace a line from her shoulder to her hip. Then he stepped over her and knelt at the jamb, taking one side of it with each of his hands. With his fingertips, he explored the corner between the wall and the edge of the fireplace, but didn't find anything.

It wouldn't be like that, though.

If it was as simple as a hidden latch, a maid would have found it while polishing the hearth; a child would have tripped it in the midst of a game. It wouldn't be a secret anymore. He leaned against the jamb and used his palms to press it down, into the floor. From somewhere inside, he heard a click, and when he stood up and pulled, the jamb swung out on internal hinges.

It revealed a doorway no more than a foot wide and five feet high. The passage stretched into darkness.

"See?" Emmeline said. "But you know how to find things."

"How do you know that?"

"You found me."

She'd opened her eyes now, and was looking at him. She lay on the cushions with her finger circling the rim of her empty prosecco glass. There was color in her cheeks from the fire's heat, and he knew that if he came to her and lay next to her, he could put even more color there. But he could smell the mildew and dust in the dead air he'd just exposed, could feel the cold leaking from the secret room, and he knew he had to go there.

She wanted him to — he knew that, also. There were a thousand places she might have brought him tonight, but she had chosen this place. This house of echoes.

"You'll want a candle," Emmeline said.

There were half a dozen of them on the coffee table next to her. He took one, shielding its flame with his hand, and stood in front of the passage. He looked at Emmeline once more, and then ducked into the tunnel.

It was only four feet deep and then it opened into a room no larger and no less austere than a monk's cell. The floor and walls were made of stone, and overhead were the bare redwood beams holding up the mansion's second story. He held the candle above his eyes and turned slowly.

There was a cot in one corner, its blankets tossed in a pile by the last person who'd slept in it. But that must have been long ago, because the blankets and the cot were each covered in drifts of spider silk and dots of dark mold. On the floor was a dust-covered water glass, and next to that was a silver spoon coated with a black crust. There were sheets of drawing paper scattered under the cot and on its thin mattress. He crouched to look at one, but it was too filthy with mildew and the leavings of insects to see what had been drawn on it. Whatever had once existed in the charcoal was forever gone. He didn't look at the others.

Caleb stood and turned all the way around to make sure he had missed nothing, and then he went out the way he had come.

Emmeline was where he'd left her.

After he shut the secret door, he put the candle back on the coffee table and then knelt next to her. She rolled to him, opening her eyes again. She took his hand and brought it to her lips, and when she kissed his knuckles, just underneath the line of cuts, he could feel the gentle touch of her teeth.

"Hello," she finally said. "How was it?"

"What was it?" he asked.

"I don't know."

"Something to do with Prohibition?" he asked. "Like a hiding place?"

She shook her head.

"I don't know. It's a secret."

"But you knew about it."

"I found it," she said. "The same way you found it. So that makes it our room — our secret room. It'll be ours until we're both gone, and then it'll just be a blank space again. A darkness."

She let go of his hand and put her palm against the back of his neck, pulling him to her.

"You're going to tell me to go," Caleb said.

"It's time."

There were too many questions to ask. Why this house, with its dead room and its strange echoes? And why him, of all the men in the city, when her knowledge of him was limited to his first name and his telephone number? When he'd started a question like this before, she'd shushed him with a finger to his lips, and then a kiss. It was better not to know, she'd said. So he asked nothing at all.

"You go home," she said. "I'll clean up."

"And you'll call me?"

"It won't be long," she said. "And then you'll see me. And, Caleb?"

"Emmeline."

"I'm yours. So don't forget."

He nodded, his forehead against hers. He stood and straightened his pants and his suit jacket, then looked down at her. She was still on the cushions, reclined in front of the fire, one elbow on the coffee table. The hem of her dress had slipped up to her thigh, well above her knee. She pushed it down and looked up at him.

"Soon," she said.

He nodded again.

Then he turned, and showed himself out.

Now he was crossing the street, his hands in his coat pockets, his key ring bouncing in his cupped fingers. Twice, she'd frozen every physical process in his body with just two syllables: *I'm yours.* He'd never met anyone who could do that, who could stop time with a word. She could probably run it backwards if she wanted to.

He stepped up to the sidewalk on the far side of the street, then turned and looked back at the Haas-Lilienthal House. The memory from earlier in the night rose up and wavered before him, the image of his mother, running down this sidewalk with a policeman in tow. They turned to vapor and blew away on the wind before he could decide if he'd seen a true memory or just the ripples of a dream.

Caleb steadied himself against a streetlamp and stared at the house.

The first level was still dark, but he saw a light moving behind the curtains on the second floor. The firelight of the hurricane lantern went past the three curved windows of the corner tower, paused a moment in the center, and then withdrew.

She was going deeper into the house. All the upstairs windows went dark as she carried the light away. But Caleb didn't turn. Not yet. He didn't know what he might be waiting for, but he knew there would be something. A sign, a hint.

He waited, leaning into the streetlamp's damp metal pole.

From behind the curtains there was a blue spark, like the flash-bulb of an old camera. No sound at all. Just a burst of light.

Then it was dark again, and silent. The fog rolled past, clipping the northern edge of the city as it pressed from the Pacific to the bay. At the corner of Franklin and Jackson, one of the streetlamps flickered and went out. His car was parked up there, in the new shadows under the dark eye of the lamppost. He turned back to the house, watched the curtain-bound windows on the second floor for another minute, and then gripped his keys inside his fist and went on.

The doorbell rang at ten thirty in the morning. Caleb rolled off the couch, took the bathrobe off the armrest, and threw it on. Because he'd broken and then boarded up the window next to the door, he couldn't see who was out there. Kennon, he imagined. Or maybe Bridget. Someone from the lab.

He opened the door.

"Henry — what the hell are you doing?"

His oldest friend looked at him. His shoes were wet and muddy, and Caleb guessed he must have parked somewhere else and then walked up to the house on one of the footpaths through the eucalyptus groves.

"Better come inside before someone sees you on my porch."

"Lemme take these off first."

Henry bent and untied his shoes, slipped them off, and then stepped into the house when Caleb stood aside for him. Caleb shut the door and followed Henry down the hall to the kitchen.

"Coffee?"

"Sure."

Caleb got the bag of ground coffee from the freezer and took the French press from the dish drain next to the sink.

"What happened to the machine?"

"Bridget."

"Sorry."

Caleb shrugged.

"The least of my problems. Anybody follow you up here?"

"Not that I know of."

"Vicki know what's going on?"

"Some. But, Caleb —"

Caleb cut him off.

"Shouldn't you be with her and the kids? It's Christmas Eve, right?"

Caleb lit the burner under the teakettle, then turned his back to Henry while he poured coffee into the French press.

"She asked me to come," Henry said.

"What?"

Caleb turned around. Henry was sitting on one of the stools opposite the kitchen counter, the same place Kennon had been sitting.

"To be honest, I didn't want to," Henry said.

"I'll bet."

"But some things matter more than work. More than careers. Like sticking by your friends when they need you."

"Vicki told you that."

"That's right."

"Nice."

Henry half smiled, then looked down at the counter. There was the hushed sound of the gas burner and the teakettle ticking as it heated.

"What's wrong, Caleb? I mean, what's *really* wrong? It's not just Bridget, is it?"

"Oh, come on, Henry."

"I'm serious, Caleb. Is it work? Something else?"

"It's nothing."

Caleb sat on a stool opposite Henry and put his elbows on the stone countertop.

"Look at yourself," Henry said. "At this place."

Henry nodded at the quarter-full bottle of Berthe de Joux on the end of the dining table, at the mostly empty bottle of Jim Beam near the sink. Caleb had spent some time sketching last night when he'd gotten home, drawing Emmeline as he'd last seen her, reclined on the cushions in front of the fire. Her sad eyes telling him to go home, but the shape of her body begging him to stay. He remembered the way it had smelled in the secret room, the heavy scent of dust and dead memories. And the way it felt when Emmeline had pressed against him, her skin cool and alive, her pulse as quick as a fawn's as they lay together in front of the fire, a few feet from the hidden door she'd hoped he would find. He understood now that meeting her must have been more than chance, more than a brush in the dark at House of Shields.

"It's not messy," Caleb said, and that was true.

"No. But how much've you been drinking?"

"Of that? Not much. Last night I just had one. I was working on something."

"For the lab?"

"Something else."

"All right."

"The lab's fine. I've got till the end of January to get the data sets to the NIH. It's all on track."

"They still giving you trouble?" Henry asked. "End of September, you were really worried."

"It's fine. I got it under control."

"In September, I thought maybe the real issue was the auction."

"Christie's can sell what it wants."

"Yeah," Henry said. "But you keep track."

Caleb shrugged, then nodded.

"It was the first time one of his pieces went for over a million," he said. "So I followed it. But so what? It's just art collectors trading them back and forth. They go higher every time. It's got nothing to do with me."

"Except they'd never sell for so much if your father had just been a normal man," Henry said. "Or if he'd just stayed a normal man. I don't know — I mean, I don't know how it was. I only saw it from the outside. And from the outside it looked fine, until it wasn't."

"And then every time one sells at an auction like that, there's a story in the *Times*," Caleb said. "And it all comes up again, and I have to talk about it with you. Or try to talk around it. We have to say how disgusting people are, to want to pay to own a piece of that. So let's just say it and get past it. People are evil. They're twisted. Can we move on?"

"I'm not saying we have to talk about it."

"Fine."

When the kettle started to steam, Caleb got up and poured the water into the French press. When it was done brewing, Henry accepted the mug that Caleb slid across the counter. Caleb sat again, took a sip, and waited for Henry.

"The patients in your data sets, those are mostly what?"

"End-stage cancer," Caleb said. "Postoperative patients. The more stitches, the better. People coming into the emergency room with traumas."

"How do you sign them up?"

"It's not easy."

"Something like, 'Hey there, instead of a morphine drip, how about two hundred bucks and a chance to tell me how much it hurts?'"

"Pretty much."

"What about the batrachotoxin study? You still doing that?"

Caleb nodded.

"We're building a 3-D model. It'll help other labs study it in computer simulations."

"So they don't have to worry about contaminating the building," Henry said. "Drop a vial, kill the whole staff."

"That's right."

"You want to come over for dinner tonight? Vicki wanted me to ask. It's why I came."

"No," Caleb said. "I mean — no, but thanks. I ought to stick around here."

"What for?"

"I just ought to be here," Caleb said. He was looking at the countertop and not at Henry. "In case she comes."

"All right."

Henry glanced around again, then focused on the dining table.

"What is that, anyway?"

"What is what?"

Henry pushed up his glasses and squinted as he read the label on the bottle.

"Berthe de Joux."

"French absinthe."

Henry turned and put both elbows back on the counter. He brought the mug to his lips, sipped the coffee, then set it down.

"Little experiment with thujone, trying to get inside the mind of our killer?" Henry said.

He said it lightly, like a joke, but Caleb's insides tightened and his eyes narrowed.

"You said — wait. What?"

"Thujone? What the killer's been giving all the victims, after the vecuronium wears off?"

"What about it?"

"That's what makes absinthe, right? That's the chemical in wormwood. They used to think it was the wormwood — the thujone — that made guys like van Gogh insane. I think it's a GABA receptor antagonist. Which, if you think about it, would be a pretty good thing to give someone you were about to torture."

Caleb looked at Henry and then at the bottle on the table. Its cold green glow.

"Thujone," Caleb said.

It was all he could think to say, but his mind was going a lot faster. Henry was right about one thing. Blocking a person's GABA receptors would be a perfect first step before lighting him up with pain. The nerves would be primed and ready to fire, the pathways cleared all the way up.

"Yeah," Henry said. "Thujone. Don't tell me you didn't know it's in absinthe."

"No," Caleb said. "I didn't."

"Look at you. Big chemistry guy, learning something from a lowly coroner," Henry said. That half-smile was back on his face, but there wasn't much joy in it. "Who got you drinking that stuff, anyway? Bridget?"

Caleb shook his head.

"Not Bridget. It was just — I don't know. An idea I had. Something I wanted to try."

"Looks like you enjoy it."

"I guess so."

When Henry finally left, Caleb dumped his coffee in the sink and then went to the dining table. He pulled out a chair and sat before the bottle of absinthe, turning it to read the label. There was nothing helpful there, no breakdown of the bottle's contents. But what had only been a whisper for the last week was now a steadily building roar. He supposed he'd been walking toward this, that it would not have been possible to ignore it forever. His job was to make inferences based on known facts, to build bridges that connected the known to the white space beyond it. He wasn't like Kennon — being good and being right were not disconnected concepts in Caleb's profession. He looked at the bottle and knew what he had to do.

He went down the hall to his bathroom, showered, then dressed in a hurry. The lab would be empty on Christmas Eve, so he didn't bother shaving. He took a leather briefcase from his study, then went back to the dining table and put the bottle of Berthe de Joux inside it. He paused a moment then, before going to the garage, to think about what he was doing. His place in all this. He looked at the scabs on the backs of his fingers and touched the bruise on his forehead. He thought of Emmeline's arms around him, and the waxen corpse of a man who'd been tortured before the ebbing tide wedged him under a sewage pipe, and the sound of Bridget crying into the phone from the lonely cold of her studio on Bush Street.

There was more.

There were the two hundred and fifty unanswered emails from Joanne Tremont with questions about the NIH grant application. The sad way Henry had nodded to him before stepping onto the walkway and going to his car with his back hunched against the rain.

EIGHTEEN

THE LAB WAS empty, but not quiet. Sounds could travel through the air ducts, could echo along the dark utility tunnels from other parts of the hospital. And no hospital was ever silent. Over the hum of the equipment powering up, Caleb could hear the din coming from the ceiling vents. Another murmur came from under the floor, where a trapdoor to the utility tunnel lay hidden beneath a lab tech's workbench. Voices and machines. A woman's distant crying. Footsteps rushing down a hard-tiled hallway. All this was blended together and piped in, like strange elevator music.

He poured a drop of the absinthe into a sample vial, then loaded it into the mass spectrometer's automatic feed tray. The machine was programmed to start its cycle as soon as the power-up was complete. He watched it a while, listening as its circuits warmed, then went into his office.

There were emails from Bridget, four of them within the last hour. The subject lines said enough: *Please.*

Please, Caleb.

I understand.

He didn't open them, didn't read them. Instead he brought up a database of organic compounds and searched for thujone. He sketched the skeletal structures of its two most common isomers on a notepad, drawing wedges and hashed lines to differentiate the three-dimensional angles of their carbon bonds. He looked at the lines and tapped his pencil eraser against his chin, thinking it through.

Later, if he needed to, he could run more delicate tests to probe at the molecular structure of the samples. He'd be able to tell if the thujone in the victims' tissues matched the isometric fingerprints of Berthe de Joux. But the first task was simply to find out how much thujone, of any isometric form, was in a drop of Emmeline's absinthe. He pulled up the results from his tests on Richard Salazar's tissue samples, studied the spectral lines. The man had been pumped full of the chemical, something close to sixty milligrams per kilogram of body weight. Enough to send a jolt through all his neural pathways, to fire his muscles into painful convulsions.

Caleb looked at his computer monitor. The blinking window in the corner told him that his first sample run was complete.

He pushed back from his desk and walked into the lab, crossing the darkened space to the printer. He pulled the pages as they came out, then stood under the reddish glow of an exit sign to read them. His head cast a shadow over the paper so that he had to hold it out and lean back to get enough light to read it. There were scores of organic compounds in the absinthe, but there was only one line he cared about.

He found it and followed it with his fingertip, tracing the line to its end and then scanning back to read its value. He'd been trembling since he left the house, buzzing with panic. But after he saw the numbers, he could hold the pages without shaking.

He went back to his office with the printout and compared it to Richard Salazar's test results, holding the two graphs side by side. He'd read the values correctly the first time. The charts were accurate. He'd run all the tests himself, had used equipment no other lab could match. There could be no mistake. Richard Salazar was full of thujone, but he couldn't have gotten it by drinking Berthe de Joux. There simply wasn't enough thujone in the absinthe to make it work. He'd have dropped dead of alcohol poisoning long before getting anywhere close.

Caleb sat down and closed his eyes.

The warning that had grown to a roar was fading again to a whisper. It didn't go away completely, of course. There were still too many connections, too many loose facts. But he could live with the whisper. They had made promises, after all, and promises had mass. A true weight that could be measured. If he could isolate the words in their hearts and run them through his machines, he could show their real values.

I will never lie to you, she'd said. *I will never hurt you.*

And early this morning, a new one: *I'm yours.*

His computer chimed and he looked up at the screen. Bridget had emailed again. It was too much. He switched off the monitor and stood.

It was dark, and he was sober again, when he got back to the medical center. He'd left the seawall just before sunset and had walked back through the avenues, looking at the blur of Christmas lights, at the flickering menorahs in the front windows of a few scattered homes. Then he was climbing the steep hill up to the hospital, the Muni tram on the N-Judah line grinding east behind him, blue sparks falling from the overhead wires.

He stopped and looked across the street at the front entrance to the hospital. There were no cars moving. Two of the closest streetlamps had blinked and gone out, so that the center of the block was dark. A half-circle turnabout led to the main hospital doors. Parked there, idling in a cloud of steaming exhaust, was a ghost-gray coupe. A car from the thirties or forties, polished and gleaming in the soft light that came from the hospital. Its headlights lit the falling rain. He looked past the long hood, past the white-walled front tire, to the woman who was leaning against the driver's side door, one foot perched on the narrow running board.

Emmeline.

She wore a black cashmere cloak over her dress, and that fell away to reveal the bare white of her arm when she raised her hand to greet him.

He crossed Parnassus, stepping past the puddles, and came to her. She took his free hand with both of hers, pulled him close, and kissed him. He'd been in the rain for three hours, but her hands were cold around his.

"Hello, Caleb," she said, when she broke off the kiss. She didn't let go of his hand, and used it to hold him closer.

"Emmeline."

"I said it'd be soon, didn't I?"

"You did."

"I couldn't wait any longer," she said.

"Neither could I."

She pressed her lips together as she looked up at him. He'd seen her do that once before, when she came into the Pied Piper and studied the Maxfield Parrish painting, looked over each man in the room, and walked out.

"Would you like to play a game?" she said.

"All right."

"Do you trust me?"

"Yes."

"And you remember everything I promised you?"

He nodded, and she smiled. Her cheeks were flushed with cold, and there were droplets of mist in her hair and on her eyelashes. She released his hand, reached into the folds of her cloak, and came out holding a black silk scarf. She handed it to him.

"Get in, Caleb. And then tie that on."

"Over my eyes?"

She nodded.

"Your telephone. Are you carrying it?"

"In my pocket."

"Turn it off," she said. "Show it to me. Let me see you do it."

He did as she asked, and afterward, she took his hand again and squeezed it, briefly tightening his grip on the blindfold. Then he was walking around the hood of the car, feeling the heat coming off the front-mounted radiator and seeing the steam rise away from the four chrome-plated headlamp housings. The statuette on the radiator cap was an armored knight, holding a sword and shield. He got to the passenger side of the car, this time machine that had rolled out of the early half of another century, and pulled on the solid silver door handle. The heavy door swung out, balanced on its hinges. He set his briefcase in the foot well, pulled off his coat and shook the rain from it, then got inside and shut the door. Emmeline was already behind the wheel. The car smelled of her perfume, and of well-oiled leather. Its coachwork looked as new as the day it had rolled off the line. Beneath his feet, he could feel the idling engine, its power coming in loping waves through the soles of his shoes.

"We'll get some heat going," she said. "But first, the scarf."

"Okay."

He unfolded the scarf, doubled it down its length to give it thickness, and closed his eyes as he tied it around his face. He knotted it at the back of his head.

"Nice and tight?" she asked. Her whisper was close enough that he could feel her breath against his neck.

"Tight enough. I can't see anything."

"No peeking. That's against the rules. All right?"

"Okay."

"You know why?" she asked.

"No."

"Guess, Caleb. It's easy."

Her fingertips traced his lips, glided down his chin to his neck. Then the flat of her hand was moving across his chest. Over his sternum and down. He hadn't liked the blindfold, hadn't wanted to play the game of putting it on. But her touch was gathering the fear from him, sweeping it away like dust.

"You're ready to show me where you live," Caleb said. "But you're not ready for me to know how to get there."

Her hand stopped at his belt buckle, and then she was whispering into his ear again.

"Get comfortable, Caleb," she said. "It's a bit of a drive."

She took her hand off his belt, and then Caleb heard her shift the car into gear. The old coupe, heavy and powerful, rolled with the smooth motion of a ship. He'd never been in a car like it. Even with the blindfold, it was like falling into another time. He felt safe here, in the car, with Emmeline next to him. That was as warm and as good as the heater blowing across his knees and onto his lap. He held his hands together atop his coat and leaned back in the bench seat.

Emmeline took a left on Parnassus and drove west for a minute or two before taking another left. He guessed they were on Ninth or Tenth Avenue, but then Emmeline began taking rights and lefts until Caleb lost all sense of place. Five minutes went by as she wound the car through the quiet avenues, circling and jagging, block by block.

"If you're wondering whether I'm lost yet, you can relax," he said. "I am."

"Good."

She made another turn and then he felt her hand on his knee. He covered her fingers with his.

"This car," he said. "I've never seen one like it."

"An Invicta," she said.

"British?"

"I think. *He* got it. When we were in Victoria, or maybe Vancouver. We brought it back on the ferry, into Seattle. That was when I was little."

"So this was his car."

"But now it's mine," she said, and her voice brightened with the words. "Do you like it?"

"It's beautiful," Caleb said. "Someday, maybe I'll even get to see it."

She laughed a little and moved her hand higher on his leg, tracing a figure eight against the cloth of his khakis.

"Someday," she said. "And that'll be soon."

Now she was driving in a single direction, following one road. She went a long stretch without slowing or stopping, so that Caleb guessed either they were crossing Golden Gate Park, or she'd hit it lucky with the lights and hadn't been caught by a red. Or perhaps she was just running through the reds without stopping. That would be easy enough tonight. Before he'd gotten into the car and put on the blindfold, the city had been as dark and empty as the beginning of a dream. A stage, maybe. A set for Emmeline, where she could make anything happen. He pictured the row houses as simple façades, propped up in the back by angled two-by-fours, lit from behind with stage lighting. Hidden wires and trapdoors to fill out the illusion.

"You're smiling about something," Emmeline said.

"Are you watching me or the road?"

"You," she said. "I'm always watching you."

Now they went into a series of curves, and Caleb could tell the road was banked against the outside turns. The car stuck to the pavement like it was on rails, its motion so stately that Caleb had no idea of their speed.

"This is where you ask me, 'Are we there yet?' and I tell you, 'Soon, Caleb.'"

"Are we there yet?"

"Not even close," she said. "Relax."

She slowed the car and he felt them turn onto a new street. Then they must have been in a neighborhood of right-angled avenues, where Emmeline once again took them on a route of turns so frequent they could only be random. At one point, she slowed the car and did a U-turn, pausing before accelerating in the new direction to lean across the seat and kiss Caleb's neck, just beneath his left earlobe.

After ten minutes of wandering, they were moving again, holding steadily in one direction. Caleb heard rain hitting the windshield and then the rhythmic swipe of the wipers. Emmeline accelerated through a turn and the road straightened out and leveled. The sound of the engine and the tires changed abruptly, as if someone had taken all the bass away from the notes they sang. Once a second there was a double thump as the car's front tires crossed to a new section of the roadway, followed immediately by the rear tires doing the same. In all of San Francisco, there was only one span of road that sounded like this.

As surely as if he'd taken off his blindfold, Caleb knew she was driving him across the Golden Gate Bridge. She couldn't have known how well he knew that route, how many times he'd made that crossing.

But he lost track of things again after they got off the bridge. Emmeline drove him for another twenty minutes. Steep, winding roads in the Marin Headlands. Then they were going down for a long time, and she took a final right turn and pulled to a stop.

"Wait here."

She got out of the car but left the door open. He heard the sound of a rolling gate sliding on its track. Then she was back inside, and they pulled forward, moving slowly for a few seconds before she stopped again.

"Stay there and keep the blindfold on, all right?"

"Okay."

She shut off the engine and stepped from the car, shutting her door this time. For a moment, he was alone, and could hear nothing from outside. Then his door opened and he felt her hand on his shoulder.

"I'll help you out," she said. "Watch your head."

He stepped from the car, her fingers on the back of his head until he was clear of the doorframe. When he stood to his full height, she guided him two steps back so that she could swing the door shut. Then she took his left arm in hers and started him on a slow walk, away from the car.

He heard the bridge's foghorn, a long, low note in the distance to his right. The wind was salty and damp.

"There's a set of steps," Emmeline said. "Here. Feel the riser?"

"Yes."

"Careful — they're tall."

They climbed a wooden staircase, the steps loose and wobbly underfoot. The side of the building was to his right. He trailed his fingers against its clapboard wall as they climbed. Sixteen steps in a straight line, and then they were on a landing of some kind.

"Stay there. You can hold on to the railing. Here."

She put his hand on the splintered rail. He heard a jangle of keys, then deadbolt locks sliding past rusty strike plates. Three of them.

She worked the door handle, and he heard the hinges move, felt the swish of air past his face as the door swung by.

"Do you mind much? Doing all this for me?" Emmeline asked. The keys clattered again as she pulled them from the last lock and put them away. "You still want this, right?"

"God, yes. I want it."

"Then come inside," she said. She took his arm again and led him the last few steps into her home.

"There's a little step at the threshold. But we're almost there."

"Okay."

"Stand here."

He stood, swaying in the darkness behind the blindfold.

Behind him, the door closed and the locks turned. It was as cold in here as it had been outside, but the wind was gone. He heard her walk around him, deeper into the room. It must have been a big space. Her footfalls tracked thirty, forty feet away from him, but there were no barriers that separated them. No doors opening and closing, no partition walls to block the sound of her heels. She struck a match against the rough side of a box. A moment later he could smell the smoke. Otherwise, the room smelled of clean linens, and perfume. Cut flowers and polished wood. A clock was ticking from somewhere off to the left. A longcase clock, maybe. He could hear its pendulum swinging.

"All right, Caleb," she said. "Take off the blindfold. I want you to see me."

NINETEEN

THREE CANDLES LIT the space around her bed. Otherwise, there was no light. Windows ran down each side of the long room, but they had been boarded up from the inside. Roughly sawn, mismatched pieces of lumber were nailed in place across the casings. As for the candles, two were in thin glass globes that sat on a narrow table next to the bed. The third was inside an iron birdcage on a stand near the foot of the bed, and this candle was thick enough, and had burned long enough, that its flame flickered out of sight, setting the waxen cylinder aglow. It cast the shadows of the cage's bars throughout the room. Into the exposed rafters and across the bed's white duvet cover.

Emmeline stood next to the caged candle, at the foot of the bed.

She'd taken off her cloak, had draped it over the winding, wrought-iron vines of the bed frame. She stood with her arms crossed beneath her breasts and her head down, so that her dark hair partially hid her face.

She looked up at him, used one hand to tuck a lock of hair behind her ear.

She wore a diaphanous black dress that was tied in place with a long length of crimson ribbon, like a ballerina's pointe shoe. She leaned her head to the side and closed her eyes as she undid the bow on her right shoulder, slowly unwinding the ribbon from the bodice of the dress and from around her waist until it was free. She let the ribbon fall to the floor. Without it, the dress slipped down the length of her body, spreading into a silken pool at her feet like a shadow. She stepped out of it, toward him, her heels tapping lightly on the old wooden floor. Her corset was black, but was so thin and sheer that even by the uncertain candlelight he could see the white curve of her breasts, the dark circles of her areolae.

"Caleb?"

"Yes?"

"I'm cold."

For the second time this evening, he thought about dreams, about their subtly embedded signals, the unconsciously posted signs that labeled chimeras for what they were. As he walked to her, the signposts were everywhere. The candlelight was too dark. The air was so viscous, he had to swim through it to reach her. The floorboards expanded as he crossed them, the shadows hiding the true distance between them. Time was stopping. But this was no dream. He closed the gap — five feet, three feet. He reached the ambit of her arms, and then she was pulling him in, as if taking him from deep water. He swept his hands down the curve of her hips, tracing their shape, his thumbs slipping between her skin and her garter straps. As she kissed him, he found the front clips that released the tops of her stockings, and he let them both go at once. He lifted her, making a seat for her with his interlaced fingers. Her legs wrapped his waist, encircling him as he kissed the tops of her breasts. He carried her to the side of the bed and put her down.

"When I picked you up, at the hospital, I said it was a game," she said, between kisses. "I asked you if you wanted to play a game. Do you remember?"

"Yes."

"It was wrong of me to say that," she said.

He was standing at the side of the bed, her ankles crossed at the small of his back, locking him to her. Her right arm was hooked behind his neck and she was unbuttoning his shirt with her left hand. She spoke with her lips against his neck.

"This isn't a game, is it?" she said.

"No. It's not."

"I want you too much," she whispered. "If I can't afford to lose, it's not a game."

"It's not a game," Caleb said. "I know that."

"Promise me."

"I already did. I'll never hurt you."

"That's all I need."

She pulled his shirt free from the waistband of his pants and then pushed it off his shoulders, running her hands down his arms until the shirt fell on the floor behind him. He grabbed the neck of his undershirt, pulled it over his head, and dropped it. Then she was pulling his belt back until it was free of the buckle's chape, and she let go of his neck and used both hands to unbutton his pants.

He ran his hands into her hair and looked up a moment, needing his bearings.

Emmeline's home was a huge loft space, a hundred feet long and half as wide, most of it lost in shadow. It was entirely open but for a carve-out in one corner, which may have been the kitchen, and a smaller alcove opposite, which might have been a bathroom. Most of the furniture was clustered in the area around the bed. There was a big cedar armoire and a pair of sea chests. An antique-looking table was encircled by high-backed chairs. A china cabinet backed with silvery, time-corroded mirrors. Other sheet-covered shapes evaporated in the shadows beyond the candlelight. Except for the bedspread, which was soft and new, there didn't seem to be a single thing in the room that was less than two hundred years old.

Emmeline lightly raked her nails down his chest, trying to get his attention. He started to turn back to her, and then the clock he'd heard earlier began to chime. He spotted it on the far side of the room, behind the table. It was taller than he was, its French Comtoise–style case gorgeously curved like a cello's body. Candlelight shone on its golden hands.

Six o'clock.

He turned back to Emmeline. She had unzipped his pants and was kissing a line downward from his chest. He put his hands on her shoulders and pressed her gently back onto the bedspread. Her hair painted a dark swath across its white surface. He unwound her legs from his waist, held both her ankles in one hand, and slipped the high-heeled shoes off her feet. She met his eyes and held them, and then she brought her ankle up and rested it on his left shoulder.

She gave him a half-smile, with one corner of her mouth. She pointed at her stocking.

He nodded and took hold of the top edge, rolling it upward from her thigh to her toes. The skin on her calf was soft and responded with goose bumps when he brushed his fingers along it. She shifted her legs so that he could roll the other stocking off.

It came easily, silk gliding along her alabaster-smooth skin.

"Hurry, Caleb," she whispered. "It's so cold."

"You want to get under the covers?"

"Yes."

She slipped off the mattress so that she was standing on the floor. Without her heels on, the top of her head was just beneath his chin. She bent and slid off her panties and garter belt, then turned her back to Caleb.

"Help me."

At first he didn't understand, but then he saw.

The back of her corset was held tightly together with a line of small hooks and eyelets. He unfastened them, wondering how she'd gotten them together to begin with. He dropped the corset into the pile of their clothes. She turned to him, naked now, her right hand cupping the full curve of her left breast, her left hand crossing her stomach and clutching her side as she shivered.

"Quickly," she said.

She turned back the duvet, climbed beneath its down-padded bulk, and moved to the center of the bed. Caleb knelt and untied his shoes, then pulled them off as he stood. He sat at the edge of the bed and slid out of his pants and socks in a single motion. Then he lifted the covers and rolled beneath them.

They met in the middle of the bed, on their sides.

Emmeline lifted herself to allow his arm to get under her, and then they were holding each other, no space at all between them. Her body trembled against his, whether from cold or desire, he couldn't say.

"Make me warm," she said.

She held on to him and rolled, to bring him on top of her. She didn't need to guide him, didn't need to tell him what to do or how to move. She lifted her knees and brought her hips up, and then all at once, as though he'd never been anywhere else, he was inside of her. The moment he entered, he realized —

She wasn't cold everywhere. Not at all.

He thought of a fire — a fire inside a ring of stones, left untended through the night. At the coldest moment of dawn, its embers would still be there, buried under ashes. Waiting for the right stir. The right touch of breath and tinder to bring them alight. As he moved inside her, holding her close and working a counter-rhythm to the cadence of her hips, he focused on that: bringing the fire back. It was a slow and steady build, until her breasts and cheeks flushed pink with heat and even her feet against the backs of his knees were warm, and then, finally, she burst into flames beneath him.

This wasn't Spondulix, where she had to sing in a secret whisper. And there'd be no way to whisper this. Her fingers dug into his back, and she bit into his shoulder and cried out his name. His own release approached, became inevitable, and he tried to pull away. Tried to keep it from her. But she sensed it the moment it began to build in him, and she held him inside with her hands, with her wrapped legs.

"Stay with me," she gasped. "Stay in me. It's all right to stay in me."

Beneath him, her hips bucked and then relaxed in time with him, and at the last, she melted into the soft down mattress. The duvet settled slowly around them, a cushion of warm air beneath it. He stayed with her until long after they were finished. What they had created, the heat between them, stayed too. When he finally moved off of her, he put one of the pillows against the iron headboard and rested his shoulders against it. She laid her head on his chest, and he put his lips into the dark halo of her hair.

He looked across the room, past the birdcage and the ancient table, to the longcase clock on the far wall. He had to squint to read the time from here, and when he finally saw it, he sat up a little higher.

It was a quarter after five. Which, of course, could not be.

"What is it?" she murmured.

"That clock. Does it run backwards?"

"Yes," she said. Her voice was sleepy. "There are strange things. In here."

"Strange like the car. The Invicta."

"Like that. He collected things. Whatever he saw that was different, that he liked. The car, the clock . . . me."

He held her tightly, but lifted his head and looked around. The candle flames had grown taller as the wax melted around them.

The circle of light stretched a little deeper into the space. He saw some of the shapes beneath the sheets and imagined what they might be. Wooden chests and suitcases, full-length mirrors on swiveling stands. He thought of something and the truth of it seemed very close. A dancing light, just out of reach.

"He was a stage magician of some kind, wasn't he?" Caleb said. "A performer."

"No," Emmeline said. She stirred against his chest, moved her hands until she had a better grip on him. Then he felt all of her muscles relax. Her voice, when she spoke next, was perfectly calm. "But that's almost it."

He looked around the room again, seeing things he hadn't noticed on the first sweep. There was a dusty stuffed eagle perched on top of the armoire, its beak open and its tongue curled up as if caught in the midst of a scream. Cut-glass prisms and gold amulets hung on fine chains from the stems of the wineglasses in the china cabinet. A crystal cake stand on a side table close to the doorway held a single dried rose and a deck of cards.

"A hypnotist," he said.

She nodded.

"And you were his assistant," he whispered. "When you got old enough, he made you into his helper. At the shows."

"Yes," she said. "Did you see us?"

"No. I've never been to anything like that."

"Then how did you know?"

He shook his head. He didn't know how he knew. Guessing this history was almost like remembering it. Maybe it was hidden in the place — a magic trick forgotten at the bottom of a sea chest. There'd been other clues. The way Emmeline walked and held herself. Out of place and out of time. Or the fact that she could stop his heart with a word, with a turn of her dark eyes.

"Do you remember anything, from before him?"

"Of course not," she said. "Think what he did."

There was nothing he could say to that. It was too easy to imagine the things he'd done to her, the things he'd made her do. Caleb was starting to fill in the blank spaces, to sketch in what happened beyond the circle of Emmeline's reach while she was alone for days, limited to the length of her chain.

He was a collector. So he'd need to hunt.

He lifted her chin with his fingers and kissed her, and they held each other under the covers, the warmth between them unabated. She put her head on his chest again and he looked to his left, seeing another thing he'd missed in his rush to get into the bed with her. On the nightstand, behind the glass candle globes, there was a picture in a simple wooden frame. A charcoal sketch, one of the five he'd made in a fever before the fireplace in his living room. He looked at that, at the way her hand brushed along his as she taught him how to pour water into absinthe. He looked at the loveliness of her face in the soft darkness of House of Shields and remembered how it had been, meeting her.

He ran his fingers through her hair, then down the length of her back under the covers. She stretched out against him.

"Were you looking for me, that night, at House of Shields?"

But she didn't answer.

When the rhythm of her breath on his chest stayed warm and constant, when the long hand on the clock unwound another five minutes in its journey back through time, he realized she was asleep. He sank with her into the pillows, let her carry him to wherever she was.

He wasn't sure which of them woke first, or what woke them. He didn't know how it had started this time, this second time. But she was on top of him, and the covers had fallen to her hips, and the two smaller candles on the nightstand had gone out recently enough that their dying smoke was still in the air. The candle inside the birdcage was still guttering and flickering, casting barred shadows, and Emmeline rode him slowly, the tip of her finger between his teeth.

She knew where they were going, knew the way well, and she brought him there gently. Leading him and resting, and leading again, so that when they arrived, they arrived together. Then they were holding each other again, cupped together on their sides, her breast filling his hand as he held himself against her back.

"Sleep, Caleb," she said. "It's all right."

But the weight of sleep was too much. He couldn't answer her. So he just held her, and the second time, he was the one who carried her through the night's door.

. . .

It was her absence from the bed that woke him. The space she'd oc-
cupied was still warm, but she wasn't in it. He felt out to each edge
of the mattress and found only emptiness. He sat up in the darkness
and let the cover fall into his lap. The last candle had gone out. He
looked at his watch; it was five in the morning.

Christmas morning.

On the far side of the room, he heard a match strike. He turned
and saw Emmeline's nude profile, the flame cupped behind her hand.
She knelt and lit a candle, then another. She shook out the match and
took the candles in their glass holders, turning to him.

"You're awake."

"And now I'm worried," he said.

"About?"

"That it's time to go."

"But then, tomorrow, it'll be time to come back. If you want to."

"I do."

She placed the candles on the table and then walked to the armoire. She was lovely to watch, lit from behind by the two small
flames as she stood in front of the open shadow of the armoire. She
leaned up on her tiptoes and reached inside, then stepped back holding a long, fur-trimmed coat. She put it on, nothing beneath it.

"It'll still be dark when I get back," she said. "So this is all I need.
You should get dressed, though."

He nodded and swung his legs out from the warmth of the covers,
then knelt by the bed and gathered his clothes.

"You have a bathroom?"

She pointed to the small alcove at the end of the room.

"Down there. There's running water, but it's cold."

"Okay."

He started toward the bathroom, but she caught up to him. She
was holding one of the candles.

"You'll need this."

"Thanks."

She hadn't been exaggerating about the water. What came out of the
tap was like liquid ice. He filled the sink basin with it and used a
washcloth to bathe himself while shifting from foot to foot, trying to
keep warm. The candle threw a wavering circle of light on the stone

countertop, illuminating a scatter of Emmeline's things. He saw a bone-handled brush and a makeup compact with mother-of-pearl inlays on its lid.

At the back of the counter, there was a shelf of glassware. He saw a glass retort with its bulbous base and downward-angled condensing neck, the kind of thing an alchemist or a perfumer might use over a low flame to distill something to its essence. Next to it were crystal perfume vials filled with golden liquid.

He set down the washcloth and picked up one of the vials.

It was heavy and cold in his hand. He withdrew its elongated stopper and raised the opening to his nose.

It wasn't perfume.

TWENTY

"YOU CAN TAKE off the scarf now," she said.

He sat up, tried to answer, and realized he'd missed what she'd said.

"Sorry?"

"The blindfold. You can take it off."

He let go of her hand and reached behind his head to loosen the knot. The scarf fell around his neck. It was still dark. The headlights lit an empty section of Judah Street as they moved east, up the hill toward the hospital. He folded the scarf and handed it to her.

She took it and put it on her lap, then caught his hand and kissed it.

"Almost there," she said.

"When will I see you again?" he asked.

"Soon."

They crested the hill, and now the medical center was on both sides of the street. She turned to the sidewalk alongside a fire hydrant, put the car in neutral, and pulled the parking brake.

"Come here, Caleb."

They came together in the middle of the car, his hand moving inside her coat to hold her naked hip as they kissed.

"Sooner than you think," she said. She kissed the corner of his mouth as she pulled away from him, then smoothed her coat back into place after he'd withdrawn his hand.

Caleb took his coat and his briefcase, opened the door, and stepped out. When he closed the door, she leaned across the seat and put her palm on the inside of the window glass. He'd seen this image before, with his mind if not with his eyes. But this wasn't a child's hand, and he saw as much desire as desperation in the way her palm pressed against the pane. He leaned down and met her eyes. She took her hand from the window glass, touched her fingers to her lips, and then put the car in gear. He stood next to the hydrant with his coat over his arm and watched as she steered back into the lane. He watched until the taillights were just a red stab in the darkness, and then he put on his coat, picked up his briefcase, and walked the rest of the way to his lab.

There was a locker room in the back of the facility, and he went to it while the coffee was brewing. The shower didn't get used very often, but it was good to have on the premises. Necessary, even, considering the sort of things that came and went from his lab. Poisons and nerve agents, slices from cadavers. Three and a half vials of batrachotoxin in the refrigerated safe.

He went to his locker and opened it. He always kept a change of clean clothes in here, just in case he spilled something that could absorb through skin. He stripped, then took his towel from its hook at the back of the locker and went into the shower.

After that, it didn't take long.

As the mass spectrometer powered up, he cleared a workbench and took out his wallet. Inside it, tucked between the bills, there was an old ATM receipt, wound up tightly and twisted at its ends like a hand-rolled cigarette. He unrolled it and used a pair of tweezers to remove a pea-size wad of tissue paper. It was stained golden-amber, because he'd dipped it into the vial in Emmeline's bathroom.

Holding it with the tweezers, he smelled it again. It was aromatic and volatile, like a bitter mint. Like a blend of menthol and sagebrush. He prepared the sample chamber and loaded it, then sat at the workbench and programmed the cycle so it would run on all three Cray clusters. When it was finished, the results would just go to the printer and nowhere else. Paper could be shredded or incinerated. Electronic files were harder to find, impossible to kill. He went into the break room and poured a cup of coffee into someone else's mug, touched it up with Andrea's half-and-half from the refrigerator, then leaned against the drab gray wall and drank it with his eyes closed.

He'd meant everything he'd said to Emmeline. And then he'd found the vial.

He slid down the wall until he was sitting on the break room floor. From this angle, he could see an old bottle cap and a dead cockroach under the refrigerator. From one of the air vents, he caught a few seconds of music, something that had drifted across from one of the clinics in another part of the building. Probably a church group, singing Christmas carols.

If he found something, it didn't have to change anything. He could just ignore it. And maybe there'd be nothing. Or he could go out into the lab now, while there was still time, and pull the plug on the spectrometer. Take the sample and throw all of it into the incinerator, so he'd never know.

He sat on the floor and went through the options until he heard the printer whine into action, the pages spitting out like dealt cards, upside down. If he turned them over, he'd know. He could drop them in the shredder. Instead, he took them off the tray and carried them to the nearest workstation. There was a halogen reading lamp here on a swiveling arm. He flicked it on, then turned the pages over. It wasn't necessary to sort one line out of many, to follow it with his fingertip and read its percentage value off the y-axis.

There was only one line.

However Emmeline had done it, whether with her glass retort or some other equipment, she had made pure thujone.

And she had at least ten vials of it on the shelf behind her sink. Enough for thirty more —

"Caleb?"

He jumped back, slamming the lamp's jointed arm with his elbow. When it hit the desktop, its bulb shattered with a sharp pop, the shards of hot glass fanning across his printouts.

"Jesus Christ, Joanne."

When their eyes met, Joanne Tremont took a step back.

"I didn't mean to startle you," she said.

"It's okay. I'm sorry," Caleb said. "I thought I was alone."

"This early on Christmas morning?" she said. "I thought *I* was alone."

"You should go home."

"There's too much to do," she said. She was shifting her weight from foot to foot and talking fast, as if she'd been up all night with nothing but coffee and worry to keep her going. "And I get stuff done when it's quiet. Usually. You working on the data sets?"

"I'll have them."

"Okay. I'll be here. You saw there's a new one?"

"No."

"Another box from the VA hospital. Must have come yesterday. I don't know how they keep showing up in the fridge, but it's good, right?"

She passed through the back end of the lab on her way to the break room. When she was gone, he used the side of his hand to sweep the broken glass into a trash can. Then he grabbed the papers off the desktop and went to his office. On the way, he stopped and opened the sample refrigerator. The box was on the middle shelf, sealed with orange tape. The patient charts were in a plastic bag, taped to the front. He picked up the box and looked at the chart, reading through the plastic about the injuries this anonymous thirty-seven-year-old woman had suffered, the pain she'd endured.

He slid the box to the back of the refrigerator and shut the door.

It was three o'clock when he stepped out of the lab and checked to be sure the doors had properly locked behind him. He looked across Parnassus at the hospital's main entrance. There was an ambulance parked in the turnout where Emmeline had waited the night before. He felt sick, as if the coffee he'd drunk had been laced with something. And his mind was a flood. He'd woken from a dream to find that he was making love to Emmeline a second time, the backwards-running clock marking the moments over her left shoulder. It had been like slipping from one dream to another. He remembered the shape of her nipple in his mouth, the way she paused and waited for him, so that they would stay together.

There had been so many vials.

"Caleb!"

He looked up. There was no one on the sidewalk, but there was a car parked at the curb in front of him, its passenger window rolled down. Behind the wet windshield, he saw a hand waving him on. He walked up and leaned to look through the open window.

"Get in," Henry said. "And do it quick."

"Whose car is this?"

"Vicki's. You've been in it about eight times."

"Shouldn't you be with her?"

"Stop fucking around and just get in."

"Fine."

Caleb opened the door. When he was in, Henry hit a button on his armrest and raised Caleb's window.

"What's this about?" Caleb asked. "And why does everybody always know where I am?"

"Who's everybody?"

"You. Kennon."

"Unless you're on a bar crawl, you only go two places. Your house, and your lab. I came here first."

"What's this about?"

"You don't know?" Henry asked. "It's been in the papers since yesterday. TV, radio, everything."

"I haven't been paying attention to anything."

Henry took his foot off the brake and pulled onto Parnassus.

"There's been another one," Henry said.

"Same as the others?"

"Not entirely. This one never went in the water. But there are cutaneous current marks—"

"Stun gun marks."

"That's right. And needle marks in the neck. Other signs of torture."

They were going down the hill, into the Inner Sunset. Parnassus turned on to Judah Street, and at Ninth Avenue they fell in beside a Muni tram on the midstreet tracks.

"If the body didn't come out of the bay, what was the cause of death?"

"I'm working on it. But right now, if I had to guess, I'd say cardiac arrest."

"From shock, or from drugs?" Caleb asked.

"I don't know."

"Hasn't Marcie done the toxicology?"

"That's the thing," Henry said. "She can't."

He stopped at the intersection of Judah and Tenth, and the Muni tram rattled to a stop beside them. Henry took a manila envelope from his lap and put it on Caleb's.

"What's this?"

"The autopsy report I did this morning. *Marcie's* autopsy report."

"Oh shit, Henry — Marcie? It was Marcie?"

Henry nodded, and Caleb closed his eyes, squeezing the handgrip on the door's armrest. The autopsy report on his lap was thick and heavy, and that was no surprise. Henry was thorough, even when he was cutting apart his friends and colleagues. He felt himself opening the envelope, pulling out the stack of paper. The first page detailed Henry's external surface examination.

The body is that of an unembalmed Caucasian female adult who appears to have the stated age of thirty-seven years. Identification was made by this Medical Examiner, who knew the decedent personally. Captain Gladstone of the Oakland Coroner's Bureau assisted in the examination to ensure this Medical Examiner remains objective . . . Fresh blood is present in the external auditory canals and oronasal passages, consistent with repeated nonlethal electrocution. Needle marks on the neck and face appear unrelated to therapeutic procedures. Significant welting is present at the injection sites. Livor mortis is discernible and well developed, distributed dorsally and not blanching with firm pressure. Cutaneous current burn marks are distributed heavily on the face and chest . . .

The rest of it would only be worse. Coldly worded, rankly physical descriptions of wounds and their locations. He thought of the things she would have suffered before she died, the hours of it, with drugs in her blood to spike the agony.

"Time of death was sometime between eleven and three," Henry said. "So it was either late on the night of the twenty-third, or early morning on Christmas Eve."

"Where was she?" Caleb asked. "Where'd they find her?"

His fingers were shaking as he slid the photographs from the envelope into his right hand.

"Some old house up in Pacific Heights. Not her house. I didn't go to the scene, so I don't know the address."

"Who found her?"

"A caretaker."

Caleb turned the stack over and saw the first black-and-white photograph. It was taken by the overhead camera in Henry's autopsy room, and showed Marcie on the cadaver table. Henry had already made the Y-incision, had cracked her breastbone with the hedge trimmers, so that the sides of her rib cage and her organs were exposed. Her face was sliced up and badly bruised, and her dead eyes stared up into the camera. Henry had a name for this shot, for morgue photographs taken from this particular angle. The Give-Me-Justice pose.

Caleb looked at it, this corpse of a woman he'd known since Stanford. He thought about the scent of bitter mint. About the smell of nightshade. Deadly blossoms collecting dew in the shadows at dusk. Somehow he kept the coffee down, but his stomach was riding an ocean storm and his inner ears were telling him that he was falling.

"Why?" he asked Henry. "Why are you telling me? You wanted me to stay out of your way. Because of Kennon."

"I wanted to see you before Kennon did."

"What're you talking about?"

"Yesterday morning, after I left your place, I got around to checking my voicemail. I had two messages. One of them was Kennon, telling me to come down to Bryant Street because they'd found another body. That one was only five minutes old."

"So?"

"So, the other was from earlier. Evening of the twenty-third. And it was from Marcie."

Caleb held on to the autopsy report with both hands. The Muni tram beside them picked up speed through the intersection, and as it pulled ahead, its pantograph arm bounced against the overhead contact wire, lighting the graying afternoon with electric-blue flashes. He'd been standing across the street from the Haas-Lilienthal House, leaning against a lamppost, when the same electric-blue flash lit all the second-floor windows. He'd seen a high-voltage discharge.

Caleb closed his eyes and put his head down.

"She must've left the message an hour, maybe two hours before it started," Henry said. "The killing, I mean."

"What'd she say?" Caleb asked, though he was sure he didn't want to know.

"She was pissed off—about the virus. And she wanted to talk to the one person she trusted when it came to spectrometer software. So she called asking me for your phone number, because she was going to come see you. She wanted to call you before she showed up."

"Pull over a second."

"What?"

"Just pull the fuck over."

Henry veered to the curb and came to a stop. He checked his rearview mirror and then looked at Caleb, waiting. Caleb put his hand over his mouth and scrabbled at the door handle. He got out of the car and fell to his knees on the sidewalk in front of St. Anne's Catholic Church. He retched coffee and half-and-half in a muddy arc, splashing the concrete in front of the church steps. He pitched forward and skinned his palms as he caught himself on the pavement. For half a minute, he stayed that way, on his hands and knees. Panting for breath, his vision blurred from the tears of vomiting. Finally he stood, wiping his mouth on his forearm. When he looked up, there was a woman leading a small child down the sidewalk toward him. She changed her mind and went back the way she'd come, her hand tight on the child's wrist.

Caleb got in the car again, and shut the door.

"She didn't call me," he said. He could hardly recognize the sound of his own whisper. "Never came to see me—I haven't seen her since last July."

"Where were you that night?"

"I had a late brunch at Park Chow. Spent some time in the lab, working. I talked to Kennon. Drove around, talking to you. Then I went to the grocery store on Stanyan, came back to the house, and cooked dinner."

Henry checked his mirror again, then pulled into the lane and started rolling west. The street ahead of them was empty except for the tram, two blocks ahead now.

"When I came over the next morning," Henry said, "you told me you'd been working on something. But it wasn't anything to do with the lab. So what the hell was it?"

"What, are you Kennon now?"

"Goddammit, Caleb! If you can't tell me, what're you gonna tell him? You think he won't ask?"

"I was drinking absinthe and drawing pictures."

"Drawing pictures?"

"Yeah. I draw."

"You learn that from your father?"

"Jesus, Henry. When does it end with you?" Caleb said. "I taught myself. And I learned more from Bridget."

"You go anywhere else that night?"

"No."

"You're sure?"

"Yes, I'm sure," Caleb said. His throat was too raw to shout, but he was shouting anyway. "I'm sure I didn't go anywhere. I'm sure I didn't talk to Marcie. And I'm fucking positive I didn't kill her. Okay?"

"How drunk were you?"

"Fuck you, Henry."

Caleb shoved the autopsy report back into the envelope and put it on Henry's lap. If he'd felt bad for lying to Henry, it didn't matter now.

"Did you give Kennon that voicemail?"

"Not yet, but I'm going to."

"Jesus."

"What do you expect? That he won't check her phone records, find out who she called that night? That he's not going to know she called me and left a message? You think he couldn't get it with a subpoena to Verizon if I didn't just hand it over? You think I'm stupid enough to believe you can ever really delete anything?"

Caleb shrugged.

"That safe you've got," Henry said. "Why don't you give me the combo? I'll clean it out for you."

"What are you saying?"

"That maybe you shouldn't be holding on to that stuff right now. Maybe I should hold it for you."

"Kennon put you up to this, didn't he?" Caleb said. "Because he knows he can't just walk in and take things from me, but he can look at whatever I give you."

"It's not —"

"And you were going along with that? Even after what you said?" Caleb asked. "He doesn't care what's true or not — it's just what he can make stick."

"Caleb, you don't —"

"Is he listening in on this?" Caleb asked. "He is, isn't he?"

Henry looked in his rearview mirror again, then signaled a right turn. As they made the turn onto Sixteenth, Caleb looked in the side mirror and saw a black Suburban trailing a block behind them. He looked away.

Henry was about to say something else, but Caleb cut him off.

"Just let me out here."

"I can take you back up to the medical center. You can give me —"

"Let me out. Now."

Henry pulled over and Caleb got out.

"Caleb —"

He slammed the door and started walking in the opposite direction, back toward Judah. The Suburban was making the turn onto Sixteenth, but its driver changed his mind and swerved back into the lane to go west. Caleb watched it go, then kept walking.

TWENTY-ONE

HE EXPECTED KENNON and Garcia to roll up in their truck. Expected they'd hustle him down to Bryant Street, sit him in a white-walled room with a one-way mirror on the back wall. And if that didn't happen, then he thought Henry would circle around, make another stab at getting him in the car.

But Kennon and Henry stayed away, and he walked alone.

Still, he had no doubts about what had just happened. Considering the circumstances, he couldn't really blame Henry. He wouldn't have done the same thing if their roles had been switched, but then, there had always been an edge that separated them. They were as close as brothers, but Caleb was on the darker side of the cut. He wondered what kind of wire Henry had been wearing. Its transmission range must have been limited, or else Kennon and Garcia would have held back a little farther. Or maybe Henry had wanted them to stay close.

Maybe he was scared.

He crossed Judah Street and went south on Sixteenth, where he stole a plastic-wrapped copy of the *San Francisco Chronicle* from the front steps of a row house. He tucked the paper under his arm and took it to the Fifteenth Avenue Steps Park, the pedestrian pathway that ran at a forty-five-degree incline between Kirkham and Lawton Streets. He climbed most of the way up the steps, until he was out of sight in the heavy growth of trees near the top of the hill. When he sat down, he could see over the rooftops of the Inner Sunset, out toward Golden Gate Park. The steps were wet from the morning's rain, from the ground-clinging fog that was still drifting out of the west. He pulled the *Chronicle* from its bag and sorted through it until he found the article about Marcie.

Afterward, he followed Lawton Street toward Mount Sutro, dumping the paper in the first recycling bin he passed. There hadn't been many solid facts in the story, but there was an anonymously sourced detail that bothered him. Someone had cleaned every surface in the house with acetone. The police wouldn't be finding any fingerprints, wouldn't have much hope of finding stray DNA, unless it was on Marcie's body.

The storage areas of his lab were full of acetone, but it wasn't a hard chemical to come by. You could just go to a drugstore and buy nail polish remover. Hardware stores sold it by the gallon as paint thinner. But it was easy to draw a connection between the way the scene was cleaned and the way he'd have cleaned it, and he didn't like it at all.

He put his hands into the pockets of his coat and walked slowly with his head down. Even though he'd showered in the lab and changed into different clothes, he could still smell Emmeline on his skin, could taste her in the back of his throat. It was a bittersweet taste, like chewing on a clove, or biting through the rind of a clementine.

He didn't like the way he felt about that, either.

Bridget's Volvo was parked down the street from his house. He walked past it on his way up, backtracked to stop next to it and look inside. There were cardboard boxes in the back seat, and they were empty.

She should have warned him.

Maybe she even had. He hadn't been taking her calls or reading her emails. He walked the last hundred feet to his house, and opened the door.

"Bridget?"

He heard her coming from the kitchen, heard the stumble of her bare feet against the floor, and knew she'd been drinking before he even saw her. She came across the entry hall and leaned against the wall, ten feet from him. She looked at him and tried to smile, but her eyes were trembling, and when she tried to say something, the cry that came from her mouth was like an open wound.

She held on to the wall for support, used it to lower herself to the floor.

"Caleb — I tried — I didn't want to be alone —"

"Bridget," he said. He came to her and knelt on the stone floor in front of her. Her hands were wet with tears, and her skin was soft and pulsing with heat.

"— alone on Christmas."

"I'm here," he heard himself say.

He felt like he was still standing at the threshold, one foot on the doormat outside. But he was all the way in, the door was shut and locked, and he was helping her up.

"I didn't know where you were!"

"I'm sorry."

"I tried calling, to tell you I was coming —"

"It's all right, Bridget."

"It's not all right! I hate it. I hate *this*, what we've done to ourselves. I can't do it anymore, Caleb."

He helped her stand, started walking her into the living room. He was still holding his key ring, but tossed it side-handed into the kitchen as they passed. Then he had both his arms around her. She was wearing the same black dress she'd worn to the gallery opening when they'd met, but she'd cut her hair since the last time he'd seen her. Now it curled inward just above her shoulders.

He thought of the vials of thujone in Emmeline's dark bathroom, the electric spark that flashed through the second-floor windows of the mansion in Pacific Heights. He thought of the sliding bang he'd heard when Emmeline had gone upstairs, the droplet of blood she'd licked from her fingertip when she came back. He saw himself pan-roasting the scallops while Marcie Hensleigh was bound and naked one floor above him. Thrashing against the ropes, choking on the gag, her body riddled with current burns from the high-voltage electrodes.

He put Bridget on the couch and fell onto his knees next to her. She leaned forward so that he could get his arms around her again. He laid his face on her chest and felt her hands go to the back of his head, pressing him against her. He held her tight and felt her fingers in his hair.

"Caleb."

He raised his face, saw the shimmer of his own tears running between her breasts. Her hands were flat against each of his cheeks, and she leaned toward him, closing her eyes as she kissed him. She'd been drinking the Sauvignon Blanc he'd used two nights ago while he was making the fumet. It tasted better on her lips than it had from the glass.

She pulled back. Her nose was pink from crying, but there was color on her cheeks now that had nothing to do with her tears.

"Caleb, I'm so sorry for all this."

"It was me."

"I can live with it. With what you did. You don't have to try to undo it," she said. "I thought about it, and I talked with Paula. A long talk, things you and I never talked about. You didn't even know I knew —"

"Don't. Please."

"Shhh, Caleb."

She put her lips to his ear and whispered.

"I wasn't wrong to be mad," she said. "But I understand now — what you said, when we had the fight. That you did it because you wanted to be with me. Just me. That was true, I guess. But it wasn't the only thing, was it?"

"No."

He closed his eyes and held her. He knew they couldn't stay in the house tonight. He had to get them out. Out of the house; out of the city. They could go south and find a hotel. A bed-and-breakfast in Monterey, or in Carmel-by-the-Sea. She'd agree to anything if he said it the right way. Tomorrow morning they could decide what to do. He would call Kennon and set a meeting on neutral ground.

It was the only way.

If Emmeline had gone after Marcie, she'd take Henry next. Or Bridget.

Bridget stood, and pulled Caleb up from his knees. She put her hands on his shoulders and turned him so that the couch was behind him. She pushed him back and he sat down. She looked down at him, then lifted the hem of her dress and mounted him, her knees pressing into the cushions on either side of his waist. His hands ran along her calves, then up the backs of her thighs. He held on to her hips.

She wasn't wearing anything under the dress.

"Please," she said. "Caleb, please."

She lifted his chin and kissed him while she worked his belt buckle with one hand.

"If you have anything tomorrow," Caleb said, "cancel it."

"I don't understand."

"We're leaving tonight. I'm taking you away."

"Tonight?"

"Yes."

"But after this," Bridget said. "Okay? After this."

"Okay."

She settled down onto him, closing her eyes as she took him inside of her. He held her hips underneath her dress and guided her down, fully with her now. There was just Bridget, who was pushing aside the shoulder straps of her dress, sliding her arms free.

Just Bridget.

The girl from the gallery who'd painted his sheets with her blood, who'd loved him so completely that she'd nearly killed him last week when he'd told her what he'd done. When her arms were out of the straps, he took the bodice of her dress and tugged it down to her waist.

"Stop crying, Caleb," she said.

But she was crying too.

Near the end, she wrapped her arms around his head and held him close to her chest, sensing what lay ahead and quickening her pace to reach it.

"Stay with me, Caleb," she said. "Stay with me, stay in me."

It was too close to what Emmeline had said. For a moment, he couldn't place himself. Couldn't untangle the web. He leaned back against the couch as she rode him and looked past her side at the clock on the mantel. Its second hand ticked clockwise, carried them forward through time in the right direction.

"Caleb, stay in me."

"I'm so sorry, Bridget."

"It's all right. It doesn't matter now, does it?" she said. "Stay in me. Hurry now. I want you to."

They were together on the couch, lying on their sides, with Bridget in front of him and his hand crossing her hip and holding her stomach. The fire was lit. Beyond the sliding glass door, the lights of the Inner Sunset blinked in and out of the glowing fog.

"I was looking at that," Bridget said. "That drawing you did. While I was waiting for you. It's really good."

"What drawing?"

"That one. On the coffee table."

He raised his head and looked, and was just able to suppress a spasm when he saw it. It was the last drawing he'd done of Emmeline. The way he'd seen her when he left her at the Haas-Lilienthal House two nights ago. She was lying on cushions, one elbow up on the coffee table. The hem of her dress had flipped back so that most of her right thigh was visible. Her eyes were closed and her lips were parted just enough to see her teeth, giving her face a look of serene resignation.

"I thought I put that away."

"You did. I found it and brought it in here to look at. The light was better in here," she said. "I'm sorry I moved it."

"It's okay."

"It's really good. You've been looking at the painting, I guess."

"What?"

"You know the one I'm talking about. The Sargent. It's in the Legion of Honor now. It's the only one he ever painted in San Francisco."

Caleb shook his head, but that cold feeling was coming back. As if all the windows in the house were open, the fog slipping inside.

"I was just sketching."

Bridget got up on her elbow, propping her chin on her palm. As she looked at the sketch, Caleb had an impulse to get up and toss it in the fire.

"You know the painting. It wasn't a commission, like most of his stuff. It was, like, something he did for a friend. And then Samuel Lilienthal bought it."

"Who?" Caleb asked.

He barely got the word out, but he was close enough to Bridget's ear that she didn't notice how low his whisper had become.

"Samuel Lilienthal. That pretty gingerbread house, up in Pacific Heights? That was his. And that's where the painting used to be. The family donated it to the Legion of Honor. I wrote a paper on it, when I was getting my master's. The painting's history."

Caleb felt it again, the abyss waiting underneath the paper-thin skin of his house. A move in the wrong direction, the slightest tear in the structure holding him up, and he would rip through it.

He spoke slowly, cautiously.

"I've seen this painting?"

"I don't know," Bridget said. "You just drew it. Like, exactly. So I guess you've seen it. That time we went to Angel Island with Henry? I was trying to tell you about the paper I wrote. But Henry kept changing the subject. Like he was worried it'd bother Vicki — it's a sad story."

Caleb untangled himself from her and stood, tucking his shirt into his pants as he rounded the coffee table. He took the sketch and put it on the mantel above the fire. He'd burn it later, when she wasn't watching.

"I guess I saw it," he said. He didn't sound very sure about it, though. "You're positive it was in that house?"

Bridget nodded.

"I saw it there," she said. "Before it went to the museum."

"Where was it?" Caleb asked. He was struggling to keep his voice level. "Where in the house, I mean."

"In the living room. Over the fireplace."

He glanced at his drawing. The fireplace was in the background, behind Emmeline. No one but Caleb would know it, but the door to the secret room was ajar by a millimeter or two. It needed him to lean against it, needed him to push it back into place. Just as Emmeline needed him to lie down with her, to wrap her in his arms.

"Maybe it was a long time ago and it just kind of sat with you," Bridget said. "That's something I worry about, when I'm working."

"I don't understand," Caleb said.

"When I'm painting, I ask myself, 'Is it all mine? Or is it something I've been carrying for so long, I don't even remember where I picked it up?'"

"I must have seen it."

But he couldn't look at her when he said it, and his heart was beating so hard it hurt. He didn't like to look her in the face and lie. And there was going to be a lot of lying, if he was lucky.

"So where are we going?"

"Down south," he said. He had to get control of this, had to get them out. "Big Sur somewhere."

He turned to her and saw the look she was giving him.

"We don't have a reservation."

"We'll make one on the way," he said. "But I walked up here from the lab, left my car there. And I think I left my wallet on my desk."

His wallet was sitting on the workbench, next to the ATM receipt he'd used to wrap the tissue from Emmeline's bathroom. He stood behind the couch and looked down at Bridget. She was still naked from the waist up, and she rolled onto her back, her fingers laced behind her head as she looked up at him.

"You brought clothes and stuff?" he asked her.

"Mm-hmm."

"Okay. You go pack. I'll run down the hill, get my wallet and the car. Then we'll get out of here."

She got up on her knees and leaned over the back of the couch, holding out her hand to him. He knew how much she loved Carmel and the little spots south of it, loved to walk on the shoreline and stay at inns overlooking the sea. He'd settle for any trucker's motel off the highway, as long as it was far from the city. But he'd promise her anything if it would get her moving without questions. He took her hand and she pulled him in, kissing his neck and then his lips.

"Thank you, Caleb."

"It's not much of a Christmas."

"It's perfect," she said. "It'll be good for us. To be together."

He nodded and felt his pocket for his keys. They weren't there. Then he remembered tossing them onto the kitchen counter on his way to the couch. He let go of Bridget and walked down the entry hall to the kitchen. It got progressively darker as he went away from the fire's light in the living room.

Darker, and colder.

The kitchen was like a meat locker, so frigid he expected to see his breath cloud the air in front of him. He found the keys on the counter without switching on the light, and was about to turn toward the entry hall when a shape on the dining room table stopped him like a cold hand.

The bottle of Berthe de Joux was sitting there, exactly where it had been when he'd spoken with Henry yesterday morning.

One of the dining room windows behind the table was open.

He must have made a sound, some small sound of fear or pain, because Bridget called out from the living room.

"Caleb, are you okay?"

"Yeah."

"Thought I heard you say something," Bridget said.

"Nothing. Just coughing."

He went around the counter, stepped to the bottle, and picked it up. The green glass was so cold, it stung the fresh scrapes on his palm. It was a quarter full. Half-moon scratch marks pocked the label where he'd picked at it with his thumbnail while sitting at the table. Drinking alone and drawing. But he'd taken it to the lab in his briefcase, had left his briefcase sitting in his office after his blind-folded ride with Emmeline.

This bottle could not be in his house.

He closed his eyes and held on to the edge of the table, trying to understand what was going on. The sketch he'd made was a copy of a painting that had hung for years at the site of Marcie's murder. This bottle had appeared in his house, when it couldn't be here. There was Emmeline, and everything that had happened since he'd first laid eyes on her.

Christ, he thought, *make it stop.*

Please.

He smelled her before he saw her.

He opened his eyes and looked into the shadows to his left. The fire in the living room was too far away. It was cold enough in here that frost was growing from the edges of the dining room windows, feathery crystalline fans. Before he could turn in the other direction, there was a sharp twinge in the side of his neck.

"Hello, Caleb."

The whisper across his ear was as light and dusky as a moth's wing.

And he was frozen, pinned in place by the needle in her hand.

She gently caressed him, her fingers tracing the tendons in his wrist, back and forth in shortening strokes until she found a point of balance midway along his forearm. It was a tender and familiar caress. A lover's touch.

She was right behind him.

He could feel her chest pressing against his back, feel the brush of her hair on his neck. He couldn't move, and it was more than just the needle or the drugs flowing from it. It was the way she touched him, the way her perfume wrapped him like spider silk enveloping paralyzed prey. The way her heart beat against his back, a calm and steady throb.

Her breath tickled across his ear again.

"You asked when you'd see me again," she said. "And I told you: Sooner than you think. Did I keep my promise?"

The needle lost its sting. In fact, everything faded to a low murmur. There was just the cold pressure of the syringe's metal hub against his skin. The rush of fluid running into him. But there wasn't any pain. She held him up with one arm around his waist and took the bottle of absinthe before it fell from his slack hand.

"I had such a good time on our last date," she whispered. "I wanted to see you again, right away."

She withdrew the needle.

He watched as she reached around him, one arm still encircling his waist. She set the syringe on the table in front of him. While still holding him from behind, she leaned up and kissed the puncture hole in the side of his neck. The spot was already going numb, but he felt her lips there. Felt the gentle, cold bite of her teeth.

When she let go of him, he went face first into the table's edge, then rolled off that, knocking over two chairs before he hit the floor.

It was all completely painless, but he could feel a sticky trickle of blood above his left eyebrow.

Emmeline knelt next to him, her face floating above his. She hooked a lock of her hair behind her ear so that it wasn't hanging in his eyes. Then she put two of her gloved fingers on his lips, and traced them down his chin to his neck. She held them over his jugular, her eyes closed and her lips moving silently as she counted. He could feel his pulse hammering against her fingertips. She was wearing the same dress she'd worn the first time he'd seen her. The silent-

202

film-star dress, the one with no back to it at all. Her hair was dark and shining, like freshly broken obsidian.

"Caleb?" Bridget called.

Emmeline turned and looked over her shoulder, then looked back at Caleb. He had seen her face in the grip of true pleasure, had seen her trembling at the edge of ecstasy. This wasn't it. She wasn't enjoying this at all.

"I'm sorry," Emmeline whispered. "I'm sorry for this."

She stood, and Caleb watched as her shadow crossed toward the living room. He couldn't turn his head to follow her, couldn't see her. There was only her shadow, stretching long across the floor. Then that disappeared and there was silence for a moment, until Bridget cried out again.

"Caleb!"

The air vibrated with an electric-violet flash, followed an instant later by the crack of a high-voltage discharge.

Bridget's scream floated out of the living room, high and sharp.

He tried to move, but couldn't. He could only stare at the underside of the table, at the up-ended legs of the chairs.

And still, there was no pain.

TWENTY-TWO

FIRST, THE SOUNDS came back. Much later, there was light as well.

The sounds were sharp and close, but the light was diffuse. Diluted by shadows and vague crosshatches, blurred by a prism of fog.

Directly to his right, he heard the ripping clicks of a heavy zipper. Then small objects tapped one at a time onto a wooden surface. Glass vials, metal instruments. He heard a pair of heels clicking across a hardwood floor, the whisper of silk on smooth skin.

There were smells, too: a match's lingering, sulfurous smoke; the probing, cold fingers of rubbing alcohol and liquid iodine. Emmeline's perfume, as subtle as a hypnotic suggestion.

The light was just a flicker of low candle flames. He tried to blink, tried to rectify the wet glow clouding his vision. But his eyes would neither blink nor focus.

There was pressure on the side of his head, then on his forehead. Pushing and tugging. A pair of scissors made a series of snipping clicks over his eyebrow. Then he saw hands lifting a strip of wet gauze from his eyes, and he was looking at the redwood beams crossing his bedroom ceiling. The hands came back into view and lifted his head, placing a rolled towel underneath him. He felt nothing but the pressure of the hands moving his head.

His neck was a limp stalk.

But now, with the towel under him, he could see down the length of his body.

He was lying on his bed, naked. The hand came back, settled on his left cheek, and gently tilted his face to the right. His head swiveled over, like a vase toppling. Something inside his neck made a popping sound, but he didn't feel it. It was like hearing a twig snap on the other side of a forest clearing.

Emmeline was sitting on a wooden chair between the bed and the wall. She took her hand from his cheek. There was a black leather satchel on his bedside table, surrounded by votive candles. The bag was open, but he couldn't see what she'd taken from it.

"Hello, Caleb," she said. "Don't try to move, all right?"

He tried to work his mouth, but nothing was connected. He couldn't answer her. He wondered if he'd been paralyzed, if the painless snap in his neck had clipped through all the nerves at the base of his skull. Just severed them, making an island of his brain.

He could hear his heart running away, could barely get enough air with each breath. She'd given him something more than just vecuronium. He felt the sandy prickle of morphine. What else, he couldn't even guess.

"You can't talk," she said. "But you don't need to. I know what you need. And I'm taking care of you. Because I'm your friend, remember?"

She reached to him, her hand disappearing above his eyes.

He felt light pressure on his forehead, felt it as she pushed his head into the rolled towel. But he couldn't tell what she was doing. Maybe she was only petting his hair away from his forehead. Stroking him, comforting him. There was no way for him to be sure.

"I didn't mean for you to hit the table that way," she said. "I should have let you down more gently. But I fixed it. Look."

She reached into the leather bag and came out with the mother-of-pearl powdering compact he'd seen in her bathroom. She flipped it open and looked at herself for a moment in the small mirror, using her little finger to dab at the lipstick on the corner of her mouth. Then she turned the mirror to him.

At first she held it too close, tilted the wrong way.

He just saw his mouth, slack and open. A trickle of drool ran from the left side of his mouth toward his ear. Emmeline brought the mirror back a few inches and angled it upward, and then he saw his forehead.

The edge of the table had put an inch-long gash above his eyebrow. She'd sutured the wound with black thread, six stitches. The surgical knots were perfectly spaced along the top edge of the laceration channel. His forehead was swollen and pink, glistening with whatever ointment she'd spread on it. But it wasn't bleeding.

She'd fixed it.

Emmeline snapped the compact mirror closed and put it on the bedside table. She stood and walked to the dresser at the other end of the bedroom, her hips swaying coolly with her footsteps. He could follow her with his eyes, though he couldn't move his head at all. The bottle of absinthe was on the dresser, along with a glass and pitcher of ice water. She made a drink, taking her time to drip the water over the sugar cube.

She must have brought her own glasses, her own spoons. She had the correct absinthiana laid out on the dresser — the heavy crystal reservoir glasses and the slotted silver spoons. Two of each, but she only made one drink.

Then she came back and sat next to him, crossed her legs, and perched the drink on her knee. She closed her eyes when she sipped the absinthe. Afterward, when she breathed out, he could smell the wormwood, the sweet anise.

"When we went to Spondulix, I sang a love song," she said. "Do you remember? Did you understand that's what it was — a love song? For you?"

She looked at him, searching his face for an answer. She took another small sip. Granules of sugar swirled at the bottom of the glass as she tilted it.

"I needed three drinks to do that," she said. "It was hard, singing for you. Getting the courage to do it."

She put the drink down and looked at her fingernails, then met his eyes again.

"This is going to be hard too."

Caleb watched her lean toward him, watched as she took ahold of his chin with her thumb and forefinger. She tilted his head back to the center, so that he was staring at the ceiling again. Then she kept turning him until he was facing the bedroom's other wall.

Bridget was tied to a chair on the left side of the bed.

Her face was beaten and bruised, her mouth stuffed with a washcloth. Their eyes met. She tried to speak behind her gag, and what came out sounded like his name. Like she was pleading his name. There was pressure on his chin again, and his field of view swiveled up to the ceiling, then down the right-hand wall to Emmeline. She withdrew her hand from his face and picked up the drink.

"We made promises," Emmeline whispered. "Promises that meant something. You said you'd never hurt me. But you did."

She took a sip.

"Don't you think it hurt, what you did tonight? What I saw tonight?"

She wiped her cheek with the back of her hand. In one ear, Caleb could hear Bridget choking out his name, over and over, behind the gag.

"Don't you know how alone I was?" Emmeline asked. "How good it felt, to give myself to you? But, Caleb — I'm going to give you another chance. And I'm not going to break my promises. I'm not going to hurt you. I just had to think awhile, had to decide what to do. I had to figure out how to make sure you'd remember. That you can never see her again. Never talk to her again."

Emmeline picked up his hand from the mattress and held it in hers. It might as well have been a mannequin's hand. He felt a tickle of pressure in his elbow, and that was all.

"And I figured it out."

He watched as she kissed each of his fingers and then laid his hand on the mattress alongside his hip. She reached into the bag and brought out a clean white hand towel, which she spread on his chest. Then, from the bedside table, she took a pair of tweezers and a stainless-steel needle driver and laid those on the towel. She reached into the satchel and brought out a small foil-wrapped package, tore it open, and took out a curved needle attached to twelve inches of black suturing thread. Finally, she took a syringe from the table and held it between two fingers, her thumb inside the stainless-steel ring of its plunger.

"Like I said, this is going to be hard," she said. "But I promise you, it won't hurt at all."

She took hold of his lower lip with her thumb and forefinger, pulled it out, and slid the hypodermic needle in. She gave the plunger a small push, then withdrew the needle and reinserted it into his upper lip. When she was done, she put the syringe on the towel. She finished her drink and walked slowly back to the dresser to make another one.

She was killing time, waiting for whatever she'd injected to take effect.

From the left corner of the room, Caleb could hear Bridget. She wasn't trying to say his name anymore. She was just crying. Emmeline stood with her back to both of them, dripping the water over the sugar cube. Because her dress had no back, her pale skin was visible from her neck to the smooth, inward curve of her lumbar vertebrae. There were scratch marks underneath both her shoulder blades. He must have done that himself, without meaning to. Must have been clinging to her the second time they made love. Pulling himself up to kiss her breasts and her neck.

Emmeline spoke to Caleb without turning.

"She'll be all right. When I'm finished with you, I'm going to take care of her, too."

Bridget went on crying.

When she sat down again, she had the drink in one hand and a wash-cloth in the other. She dabbed the side of his mouth with the cloth, then folded it under his chin. She took a sip of the absinthe but didn't swallow it. Instead, she slid off the edge of the chair and knelt on the floor next to him. She leaned over him and kissed him, letting the cold absinthe move from her mouth into his. She had her hand on his cheek and she kept her lips over his until the absinthe went down his throat.

She pulled away until her nose was an inch from his.

"You were looking at my back," she said. "You gave me those scratches. But I didn't mind. That didn't hurt me. You can do it again sometime, if you want. Whenever you want."

She leaned in and kissed him again.

Then she got back into the chair and used her fingertips to straighten her dress over her knees. She took the needle driver from the towel on his chest, and used its plierlike grips to clamp onto the middle of the curved suturing needle. She picked up the tweezers in her other hand, gave him half a smile, and then used the tweezers to pull out his upper lip.

"So you remember," she said.

With a slow twist of her wrist, she brought the suturing needle through the middle of his lip.

"Never talk to her again."

The driver's locking mechanism made a sharp click when she released the needle, then clicked again when she grabbed its tip from the inside of his upper lip. There was no pain, but he felt a tug as she pulled the needle through. Bridget was so silent that he could hear the whisper of the thread as Emmeline drew it through him. She held his bottom lip with the tweezers, twisted her wrist again, and then he was watching as she pulled the needle out and brought the thread up. She let the needle dangle as she threw two loops of thread around the driver. Then she used its plier jaws to grasp the thread's free end, which she pulled through the loops, tugging until the first half of the knot was tight. She threw another loop to complete the knot, cinched it, and used a small set of scissors to cut the thread.

She sat back.

"That's the first one," she said. "Eight to go. And then we'll talk about your eyes. So you remember never to look at her again."

When she was done with his mouth, she picked up the powdering compact, flipped its mirror open, and held it for him. His mouth was outlined with blood. Already, his lips were swelling and puckering around the needle holes. Emmeline snapped the mirror shut, tossed it into her leather satchel. She sipped her drink, then picked up the syringe.

"We won't need the mirror again. Because you won't be able to see. But I swear, Caleb," she whispered. "This won't hurt."

She started with his left eye.

And she was right: a few minutes later, when she pulled out his upper eyelid with the tweezers, twisted the suturing needle through it, and sewed his eye shut, it didn't hurt at all.

He was in the dark now, but Emmeline was still with him. Just holding his hand. He couldn't feel her fingers laced with his, couldn't tell whether her hand was cold or warm, but he could feel the pressure as she massaged his palm.

Then she was whispering to him, her breath in his right ear.

"I'll take care of Bridget. But first you get to have this . . ."

There was pressure on his neck, something expanding underneath his skin.

"It'll take about a minute. You'll sleep. And that way, you won't have to hear. I don't want you to know. It'll be better if you don't."

He finally tore through.

The bed was gone. The floor under it had just been an illusion, fooling him all these years with feigned solidity. He'd slipped right through it, had found the void he'd always feared. The true foundation of his house was just a vacuum.

TWENTY-THREE

CALEB WAS RUNNING.

Tripping over the curb and falling to the wet pavement, getting to his feet and stumbling on. He hit the retaining wall on the opposite side of the street, scraped along it, skinning his shoulder, opening new cuts on his palms. The scream trapped behind his lips was a wet, gurgling hum. He kept running. His shins slammed into the bumper of a parked car and he went sprawling across its hood, knocking his head on the windshield.

The car's alarm went off.

He slid off the hood and fell into a fetal ball on the asphalt. The alarm went through its full cycle, so deafening that it covered the pain, overwhelmed it. He lay on the ground and screamed.

Then, with two final beeps, the alarm shut off. There were footsteps, someone running on cement in hard-soled shoes. He curled himself tighter, his hands around his shins. Another group of people came at a run from a different direction.

There was a moment's silence, broken finally by a woman's high, wavering scream.

"It's Caleb Maddox, I think, he's —"

"Holy shit."

"Did you see his face?"

"— call them yet? Did somebody call —"

"— his *eyes,* oh shit, Terry, look at his *eyes* —"

"Don't touch him. Stay back from him. They're coming."

They cut the stitches from his lips in the back of the ambulance, and someone turned his head to the side and let him vomit out the blood and bile he'd swallowed. He felt the thick gouts of it coming out, felt the cold metal bowl pressed against his cheek. They held him down and let him scream, held him tight to the padded stretcher and listened to the incoherent torrent spilling from him.

"Emmeline — it was Emmeline. And she's got Bridget. You have to look for her. The police — Kennon. I couldn't find her — tried — but I can't see."

"Sir —"

"*I can't see!*"

And then he was just screaming again, and the paramedics were wrestling his arm down, strapping him in place, jabbing him with something. He screamed all the way down the hill, and was thrashing against the restraints when the ambulance pulled to a stop outside the emergency room. He was bucking and writhing while they wheeled him inside. Yelling for Bridget, for Kennon.

But warmth was spreading from his right arm, a soothing glow, so that by the time the first of the doctors reached him, he was able to lie still for them while they snipped the stitches from his eyes and pulled the threads out with tweezers.

Somebody, maybe a nurse, was standing behind him, her hands on his ears to hold his head steady.

"Be still, Caleb," a voice said. "We're almost there."

The hands on the sides of his head didn't let go. He could smell latex on the doctor's fingers. The press of instruments against his lower eyelids was steady and sure. The scissors made their sharp clicks above his right eye, and the threads stung as the doctor pulled them out.

"That's it."

"I still can't open them," he whispered.

"Here."

He felt new hands on him, felt a warm washcloth gently circling his eyes, wiping out the crusted blood that was sealing his eyelids shut. He blinked into the white light, closed his eyes again, then looked out under the shade of his hands.

"Get that light off him."

There were six people in the room with him. Two of them were uniformed police. Hospital police. He looked at the older of the two, a woman whose hair was tied in a thick blond ponytail.

"Inspector Kennon," Caleb said.

"On his way," the officer said. She looked away from him.

Caleb looked down his side. There was an IV catheter inserted in the vein of his forearm, held in place with loops of white tape. The tubing led up to a saline drip on a stand next to him. He remembered crashing through his house. Upending tables and chairs, knocking over bookshelves. Crawling on his hands and knees, groping for Bridget.

"Someone has to go into my house," he whispered to the officer. "Bridget might still be there."

"SFPD went in. It was empty — I'm sorry."

Caleb looked at the doctor. He knew the man, ate lunch with him sometimes in the hospital's cafeteria. But he couldn't think of his name. And he couldn't lift his head. For all he could feel, he might have been floating three feet above the hospital floor, covered in a blue sheet.

"What time is it?"

"Two thirty."

"Morning or afternoon?"

"Morning."

Caleb closed his eyes and tried to do the math, tried to remember when he'd gotten home. He couldn't do it.

"Where the hell is Kennon?"

"He's coming, Dr. Maddox," the officer said. "You wanna tell us what happened to you?"

"I'll tell Kennon. Just get me Kennon."

A nurse had rubbed antibiotic cream around his eyes and lips, and had turned off the overhead fluorescent tubes for him. Before leaving him, she had taken a roll of lightweight gauze and wrapped his eyes.

"Just for a little while," she said. "Till the bleeding stops."

"Okay."

"Can I get you anything else?"

"No."

If he opened his eyes behind the loose weave of the gauze wrapping, he could see a square of light from the door's window, could see the shape of the IV stand. He lay under the sheet in the semidark, listening to the heart monitor, to the sounds outside his room. He thought about what might be in the IV drip. Diazepam, midazolam. Something to settle him down, to stop the screaming. The last thing he remembered with any real clarity was Emmeline slipping a sip of absinthe into his mouth with a kiss.

When he tried moving his hands and feet, they responded. He brought his left arm across his chest and probed at his right forearm until he found the IV catheter port. He unstrapped the tape from his arm and slid the needle out of his vein. He jabbed it into the mattress next to him, where it would be hidden. Whatever the tranquilizer was, he didn't want it.

The door opened.

Through the gauze, he saw a silhouetted figure lean a moment against the edge of the lighted rectangle before coming into the room. He heard a chair slide across the tile floor, heard the man settle in beside him.

"That you, Kennon?"

"Yeah."

"Bridget — she's — she wasn't —"

"They found her. An hour ago. I came from there."

Kennon stopped, fiddled the notepad out of his back pocket and set it on his knee.

"Go ahead and say it."

"She's alive. Somebody shot her full of drugs and dumped her down the hill, off your back deck."

"Where's she now?"

"Safe," Kennon said. "And that's all you get to know."

"Did she tell you about Emmeline?"

Kennon didn't answer him at first. He just sat in silence, in the dark to Caleb's right. The heart monitor beeped slowly.

"She's safe," Kennon finally said. "I've got good people with her."

Caleb had been trying to sit, but he gave up. He let his head rest on the pillow and pulled the sheet up, making sure the needle and tubing didn't slip into sight.

"I haven't been telling you the truth," Caleb said. "All those times we talked. I've been leaving something out."

"There's a surprise," Kennon said. "Try telling me something I don't know."

"There was a woman in House of Shields that night," Caleb said. "I went looking for her."

"And you found her."

"Yeah."

"I'm going to record this, Mr. Maddox."

"All right."

Caleb heard Kennon shifting around. There was a click as he hit a button on his recorder. A blurry red glow appeared in the darkness to his right.

"Tell me from the start," Kennon said.

Caleb talked to the inspector for an hour and a half. Kennon asked a few questions, but mostly he just listened. A nurse came into the room once, but backed out and shut the door when Kennon waved her off. As he spoke, he felt the drugs lose their sway on him. But he never sat up, never took off the gauze. He spoke in a low whisper and left nothing out.

Except a few things.

If they hadn't found Bridget already, he would have told Kennon about the Golden Gate Bridge. But they had Bridget, and she was safe. So he left that out. He thought of the cool last kiss Emmeline gave him, before she sewed his mouth shut. She was crying as she did that. He'd felt her tears fall onto his cheeks.

And he didn't tell Kennon what Bridget had said about the John Singer Sargent painting, the one that had spent decades in the Haas-Lilienthal House before moving to the Legion of Honor. He didn't know what to think about that.

At the end, Kennon finally spoke.

"Mr. Maddox — Dr. Maddox — did this Emmeline person know anything about computers?"

"What?"

"You think she was raised by a man who kidnapped her. Some kind of hypnotist — basically, a guy doing parlor tricks. You think this guy, this hypnotist, could've taught her anything about software?"

"I don't know."

"Seems like a stretch, doesn't it?"

"I don't know."

"And you never went upstairs in the Haas-Lilienthal House?"

"No."

"Not even for a minute, to use the restroom?"

"I never used the restroom there. I don't even know if there is one upstairs."

"So we wouldn't find any of your DNA upstairs, then, right? Any of your hairs?"

Now Caleb was all the way awake. He felt the electric current ride the nerves down his spine, charge into his fingers and toes. He lay perfectly still and spoke in the same low whisper.

"If there is any — any of my hair — it came off Emmeline. We were kissing. She ran her hands through my hair."

Kennon didn't answer him. The long silence was broken only by the beeping heart monitor. Its rate was faster than it had been a few seconds earlier.

"How you feeling, Dr. Maddox?"

"How do you think I'm feeling?"

"You don't look so great. But your mind seems pretty clear. You're lucid? You'll remember this conversation?"

"I think so."

"When you and Bridget had the fight last week, what started it?"

"Come on, Kennon. That had nothing to do with this."

Kennon yawned and stretched his arms out. Caleb had lost track of the time. Other than the small square of glass on his room's door, there were no windows.

"I asked Henry," Kennon said. "Since you guys are old friends, I figured he might know."

"Then he probably told you the truth."

"When you got it done, were you planning to keep it a secret from her forever? I mean, what were you thinking?"

"I don't know."

"She wanted kids," Kennon said. "You didn't. But you didn't want to have that conversation. So you just went and got it done while she was out of town. That it?"

"Pretty much," Caleb said. He didn't want to explain it, didn't want to make Kennon see that it hadn't been a selfish act. He'd done it for both of them. He'd done it for the children who would never be born and would thus never have to blame him for their inheritance.

"Then you told her, later on. And she didn't take it so well."

Caleb didn't answer. After a while, he heard Kennon flick a switch on the recorder. He'd turned it off.

"And what about your father, and the months you and your mom spent in Langley Porter? Or the time you disappeared. You tell her any of that?"

Caleb held still and listened to the heart monitor, willing it to slow down. Waiting for the dragging pace of his pulse to tell Kennon that he'd passed out. Kennon sat with him, perfectly still and silent. A patient man.

"Did Bridget understand what it was like for you?" Kennon asked. "I was in there, right after your dad did it. I found you chained to the floor. Did you know that?"

The legs of his chair scraped against the linoleum as Kennon dragged it closer to the bed. He leaned to Caleb's ear and spoke in a low whisper.

"I don't know what your life was like before that day. But I've got a good idea. I saw the basement, saw everything he had for the two of you. The dog collars, the tie-downs — everything," Kennon said. "He didn't snap all at once, did he? I mean, you don't just wake up one morning and put eyebolts in a concrete floor without having thought it through."

Kennon leaned back and was silent. Shadows fluttered past the door's small window as a group of nurses rushed up the hallway, their soft-soled shoes squeaking on the clean floor.

Then he was bending close again.

"It was years in the making, wasn't it?" Kennon whispered. "Thinking about it was probably like picking at a scab. He might not have wanted to, but he couldn't help it. He never stopped painting, never took a break from the galleries and the shows. But that whole time, he was following a secret staircase down to hell. And you and your mom were going with him, whether you wanted to or not."

Caleb closed his eyes behind the gauze and let himself drift into the shadows. He knew his way through them, had been navigating the darker end of the spectrum most of his life.

"You're done talking now, I guess," Kennon finally said. "After I found you the first time, they said you didn't talk until you'd been at Langley Porter a week. So that's okay — we're used to it, I guess. Par for the course, for Caleb Ellis — excuse me, Caleb *Maddox*. But if you think of something you want to tell me, just let the police officers know. There'll be two of them sitting right here."

Kennon stood. Through one eye, Caleb watched him put his recorder in his pocket, take his coat off the back of the chair, and leave. As he was walking out the door, a man was walking in. Kennon took the man's arm.

"Step outside a minute, Doctor," Kennon said. "Wanna ask you something."

As soon as the door closed, Caleb sat up and let the sheet fall to his waist. He pulled the gauze off his face, felt the scabs rip off and the bleeding start again around his eyes. He didn't care about that. A tangle of wires led to adhesive electrodes stuck to his chest. He reached across to the heart monitor and switched it off. He didn't want it to sound an alarm when he tore off the leads.

When he stood, his legs were trembling. But he could walk.

He wrapped the sheet around himself and went to the door, standing to the side of the window. Kennon's back was to the door. He was writing on a notepad.

"Ten milligrams," he was saying. "Diazepam — that's p-a-m, *m* as in *Mike*?"

"That's right."

"What's that do? Diazepam."

"It's a tranquilizer. Valium. Came in here, he was screaming. Had to calm him down, stop the thrashing."

"A dose like that — he's not hallucinating or anything, is he? He can understand questions, answer them?"

"Sure," the doctor said. It was the man whose name Caleb couldn't remember. "He might be a bit confused. Like talking to a guy coming off a long night of drinking. He might not remember what he said to you."

Kennon nodded, put the notebook away.

"Good," he said. "I got one more question for you."

"Shoot."

"Could he have done that to himself?"

The doctor looked up from his clipboard and took a step back. Caleb leaned against the doorjamb and listened. It was cold in the room. As cold as it had been in his kitchen when Emmeline came up from behind him. He remembered the scent of her perfume, the way it slipped over his shoulder and wrapped him, like a fast-growing tangle of vines.

"The sutures?"

"Yeah. The eyes and the mouth. Could a guy do that to himself? Sew his own eyes shut?"

The doctor looked at his feet as he thought about it. He ran his thumb over his lips, closed his left eye and pulled out the eyelid. When he looked up at Kennon, Caleb flinched back from the window.

"The mouth, that'd be easy," the doctor said. "If you were standing in front of a mirror. One of the eyes, maybe. But — Jesus, Inspector — you'd have to be fucking nuts."

Caleb leaned back to the window in time to see Kennon coughing into his fist.

"I'm not worried if he's fucking nuts. That's not my problem. I just want to know — could he have done it?"

"Maybe."

"And he wouldn't need to be a doctor?"

"You can learn anything online. Or if you spent a lot of time in hospitals, you could watch. It's an easy knot."

"Were the stitches in both eyes the same?"

"Come again?"

"The stitches," Kennon said. "Were they the same in both eyes?"

"The right eye, it was a little uneven," the doctor said. "Not quite as perfect as the mouth, the left eye."

"You got pictures?"

"Paramedics took them. In the ambulance."

Kennon pulled out his wallet. Caleb pressed himself against the edge of the door, looking out the square window with one eye.

"This is my card. See my email address there? Those pictures get emailed to me before sunrise."

"Okay," the doctor said. "And, look — the uneven stitches? That could've been anything. He was running into stuff, falling down. He could've pulled the knots loose, could've ripped something."

Kennon looked at the doctor.

"I asked you if he could've done it himself," Kennon said. "You didn't say no."

The doctor stared back, then nodded.

"I didn't."

Kennon put his wallet away.

"Where'd those two officers go? Those hospital police?"

"They're waiting in the lobby."

"You go get them," Kennon said. "Put them outside this door. He wakes up, they call me."

"Got it."

"Thanks, Doc."

TWENTY-FOUR

CALEB KNEW HE had about a minute, maybe less. His options were narrowing with every second, and when the hospital police got to his room, there would be none left. He opened the door and looked out. Kennon and the doctor had walked away in the same direction, going down a wide corridor that led to the emergency room's triage desk, which was near the front entrance. A red plastic sign on the wall opposite his room gave directions to the different departments on this floor. The arrow underneath *RADIOLOGY* pointed deeper into the building. He pulled the blue sheet around himself, looked one more time to be sure the hallway was empty, and went as quickly as he could.

He rounded the corner and limped through the double-leafed, lead-lined doors that opened to the CT scanning suite. It was dark in here. The scanning machine was an empty hulk in the center of the room, its sliding bed poised to send a patient into the machine's oculus.

He went through the service door into the control room. There was a white lab coat on a wooden hook. He dropped the bed sheet and put on the coat, which almost reached his knees.

Another lead-lined door exited from the control room to the power supply closet. As he opened the door, he heard the intercom system crackle once, and then a woman's voice spoke out of the ceiling.

"Uh . . . we got a code gray in the ER," she said. "That's a code gray in the ER."

The intercom cut out.

They were looking for him now. They'd fan out from the triage desk, cover the exits first, then move inward. It might be a while before anyone thought to check in here. But he didn't plan to stay any longer than he had to. He stepped into the power supply closet, switched on the light, and closed the door.

The access hatch to the utility tunnel was at the back of the closet, where heavy-duty conduit pipes rose out of the floor and into the distributor box. He knelt and lifted the trapdoor on its hinges, straining to get it all the way up. A steel ladder led down the shaft to the base of the utility tunnel. There was some light down there, a soft glow. He stood and turned off the closet light, then descended, shutting the trapdoor as he went.

The medical center had its own power plant, at the back of the campus, abutting the slope of Mount Sutro. He could hear it ahead of him, the low whine of its generators and the rush of the fans and the water in the forced draft cooling towers. There were caged light bulbs mounted on the cement walls at the tunnel junctions. When he got to the first junction, he read the numbers on the conduit pipes, looked back along the route he'd followed, and figured out where he needed to go. There was a smaller, unlit passage that went off to his left. This burrowed under Parnassus Street, and it carried power and heat to his own lab. He followed it, crawling in the dark now, pausing every thirty feet to listen to the tunnel behind him.

He was waiting to hear voices, running footsteps. But neither came.

He climbed out of the power supply closet behind the mass spectrometer and stood in the main room of his lab, wearing nothing but the dirt-streaked lab coat. His wallet was where he'd left it, flipped open on the workbench. He took it and walked to the locker room. When Emmeline dropped him off after their single night in bed together, he'd changed clothes and left his old ones in his locker. The only thing missing was a pair of shoes. He sat on the wooden bench and dressed, then tossed the lab coat in the trash on his way to the sink.

Before he left, before he went looking for a place to hide, he knew he needed to see his face. So he stood in front of the mirror and looked. His eyes were swollen and ringed with blood. His lips were puckered and bleeding in a dozen spots, and his face was smeared with charcoal-gray dust from the tunnel. Grains of sand and the wings of dead insects were stuck in the antibiotic ointment. At least the bathroom had paper towels and soap. He didn't have time to do much, but if he didn't clean up a little, he might not get far.

When he left the lab, it was four thirty in the morning.

Caleb's car was in the garage, but he didn't have his keys. Even if he'd had them, he didn't think driving it would be a good idea. Kennon would put out a BOLO for it, and every patrol car in the city would be looking. Going home was out of the question too. Kennon's men would be there, picking through it. Putting evidence in zipper-lock bags, snapping pictures. He came out of the parking garage at the lower level on Carl Street, crossed the Muni tracks, and walked down the hill on Arguello. Heading north, toward the park. He had no jacket and his socks were soaked before he made the first block.

He stayed in the shadows close to the row of houses, and once, when a police car passed, he had to crouch behind a parked minivan. It took him fifteen minutes to find what he was looking for. The motorcycle was at least ten years old, a cheap sport bike that had never been much to start with. It was parked between a Jeep and a beat-up Honda beneath the spreading shadow of a cypress tree on Frederick Street. Leaning on its kickstand, not locked to anything.

He knelt next to the motorcycle and felt the wires running between the headlight assembly and the handlebars, following them down under the plastic fairing cowl. He traced the wires until he found the three-pronged, male-female connector plug. The plastic was so old that the locking clip broke when he disconnected it.

It didn't matter.

Caleb took a paperclip from his pants pocket. Before leaving the lab, he'd broken it to the right length. Now he bent it into a U. He'd learned something of value in every California institution that had held him between four walls. University High School, Berkeley, Stanford. But this trick was purely thanks to the buildings and grounds superintendent at the Langley Porter Psychiatric Institute, who'd allowed Caleb to shadow him for two months while his mother sat in the dark and wept in between surgeries.

He pushed the wire into the female half of the connector plug and heard the motorcycle's ignition click once. There was still medical tape on his right arm from the IV catheter. He took a piece of it and taped the paperclip in place so it wouldn't slip out while he was riding. He stood, mounted the bike, and brought up the kickstand.

It started on the first try.

Six a.m., and the rain still hadn't let up.

He lay on the mattress and stared at the water-sagged ceiling, listening to a garbage truck emptying dumpsters in the alley behind the hotel. Riding down Eddy Street, in the heart of the Tenderloin, he'd seen ten hotels just like it. But the Coburn Arms had a light in the office, and the clerk behind the bulletproof window took cash without asking questions.

After paying for the room, Caleb had three hundred and fifty dollars left. The ATM on Castro Street had a daily withdrawal limit, so he couldn't get any more until tomorrow. Assuming Kennon didn't freeze his account between now and then. He had no idea how big this might be, how wide a net Kennon would cast. There was a TV in his room, but it didn't work. In fact, its tube was shattered and the room's prior occupants had been using the hollowed-out box as a wastebasket. It was crammed with empty whiskey bottles and used needles. Little twists of bloody toilet paper.

Caleb was too cold to do anything but get into the filthy bed. He wrapped the stiff blankets around himself and lay shivering. He was tired enough to sleep, but knew what would happen if he did. He'd hear Bridget screaming behind the gag, would see her tied to the chair. He was afraid if he closed his eyes, he'd see her face. He couldn't bear it if she'd been cut up like his mother, sliced up and left for Kennon to find.

Or he'd see Kennon, sitting in the dark, the single red eye of his recorder glowing.

The police couldn't have found one of his hairs on the second floor of the Haas-Lilienthal House. That was impossible. But if a bottle of

Berthe de Joux could carry itself from his locked lab to his locked house, a piece of hair might get anywhere.

He looked at the window. The streaking rain flashed amber with each pulse of the garbage truck's rotating warning lamp. He wondered where Bridget was. Wondered how badly she was hurting right now. Sometime soon, she might start talking. For Kennon to have come at him that way, she couldn't have said anything yet. Maybe she'd been in shock, or delirious with drugs. Screaming gibberish, seizing up and rolling her eyes backwards. Maybe she'd never been conscious at all. But soon, she could tell them about Emmeline. She had to tell them.

Dawn was still hours off. He didn't sleep.

At ten in the morning, he walked toward the Goodwill on Geary Street. Halfway there, he looked at his wrist and saw he was still wearing a plastic bracelet from the hospital.

He hooked his finger underneath it and popped it off. It fell in the gutter with the rest of the trash.

The bell rang when he walked in, and the man behind the counter glanced up from the magazine he was reading. He looked at Caleb. At his shoeless feet, his bloody shirt. His pincushion face. He set down the magazine and brought a nightstick from under the counter. He pointed it at Caleb's chest.

"You bringing trouble, you can take it the fuck back out."

"Bringing cash," Caleb said. "Not trouble."

He brought out his wallet and fanned the bills.

The man put down the nightstick and nodded. He sat on his stool again and picked up the magazine.

"Boots are in the back. Jackets, too."

Ten minutes later, he had boots on his feet and a jacket that kept out the rain. Gloves and a stocking cap. The dark sunglasses were a blessing on his eyes, though the day was cold and the rain was coming back. On his way to Eddy Street, he spotted a pharmacy. It would sell makeup, and if he could stop the bleeding, he could use it when it was too dark to wear the sunglasses.

He spent the day hiding in his room at the Coburn Arms. Staring at the smashed TV set and holding chips of ice against his face. Picturing Bridget in her hospital room, the remnants of Emmeline's drugs covering her like a heavy blanket. But she was okay — Kennon had said she was okay.

As for Emmeline, he couldn't even imagine what she did by day.

Maybe she slept in her bed of wrought-iron vines, and with each breath brought the smell of candle smoke into her woodland dreams. When it was dark enough, she could glide into the city in her Invicta Black Prince to descend to underground bars. To hunt, to collect.

He sat on the bed and thought of these things, and rubbed the ice against his wounds. He sipped Jim Beam from the bottle he'd bought, but it didn't even touch him. He was still numb from the hospital. He tapped his fingers against his swollen lips, and listened to the sirens prowling the Tenderloin streets like packs of wolves.

Like Emmeline, he waited for dusk.

The California Palace of the Legion of Honor was up in Lands End Park, in the northwest corner of the city. He parked the motorcycle on El Camino del Mar, a five-minute walk from the museum. At four thirty in the afternoon, the park was windswept and cold.

There were only a few cars parked near the trailheads. It wasn't a day for walking. He could hear the waves eating at the base of the cliffs down beneath where he'd parked the bike. Steady crashes, the breath of wet air sucking through holes in the rocks. He pulled the paperclip from the ignition wires so the short wouldn't drain the battery, and then leaned against the bike's seat, looking northeast, toward the bridge.

While there was still enough light, he took the tube of concealer foundation from his pocket, squeezed some onto his finger, and leaned close to the motorcycle's mirror so he could paint over the bruises and the needle marks around his eyes and above his eyebrow. The foundation wasn't perfect, but after he blended it back toward his temples and down his cheeks, brushing it lightly, as if giving depth and shading to a charcoal sketch, it was acceptable. He could get in and out of the gallery, at least.

He waited until sundown, then started toward the museum. It would be open for another half an hour. He cut through the parking lot and then went up the entry ramp, passing beneath the stone arch into the courtyard, where a bronze Rodin hunkered naked in the blowing rain. At the main entrance, a security guard opened the door for him.

"Closing soon," he said.

"I'll have time. Just wanna see one thing."

He paid the admission price at the ticket desk and accepted the brochure the woman handed him.

"Looking for something in particular?"

"A John Singer Sargent painting. I don't know what it's called."

"We have two, and they're both in gallery seventeen."

He started to unfold the brochure, looking for a map. But the woman caught his hand and pointed across the entry hall.

"You go that way, turn right. It's midway down the east wing."

"Thanks."

He passed two more security guards on his way to the gallery. His Goodwill boots squeaked on the parquet floors. He looked back and saw that he was leaving wet tracks. The second security guard was watching him, his thumbs hooked in his belt.

Gallery seventeen, when he got to it, was empty. There was a large bench in the center of the square room. Five paintings on each wall. He saw the one he was looking for right away, in the far corner.

If there had been a clock in the room, he was sure it would run backwards. Unwinding time. Because this couldn't be real. Every other gallery he'd passed through had been lit brightly, but this one was missing two of its halogen bulbs. The light in here was heavy and honeyed, like candlelight. He walked slowly to the painting, the floor growing beneath him as he went. It was like walking against the flow of a moving sidewalk. He didn't want to see this, didn't want to get any closer to it.

He crossed the room until he stood directly in front of it.

Bridget had been right: he'd drawn it, almost exactly. But that had to be because of what he'd seen in the Haas-Lilienthal House, the way Emmeline had propped herself on the cushions to watch him leave. He couldn't remember seeing this painting before. The room was reeling now, the walls spinning up and back as if he'd just finished off a bottle of absinthe. Only the painting held steady.

It was Emmeline, reclined on the thin mattress of a cot. Her lips were slightly parted and a look of serene sadness lay in the angle of her eyebrows and the tilt of her eyes. The woman in the paint-

227

ing was lying in a prison cell instead of a mansion. The floor was made of flagstones; straw poked through the tears in the old mattress. But otherwise, his drawing was an exact copy of the painting. And Emmeline was an exact copy of a woman John Singer Sargent had painted in 1917. Caleb's stomach was a frozen fist.

There was a glass plaque fixed to the wall alongside the painting.

John Singer Sargent
American, 1856–1925
Miss Emmeline Ponurý, on the evening before she was hanged at San Quentin, ca. 1917

Oil on canvas
Signed lower right corner: John S. Sargent
Gift of The Haas-Lilienthal Trust.

He stumbled backwards until he got to the bench at the center of the room, then sat down, still facing the painting.

He had to hold on to the edge of the bench so that he didn't pitch forward into the floor.

"They're shutting down now."

He looked to his side, startled.

It was the woman who'd sold him the ticket. He hadn't heard her come into the gallery. She'd put on a red raincoat and was carrying her purse over her elbow. A set of keys dangled from a pink lanyard in her hand. She crossed the room and sat on the bench, leaving four feet between them.

"That's the one you came in to see?" she asked, nodding toward the painting.

"That's it."

"It gets me, too," she said. "It's so different from all his others. Except maybe the one of the beggar girl, in Paris. You know that one?"

Caleb nodded. Bridget's copy was hanging in his bedroom. It was the only thing she'd left behind.

"It's like that," the woman said. "It has that same look."

"Haunted."

"Yeah," she said. "That haunted look."

"Who was she?" Caleb asked.

He was whispering, looking at the painting. He couldn't take his eyes away from it. Beside him, the woman shrugged. Her raincoat made a crinkly sound in the quiet gallery. From farther away, there were hollow booms as the security guards closed metal doors in the lower galleries.

"There was an art student who used to come in here, six or seven years back. She told me the story. She'd studied it. But I don't remember everything she knew."

"Whatever you remember," Caleb said.

"Something about a poisoning — she poisoned a guest, I think, at the Palace Hotel, in that bar they have there. The one with the painting. And then at her trial, the girl said she'd been kidnapped. By a showman of some kind. A man with a traveling act, who took her state to state. She'd never had a choice, she said, because of the things he'd done to her — horrible things. But no one believed her," the woman said. "And she hung for it."

She spoke softly, without looking at Caleb. He waited for her to go on, and eventually she did.

"John Sargent was friends with her attorney. He did the sketch when they visited her in San Quentin, on the night before. He did the painting the next day."

"Without a model to sit for it."

"Yeah," she whispered. "By the time he painted it, she was gone."

They sat in silence for a moment with Emmeline Ponurý, who was waiting to be hanged.

"What happened to it?" Caleb asked. "What are those scratches?"

It looked as if someone had put his fingernails into the paint next to Emmeline's arms. A few of the scratches went as deep as the weave of canvas.

"Vandalized," the woman said. "Twenty-five years ago, maybe. Before it came to the museum."

"Why?" Caleb asked.

But he could guess. It looked like someone had been trying to dig Emmeline off the canvas. Like someone had been clawing near Emmeline's wrists, trying to break through the barrier of paint, to help her through the frame and into the world.

On the bench beside him, the woman shook her head.

"I don't think anyone knows what happened," she said. "That girl, the art student, even she didn't know. It looked worse before the restoration."

"She was a pretty girl, the student?" Caleb whispered. "Blond hair to her shoulders, blue-gray eyes?"

"You know her?"

"I used to."

The woman stood.

"They've locked the front doors now. I can walk you out."

But Caleb didn't get up right away. The painting was such a perfect rendering of Emmeline, he could almost smell her perfume. If she came to him now, if she kissed him, her lips would be cool on his wounds.

As cold as absinthe, and as soothing as morphine.

It'd be easy, wouldn't it? she might whisper. *Here, on this bench. You could have me any way—*

"Sir?"

"I'm sorry. I'm coming."

Jesus, he thought. *Please let this stop.*

There was only one person who might know what was going on. To see him would be dangerous, but Caleb knew there was no other choice.

TWENTY-FIVE

CALEB STOOD IN the shadows on Bay Street in the Marina District, pacing to keep warm, watching the lights in the house across the street. He hadn't come to commit theft, but he'd already stolen something. And now that he'd thought about it, he'd probably do it again before he left. There was at least one other thing he wanted, and he could get it here.

He was two blocks from the Vespa scooter now. That had just been luck, coming across it, forcing its seat compartment open, and finding the motorcycle helmet inside. The helmet would be necessary later tonight when he crossed the Golden Gate Bridge. There were usually police around the toll plazas. Riding past them without a helmet would be too dangerous.

He watched the house.

Like the rest on this street, its ground floor was a garage, and next to the garage door, a set of steps led upward to a little porch and the main entrance. The living room's bay windows were on the second level, directly above the garage. A woman came into view. She pulled the curtains back, cupped her hand to see past the inside reflection, and looked up the street. After a moment, she disappeared toward the back of the house.

Five minutes later, a car slowed in front of the house, and then the garage door started up on its tracks. As the car turned into its drive, Caleb crossed the street, staying off to the right where the driver wouldn't see him if he happened to check the rearview mirror. Caleb stepped into the garage after the car pulled inside. He pressed against the wall as the rolling door started down.

The driver's door opened and Caleb came out of the shadows, moving around the back end of the car.

"Have a seat, Henry. But keep the door open."

He put five fingers on Henry's chest and pushed him back into the driver's seat. Henry's feet were on the garage floor.

"Caleb — Jesus."

Caleb leaned down and looked into the car to be sure no one else was in it.

"Keep your hands on your knees," he whispered.

"What is this?"

"What's it look like?" Caleb said. He was holding the motorcycle helmet behind his back with one hand, keeping it from Henry's view.

"You should turn yourself in. I could call it in for you. We could wait outside."

"That's funny, Henry," Caleb said. "Give me your phone."

"What?"

"Your phone. Take it out of your pocket."

Henry dug the phone from his pants and started to hand it across to Caleb.

"No. Turn it off first. Show me. I wanna watch you do it."

"Jesus, Caleb." Henry turned off the phone. He handed it to Caleb. "You happy now?"

"Not yet. What's the password?"

"I don't have one."

"We'll see about that."

Caleb turned on the phone, watched it reach its home screen without asking for a password.

"Put your hands back on your knees," Caleb said. "And be quieter. I don't want Vicki coming down here."

"What do you want?"

That was a fair question. Caleb didn't know exactly what he wanted. He wanted answers. He wanted to know who Emmeline was — or what she was. He didn't think Henry would have that, but he might have something.

"The Haas-Lilienthal House, where Marcie was killed. Have you and I ever been there together?"

"What the *fuck*, Caleb?" Henry whispered. "Kennon's running the biggest manhunt in Northern California since the Zodiac killings. Looking for you. And you show up at my house, jump out of the garage, and want to know about that?"

Caleb cocked his head.

"We were there?"

Henry stared at him open-mouthed.

"With our class," Henry said. "Caleb, you don't remember this? You really don't?"

"No."

"When you disappeared, that's where it happened. One minute we were upstairs with Mrs. Copenhagen, with the other kids, and then when we went into the next room, you were gone."

"I don't remember."

"They searched the place, tore it to pieces. And when they didn't find you, they made us wait on the school bus. The police and the chaperones went through the neighborhood. Door to door."

Henry had been looking at his feet on the garage floor, but now he looked up and found Caleb's eyes.

"The hardest thing to see was when they brought your mom," Henry said. "She was barely back on her feet. She dropped her cane and fell in the street. She was screaming. You have to know this, Caleb."

"I don't."

"But the newspapers talked about it. And I know you've read the stories."

"The stories just said it was a museum," Caleb said. "They didn't say which one."

"It was Haas-Lilienthal."

"You're sure?"

"Caleb, come on," Henry said. "I was there. When you were gone, when we couldn't think of anything else to help your mom, my parents and I would hang flyers. We put them up and down Franklin Street. On the telephone poles and the parked cars. I taped one to the Haas-Lilienthal's front porch."

Suddenly, the memory was so clear, he could see them: flyers covered both sides of Franklin Street. They were stapled to telephone poles and taped to lampposts, their bottom edges fringed with tear-away strips waving in the breeze. Smaller leaflets were tucked under the windshield wipers of parked cars, where an earlier rain had soaked them to the glass.

They all asked the same question, in oversize, bold print:

HAVE YOU SEEN CALEB ELLIS?

When Caleb was fourteen and his mother could walk again without a limp and could show her face in the daylight once more, she remarried. He became Caleb Maddox. In the years between — after he reappeared but before she remarried — they went back to her maiden name. For those years, he was Caleb Bellamy. But in the two weeks he was missing, his mother was only half alive, with another year of surgery in front of her. It had not yet occurred to anyone to legally drop the monster's name. So Henry and his parents would have printed *Caleb Ellis* on their flyers, the text running above a black-and-white school photo.

Caleb looked at Henry, his eyes pulling back into focus. He wanted to rub them clear, but it stung too much to touch them.

"They found me outside," he whispered.

He didn't remember that either, but he'd read it. Henry looked at him and nodded.

"You'd been gone exactly fourteen days," Henry said. "Almost to the minute. Your fingers were scratched up, the nails all broken. You were covered with dirt, had spider bites on your arms and face. But otherwise, you were fine. They never got anything out of you that made sense. A lot of people thought a man must have grabbed you."

"Kidnapped me."

Henry nodded.

"Then, either he let you go or you escaped. They figured sooner or later, you'd start talking. But —"

There were footsteps from upstairs: Vicki was crossing the hardwood floor above them. They both looked at the garage ceiling, then at each other. Over their heads, Vicki opened the front door and let someone in.

"But what?"

"But it never felt right," Henry whispered. "That kidnapping theory. And I had a hunch. With the job at the ME, I could finally do something about it. Last night I started checking the police reports up in Pacific Heights, from back then."

"You always want to dig through my life, or is this a new thing?" Caleb asked. "And don't you dare shout out. I don't care who's up there with Vicki. This is just you and me."

Henry ignored him and went on. But he kept his voice low.

"In the two weeks you were gone, there were ten break-ins within five blocks of Haas-Lilienthal. That was like a one thousand percent spike for the neighborhood. They never caught anyone," Henry said. "But it stopped after you came back."

Caleb was gripping the motorcycle helmet so tightly, he thought it might crack.

"You're saying it was me?"

Henry held up his hand, and Caleb had to fight back an urge to grab it.

"What do you think I was stealing?"

"Food," Henry said. "You were stealing food. That's the only thing that was missing from the houses."

Half a minute passed. Caleb wanted to shout that he didn't remember, that this was crazy. He wanted to beat Henry with the motorcycle helmet until he started making sense. Finally, he took a step back, to be farther from his friend.

"Everyone said I was kidnapped. I spent my whole life feeling dirty, wondering what he did to me. Looking over my shoulder, expecting either my father or something even worse — and you think I was hiding in the house the whole time?" he asked. "Sneaking out at night, breaking into people's pantries? That I was just playing some kind of sick prank?"

Henry shook his head. Not in disagreement, but in pity.

"It makes as much sense as anything else," Henry said. "If you think about it, try to process it."

"Now you're a therapist."

"You never went to therapy. Maybe you should've. Or maybe we should've just talked," Henry said. When Caleb didn't respond, he went on. "I think you found a crawlspace or something. A hiding place that everyone missed. And then when the cops were finally gone and the house was empty, you could do whatever it was you wanted to do."

"Which was what, Henry?"

"Be in another world for a little while. Of all the kids who ever needed another world—"

"That's crazy."

"It isn't—and I'm not saying it was a prank you were playing. I started researching last night, when you escaped the hospital. Reading case studies. I should've done it years ago. But it wasn't a joke you were playing. I think it was something else. A dissociative fugue, maybe."

"A fugue?"

Henry nodded and looked up at Caleb.

"It's like a complete break, a kind of—"

"I know what it is."

"Then you know it fits."

"Henry—you need to drop it."

"I'm just saying. Because in the right person, trauma sets it off. Extreme trauma, in your case. You disappeared the first day you went back to school. The first time you had a chance, when no one was watching every move you made. You can't tell me they're not linked, the disappearance and what came before it."

Caleb shut his eyes and bit on the tip of his tongue. He had to focus. That was the way back. He shook his head and opened his eyes.

"You can think whatever you want, Henry," he said. "It doesn't matter. I just want to know about the house. You saw me go upstairs? Back then?"

"You want Kennon to believe that's how your hair got there? That no one's used a vacuum cleaner in that house since then?"

"You didn't answer my question."

"We went upstairs."

"And before that, did we see the painting? The one of the girl?"

Henry nodded.

"We saw it."

"Last summer, you took us for the weekend on *Toe Tags*. We spent the night at Angel Island. You remember that?"

"I remember," Henry said.

"Sunday, we went to Sausalito and had lunch at the Trident. That restaurant on the pier."

"So what?"

"Bridget told us a story, didn't she? Or, she tried to. About a paper she wrote, for her master's."

Henry shook his head.

"Caleb — you've been circling the same thing for decades, and you don't even know it. It was a mistake, that we never talked about it. I thought you were doing okay. Grad school, the lab, Bridget — why talk about it when it was all going so well?"

Caleb was barely listening.

"The Trident's been closed since then, hasn't it?"

Henry nodded, and Caleb wasn't sure what was on his friend's face. It wasn't fear anymore. It might have been sadness, or pity.

"Pier got hit by a loose barge," Caleb said. He'd read it in the paper the weekend after their trip. "Snapped some of the pylons — building's not safe anymore."

Caleb massaged his temple with his thumb. His eyes were stinging and his lips felt like he'd touched them to a live wire. They were cracking and splitting between the needle holes. He'd forgotten their lunch at the Trident, forgotten what they'd talked about. Now he had an image of the table where they'd been sitting, out on what used to be an upstairs deck. Bridget had told them something, pointing once up to the north end of Richardson Bay, toward San Quentin. It hadn't seemed important at the time.

He looked up at Henry.

"Why'd you change the subject that day?" he asked. "You cut her off. Why didn't you let her finish?"

"Why do you think?" Henry said. "I know what's good for you to think about, and what isn't. And you never told her about your father, or what happened at the house, after. You can't talk about that painting without going there."

Part of that was true, anyway. He'd left a lot out for Bridget. He'd never told her why Henry sometimes looked at him sideways when he was quiet for too long. Why Henry concerned himself with what Caleb should think about, and what he shouldn't.

"They really found my hair upstairs?"

"Kennon says he did."

"Shit."

Caleb backed up and leaned against the wall, pinning the motor-cycle helmet against it with his back.

"You should turn yourself in, Caleb," Henry whispered.

"I told Kennon how that got there," he said. "She kissed me in the kitchen."

"Who kissed you?"

"Emmeline," Caleb said. "The girl from the painting. It could've gotten on her dress when she kissed me. My hair, my DNA. Then she went upstairs. Said she needed to close a window. I was cooking the second course."

"Caleb," Henry said softly, "please turn yourself in. If you want me to, I can drive you there now."

Caleb stood again and picked up the motorcycle helmet.

"No," he said.

He stepped up to Henry, then reached past him, into the car. He felt along the sun visor and hit the remote for the garage door. The door started to roll up slowly.

"I saw Bridget tonight," Henry said. "Saw what you did to her. She'll be okay. But, Caleb —"

"Henry, I didn't do that."

"Then who the fuck did?"

"Ask Bridget."

"She doesn't remember anything. Which is how you wanted it. You knew what those drugs would do," Henry said. He wasn't whis-pering anymore. "When she was already drunk, you pumped her full of BZDs. Then you either pushed her, or she was running away from you and went off the deck. God knows what you would've done if you'd caught her — but it's all a little too close to your father, isn't it? The sewing, the chisels you left in the bedroom."

"It was Emmeline!"

He started for the door. Henry stood up from the car and grabbed his wrist.

"Where you gonna go, Caleb? You can't run from this!"

Caleb tried to pull his arm away, but Henry was too strong. In-stead, they fell together into the utility shelves that lined the wall. Caleb dropped the helmet and scrabbled with his free hand along the upper shelf until his fingers touched a wooden handle. Tools rained across the concrete floor when he brought the hammer off the shelf. He cocked his arm but didn't swing. He'd never swing at Henry. Surely they both knew that. But Henry dropped his wrist and went backwards until he was pressed against the car.

"I can find her," Caleb said. "And I can end it."

Caleb didn't take his eyes from Henry as he knelt to retrieve the helmet. Then he turned and ran up the street, and didn't hear whatever Henry was shouting behind him.

It was a mistake to have let Henry see the helmet. It was a mistake to have gone to see Henry at all. Now they'd know what he was wearing, and how he was getting around. So he couldn't waste any time now.

He had to get across the Golden Gate Bridge.

He sprinted the last three blocks to the motorcycle, knelt next to its front tire, and fiddled the paperclip into place. He put on the helmet, mounted the bike, and started it. From Bay Street it was easy to reach the Golden Gate Bridge. On the bike, it would be two minutes across the Presidio.

There wasn't much traffic, but when he came to slower cars, he veered around them, doing his best to outrun his own headlight. The streets were slick with rain, so that he skidded through the turns, but he didn't spill the bike. When he came to the toll plaza he slowed to thirty and rolled through it, knowing the cameras were scanning his plates. If this bike's owner didn't have a bridge pass account, he'd be getting an invoice in a few weeks. By that time, it wouldn't matter.

Then Caleb was on the bridge itself, listening to the change in pitch as the ground dropped from beneath the road. The bike thumped over the segmented sections of the roadway and he cruised under the south tower doing the speed limit. He checked his mirrors and saw nothing. Just the electric gloom of the city lost in its weather.

There was a scenic overlook about a quarter of a mile after the bridge reconnected with land. Caleb pulled off and parked the bike, then sat straddling it as its engine idled. When Emmeline had escorted him from the Invicta to take him upstairs, he'd mostly been focused on her. On the touch of her arm, and the shape of her body beneath the soft cloak. But he'd heard the foghorn on the Golden Gate Bridge, and he'd smelled the bay. He was sure it had been the bay and not the open ocean on the other side of the peninsula. There were no buildings on the ocean side.

So Emmeline lived in Sausalito.

If she were any farther north — in Tiburon or Mill Valley — the foghorn would be too far away to hear. And Sausalito fit the rest of the facts. He and Henry had cruised all over the bay sampling sewage treatment plants, and he'd proved beyond a doubt that Charles Crane had been lodged under an outflow pipe between Sausalito and the bridge. Emmeline had five thousand square feet on the second floor of a wooden building on the Sausalito waterfront, and her windows were boarded up from the inside. He had a good idea where that was.

Not just a general area, but the exact building.

Before he put the bike back in gear, he took Henry's cell phone from his pocket. It was still on. He switched it off, then put it away.

From the scenic pullout, it was only two miles to downtown Sausalito. He took it slowly, the wind in his face carrying night smells of wet eucalyptus and bay laurel. A coyote ran across the road in front of him, stopping long enough to flash its eyes before disappearing up the hillside. When he got to the last curve before the center of the town, he could see his destination ahead. He parked the bike three hundred yards short of the restaurant, and finished the distance on foot.

Both the pier and the building were still standing, but the angles were wrong.

It was six months since the accident, and the Trident didn't look any closer to reopening. The windows were boarded up because every pane of glass had shattered with the force of the barge's impact. There was a chainlink fence across the front of the wooden pier. Beyond that, the contractors hadn't done much.

One car passed, and then the seafront promenade was empty. Caleb walked along the fence and came to its center. The gate stood open, the chain and lock hanging over the latch. He took the phone from his pocket and turned it on as he walked across the pier's disjointed wooden deck.

On the planks next to the restaurant, someone had erected a

dome-top temporary garage tent. Caleb's shadow disappeared from beneath him as he walked past the reach of the streetlamps. When he pulled back the tent's canvas flap, rivulets of beaded rainwater ran off to his feet.

For a moment, he thought the tent was empty. But then his eyes compensated for the shadows and he was looking at the back end of the Invicta, at its elliptical rear window. Its trunk stood open an inch, as if it hadn't been shut hard enough. He lifted it, and used the phone's screen as a light.

The only thing in the trunk was a black dress shoe. A man's shoe.

He backed out of the tent and looked up at the side of the restaurant. Of course there was no light coming from it. There was just enough space between the side of the tent and the building for two people to walk side by side. Emmeline had led him through this gap when she brought him upstairs to make love to him. Her hands had been on his arm, her body pressed close. He followed her route a second time.

In the back, near the drop-off where the end of the pier had collapsed into the bay, he found the staircase. He stood at its foot but didn't climb it. He heard the foghorn, three miles away on the concrete fender of the bridge's south tower. A few feet below him, the bay rippled between the pylons. When the tide went out, the current would run away from the shore before bending due south. Kennon's number was in Henry's phone, and he dialed it.

Kennon picked up immediately.

"Inspector?"

"Yeah."

"This is Caleb Ellis — Caleb Maddox."

"I know."

"I'll tell you where I am, if you come alone."

"You don't have to tell me anything. I'm looking at you."

Caleb jerked around, looking back toward the streetlights where the pier met the shore. There was a dark SUV parked at the curb, the silhouette of a man standing at its bumper.

"Come around and stand in front of the tent," Kennon said. "Keep the phone on your ear and put your other hand on your head."

Caleb did as he was told.

Standing in front of the tent, with his back to the Invicta, he watched Kennon come through the gate. He had his gun drawn but was holding it by his thigh, its muzzle pointed at the planks. He hung up his phone and pocketed it. Caleb kept his phone where it was.

"Step to the building, put your hands on the wall."

Kennon gestured with the gun, using its barrel to point to the restaurant's wood-planked side. Caleb put his hands on the boards and stood with his feet apart.

"You were at Henry's?" Caleb asked, over his shoulder. "That was you coming in?"

Kennon nodded.

"He didn't know or he'd have shouted. But Vicki's phone can track his. Handiest app I ever saw. Put your nose against the wall."

Kennon started patting him down: arms, sides, crotch, and legs. He pulled out Caleb's wallet and rifled through it. Then he stood and took the phone from Caleb's hand, and in the same motion brought Caleb's left arm around behind his back. When he had the cuffs on, he stepped back.

"Turn around," Kennon said.

Caleb leaned against the wall and watched Kennon holster the gun. After he snapped the leather band in place, he held his palm a moment over his chest. He took a step back from Caleb and looked down, breathing hard through his nostrils.

"You okay, Inspector?"

"Fine."

But he wasn't fine. He was sweating all over, though the air couldn't have been more than forty degrees. He took his hand off his chest and used it to wipe sweat from his forehead.

"You gonna read me my rights?"

"You know 'em?"

"Sure."

"Then we'll skip it. Save it for when we get to the station," Kennon said. "You called me. So what's on your mind?"

"Look in the tent."

Kennon backed toward the front of the tent, not taking his eyes from Caleb. He took the front flap and pulled it back, then looked inside. He glanced back at Caleb to be sure he wasn't moving, then pulled the flap back farther. He stared into the tent for half a minute, then let the door flap fall closed.

"Jesus," he said.

He stopped midstep on his way back toward Caleb, pausing to twist his neck side to side, like a boxer working out a kink between rounds. He looked at his right hand, running the pad of his thumb against the four fingers. Then he touched the lapel pocket of his jacket, where he'd put Caleb's wallet.

The sweat was back on his face.

"That's a Black Prince," Caleb said. "Invicta only made fifteen. And probably only one like that."

"There's nothing—"

The scream cut Kennon off. He jumped, but Caleb wasn't surprised at all.

It was a man's scream, low and rattling. The kind of sound a bull might make in an abattoir. It fell away, then came again, louder the second time—the man had only paused to draw a deeper breath. It was coming from inside the building.

Kennon drew his gun and grabbed Caleb's shirt collar.

"The stairs—where are the stairs?"

"In back."

"Get in front of me. Go!"

Kennon spun Caleb by his shoulder and shoved him forward, the gun's muzzle digging between his shoulder blades. They ran between the tent and the building and turned the corner, and then Kennon was hitting him on the back of the head with the side of the gun.

"Go up! Don't even try to get behind me."

He ran up the stairs, taking them two at a time, not trying at all to be quiet. Kennon herded him from behind. When they reached the landing, Kennon grabbed the chain between Caleb's cuffed wrists and yanked him away from the door. Then Kennon reared back and kicked the locks. The door frame's dry wood splintered with the first kick and cracked in half with the second. The frame spun inward with the door, carrying the three sets of deadbolts with it.

Kennon was breathing in a whistling gasp so loud that Caleb could hear it over the screams from inside. But the inspector didn't pause. He swung Caleb into the room, pushing him down and to the side so that Caleb went sprawling across the floorboards, taking most of the weight of the fall with his left shoulder.

• • •

At first, he thought the place was on fire. That the whole floor was on fire. But then his eyes found a reference point and focused. He was looking at a sea of votive candles. Thousands of them. Everything that had been here before was gone. The only things left were candles, and a mattress in the center of the floor.

Emmeline was getting up off her knees. She'd been kneeling at the head of the mattress. The skirt of her black dress was spread on the floor, a shrinking circle as she slowly rose up. A cobra, coiled and rising. Next to her, tied up on the mattress, was a fully dressed man. He was twitching, his whole body coming off the bed in the worst of the spasms. There was something on his face.

Caleb struggled to get up but couldn't. He got to his side and fought against the cuffs. Kennon stepped into view. He was trying to hold the gun on Emmeline but his arms weren't steady. The gun was pointing closer to Caleb than to her.

"Stop," he said.

His voice was choked. He had to work to get the words past some obstruction in his throat. He bent forward, suddenly, and caught himself with one hand on his knee. Like a runner who hits his limit. Winded and beaten. When Kennon looked up, Caleb could see veins and tendons bulging on his neck. Their eyes met.

"Don't move," Kennon said.

This time, his voice wasn't much more than a whisper.

Emmeline stood to her full height and took a step toward Kennon. He fired the gun at her. Caleb didn't know if he was trying to hit her or not. A candle inside a glass sphere exploded three feet from Emmeline's ankle. Closer, in fact, to Caleb's head. Behind her, the man on the mattress went on twitching. The device clamped to his face was made of iron. Thumbscrews ran along both its sides in double rows.

"Inspector, you'll hit somebody," Emmeline said.

She kept coming toward him. Her dress was cut long in the back, so that its hem trailed on the floor behind her, a black train. Emmeline stepped carefully between the candles, but her dress swept over them. They tipped, spilling wax, sending up smoke as they went out. Caleb got to his back and struggled until his cuffed hands were behind his thighs. He didn't take his eyes off Emmeline.

"You look sick, Inspector," Emmeline said. "I could get you some-thing to drink. A glass of water, maybe? Something a little stronger?"

Kennon fired again and Emmeline didn't even flinch.

The bullet missed her by ten feet, punching a hole in the back of the building.

"Stop—"

"You should be more careful what you touch," Emmeline said. "Some things can go right through the skin."

Kennon fell onto his knees. His face was purple.

"Maddox—" he said.

But Emmeline just shook her head.

"If you want to talk to Caleb, look at him," she said. "You're look-ing at me now."

Kennon took one hand off his gun and held his throat. But with one arm, he wasn't strong enough to hold up the gun. He dropped it, then tipped over as he tried to get it again. Emmeline walked slowly to him, her dress flowing with the sway of her hips. When she got to the gun, she moved it beyond Kennon's reach with a slide of her high heel.

"It's dangerous to take a man's wallet," Emmeline whispered. "You never know what might be on it."

Caleb bent his knees, then brought his hands up and pulled his legs through the loop of his arms. With his hands in front of him, he rolled to his knees. Then he picked up Kennon's gun.

Emmeline finally turned to him.

"Hello, Caleb," she said. "I think your friend's been poisoned."

He held the gun on her, and she just looked at him. He was on his knees still. Kennon lay between them, and had stopped moving. They both looked at him.

"Maybe he's done now, though," she said. "Do you think so? He looks done to me."

"What are you?" he whispered.

"Yours," she said. "All yours."

The man on the mattress had finally stopped screaming. Blood was spreading from beneath his encapsulated head.

Emmeline walked past Caleb to the door. The train of her dress was smoldering in the back, where it had dragged through hot wax and candle flames. She paused on the landing and looked back through the open door. She raised her gloved hand to him. He thought of the way she'd held it against the window glass when she dropped him off. It was a goodbye, but it was also a promise. And Emmeline kept her promises. All of them.

She nodded at him, reading his thought straight from his eyes. "Soon," she said.

Then she was out of sight, going down the stairs. He looked at his shaking hands on the gun. He'd never put his finger on the trigger.

When it started, the Invicta's big straight-eight sounded like thunder.

Like thunder at night, when the storm is close enough to wake you up and rattle the windows. He closed his eyes and listened to it move away, listened until it was gone. Then he dropped the gun and went to Kennon.

But Kennon was gone too.

TWENTY-SIX

SAUSALITO'S POLICE STATION was a little brick building on Johnson Street, so close to the Trident that he was in the car with Garcia for only a minute before they pulled him out and walked him upstairs from the sally port. The interrogation room was about the size of his bathroom. He was sitting on a lightweight plastic chair with his wrists cuffed to a metal handrail mounted on the wall. There was a white-topped table in between him and Garcia. None of the others had come into the room, but he guessed they were standing in the viewing chamber on the other side of the mirror. Or watching through the camera mounted in the corner.

Garcia finished reading aloud from the back of a white postcard.

"You understand your rights as I've read them to you, Dr. Maddox?"

"Yes."

His left eye was swelling up, so he had to pivot his neck to see Garcia clearly. The clean line of stitches on his forehead had broken open, either when Kennon threw him into the room, or when one of Garcia's men tackled him and broke his shoulder.

"I don't know if I can help you, if you decide to talk," Garcia said. "I've got so much shit on you, I don't even need to ask questions. But if you want to explain, want to take a shot, I'll listen. Maybe you know something I don't."

Caleb looked up at him.

"I didn't do this," he said. "Kennon had a heart attack. When you got there, I was trying to help him."

Garcia raised his eyebrow.

"He came in, arrested you, and then he just dropped dead?"

"It wasn't like that. He'd just run up the stairs — kicked in the door. He threw me across the room to keep me out of the way. And then he saw her. Saw what she was doing to the man."

"That man," Garcia asked. "When'd you find him?"

"When we came in the door — when Kennon kicked in the door and we went in. He was on the mattress."

"I meant before that. Did you see him before Marcie Hensleigh, or was it right after?"

"I never saw him before tonight, when Kennon and I found him."

"Yeah," Garcia said. "Okay. We'll get to that."

He looked over his shoulder at the mirror on the wall behind him. He made a hand gesture Caleb couldn't see. Then he turned back to Caleb.

"And Kennon — autopsy's gonna say it was a heart attack?"

"Yes," Caleb said.

"Because you know all about autopsies, don't you, Dr. Maddox?"

Caleb shifted in the chair. If he scooted it closer to the wall, he could fold his hands in his lap.

"I know about autopsies," Caleb said. "But I also know what I saw. And it was her."

"Great," Garcia said. "Now you're going to tell me about the girl. Elvira, Mistress of the Dark."

"Emmeline," Caleb said. "Her name's Emmeline."

"I listened to Kennon's tape," Garcia said. He had a notepad on the table, but he wasn't writing on it. He was just watching Caleb. "His conversation with you, at UCSF. So I know what you said she looks like. And I talked to everybody who was in House of Shields the night you said you met her. So here's my question. Bear with me, because it sounds like a joke."

Garcia stared at him, and Caleb didn't look away.

"It's one in the morning," Garcia said, "and there's nine straight guys in a bar. Not a girl in sight. Then Bettie Page walks in, wearing nothing but a nightie and some heels. And not one guy in the place — *not one,* including the bartender — notices her."

Caleb looked away, looked at his hands and the cuffs biting into them. Garcia paused and waited until Caleb raised his face. Then he went on.

"Except you," he said. "You noticed her. So what I want to know is, how am I supposed to believe that?"

"I can't tell you what anyone else saw."

"You know Spondulix? Place on Nob Hill?"

Caleb nodded.

"Kennon sent me there to check it out. You know they got a video camera behind the bar?"

"No."

"It was recording."

Caleb held on to the metal bar so Garcia wouldn't see his hands shake. But Garcia wasn't looking. He was reaching down, taking something from his briefcase. When he sat up again, he had a tablet computer. He turned it on and scrolled through a menu, then set it on the table between them. On the screen was a black-and-white still frame.

The camera must have been mounted well behind the bar, where it could keep an eye on the cash register. But in the background, Caleb could see himself. He was holding a votive candle and a glass of absinthe. From the camera's angle, you couldn't see the piano. Couldn't see the piano bench.

"You want me to hit play? You wanna watch it?"

Caleb didn't say anything, but Garcia's hand went to the screen and hit a button. The still frame came to life. There was no sound, just the pixelated, low-quality video. Caleb watched himself on the screen. He was swaying back and forth.

His lips were moving.

"Weird, don't you think?" Garcia said. "I wonder what you're singing."

"I wasn't. There's a piano there. Outside the shot. She was playing it for me."

"Kennon dies of a heart attack, and no one sees it but you. Emmeline walks into House of Shields, and no one sees her but you.

249

Bridget gets thrown off your back deck but doesn't remember a thing. And Emmeline goes to Spondulix, has three drinks, plays the piano, cleans the place up after you leave, and never once walks across this camera's line of sight?"

Caleb shook his head.

"I don't know what she did after I left."

"You know what else is on this tape? If you scroll it back another two hours before your little song and dance there?"

"No."

"Justin Holland. He went out for dinner with a client that night. Afterward, he stopped in Spondulix for a drink, by himself. We'd never figured out where he went, until just now, thanks to you. But he was sitting there for fifteen minutes — wait, you know who Justin Holland is, right?"

"I know who he is."

"Of course," Garcia said. He bounced his palm off his forehead. "Because you just happened to find him in San Francisco Bay the next night, right? That's what you told Kennon, and Henry backed it up."

Caleb looked at the tablet's screen. In the video, he was setting the candle on the corner of the piano. Then he walked out of the shot. Because it was happening off screen, Caleb couldn't explain it to Garcia. But Emmeline was holding him right then. Putting his jacket around his shoulders and pressing herself against him. Nothing between them at all, except a little bit of fabric.

Garcia pushed the tablet closer to him.

"How many patient data sets were you missing for the NIH grant application?" Garcia asked.

"What?"

"We've been talking to Joanne Tremont. Talking with her a lot. She's been hounding you to finish the data sets. You needed patients in pain — folks willing to skip any kind of meds."

"That's true. And I have the data."

"But hardly anyone volunteers to skip morphine when they need it. Or they'll hold off a little while, and then cheat on you. Or they weren't in any real pain to begin with. So you didn't have enough backup. The NIH thought your data was thin."

"It's good data. I have the backup."

"Sure you do. You found a nice way to beef it up, didn't you?" Garcia said. "You made sure they didn't get anything for the pain. And there was plenty of pain."

"That's bullshit."

"Joanne told us about the samples. How they just started showing up in the lab, with VA hospital patient charts. Special deliveries, huh?"

"I have a contract with the VA."

"Maybe that's why we found a stack of blank VA charts in the Sausalito kill house. The sample tubes, the needles," Garcia said. "How much money's riding on the grant?"

Caleb looked at the cuffs on his wrists. The locks that held him were so simple. He could open them in a minute if he had the right tool. He looked back at Garcia, who was answering his own question.

"Funding for years — millions of dollars. Right?"

Caleb nodded.

"It was a lot of pressure, wasn't it?" Garcia asked. He was leaning forward, his elbows on the narrow table. "A lot of stress. Not knowing if you were going to lose it. All those people counting on you to get it. Joanne, Andrea. Half a dozen lab techs."

"Anyone who's in charge of anything has people counting on him," Caleb said.

"But not everyone cracks," Garcia said. "You cracked. But you've got special circumstances, don't you? Maybe it wasn't really even the money. Maybe that was just an excuse you gave yourself and it would've happened anyway."

Caleb didn't answer, but he didn't look away. He thought of Bridget, exploding in anger when he told her about the operation he'd gotten. She'd shoved him back, ripped his hands away from her shoulders. Screamed that he was a liar, that he'd been leading her on. The tumbler was the first hard object she found, and she'd thrown it blindly, as hard as she could —

"Dr. Maddox?"

"What?"

"Did you hear my last question?"

"I guess not."

"You went to see Henry Newcomb in his office in September, right after you got the operation, didn't you?"

Caleb nodded.

"You were upset — and drunk. In fact, you were so worked up, he took notes after you left. You told him Bridget was pressuring you, but you couldn't do what she wanted. And you were worried about the grant. So much money."

The video clip on the tablet computer was looped. Caleb stared at the grainy image of himself, swaying in the darkness with a candle and a drink. He didn't look well. His shirttail must have come out of his pants while sitting with Emmeline, and his pale face glistened with sweat. Without the piano's sound, his movements made no sense: he might have been too drunk to stand still. He might have been muttering to himself. But if he looked bad, it was because the shot was too tight to bring in any context. Had the camera been three feet back, it would all make sense.

"You know what else he told me?" Garcia asked.

"I couldn't guess."

"He thinks he's figured out what's wrong with you," Garcia said. "So let's talk about that."

"You're not making any sense."

"The girl in the painting," Garcia said. "The Haas-Lilienthal house, where you disappeared."

Caleb looked up from the video screen and met Garcia's eyes.

"I was twelve when that happened. When I was taken."

"Taken?" Garcia asked. "That's the story you're sticking with?"

"You've been talking to Henry too much. And if you read the file, you know I don't remember any of it."

Garcia looked at his watch, then looked at the mirror behind him.

"That field trip your class took, Henry said it was your first day back in school. You'd been out two months," Garcia said. "You remember why."

"That's got nothing to do with anything."

"When you're twelve years old, and you watch your father tie your mother in a chair, watch him cut and sew her for three days before he puts his brains on the ceiling with a shotgun — that has something to do with everything. So it's not like you weren't carrying some weight," Garcia said. "Breaking under the strain of it, maybe. Even without that last act, your dad's masterpiece, you might've broken.

Kennon told me what it was like in there, inside your house. Henry, too."

"Why don't you just bring Henry in here? If you're going to sit there and tell me what he thinks."

Garcia nodded.

"He's here. But I don't think he wants to see you."

"That's big of him."

"Kennon took a picture of your mother's face, after your father finished with her. And after he finished with himself, I guess. I saw it, the picture, and you know what it made me wonder?"

"No."

"Bridget," Garcia said. "Were you really going to do all that to her?"

Caleb sat without saying anything. He stared at the tabletop, the bland whiteness of it, and tried to fight down the heat he felt flooding into his cheeks.

"No one knows everything your dad used on your mother. But you'd know, wouldn't you? What he used on your mom. He made you watch. Did you have that all lined up for her? The chisels and everything else?"

Caleb didn't answer. He could still hear her screaming: *Wake up, Caleb!* But he hadn't been able to do anything for her when Emmeline got up from the bed and turned to her. When he looked up again, Garcia was talking. He wasn't sure how much he'd missed, but didn't really care.

"— know that about fingerprints, right?" Garcia was saying.

"I didn't hear you."

"Fingerprints? How they stay the same your whole life? The way they look right now is the way they looked when you were twelve, except back then, your hands were a little smaller."

"And so what?"

"So, we found your room, in the Haas-Lilienthal house," Garcia said. "Henry said you were good at finding things, but I don't think any of us understood it — really understood it — until we saw that door. I'd never seen anything like it, that room. And your prints are all over it."

"I only went in there once, and I didn't touch anything."

"Maybe you've only been once lately. And haven't touched anything lately. But you were touching all kinds of stuff back then. When your hands were smaller."

"What difference does it make?"

Garcia shrugged.

"It meant a lot to Kennon, to finally figure it out."

"I bet."

"You know it was him who found you?"

Caleb nodded.

"He mentioned it."

"He was there all three times. When your father finally did what he'd been working up to. When you disappeared. And then when you came back, he was the one who found you. Your neighborhood was his beat. So when you got the gag off and started screaming, he was the first one."

"That's great."

"If he hadn't come and untied you and your mom, she'd have bled to death and you'd have starved. And then after the hospital, when you disappeared, he never stopped looking. If he hadn't seen you on the porch, who knows? You might've wandered off again. Gone back into your room."

Caleb squeezed the bar in his hands and looked back at the tabletop. For the last week, he'd been terrified that the floor beneath him might give way and drop him into oblivion. Now he'd have given anything for that to happen.

"So I hope for your sake you didn't actually kill him. That it was just a heart attack. Because if you killed the man who saved you twice?" Garcia said, leaning across the table and whispering. "The man who lifted your mother into the ambulance? Who found the bolt cutters to let you loose? I don't know. I don't know what they should even do to someone like that."

"Fuck you, Garcia."

"You don't have to tell me about the batrachotoxin," Garcia said. "Henry already did."

"Then fuck him, too."

"You left the safe open, after you escaped the hospital. Before you left, you smashed the vials all over the floor. But we wore hazmat suits when we went in. So nobody else died. You can thank Henry for that," Garcia said. "And Henry? He's been a good friend to you. Said you're the smartest person he's ever known — also, the most delicate. Maybe that's over now, the friendship. But he tried."

"I didn't —"

Caleb stopped and looked up. He finally met Garcia's eyes. For the first time in this conversation, he was absolutely sure about something.

"No one can get into that safe. No one."

It was so easy to say, because it was the truth. But then, in the long silence, he had to think about what it meant. He glanced down at his hands, which had gone pale and cold from the pressure of the cuffs.

Finally, Garcia answered.

"Exactly," he said.

He tossed his notebook onto the table. He still hadn't written anything down.

"Emmeline — is she like a voice in your head, or can you really see her?"

Caleb watched the video screen, remembering the first notes of the song she'd played. Like a patter of rain against the windows of a house that lay far from any other. If they could go away somewhere, just the two of them, the rain would sound like that against the windows of their bedroom.

"Not gonna bite at that?" Garcia asked.

Caleb shook his head and leaned closer to the screen. Emmeline wasn't in the shot, but maybe he'd be able to see her shadow. Something. Anything to show she was there. The glass sphere had been so warm in his hand. Heat and light against the cold green of the absinthe in the reservoir glass. He watched his lips move to the words as Emmeline sang them.

Garcia reached across the table and pulled the tablet computer away. He shut off the looping video and put the tablet into his briefcase.

"She's real," Caleb said. But he could hear the threads of fear and strain woven into his words. He sounded like a man holding on to a high ledge by his fingernails. "I've met her. Touched her."

"Sure you have," Garcia said. "Problem is, nobody else has. Because she doesn't exist, except in your head and in a painting."

Someone knocked on the door.

Garcia pushed his chair back and crossed the room. He stood

with his back to Caleb, blocking the doorway as he leaned through it. Whispers batted back and forth. Then Garcia stepped out into the hall and let the door click shut behind him. Caleb sat with his hands cuffed to the rail and tried not to look at the mirror on the other side of the room. There'd be a crowd on the other side of it, watching him. He hung his head low, so they wouldn't see his face.

Garcia came back after five minutes. He set a few sheets of paper face-down on the table, then slid into the chair and put his elbows on the table, his fists leaning in to each other. He went straight to it.

"Back in September, you were in the morgue," Garcia said. "You told Henry about the operation, told him about all these—how would you say it?—these *concerns* you had. Bridget. The NIH, breathing down your neck. And then, right in the middle of that, Henry got a phone call. Had to take it. So you stepped outside his office, didn't you?"

Garcia was staring at him so hard, it was like being in the searchlight of Henry's boat. The shadows were darker for it.

"You had ten minutes, maybe fifteen. Totally alone in the morgue. And that's when you put the virus on Marcie's mass spectrometer. Because the killings started that night. Charles Crane walked into a bar and stepped right out of this world. He was the first, wasn't he?"

Caleb sat in silence for a long moment, staring at the table. He thought about what it might feel like to fall through the floor. The darkness underneath everything was terrifying, but once you were in it, it was like a black cashmere cloak. Warm and safe.

She'll take care of this, Caleb thought.

"Dr. Maddox?"

"I didn't do that."

"We'll see," Garcia said. "Electronic data's hard to erase. Even for a clever guy like you. And the FBI's all over this."

"Then they'll clear me."

"I doubt it," Garcia said. "But maybe you can explain this. How many people called you on December twenty-third?"

Caleb didn't have an answer, and shook his head to show it. He wasn't even sure of today's date, couldn't begin to track backwards through the days and nights of this week.

"I'm talking about the day you made dinner for Emmeline. How many people called you?"

"Just two. Bridget and Emmeline."

"Emmeline called you while you were eating brunch at Park Chow, right?"

"That's right."

"Called you from a pay phone, from a number you didn't recognize."

Caleb nodded.

"And you talked to Henry while you were driving around. You called him. Before you went to the grocery store on Stanyan and ran into three of Bridget's girlfriends."

"Yeah," Caleb said. "That's right. I called him."

"That's it for phone calls on the twenty-third, right?"

"That's it."

Garcia took the paper and flipped it over. He slid it across the table so that it was in front of Caleb.

"We found your cell phone, in your house. That's a printout of your call log, from December twenty-three."

Caleb looked at the page. The first entry was an outgoing call to Henry's number. There was nothing earlier than that, but there should have been a short call in the morning. An incoming pay phone call.

"This isn't complete," Caleb said. "You didn't write them all down."

Garcia shook his head.

"It's all there."

Caleb looked at the other two items on the list.

There was a missed call from Bridget, and then, later in the evening, there was a call from a San Francisco number he didn't recognize.

"That one," he said. He couldn't point at it because his wrists were cuffed to the bar. "On the bottom. And that's when she called me. Just after eleven o'clock, to tell me where to go."

"You think?" Garcia asked. He leaned across and took the paper. "You think that was Emmeline?"

"It's when she called. At eleven o'clock. That's the only phone call I got at eleven."

"That's Marcie Hensleigh's number," Garcia said. "She called you, just like she said she would. She waited awhile for Henry, for him to call back with your number. And when he didn't come through, she figured it out some other way."

Caleb didn't look up. He closed his eyes and leaned in to the wall.

When Emmeline left the Trident, as Kennon lay dying, she'd held her open palm against an invisible pane of glass that separated them. She'd been waving goodbye, but it was a promise, too. She'd kept all her promises to him so far.

Soon, she'd said.

Caleb looked up at Garcia and pushed himself away from the wall. "I want to call a lawyer."

"You know what's a pity?" Garcia said. "There's only one guy in the world who knows everything that happened in that room tonight. You. And you're out of your fucking mind."

TWENTY-SEVEN

IT WASN'T UNTIL three thirty in the morning that they finished the jurisdictional paperwork to transfer him to Bryant Street. Sausalito's police station was mostly empty as they filed through it, though a few men and women stood up from their cubicles to watch him go by. Garcia walked behind him, his hand on Caleb's shoulder as they went down the stairs. A uniformed cop named Gedarro was in front.

Then they were in the garage bay at the sally port. An SFPD cruiser was parked inside. The patrolman opened the rear door, then put his hand on the back of Caleb's head.

"Easy now."

His hands were cuffed behind him again, so that he had to lean forward, his face close to the metal grate that separated the back seat from the front. He didn't move far enough inside. When the officer slammed the door, something was jabbing him in the thigh.

Garcia sat in front. He leaned around and looked at Caleb through the cage wall.

"Comfortable back there?"

"Fine."

Gedarro got behind the wheel and started the engine. They pulled out, took a right, and started rolling toward the water. Gedarro was looking in the rearview mirror.

"No escort?"

"They didn't tell you?" Garcia asked. "Some traffic thing, near the bridge. They knocked on the door and told me before everyone cleared out."

Caleb had moved away from the door now, but something was still stabbing his leg. It was the paperclip, the little U of wire he'd been using to short the bike's ignition circuit. He'd been frisked twice tonight, but both Kennon and Garcia had missed it. It was wrapped in a fold of medical tape, and had probably been stuck inside the seam of his pocket lining. They'd been looking for knives and tools, not pocket lint.

"You want sirens?" the patrolman asked.

"That's okay," Garcia said. "No sirens. I think Sausalito's had enough tonight."

Caleb leaned against the window and brought his left arm as far toward his right kidney as it would go. That fired a starburst inside his broken shoulder, but he didn't say anything. He got his fingertips into his right pocket and started pulling the lining.

When they passed the Trident, Caleb turned away. He didn't want to see the building again. Instead, he saw the dashboard's digital clock, reflected in the dark window beside Garcia. He read the backwards numerals.

3:31.

It had been 3:33 when they got in the car.

Soon, Emmeline had said. And as he remembered her voice, the promise she held in the palm of her hand, he smelled her perfume. Not in the car. The car smelled of sweat and bleached-out vomit. Gun oil. But she was coming. He knew that. He looked to the front of the car again. Officer Gedarro was a tall man, and the back of his uniform collar spilled over the top of his seat and pressed against the expanded metal grate that separated him from Caleb. A little bulge of the blue-black cloth was pushing through to Caleb's side.

Garcia wasn't wearing his seat belt.

As they came into the last turn of Alexander Avenue before the underpass and the ramp to Highway 101, the swirl of siren lights and road flares came into view.

"Oh shit," Garcia said. "No one said it was here."

"Said what?"

260

"Just slow up. Stop next to this guy."

Gedarro hit the brakes. Caleb's fingertips touched the paperclip. He pulled it out, let it fall into his palm.

He looked up at the clock's reflection.

3:30.

Gedarro came to a stop at the first line of flares and put down his window. A patrol officer came over and leaned in. He nodded at Gedarro, but spoke to Garcia.

"There's no way around, sir. Some kind of motor coach, like a private bus — it's flipped just around the bend. You want to get on the bridge, you'll have to go back through Sausalito, go down Spencer and get onto the highway from there."

"You can't just get us through?"

"No, sir. I would if I could."

"All right," Garcia said. He looked at the flashing lights, and then at Gedarro. "Turn us around. We'll go back through town, then use the ramp at Spencer."

Gedarro did a three-point turn on Alexander. They hadn't gone far before he spoke.

"We could take the tunnel on Bunker. Save us going back."

"Bunker's faster?" Garcia asked.

"Should be."

"Up to you. I know I don't like going back."

In thirty seconds, they reached an intersection. Caleb couldn't see the name of the crossroad, but Gedarro turned left onto it. They passed a turn circle and the entrance to the Bunker Road Tunnel was ahead of them. Its small black mouth opened into the hillside. Then they were rushing underground, burrowing west in a one-lane tunnel as narrow and as dark as a hand-hewn mineshaft. The closely spaced overhead lights streaked past, and the curved concrete walls threw the engine's roar back at them. Caleb worked his wrists against the cuffs and stared ahead at the rushing dark, at the back of Gedarro's neck.

He heard her before he saw her, the Invicta's straight-eight thundering up from behind them. Caleb looked to his left. He saw the chrome-plated headlamps, the upright radiator grille, capped with a statue of an armored knight. The hood came next, ghost gray and impossibly long. To fit alongside them in this tunnel, she'd have to be driving with her left wheels riding on the tunnel wall.

Something behind Caleb's back clicked. There was release of pressure from his left wrist, the relief of fresh blood flowing into his fingers.

He ignored it.

His eyes were on the Black Prince. The tunnel lights glared off its windows, flickering and orange, as if someone had set the leather coachwork aflame.

Caleb glanced ahead.

Gedarro was wearing a gold chain beneath his uniform shirt. Some of the electroplating had worn away from the links crossing the back of his neck. The metal underneath the gold was steel. The chain's clasp was out of Caleb's reach, beyond the grate. But with the paperclip in his fingers, Caleb knew how he could get it, how he could catch the links with a hook and pull the chain through. The thought that came next was just an image, not a plan: he had the chain in his fist and was yanking it backwards. It would feel like a blade against Gedarro's soft windpipe.

The Black Prince was right alongside him now, riding the tunnel wall like a scurrying insect, so close he could feel the pulse of its cylinders in his gut. Then he saw her behind the wheel. Her left hand was out the open window, one lacquered fingernail resting on the door-mounted mirror. In the roaring tunnel wind, her dark hair swirled about her head, like starlings at sunset.

Emmeline.

He let his lips soundlessly shape her name as he leaned toward the grate.

When Emmeline swerved into them, there was really no contest. The Invicta was bigger and heavier, and it was going faster. The patrolman hesitated between the brakes and the gas, and that decided everything. The Invicta's bumper slammed into the driver's-side door of the cruiser, pinning the car against the tunnel wall. A horizontal shower of sparks filled Caleb's window before it shattered. He hit the grate behind Garcia's head, felt his nose break inside the weave of the heavy wire. Then the patrol car's right tires were in the air. Caleb flew to the low side of the car and bounced off the barred window.

He heard an engine running, but he wasn't moving. Nearby, a pane of glass shattered, but nothing hit him. He sat up, and when he did, his neck popped and all the sound and light exploded away for a second.

Then everything came back.

There was blood on the window next to him, a spatter of it so thick he could barely see through the cracked glass. Something was moving out there. He heard footsteps. High heels on concrete. But there was nothing moving in the front seat: Garcia was halfway through the windshield. His feet were still inside the car, and they kicked a little. That was more than the other officer could muster. The patrolman had snapped his neck. His head was bent around backwards, wide eyes staring at Caleb.

Caleb's door swung open, and then he smelled her: that enthralling scent of midnight dew. Flowers that can't exist. That never have and never will. He looked at his hands. He didn't remember getting the cuffs off, but they were gone. He was gripping a broken gold chain in his left hand. He let it go, then wiped his bloody hand down the front of his khakis.

"Hello, Caleb," she said. "I promised I'd come soon. Didn't I?"

He turned and looked at her. She was still wearing the same dress, its black train burned through with holes. She held out her hand to him. The dashboard clock glowed 3:28.

"Are you coming?"

Her voice was only reaching him through one ear. The other ear just registered a high-pitched ring. He stared at her hand. The fine lines on her palm, the veins barely visible under the smooth run of her skin. He'd drawn that hand once. He tried to remember when. It was a picture he'd carried with him for so long, he couldn't say where he'd picked it up.

"Are you coming?"

When he spoke, the words sounded as if they were coming around a mouthful of melting ice. That was blood, probably. Bits of broken teeth.

"You're not standing there," he said. "You're — you didn't do this."

"Does it matter, Caleb?" she asked. "Do you care what any of them say?"

His vision split into doubles whenever he moved his eyes. He closed them, blinking away the blood. When he looked again, she was still standing at the open door. The two separate images of her floated into each other and made one. A solid, beautiful whole.

"I loved you," he said. "The first time I saw you. I was just a little kid."

"I know."

"And I wanted you — to save you — for you to save me."

"Do you remember when we found each other?"

He tried to shake his head, but his neck was a knot of twisted nerves, and the motion shot fiery bursts of pain down his arms. He screamed until his breath was gone. When he could, he looked up at her again.

"I can give it to you," she said. "Do you want it?"

"I can't do this. Not alone."

"Close your eyes, Caleb. I'll give it to you," she said. "We made time stop, that morning. Let me show you."

He closed his eyes. Her fingertips touched his forehead, tracing a circle in the blood. It was there, the memory. It was on her fingers, and then it was mixing with the blood on his skin, and then it was soaking into him. It hadn't been lost for twenty-five years. Emmeline had been keeping it for him. Saving it, until he was ready to take it back. She pulled her hand away when she was finished.

"Do you remember it, Caleb?"

They filed out of the bus and stood on the sidewalk in a light rain while their teacher and the two field-trip chaperones did a head count. Then they went up the steps, Caleb walking beside Henry, who pushed his glasses up to read the plaque next to the door.

They were in the kitchen when he saw it.

The repairman must have stepped out for lunch. Tools were sitting on the floor around the sink. Wrenches and a soldering torch, a long flathead screwdriver with a chip of carbon steel missing from its blade. Caleb was standing at the back of the group. No one but

Henry noticed when he took a step closer to the toolbox. The docent was talking about ice delivery wagons.

There was a knife on the floor, its curved blade as black and as sharp-looking as a tiger's claw. It was exactly like his father's knife, except there was no blood on this one.

"Caleb," Henry whispered.

Caleb heard the guide leading the class out of the kitchen and into the dining room. The repairman had wrapped the knife handle with black electrical tape to give it a better grip. His father had done that too. Near the end of his father's work, the handle would have been very slippery, without the tape.

Caleb closed his eyes tightly and then opened them.

He was in the museum house, alone in its kitchen. It couldn't really be the knife. His mother was at the new apartment, her face in bandages. The other children were in the next room. He knew that, but he couldn't hear them. There was just his father, his barking cries.

The knife was on the floor where his father had dropped it. But that wasn't right. He wasn't in the basement anymore. A man had come and had let him out. He was in a museum. A kitchen in a museum. The knife was where the repairman had left it.

It belonged in the dump, where his father's ashes had gone. He knew he had to get rid of it. The blade couldn't be burned, but at least it could be buried.

Caleb thought he was alone, until the shadow fell across him. He looked up, then quickly got off his knees. The kid taking the knife from the floor was named Drew. Until today, he'd just been a face in the back of the room. The kind of boy who still followed the words with his finger when the class was reading, who wore shoes with Velcro fasteners because laces confounded him. But now Drew held the knife so that its clawed blade pointed to Caleb's stomach.

"Was it one like this?" Drew whispered. "What he used?"

Caleb stared at the knife. His throat was locked so tightly, he might have been dangling from a gallows.

"It was, wasn't it?" Drew said. His voice was just a hiss. Their teacher was in the next room. "And you wanted it."

Even if he could have spoken, he wouldn't have. The boy had it wrong, but Caleb knew he didn't owe him anything.

"Did you like watching it?" Drew asked.

He let the blade slide back and forth in the air, an inch or two from Caleb's eyes.

"Did you like to see him cut her?"

Caleb felt a hand on his shoulder. He didn't turn, didn't take his eyes from the wavering blade, but he knew the hand was Henry's.

"Put it down, Drew," Henry said.

The kid took a step back. Henry was the tallest boy in their grade, and he had nearly a foot on Drew.

"I wasn't —"

Henry was also the fastest boy in their class. He darted around Caleb and caught Drew's wrist, yanking his arm upward and twisting it. Henry shoved him against the sink and clapped his palm over the boy's mouth. The knife fell to the floor.

"You shut up," Henry whispered. "I'm gonna let you go, and then you get back to the class. You got it?"

Drew nodded, his eyes bulging.

"You don't say shit," Henry whispered. "I see you on Caleb again, I'm not telling the teacher. It'll just be me and you."

Henry let the boy go, and watched as he hurried from the kitchen. Then Henry put his hands on Caleb's shoulders.

"You okay?"

Caleb didn't answer. If anything, the noose had drawn tighter. But Henry could read him, whether he spoke or not.

"Just breathe," Henry said. "It's gonna be all right. You know?"

Gently now, Henry turned him toward the door. They went into the dining room, where they caught up to the class. Several of the children turned when they came in, marking him with their dark eyes.

He'd understood, then, that he could never come all the way back. Drew knew it, and so did the others. Maybe Henry most of all. They'd found a nightmare, and a monster. It was safe for them, because it was over. It was just a story, a fairy tale. And though Caleb would never belong with them, now a part of him belonged to them. They would tear out his history, cut it from him before it stopped beating. Claim his darkness for themselves. Something to marvel at, and then throw away.

It was too much, trying to meet their eyes. He looked around the new room. His throat was still closed off, and he might not have drawn a breath since he'd seen the knife. There was a fireplace, and above it was a painting. The young woman was looking at him, but her gaze didn't hurt at all. The pain left his throat. Light poured from the painting into the room. As he watched, the woman moved her left hand. He stepped back and bumped into Henry.

"Caleb," Henry whispered. "You need to breathe."

He turned to his friend, eyes wide, and then he looked back at the painting. Now she was using one elbow to prop herself off the straw mattress. Her left hand reached toward him, palm out. Three times, she curled her forefinger in. She wanted him to come nearer, but Henry was leading him away.

He knew enough to stay quiet.

But in the next room, he slipped from Henry's grip and drifted to the back of the class. And then at the top of the stairs, he left them altogether. At the landing, he heard a whisper. She was calling him from the mantel. All she said was his name, the two syllables drawn out as if spoken by the wind.

Caleb.

He went to her. How couldn't he?

Downstairs, it was as though the sun had set. A servant might have passed through, lighting unseen candles. Above him, the children's voices rose skyward, fainter and fainter. When they disappeared, the house sighed.

He crossed the room and stood before her. The moment stretched to infinity. He didn't even feel himself fall past the horizon, because he was alone with her. Just Caleb and Emmeline, inside the cataract. Warped space and looped memory. Time was so soft, the clocks might hang like limp rags. They were a foot apart, their eyes on each other. He wanted her so badly, it ached.

She was hauntingly lovely. And waiting to be hanged.

He wasn't afraid when she sat up in the painting, swiveled to the mantelpiece, and bounced down as lightly as a dancer. She took the cushions from the couch and stretched out on the floor. That was the image that would become so treacherous, so persistent in his thoughts and deepest memories, waiting for the right season to sprout and grow anew. Her eyes were half closed, the ghost of a smile on her lips. She was waiting for him, begging for his touch. Pleading him to make the clocks run backwards so that he could come to her. So that he could take her away. Save her from the dawn. No chains could stop him this time. There were no eyebolts in this floor.

The fireplace fluttered alight behind her as she opened her arms to him.

Before going to her, he looked at the mantel again. The prison cell in the picture frame was empty. He fell on his knees in front of her, shaking with tears he'd never have to explain, because he knew that she was —

"Caleb?"

He looked up. They were in the tunnel. She was holding her hand out to him, palm up. Her fingertips were painted black-red with the blood from his forehead.

"A part of me," he whispered.

"So come," she said. "Please come. We have to hurry now. You have to drive the police car. Get it out of the tunnel. I'll meet you."

"Henry told them about me — about us."

"You have to hurry, Caleb. You have to go north. Hide the bodies and switch cars. I'll meet you. But you must hurry."

He closed his eyes again and reached for her hand. It should have been right there, should have been so easy to catch. He'd found her hand while blindfolded. He'd found her in the dark half of San Francisco with nothing to track but the scent of her perfume, the memory of her fingers on his wrist. He'd found her secret room — their room.

But now when he reached for her, his fingers caught nothing but air. When he looked up, he just saw the tunnel wall.

She was gone. The Black Prince was gone.

"Emmeline?"

The tunnel's sounds dropped away. The ventilation fans and the squad car's engine ran in silence. Garcia's feet kicked soundlessly against the dashboard. The only noise was a dry scraping: the sound of autumn leaves swirling on a sidewalk in a cat's paw of wind.

He leaned from the car's open door and looked back along the roadway.

A piece of paper was sliding toward him along the pavement, riding the air current that flowed through the tunnel. He couldn't read the text on the page yet, but he knew what it was and felt his skin go cold in dread of it. And he understood, too, that this was from Emmeline. She wanted him to see this, as she'd wanted him to find the secret door. He hadn't needed a key to enter the room behind the fireplace; the room required no key because it was itself a key. She'd known that if he ducked inside and breathed the decades-old dust and mold, if he saw the scatter of drawings and the web-covered cot, then he would open a more deeply hidden door. Now she was asking him to open one more.

He lifted himself from the back seat and stood, catching the paper with his foot before it slid past.

It was a flyer. The same kind of flyer he'd seen on Haight Street, and up near Fisherman's Wharf, and along half a dozen other avenues in the last few months. Since September, they'd been taped to the lampposts and stapled to the trees. He'd seen them pasted to shop windows, block upon block. Walls of paper covering entire storefronts, wrapping full-grown trees to their highest and most insubstantial branches. He'd seen crowds of people walk past them without slowing, without turning their gaze for even the half-second it would have taken to read the names of the missing.

He bent and took the flyer in his hand. Its bold print ran above three black-and-white photographs.

HAVE YOU SEEN INSPECTOR GARCIA OR OFFICER
GEDARRO? WHAT ABOUT DAVID HANEY?

The first two photographs could not have been taken. Garcia's face was smashed and lacerated, one eye punctured by a shard of glass that still protruded from the socket. Officer Gedarro stood with his back to the camera but was nonetheless looking straight into the lens, because his neck was broken and his head had turned all the way around. The skin around his throat was twisted into a spiral, like the strands of a rope. The last photograph showed the man who'd been on the mattress in the Trident, his face still enclosed in the metal apparatus. Caleb let go of the paper and watched it skid away, watched it follow the tunnel's gentle curve until it evaporated into the fog that waited outside.

Twenty-five years ago, his father might have seen the flyers too. There'd been missing men on his conscience, fifteen of them, going back to the day of Caleb's birth. Their faces might have covered the walls of his basement cutting room during his last three days of work. Flyers and handbills and leaflets everywhere, like the guilty debris after a flood. His father, bloody up to his elbows and singing as he shaped his final sculpture with a wooden mallet and an improvised chisel, might have been staggering through a sea of flyers, might have been fighting off a whirling storm of them whenever he paused and waved his arms at the ceiling, whenever he spun in circles and punched the air while shouting in languages no one spoke.

Perhaps the collectors who bought his paintings wanted to search them for hints. Wanted to stand before them in quiet rooms and study them for signs and forewarnings. Hidden images full of dark potential, like buried seeds. The same way Henry and the rest of them would pick through his house and his lab, would reread his articles in a hunt for the genesis of this darkness named Caleb they'd found like a weed in their ranks. They would catalog their discoveries and write about them in journals, and perhaps someday a different class of collectors would begin trading in his charcoal sketches, buying them at private auctions and taking them home to study the chiaroscuro shading in his series of Bridget Laurent nudes, hoping to divine the point at which the spectrum went to full black.

He looked down the empty tunnel.

"Emmeline?" he whispered.

She didn't answer. She couldn't answer, because she was gone.

He closed his eyes again and held on to the roof of the car so he wouldn't tip over. He had to breathe, had to focus. That was the way back. To focus on her. To focus on anything at all, but especially on her.

"Emmeline."

Whispered slowly, her name lapped like three low waves against a welcome shore. He set the word loose in his mind, let it wash through him.

Even though she was gone, he could still smell her.

I'm yours, she'd said, and so far, she'd never lied to him. Everything had been true, every promise had been kept. Her perfume, lingering above the smell of twisted metal and burning rubber, was a new promise. A promise that if everything else was gone, if no hope or plausible future remained, there was Emmeline.

He opened his eyes, then turned and shut the squad car's passenger door. He stepped up to the driver's door and looked at Officer Gedarro through the cracked window. Then he looked at the car's front end. Shattered windshield glass was spread in a fan on the hood and in Garcia's hair. The glass shard in Garcia's right eye glittered in the amber light. But the engine was still running. If he reversed away from the wall and put the car back into forward gear, he'd be able to drive it. Perhaps not far, but he didn't need to go far. The first thing was to get out of the tunnel.

He opened the driver's door and shoved Officer Gedarro into the passenger seat, behind Garcia's dangling legs. Emmeline was his. That was the truest thing of all. And she'd be waiting for him, up north, or wherever he went. He dropped into the seat and slammed the door. The rest of the glass fell out of the window frame. After he backed away from the wall and straightened the wheel, he checked the side-view mirror. There were no headlights yet, but there would be, and when they came, they'd come fast.

He'd have to hurry now. Emmeline hadn't been lying about that, either.

He put the car into gear and pressed on the accelerator, then reached past the steering wheel to clear away the opaquely shattered glass hanging in the windshield's frame. Then there was the wind, fresh against his bleeding face.

Out on the hood, Garcia was watching him with his good eye. He blinked and stared, blinked again. His feet kicked a rhythm against the dashboard.

"North," Caleb said, looking at the detective. "She'll be there. You'll see."

The cruiser was riding on two flat tires. Any faster than ten miles an hour and he couldn't stop the fishtailing. They came limping out of the tunnel, the wounded car and its cargo of men, and when he hit the wall of fog outside, he saw how it would be when he got to the north, how it would go when he found her again. A week or a month from now, he might be sleeping in a storm culvert beneath some empty stretch of highway, but when he woke at night and raised his head to look around, he wouldn't see a cement drain. He wouldn't see the sticks and old animal bones he'd shoved aside to make his bed.

None of that.

He'd see a candle guttering in an iron birdcage, would see the crystal cake stand with its dried rose, the stuffed eagle frozen in its scream. Persian carpets would blanket a wood-planked floor. Somewhere in the wavering shadows, he'd hear the Comtoise clock as it marked the backwards time of nowhere.

He might have stolen an old blanket from a laundromat, but when he woke in the light of Emmeline's caged candle, when he heard the swing of a pendulum and the click of well-oiled clockworks, he would be ensconced in white down rather than pilled wool. If he explored beneath that duvet, he'd find Emmeline's hip, would trace with his fingertips that fine, cool curve until she stirred and woke and turned to him.

They'd travel by night.

North and beyond, until they found woods deep enough to hold them. He might be sitting in the passenger seat of a pickup truck after daring to hitchhike, the old man behind the wheel smelling of sweat and chewing tobacco, smelling of thoughts kept to himself. But if Caleb closed his eyes, the truck's rattle would die away until it carried them as if it ran on smooth rails. The engine would tighten up until its knocks blurred into the roar of a finely tuned straight-eight. If he opened his eyes, Emmeline would turn to him and smile, one hand on the Black Prince's leather-wrapped wheel.

Don't look in the back seat, Caleb, okay? she might say. *I don't want you to be angry with me. The old man —*

Garcia was still watching him from the hood.

"She'll take care of me," Caleb said to him. "That's all it is."

Ahead, he saw a pullout, a wide place in the gravel shoulder where the car could easily slip through a gap in the guardrail and go down the embankment. There was only one thing left to do. He reached across to Gedarro and unsnapped the holster on his hip. He pulled out the gun and held it in his right hand. Then he slowed the car to an idle, pointed its hood at the shoulder where the hill sloped away to a brushy ravine, and tumbled out, rolling clear of the car as it passed. He watched it pitch down the slope until it disappeared. The last sound was a weak scream, and he wished he hadn't heard it.

It would be okay, though.

He could give it to Emmeline and she would carry it for him, beyond his reach. She could carry a lot of screams for him. But there was another way too. His father had been wrong in everything he did, but surely his last decision was the correct one. No one had ever doubted that choice. He looked at his feet. On his way out of the car, he'd dropped Gedarro's gun. Now he searched the road's shoulder until he found it.

He stooped and picked it up.

Either way, he'd need the gun. He brushed it off and put it in his waistband, then began to consider his route toward the nearest neighborhood. If he hurried, he might find a motorcycle before dawn, might be far into the north by first light. She was waiting for him, up there, where the deeper woods turned back even the afternoon sunlight, and the morning fog caught in the tree crowns and fell to the ground smelling of wet bark and the sea. It would be a good place for them, for what they had to do. Maybe she'd bring absinthe, and they could drink one last glass with each other, under the trees, before the dark came.

Acknowledgments

A great many people helped me to make this story into what you're holding. My wife, Maria Wang, read the manuscript countless times, always with a red pen. I could not have written this story without her. My sister, Lisa Moore, provided on-the-ground reconnaissance when I couldn't visit San Francisco myself. Dawn Barbour, at the Sausalito Police Department, answered strange questions, and Nathaniel Boyer, M.D., who was then at the UCSF Medical Center, answered disturbing questions. Bruce Nakamura, Jon Wilson, J Moore, Elizabeth Moore, and Jocelyn Wood are beta readers without equal. Most of all, there was Alice Martell, my agent. She saw what this story could be and wouldn't let me stop until I got it there. When the book was finished, she became its tireless advocate. Working with the editors — Andrea Schulz, Naomi Gibbs, and Alison Kerr Miller at Houghton Mifflin Harcourt, and Bill Massey at Orion — has been a privilege. Thank you all.

The Trident Restaurant, in Sausalito, is open for business as of this writing. It has never been hit by a barge, and is a wonderful place to spend an afternoon.

**Keep reading for a sample from
Jonathan Moore's next novel**

THE DARK ROOM

Out in January 2017

*See what happens when our deepest secrets
are unburied in a thriller that grips from
the start with "suspense that never stops."*
— James Patterson

ONE

IT WAS AFTER midnight, and Cain and his new partner, Grassley, watched as the excavator's blade went into the hole, emerging seconds later with another load of earth to add to the pile growing next to the grave. On the phone that afternoon, the caretaker of El Carmelo Cemetery had asked if they could do this at night. There were burials scheduled all day, and he didn't want to upset anyone. The time of day hadn't made any difference to Cain. Staying up all hours was his business. He just wanted this done.

After three more scoops with the backhoe, the caretaker rotated the arm out of the way and his assistant jumped down into the hole with a long-handled spade. As he did that, the van from the medical examiner's office arrived. Its headlights scanned across Cain and Grassley, and then paused over the exhumation. The caretaker's assistant climbed out of the hole, blinking against the bright light. Then he took the lifting straps from his boss and jumped back into the open grave.

Cain watched the technicians climb from the van and start up the hill. A man and a woman, young, no more than a few years out of college. Grassley's phone rang, and he checked the screen before he answered. He looked at Cain and took a few steps back.

"Yes, ma'am," he said, and then he paused a while to listen. "No, we're out at El Carmelo, in Pacific Grove—you know, the Hanley thing?"

Now Grassley was listening again, pressing his finger into his free ear to dull the excavator's diesel rumble.

"He's right here. Hold on."

Grassley handed him the phone.

"It's the lieutenant," he said. "She wants to talk to you."

He took the phone, stepping through the long shadows of the headstones toward the cypress trees at the top of the hill, where he would be farther from the excavator's idling engine.

"This is Cain," he said. "What can I do for you, Lieutenant?"

"Something came up. I need to reassign you."

"We're right in the middle of something."

"I wouldn't pull you off if I had a choice," she said. "But I don't. Grassley can take Hanley from here."

"We're two hours south."

"That's not a problem," the lieutenant said. "You're — Where exactly are you?"

"El Carmelo," he said. "The cemetery."

"Hold on, Cain."

He knew she was checking her computer, pulling up a map. There was too much noise on the hilltop to hear her keystrokes. In less than twenty seconds she was back to him.

"There's a golf course," she said. "Right next to you. They can set down, pick you up."

"They?"

"The CHP unit."

"You're sending a helicopter?"

"It'll be there in ten minutes," she said.

"What's going on?"

His mind went first to Lucy, but the lieutenant wouldn't have called about her. She didn't even know about Lucy.

"We'll talk when you get here, face to face. Not over the phone. Now give me Grassley. I need another word with him."

He started toward Grassley, then stopped when he saw the hole. He had to try one more time. He cupped his hand over the phone's mouthpiece, so she'd hear him clearly.

"I spent three weeks setting this up."

"It's a wild-goose chase, Cain. One that's been sitting thirty years. I've got a problem that's less than an hour old. Now it's your problem. Put Grassley on."

He came back to Grassley and handed him the phone. It wasn't any use wondering why the lieutenant was pulling him away. Instead, he walked to the edge of the excavated grave and looked down, shining the flashlight he'd been carrying. The caretaker's assistant was kneeling on top of the casket. He'd dug trenches along its sides and was reaching down to fasten the lifting straps.

Three decades underground, the kid wouldn't weigh much, at least. And from what Cain understood, by the time he'd finally died, there hadn't been all that much to put in the casket anyway. The assistant climbed out of the hole again and handed the ends of the four straps to his boss.

Cain checked up the hill and saw Grassley standing under the tree, one finger in his left ear to block the noise as he talked to their lieutenant.

"Inspector Cain?"

He turned around, putting his hand up to block the light shining in his face.

"That's me."

The woman from the ME's office lowered her light and came around to stand next to him. She leaned over to look down into the hole.

"You're riding back with us in the van?" she asked. "We heard something like that."

"Not me," Cain said. "I just got reassigned."

He gestured up the hill toward Grassley.

"He'll have to go. You or your partner can follow in his car."

"Reassigned? It's two a.m. and we're —"

She stopped, following Cain's eyes to look at the light coming toward them from the north. When the helicopter broke out of the clouds and into clear air, they could hear the *whump* of its rotors. Cain pointed up the hill toward his partner.

"That's Inspector Grassley," Cain said. "Make sure he gets in the van, that he rides with one of you. He might want to drive back on his own, but don't let him. We need the chain of custody. You understand. I don't want any problems later, some defense lawyer picking us apart."

"I get it," the woman said.

"I've got to go," Cain said. He looked back into the hole, shining his light on the casket's black lid. "Let's get this one right."

He paused on the way down the hill and looked back up at Grassley. They met each other's eyes and nodded, and that was all. Then he hurried across the access road, toward the long fairway that stretched between the graveyard and Del Monte Boulevard.

When he reached the golf course and felt the short grass under his feet, he checked the sky to the north and saw that the helicopter was less than a minute away. He took out his cell phone and dialed Lucy's number.

"Gavin?"

"Sorry—I didn't mean to—I thought I'd get your voicemail."

"I was up."

He looked at his watch. It was a quarter past two. The grass on the fairway was slick with dew, and he could smell the ocean.

"You're okay?"

"I'm fine."

"You're feeling sick again," he said. He could hear it in her voice.

"It's not such a big deal," she said. "Really."

"Okay."

"Where are you?" she asked.

"Down south, near Monterey. For Hanley."

"Hanley?"

"The video we got, the guy who—"

"That's enough," she said. "I remember. I can't stomach it right now."

"No more," he said. "I promise."

"Are you coming soon?"

"Something came up," he said. "They're sending a helicopter, but I don't know what's going on."

"You have to hurry?"

He glanced up at the helicopter, saw it swing around as it lined up for the fairway.

"I ought to go."

"Then call when you can," she said. "Or better yet, just come."

"As soon as I can," he said.

"Be careful," she said. "Gavin, I mean it."

"Try and get some sleep."

They hung up and he put the phone away. Then the helicopter came in just above the line of trees, and when it was hovering over the fairway, its spotlight lit up. He walked toward the white circle, one hand in the air to call the CHP pilot in.

TWO

IT WAS HIS first time in a helicopter. The SFPD had scrapped its aero division before he'd even joined the force. Now whenever his department needed helicopter support, it called the California Highway Patrol. The agencies were friendly, but arranging anything was a bureaucratic and logistical mess. Which meant that this flight, on short notice at two in the morning, could only have happened if someone far above his lieutenant had stepped in.

He put on his headset and bent the microphone toward his lips.

"Where we headed?"

"Civic Center Plaza," the pilot said, and Cain had to press his earphones tight to hear her voice over the engine. "I'm supposed to set you down on the lawn at the corner of Polk and Grove."

"They tell you what it's about?"

She shook her head.

"I'm just a taxi service tonight. That's all I know."

They were racing above Monterey Bay. Five, six hundred feet up, with wisps of fog between them and the black water. Ahead, he could see Santa Cruz, its lights spread between the bay's curved shore and the low, silhouetted mountains.

"What were you doing in the cemetery?" the pilot asked.

"Exhumation."

"Cold case?"

"That's right," Cain said.

It was no ordinary cold case, but he wasn't going to explain that

284

now. He hated to be reassigned right at the cusp, a moment before they pried open the lid and found out if they had a case or nothing at all. It wouldn't wait for him, either. The lieutenant had been clear — Grassley would handle it without him. He was supposed to be good, but he'd been Cain's partner for only three weeks. Cain hadn't seen enough to have an opinion either way, and that made him nervous.

When they reached the northern edge of Monterey Bay, the pilot came up high enough to pass above the Santa Cruz Mountains, and though they were flying toward the city's gathering orange glow, beneath them, the woods were dark and untouched.

Twenty-five minutes later, the pilot circled Civic Center Plaza once, and then put the helicopter down on the lawn, slipping easily between two rows of flagpoles. Cain took off his headset and stepped out, closing the door behind him.

Lieutenant Nagata was waiting for him across the lawn, standing clear of the wind. Behind her, on Polk Street, a yellow cab and a pair of private cars had slowed to a crawl to watch the helicopter.

Cain straightened his suit and went to his boss.

"Lieutenant," he said. "Where are we going?"

She nodded toward City Hall, which rose into the dark across the street. The gold leaf on the dome glowed against the night. Lieutenant Nagata waited for a car to pass, and then led him across Polk Street. A policeman opened the main door for them, and Nagata led Cain into the building. She stopped beneath the rotunda, at the foot of the grand staircase.

"He wants to see you alone. Go on up, and when you're done we'll talk down here. I'll introduce you to Karen Fischer."

"Who wants to talk to me?"

"Castelli."

He thought about that, what it might mean. He'd never been inside City Hall in the middle of the night. The lamps next to the staircase were lit, and there were a few spotlights farther off, illuminating the bust of Mayor Moscone and the spot of floor where he'd died. He could hear someone pacing in one of the marble-floored galleries above, and he looked around until he spotted the patrolman up there.

"Karen Fischer — who's she?"

"Your contact with the FBI," Nagata said. "Starting tonight, and until this is over. But go up. He's waiting, and he's had a long night already. It'll just get harder for him from here."

It wasn't like Nagata to show sympathetic concern for anyone holding an elected office. The one exception was the mayor. It almost never came up, but when it did, she could be fierce about it. She owed him her job and paid that debt however she could. With her hand at the small of Cain's back, she pushed him toward the grand staircase. He climbed up, passed under the ceremonial rotunda, and then nodded to the patrolman who stood between the flags flanking the mayoral suite.

Cain stepped inside the reception lounge, the red carpet thick underfoot. There was a glass-shaded lamp on the receptionist's desk, and it was the only source of light after the patrolman closed the door behind him.

There was no one else in the lobby. Cain wasn't sure if he was supposed to sit. Maybe in the mayor's mind it made sense to pull him out of El Carmelo, fly him back into the city, and then make him wait. He crossed through the lobby and found the door to the mayor's office. He knocked once with the back of his hand, then opened the door.

Harry Castelli was bent over his phone when Cain stepped in. He glanced up, then cupped his hand over the mouthpiece.

"He's here, and I'll—"

But Cain couldn't make out the rest of it.

The mayor hung up, then pointed at one of the two chairs that faced his desk. Cain pulled one out and sat looking at the man who'd brought him. He was wearing a white dress shirt and a pale blue silk tie. His suit jacket lay atop his desk. His hair was black but must have been dyed because the stubble on his face was all white. His face was fall-down tired. Nothing like the man Cain had seen on TV, leaning with his elbows on a podium in the rotunda, facing a crowd of reporters that pressed all the way down the stairs.

"You're Cain—Inspector Cain?"

"That's right."

"I called your lieutenant and asked for a name."

"Okay."

"I wanted the best, and that's why you're here," the mayor said. "I see you wondering."

"I appreciate that."

If this had happened at the beginning of December, Nagata would have picked a different inspector. But December had been a hard month, and she didn't have much choice. A pair of inspectors and the Office of the Medical Examiner had lost control of an investigation, and three of Cain's closest friends had been killed. By New Year's Day, he was the most senior man left standing in the Homicide Detail. He was thirty-seven years old.

The mayor reached halfway across the desk and lifted his suit jacket. There was a manila folder under it. He looked inside, then put it on the desk and weighed it down with his palm. He was wearing a thick gold wedding band. No scratches on it. He must have been in the habit of taking it off whenever he did anything with his hands — or else, there'd always been someone else to do those sorts of things for him. Any kind of real labor.

The mayor leaned forward. He may have looked exhausted, but when he spoke, his voice was deep, each word a jab.

"Let's make one thing absolutely clear."

"All right."

Castelli took the folder again, holding it up without opening it.

"I don't know what this is," Castelli said. "And I don't have anything to hide."

"Okay."

"We're clear?"

"I heard you," Cain said.

Usually, the first thing a witness said was a lie. This wasn't starting well for the mayor.

"This — this *thing* — it's bullshit."

Cain didn't answer. He looked at the mayor until the man put down the folder and opened it. There were only a few pages inside. Five, at the most. Cain could see a letter on top, upside down. Its author had conveyed his message in just a few lines. No letterhead, no signature. A nice, clean typeface. Cain didn't need the mayor to tell him what kind of letter it was.

"This came today, in the regular mail."

"It came today, or it got opened today?"

"Both — we open all the mail, every day."

"Who opened it?" Cain asked. He looked at the mayor's hands again. "Not you, I'm guessing."

"My chief of staff. And then she brought it straight to me."

"And she's—"

"Melissa Montgomery. She's giving her statement to the woman from the FBI."

"All right," Cain said. "Is that a copy?"

"The FBI's got the original. This is your copy."

Castelli took the top page from the stack and passed it across, closing the folder before Cain could get a good look at the photograph underneath it. Cain took the letter and turned it around.

Mayor Castelli:

1 – 2 – 3 – 4!

All this time, and you're really surprised? Or are you just feigning it, like everything else? Nothing stays in the dark forever.

I'll give you until Friday. Or else: 5 – 6 – 7 – 8. Those go to everybody. Even if they've never seen you that way, they'll recognize you. You didn't forget 9 – 10 – 11 – 12, did you?

When it's dark, you think about her. You imagine what it must have been like. Should your wife start thinking about it too? What about your daughter? Could she be the next Sleeping Girl?

There's an easier way out: *bang!*

— A FRIEND

Cain read the note twice, then put it on the desk in front of him. He studied Castelli for a moment. He looked at the note and read through it once more.

"The numbers — one, two, three, four — those are photographs?"

"Yes."

"Show me."

Castelli passed him the folder. Cain put it on the desk's edge, then flipped the cover back and looked at the first photograph. It was a copy, but a good one. A glossy, full-page print on good photo paper.

"You sent this out, had it done somewhere?"

Castelli shook his head.

"One of my staff — he's got a photo printer. Here, in the office. Melissa used that."

"It was black-and-white to start with, or just after she copied it?"

"Black-and-white."

"It would be," Cain said, speaking mostly to himself. "Wouldn't it?"

"I don't understand."

Cain lifted the photograph from the folder and laid it on the desk, sideways, so that they could each lean in and look at it.

"These distortions," he said, touching the photo with his fingertip. "Here, and here."

"Yeah?"

"This isn't digital, unless it's seriously touched up."

"It was shot on film, is what you're saying."

"You get an amateur in a homemade dark room, you see things like that — ripples, bright spots. And it's easier to develop black and white than color."

"You're a photographer?"

Cain shook his head.

"My line of work, I see a lot of photos," he said. "You know what it tells me, that he didn't shoot color? He didn't want to take these out, let someone else see them. He used black-and-white, and developed them at home. Your friend has his own dark room."

"He's not my friend."

"That's not what he thinks," Cain said. "He's pretty familiar."

"Not to me."

"And what about her?" Cain asked, touching the young woman in the photograph. "You know who she is?"

"All this, it's bullshit. I told you already. I don't know anything about this."

The mayor stood up and went to the cabinet behind his desk. He opened it, his back to Cain. When he turned around he was holding a bottle of bourbon and a pair of tumblers.

"Drink?"

"I'm on duty."

"And I'm your boss. Have a drink with me."

"I'm on duty, sir."

Castelli put one of the tumblers away, then poured three fingers of bourbon into the other. He sat again, putting the open bottle and the glass in front of him. Cain looked back to the picture, let himself go into it. The young woman wore a one-sleeved black dress held together at the front with a jeweled clasp. She held her hands out in front her, her fingers splayed in a gesture of self-defense. He couldn't read the look on her face. She hadn't expected the photograph to be taken, and she was afraid. But it wasn't the camera that frightened her. It was the man holding the camera. She was begging him not to come any closer. That was it — that was the look: she hadn't given in to full terror yet; she thought she might have a chance.

She still thought she could beg.

Behind her was a brick wall. In the middle of it, a padlocked steel door. It might have been a warehouse, the storeroom of a bar. The basement in a forgotten apartment block. It probably hadn't mattered to her where she was. She just wanted a way out, but there wasn't one.

In the left corner of the photograph, someone had used a black marker to write the number *1*. There was a loose circle drawn around it.

"You've never seen her?" Cain asked.

"No."

"She look like anyone you know?"

"No."

"Could she be someone's daughter — a niece, something like that?"

"I said I've never seen her before."

"Listen to the question," Cain said. "I didn't ask if you'd seen her. I asked if she looks like anyone you know. If she could be related to someone you know. Look at the picture — look at her face, and answer the question."

Instead, Castelli took his glass of bourbon and drank half of it. He set it down, topped it off, and then started coughing into the crook of his arm.

"Mr. Mayor."

But he was still coughing, and his face was going crimson. When he finally stopped, he took a tissue from the box at the edge of his desk. He used it to wipe his face and nose.

"Mr. Mayor," Cain said. "I need you to look at the picture."

"It's all bullshit—a hoax, whatever you want to call it," Castelli said. "I told you."

"You called me. Not the other way around."

"I'm being blackmailed."

"Because of something you know?"

"I don't know her, and she doesn't look like anyone I know."

"She's a pretty girl," Cain said. "I'd remember her if I saw her—wouldn't you?"

Castelli looked at him. Then he nodded.

"Sure," he said.

"You'd remember, if you saw her?"

"I'd probably remember."

"Because she's a knockout, right?"

The mayor glanced at the photograph. Cain wasn't sure if he nodded or not.

"She looks like one of those old film stars," Cain said. "Lana Turner, maybe."

"You got it mixed up," Castelli said. "It's Lauren Bacall you're thinking of. She looks like Bacall."

"*The Big Sleep*—that was her?"

"Bacall and Bogart," Castelli said. "Yeah."

"One of your favorites?"

"It was okay."

"I meant Bacall."

"Bacall?" the mayor asked. He took another drink. "She was before my time."

"Way before mine," Cain said. "But you see her on the screen, and it doesn't really matter."

"Maybe for some guys."

Cain took out the next picture and set it on top of the first. This one showed a cluttered bedside table against a water-stained plaster wall. He could just make out the edge of the iron bedframe beside it. At the table's edge sat an empty tumbler, a lipstick mark kissing its rim. There was a man's wallet, and a set of house keys. An empty ashtray. There were a dozen white pills in a loose pile, and next to them there was a silver flask, its cap unscrewed. Behind the flask were two pairs of handcuffs. Not the toys they sold in sex shops, but the real things, like the pair strapped to Cain's belt.

"Recognize any of this?"

"No."

"Not your keys, not your wallet?"

"Not mine."

"The flask?"

"I've never seen it."

"How about the handcuffs?"

"Come on."

"Come on?" Cain asked. "Did we read the same note? The guy who sent it, he's pretty sure this stuff means something to you. The next ones — the photos he's holding back — those might mean even more."

Castelli took a swallow of his bourbon.

"Go on," he said. "Make your point if you've got one."

"Right now, it's just you and me. But on Friday, when he sends it out? You'll be talking to the cameras."

"Or you could find him."

"That's what I'm trying to do," Cain said.

"Arrest him. Lock him away."

"I can't if you don't cooperate," Cain said. "So far, everything you've told me is bullshit."

The mayor stared at him. He glanced at his phone, and Cain thought he might call someone in. Have Cain muscled out of the office, out of City Hall. But then he shook his head. He held his glass close to the green-shaded desk lamp and looked at the glowing bourbon.

"I'm trying," Castelli said. "Nothing like this has ever happened to me. I'm not lying to you."

"The handcuffs — you own any like that?"

"Never," Castelli said. "Not like that, and not any other kind."

He set his glass down, then picked it up again. He was nervous about his hands, wanted to keep them busy. When he spoke on TV, he was always gripping the podium. If he didn't have a podium, then he was holding on to something. A cup of coffee, a rolled-up newspaper. Cain wondered if he'd been a smoker at some point.

"It's you and me right now," Cain said.

"We're not into anything like that, is all."

Cain nodded. He waited for the mayor to start talking again. Sometimes a man wouldn't answer a question but would talk to end a silence. This silence stretched for ten seconds, and then Castelli took another sip of bourbon and spoke into his glass.

"My wife and I, is what I mean. When I say *we,* I'm talking about me and her. The two of us, we're not into anything like that."

"Okay."

Cain could think of half a dozen follow-ups, but this wasn't the time. The mayor had opened the door a crack, but was ready to close it if Cain started to press. Instead, Cain opened the folder and took out the third picture, putting it on top of the others. Castelli glanced at it, then looked away, picking up his drink. Cain could smell the bourbon fumes in the air between them. Sweet and sharp, like sugar burning in a pan.

The photograph showed the woman, this time from the knees up. She was still wearing the black cocktail dress. Her back was against the wall, the nightstand at her left hip. She was drinking from the silver flask, her features caught in a painful wince. Her eyes were focused to her right. Someone must have been standing over there, out of the shot. Cain took the photograph and held it up, tilting it toward the light. He took off his glasses and leaned close to look.

"Did you look at these?" he asked. "All these pictures?"

"I saw everything in the envelope."

"You understood what's happening here?"

"I don't know."

Cain slipped his glasses back on, then set the photograph with the other two.

"The pills — they were on the nightstand before. Ten, twelve of them," he said. He pointed to the empty space where the pills had been in the second picture. "They'd be right here."

"Okay."

"They made her swallow them," Cain said. "Don't you think?"

"I don't know."

"Any idea what they were, those pills?"

"Of course not."

"You see her eyes, how she's looking to the right?"

"Yeah."

"What do you think about that?"

"She was looking at something. Or something caught her eye."

"Does she look scared to you?"

"I guess," the mayor said.

"Come on," Cain said. "We're cooperating. Right?"

"She looks pretty scared."

"Could someone have had a gun on her?" Cain asked. "Outside the shot?"

"Inspector — I don't know what you want me to say. I can't tell you what's happening outside these pictures. Not what she saw, or what she thought about it. I don't know who she is. I don't know what they paid her to pose for them, what they told her she was doing. Maybe she thought it was nothing — spread for some magazine, get a little cash."

"You think it's staged? That's what you think?"

"I don't know anything," the mayor said. "Except that it's got nothing to do with me."

"It does now," Cain said. "Sir."

The final photograph in the folder was turned face-down. Cain picked it up.

"I'm telling you —"

"You don't know anything," Cain said. "Right?"

"I just want us to be clear."

"I heard you the first time."

Cain turned the photograph over.

Now the woman was on the bed. Either she'd taken off the dress herself, or someone had taken it off for her. She lay on her back, her head on a pillow. She wore nothing but a pair of black panties. One knee was bent, so that her left foot was hooked across her right ankle. She'd painted her toenails. The polish looked black, but it was a black-and-white photograph. Cain supposed it could have been any dark color. Her right arm came up past her head, her hand shackled to the bedframe above her. There was no cuff on her left arm, which rested across her chest. If she'd been conscious, it might have been a gesture of modesty, of defense. An attempt to shield herself from the men in the room with her. But she wasn't conscious. Her eyes were closed, and her lips were slightly parted.

Cain studied her, and then looked at the nightstand next to her. It had been cleaned off. There was just the empty tumbler, the dark lipstick stain on its rim. He looked back at the woman. He'd seen enough death in the last eight years to guess he wasn't looking at it right now. It was just a photograph, and a poorly developed one at that. But he could almost see the rise and fall of her chest, could feel the warmth coming off her. She wasn't dead; he was sure of that. But she wasn't asleep, either.

There was no way to gauge how much time had passed between the third photograph and the fourth. Enough to put her in the bed, to clean the room up a bit. They'd stripped off the dress and maybe put a comb through her hair. She'd taken at least twelve of the pills, and she'd had whatever they'd put into the flask. By the time they took the picture, the drugs were working on her.